PALACE
of the
DROWNED

ALSO BY CHRISTINE MANGAN

Tangerine

PALACE

of the

DROWNED

Christine Mangan

FLATIRON
BOOKS
NEW YORK

PALACE OF THE DROWNED. Copyright © 2021 by Christine Mangan. All rights reserved. Printed in the United States of America. For information, address Flatiron Books, 120 Broadway, New York, NY 10271

www.flatironbooks.com

Book design by Donna Sinisgalli Noetzel

Library of Congress Cataloging-in-Publication Data

Names: Mangan, Christine (Christine Rose), author.
Title: Palace of the drowned / Christine Mangan.
Description: First Edition. | New York : Flatiron Books, 2021. |
Identifiers: LCCN 2020056386 | ISBN 9781250788429 (hardcover) |
    ISBN 9781250788443 (ebook)
Subjects: LCSH: Suspense fiction.
Classification: LCC PS3613.A53685 P35 2021 | DDC 813/.6—dc23
LC record available at https://lccn.loc.gov/2020056386

Our books may be purchased in bulk for promotional, educational, or business use. Please contact your local bookseller or the Macmillan Corporate and Premium Sales Department at 1-800-221-7945, extension 5442, or by email at MacmillanSpecialMarkets@macmillan.com.

First Edition: 2021

10 9 8 7 6 5 4 3 2 1

For Pippa, who told me to go back to Venice

PALACE
of the
DROWNED

PROLOGUE

Rome, November 1966

Outside the Roma Termini station, she came to an abrupt halt. It was the flapping of their wings that had initially caught her attention, as she pushed against the glass door of the station. At first, she had been unable to place it, that strange, overwhelming noise. She had stood, watching the crowd as they milled around her, wondering why no one else seemed to be aware of it—that sound like a crackling fire, so that for one mad moment she wondered whether the world might be burning, whether everything that had happened before, everything she had left behind in the watery grave that Venice had since become, no longer mattered. Tilting her head upward, she watched the flock of birds that swarmed the evening sky. They looked, she thought, their dark form molding into one, like a plague of locusts.

A stranger brushed against her as she stood, a businessman on his way home, a returned traveler—she didn't know, but she could feel the force of his impatience as it pushed up against her. She stumbled, her eyes falling on the *carabinieri* station just yards away, on the guard who stood just outside its doors. Her heart began to beat at an unsteady pace. She wondered what the guard might see

if he were to return her gaze—an innocent tourist momentarily overcome by the beauty of Rome, or something closer to the truth.

A fugitive in a foreign city.

She shivered and with hurried footsteps began to make her way in the opposite direction, forcing herself to focus on the familiar sound of her heels as they clicked against the cobbled streets, the rhythm steady and strong, urging her forward.

She told herself not to look back.

CHAPTER I

Venice, October 1966

She was on her way to the Rialto market, hoping to buy some *vongole* from one of the local fishmongers, despite the fact that it was October and therefore not really the season for them, when she felt someone grab her by the wrist.

Just moments earlier, Frances, or Frankie, as she was known to the small set of people she had called friends over the years, had been walking alongside the Grand Canal, concerned with nothing more than her aching feet crying out for a *vaporetto*. Pulling the cowl of her houndstooth wool overcoat tightly to her neck, in what she was forced to concede was a failing attempt to keep out the impending cold and drizzle, she had made her way determinedly toward the fish market—her heels clicking against the rain-splattered cobblestones, dodging the crowds of tourists winding their cameras with spools of film to capture the city's infamous candelabras, and their accompanying tour guides, wooden paddles held high into the air—all the while cursing the friend who was supposed to have been walking alongside her in this miserable weather.

Instead, weeks before, Frankie had sat alone at Victoria station, about to board a train to Dover, a crumpled telegram somewhere

at the bottom of her bag. It had been handed to her along with her ticket. RUNNING LATE STOP SORRY STOP FORGIVE ME. Frankie knew that the use of a question mark was impossible in a telegram, but still, it didn't stop her feeling needled by the assumption of the last bit, turning the latter into a declaration instead of a plea. She was used to such flightiness on the part of her friend, and yet the slight had rankled more than usual. Venice had been Jack's suggestion, after all—Frankie would never have come on her own.

When Frankie later called her friend from the telephone box at the station, Jack had begged her to cancel and wait until the following weekend, when they could set off together and be in the city of bridges in just a few hours rather than a few days. Frankie still didn't understand the reason for the delay, had heard the edge in Jack's voice when she had broached the question. It wasn't as if Jack had to clock in. Heiresses were not subject to the same grueling schedule as the rest of the world. Jack was, had always been, at the mercy of no one but herself—a fact she often tried to exert upon others. But that day, Frankie had refused. She had only ever flown once before and had detested every second. There was something about it—the whining of the engines, the slamming of air, of oxygen, of force, of gravity. The toll she could feel it taking on her body. She wondered about her insides, whether they were as clenched, condensed, as twisted and distorted as they felt. She had been, for the duration of the trip, aware of nothing so much as the feeling of being trapped in that box of tin, thick with cigarette smoke and cloying perfume, with polite conversations and sharp, quick glances. It reminded her too much of the years during the war—confined in dusty basements, listening to the roar of planes overhead. She had sprinted from her seat the moment the plane touched the ground.

Not that the ferry and train over had proved to be much better. The ferry had been an arduous journey, the inside suffocating in warmth—filled to the brim with ladies playing bridge, unsupervised children running wild, their husbands and fathers retreating

to dark corners with cigarettes and measures of scotch—while the dark and gloom of the weather outside made it impossible to step out for a breath of fresh air. Later, in Italy, Frankie had misread her connecting ticket, thinking she was leaving Torino from Porta Susa, the station where she had arrived from Paris. She realized only at the last minute that the train to Venice left from Porta Nuova, nearly a full mile away. After several panicked moments, she managed to come to her senses and hail a taxi, arriving, mercifully, just in time, although flushed and sweating as she collapsed into her assigned seat, blood pounding in her ears. Her spirits had been further dampened upon realizing her traveling companion was an elderly woman cloaked in a large and rather foul-smelling fur coat, with a miserable-looking dachshund, which was prone to fits of loud yapping every time the train lurched, perched on her lap.

When Frankie finally arrived at the station in Venice and managed to purchase the right ticket for the right water bus, she had experienced an inflated sense of triumph. Alighting at the San Zaccaria station, confident in her ability to steer herself through the city unaided, she had even gone so far as to decline the help of a smiling porter, determined to make her way through the *sestiere* of Castello all on her own. It was a decision she soon regretted, as her meticulously written directions led her down one street and then another, the width barely large enough for herself and her one leather bag, let alone the people trying to make their way from the opposite direction. And yet, somehow, there always seemed to be enough room, the person coming toward her shifting just enough to allow them both through without so much as brushing shoulders. These narrow passageways then emptied out into *campi*—the open spaces smaller than she had imagined—before leading her onward and over one little bridge, and then another, and sometimes under archways that forced her to bend forward so as not to knock her head against the stone. She had taken a few wrong turns but nothing

that had led her too far out of her way. The most disconcerting moment had come when she met with a dead end, which, unlike those she was used to at home—bricks that boxed you in and held you in place—meant she found herself standing in front of an archway that led only to water, rushing up and over the stones, dangerously close to her feet. The first time it had happened, Frankie stumbled, thrown off by the movement of the waves, by the sulfuric odor that filled the alcove. It was hypnotic, the lapping of the green water up and over the cobbles, the smell of brine surrounding her, so that instead of taking a step back, she had moved forward, as if to welcome it. The spell was broken only when a local had appeared in one of the windows, calling out something to her in Venetian. Looking up, she had seen window boxes and lace curtains, an older man looking down at her in consternation as music flooded from a record player somewhere inside the flat. Frankie backed away, embarrassed. Head down, she had pushed onward, trying to make it look as though she knew where she was headed.

That had been weeks ago, and there was still no sign of Jack.

And so Frankie was alone, in a city that was still largely unknown to her, when she felt that hand clasp on to her wrist, fingers tightening in a way that made her body go slack with fear. This reaction irked her hugely, for she had never been one to be afraid, to be skittish, or any of those other detestable feminine attributes that were encouraged in the etiquette books of her childhood, but after everything that had happened as of late, the instinct to recoil was now almost second nature.

But then—she looked up, her eyes falling on the person standing there, and she could have laughed. It was only a girl. A young woman, Frankie supposed she should say, although lately anyone younger than her own two and forty years seemed infantile.

"Frances—is that you?"

Just then a wasp, no doubt attracted to the bundle of yellow plums Frankie had in her canvas sack, purchased from the floating

greengrocers at Campo San Barnaba, dived between them and Frankie swatted it away, breaking the girl's hold in the process.

"Yes," Frankie replied. The word, she knew, sounded severe in its haste, more so than she had intended. She studied the girl, struck first by the long, wavy red hair that cascaded over her shoulders, reaching nearly to her waist. The girl's outfit, she thought, looked like it had been carefully selected from a West End shop. A shapeless mustard-colored shift with a Peter Pan collar, the dress grazed midway at her thighs, and was covered by an oversized swing coat that ended just below. Frankie felt suddenly prim, older than her years, with her short blond wisps of hair pinned tightly back, bobby pins scraping against her scalp, her face bare except for some hastily applied eyeliner. She herself wore a simple black sweater and pair of cigarette pants. She pulled her overcoat tight against her. "It's Frankie, actually. No one ever calls me Frances, except for elderly relatives and people who don't really know me." She frowned at the words, feeling the pull of the pins against her scalp.

The girl in front of her was a stranger, she was certain of it. And yet—

"I knew it was you," the girl cried, pulling her close, into something that would have resembled a hug had Frankie's body yielded to the movement. "Oh, God, it's been ages, but I knew it was you."

"Do we know each other?" Frankie asked, stepping back.

The girl's hands flew to her face and she laughed. "Oh, goodness, you don't remember."

Frankie's eyes narrowed. She met a good deal of people in her line of work, had met even more in the last year, after the publication of her most recent novel, despite its admittedly tepid reception, but the girl before her seemed too young to be involved with that crowd. Frankie had difficulty believing she could be a day over twenty. No, their paths would not have crossed in the world of publishing.

"You're not Diane's daughter?" Frankie inquired, the vision of a

schoolgirl dragged in to meet her suddenly vivid in her mind. She had never been a fan of Diane's, the wife of one of the editors at her publishing house—she couldn't remember whose at this point. The woman was far too eager, too effusive for her liking.

The girl's face brightened. "You do remember! Oh, I'm so pleased."

"Yes," Frankie replied, allowing a tight smile. In her memory the girl had been a blonde—but perhaps she was wrong. She wished that she had not mentioned Diane at all now, that she had let the girl make her own introduction, just so that she could be certain. "What are you doing in Venice?" she asked, not bothering to make the question sound anything less than pointed.

"Playing tourist," the girl responded with a smile. "And you?"

She searched the girl for any signs of pretense—for surely she knew the real reason for Frankie's presence in the city. The incident at the Savoy had been in all the papers at the time. Jack and her editor had tried to hide them from her, but she had seen a few, had even managed to glimpse a headline or two. FEMALE WRITER BECOMES HYSTERICAL. WOMAN NOVELIST LOSES THE PLOT. They hadn't been particularly clever. But, then, she imagined there had been a rush to make it to the printing press first—it wasn't every day an esteemed writer had a very public breakdown in the middle of a bar at a five-star hotel. If the girl in front of her was aware of any of this and lying for Frankie's sake, or for her own, Frankie could detect nothing, no betrayal that she knew. She shrugged. "Something like that, I suppose."

"And have you only just arrived?" she asked, to which Frankie responded yes, even though it was a lie. "It's a pity you weren't here earlier," the girl continued, indicating the market around them. "You've only just missed the *moeche*."

"*Moeche?*"

"Yes, it's a delicacy, straight from the lagoons. The Venetians called them *moeca*."

Frankie nodded, conscious that they were standing still among the crowd of the morning market, locals and tourists alike pulsating around them, although there was little chance of confusing the two. The locals appeared determined, ready to root out the best deals of the day, fortified by their morning espresso, while in the tourists she thought she could read something of disinterest in their slackened expressions, their eyes moving quickly over the architecture of the city and lingering instead on the little stalls full of postcards and trinkets. "They're already out of season, then?" she asked, trying to be polite, wondering whether they would be swept up in the movement if they continued to remain static. Frankie loathed small talk.

The girl gave a laugh. "They don't have much of a season. They're here one day and gone the next. The *moecante* know when they're ready to molt."

"Molt?" Frankie asked, turning her attention back to the girl and thinking of birds and feathers and wondering how this all made sense for something that came from the canal.

"Yes, you see, they're crabs, and when they shed their shells there is a moment, a few hours, when they're soft enough to eat." The girl grinned. "Only," she continued, somewhat earnestly, "they have to be taken out of the water at once, so that the new shell doesn't start to grow and harden."

Frankie looked at the girl then—*really* looked at her—as she tried to decide whether she was horrified or amused by the expression of excitement on the girl's face at the prospect of such violence. "That sounds terrible," she offered, her voice suggesting she did not mean it.

"Yes, I suppose it does." The girl nodded, still smiling as she spoke. "Are you in Venice on your own, Frances?"

At the abruptness of the question, Frankie's eyes narrowed. Yes, Diane's girl had been a blonde. "Why do you ask?"

The girl shrugged. "I was going to suggest that we might meet for a cup of coffee." When Frankie didn't respond, she added, "I'm here alone as well."

"A cup of coffee?" Frankie repeated.

"Yes. Shall we meet tomorrow? Where are you staying?"

"In a palazzo near the Campo Santa Maria Formosa. I can't remember the number," she lied. "But I can't make coffee tomorrow, I'm afraid."

This was obviously not what the girl had expected to hear. "Oh," she replied, somewhat more softly than before. "And the day after?" she asked, the words spoken with a slight hesitation this time.

"The same." Frankie intended to leave it there, to walk away without being coerced into making plans with the strange girl. The idea of meeting people, of having to engage in conversation with strangers, was one that rarely appealed to her—but then, seeing the crestfallen look on the girl's face and desperate to say anything that would extract her from the situation, from the crowds growing around them, Frankie felt compelled to add, "I might be able to rearrange a few things."

The girl's face broke out into a large grin.

"It's Gilly, by the way," she said, pronouncing her name with a hard *G* and extending her hand. "Just in case you'd forgotten."

Frankie had been to the Continent only once before, as a young girl.

The memories she had from that time in France were brief and scattered. In her mind it was all dazzling lights thrown against cobbled streets, the smell of bakeries in the morning. She had been lucky enough to tour the country with a friend and her parents, a loop that had taken them from the capital in a large unwieldy circle through cities, port towns, and small villages. Throughout it all, however, her heart had remained steadfastly in the city of lights. For while she had loved the quaintness of Rouen, the magic of Mont

Saint-Michel, and even the hot, sandy beaches of Nice, in the end there had been nothing that compared to Paris, to the smell of it, from the aroma of yeast in the morning to the powerful stench of the *fromageries* to the hot breath of the Métro that assaulted her every time she tripped down the stairs. There, she had felt the future stretching before her, wide and unmarked, hers for the taking.

Frankie had done little traveling in her adult life. At first, her lack of travel had been because she could not afford to do so, her parents' deaths and her decision not to marry—despite one solid proposal and another, hastily rushed offer—but to instead attend university, putting her at a distinct financial disadvantage when compared with her peers. But then there had been a bit of success with the publication of her first novel in her late twenties, and some money as well, enough for a holiday abroad. By that time, however, her interest in traveling had diminished greatly, the feeling that she had once experienced growing harder to remember as the years passed, until it was only a vague memory. And while others around her prattled on about needing to go elsewhere in order to truly find oneself, Frankie could not help but think it was all a bit of rubbish. She knew herself already—too well, she often thought—and so she knew that the dark, rainy streets of London were for her, that the high street in Crouch End and the trip down to Euston on the 91 bus, followed by a brisk walk over to Bloomsbury to show her reader's ticket at the British Museum's Round Reading Room, were the only kind of excitement she wanted. Others could keep the sizzling beaches of Positano, and even the romantic dreariness of Paris—she didn't envy them for it, not one bit. Hers was a small world and she was glad of it.

Perhaps not surprisingly, then, Frankie had hated Venice when she first arrived. It had been warmer than she anticipated, so that the palazzo had been stuffy and unpleasant—and yet it had been impossible to open the windows due to the abundance of mosquitos that seemed to lurk in both canal and courtyard. She had made

the mistake only once, awakening to find herself covered in red bites that itched and swelled, growing into blisters that wept and refused to heal. The very worst were still present, a cluster on her forearm that she had begun applying a salve to, worried that they might never fade.

But then, just a few days after her arrival, the weather had broken. The air had grown damp and chill, eerily similar to autumn in London, and the vast majority of the tourists vanished from the *campi*. With this shift in weather came the emergence of Venice's actual residents, who had somehow managed to remain invisible to her before then—older Venetian women, wrapped in fur coats, walking arm in arm with friends on the way to share a drink, and their male counterparts, making their way determinedly up one bridge and then another, a small dog often scuttling beside. Suddenly, Frankie found, the city seemed a place to be lived in rather than a place to be visited, and she had come to enjoy Venice in the days that had passed since—in particular, the emptiness of the city, something that never happened in London, no matter the season. Gone were the hurried footsteps that crowded the city, so that now Frankie could spend hours gazing upward, unfettered, unworried about bumping into someone else. She could linger in passageways, in cafes, eating brioche or sometimes *krapfen*, the Italian version of a jam doughnut, lingering over her coffee, in no rush now that the crowds had dissipated.

In Venice, Frankie found she could almost feel it again, that sensation she had experienced as a young girl in Paris. In certain places, at certain times of day. She found it when she rode the water buses, the *vaporetti*, looking up at the city, always up, her neck craning, as if the city demanded such reverence, and again when it was dark and gloomy, which it almost always was now, when she became lost in this city constructed of bridges and canals and too many tiny islands to count and too many twisty, hidden streets to know. She found it in those places marked by history, the

echo of some long-ago person or event reaching out across time to mark her, in a way that she felt she had not been since her youth.

Now, after her encounter with the girl, Frankie felt the city somehow changed, as if the luster of it had been dulled by the girl's intrusion. It was a ridiculous thought, one that was far too sentimental for even her own liking, and yet she could not help but feel that the day was altered, her presence in it now marked by the girl's own.

Moving between the market stalls, Frankie stopped at her favorite seller for *aromi misti,* that little bundle of rosemary, bay leaves, and thyme, and waited until it was her turn to order. She had learned, after her first week, not to touch the produce herself, the action having earned her a sharp slap on the hand as well as a rebuke in rapid-fire Venetian from the woman running the stall. Since then she had discovered that one had to wait—as one often did, it seemed, in Italy—to be noticed, to be served, to pay and receive any lire owed. Tasks that back home in London took only a few minutes seemed to stretch endlessly here. There was one place to buy produce, another for seafood, another for wine, and another still for cheese and pasta and eggs. And yet, rather than frustration, Frankie felt a strange sense of calm at the mechanics required in these day-to-day transactions.

She drifted toward the fish market now, where she managed to buy some *seppioline* at a good price, fresh from the lagoon, but not the *vongole* she had initially hoped for. As she handed over the coins, Frankie reflected that the purchase did not bring her as much pleasure, nor did the sight of the creature's black ink, used by the fisherman to scrawl the price. She could, she thought, still feel the fingers of the redheaded girl around her wrist.

Afterward, her shopping complete, she turned and headed to a local *bacaro* just steps away from the market. Fighting her way through the small crowd of Italians filling the one-room bar, through the chatter and cigarette smoke that hung heavy in the air, she ordered her usual *un'ombra* at the counter and took the red wine outside to enjoy on the battered wooden chairs, alongside the rest of the locals who had similarly spilled onto the streets. She waited for the drink to calm her nerves. But even hidden in the shadows of the overlooked passageway, sipping on wine, her heels tapping against the cobblestones, her mind would not quiet, would not be still.

Gilly. That was what she had called herself. Frankie thought it had a ring of falsity to it. As did her story about their supposed introduction. Gilly, with a hard *G.* It was too juvenile, too hard to believe that someone had willingly bestowed it as an actual given name. As Frankie took another sip of wine, she allowed that it wasn't the girl herself so much as the girl's recognition that had unsettled her. A reminder that while she might play at disappearing into Venice, her vanishing act could never truly be complete. There would always be someone who knew her—and who knew about what had happened at the Savoy. The two were synonymous now, intrinsically linked. No matter how much she detested the thought.

Frankie gave a small shake of her head, cursing under her breath.

If only she had never read that damned review.

She had made it a habit, ever since the publication of her first novel, of asking her editor to send her the press cuttings, once they became available. Charlotte Brontë had done it, she knew, making sure that she received each and every word written in the public about her work. Frankie had always liked the idea, had told herself it was good to know what the reviewers did and did not respond to, so that she could work on it and improve in her next book. Of course, this had been easier with the first novel, when the praise had been near unanimous.

Since then, there had been a shift—a subtle one, but still there all the same.

Her latest novel had garnered only a handful of reviews, far less than her first outing, with gentle critiques alongside lines of flattery referring, as they inevitably did, to her first novel, which Frankie wasn't certain was even still in print. They lauded her language, her skill, but they also felt that her most recent was only more of the same, the reviewers' boredom emanating from the page. Frankie could feel something unspooling within her. Her second novel had sold well, based on the success of her first, but her third had faltered, and it soon became apparent that this, her fourth and most recent, was destined for the same type of mediocrity. Frankie had grown increasingly apprehensive over the years, sensing the interest of her publishing house begin to shift, imagining it as some great beast brought to life, shuffling slowly about, sniffing at her tentatively, and then turning its back on her. She could feel it, she thought: the end, lurking just around the corner. She still had one more book left on her contract, technically. It was part of a deal she had signed after her third, when they still had a bit of confidence left in her, in her ability, when they still believed that she was something worth investing in. A contract for one more, and a first look at the one after that. If they decided not to publish, she didn't know what would happen then, tried not to let herself dwell too much—though that soon became impossible after the review.

Bundled up alongside the other publications that her editor, Harold, had his secretary post out to her every fortnight or so, the review had appeared in a weekly magazine she did not recognize, written by someone identified only as J.L.

Her face had burned as she read the opening paragraph.

The first line of Frances Croy's latest novel failed to transport me. There was something so apathetic, so resigned, so passive about her opening sentence that this reviewer could only sit back and reflect for a moment, wondering what had happened to the daring writer who was first introduced to the reading public with her astonishing debut, After the End. *There was no trace of her here.*

At first, Frankie tried to forget about the review, tried to push it out of her mind. But she had always had a tendency to fixate, to obsess. That day she had cleaned her entire flat from top to bottom. When the house was spotless and she could find nothing more to spray or polish, she decided to contact her editor. Instead of calling Harold, she paid him an unannounced visit, throwing the magazine onto his desk without so much as an explanation first. It had been dramatic, but, then, Frankie felt the moment called for it. After reading the review, Harold shrugged his shoulders and suggested that the words belonged to an overzealous admirer.

"A fan?" she had scoffed. "No, Harold, I think we can at least say *that* is impossible."

But Harold shook his head and told her she would be surprised at what he had seen during his years in the business. "Sometimes love and hate become muddied in the eyes of the beholder," he told her.

She had reached for his packet of cigarettes, the only time she allowed herself the indulgence. "That sounds like complete nonsense," she told him. Frankie had hoped he didn't notice just how much her hands were shaking as she lit her cigarette.

"Why bother yourself over a single review? Most people don't even read them."

"That isn't the point, Harold."

"I know, dear, but try not to think too much of it. The other critics, well, they—" But then he had fallen silent, cleared his throat a few times, and spread his hands in absence of words, so that Frankie wanted to snap, wanted to demand what exactly those other critics had written, as she could read between the tepid lines and general silence just as well as her editor. "Don't let it bother you," he had advised her then. "In fact, look at it as a challenge to try something new with the next one, something to perk up the sales a bit."

Frankie had blinked.

"You're not exactly the budding ingenue any longer," Harold

hurried to explain. "We're four books in now, Frankie, and what worked at first, well . . ."

It wasn't working any longer. That was what he wanted to say.

"Something new?" she asked, ignoring the better part of his statement.

After that, he had refused to discuss the review further, suggesting a strong cup of Earl Grey and a good night's sleep. "It won't seem so important in the pale gleam of morning," he promised.

Frankie had smirked at the idea and, upon arriving home, done the very opposite of what her editor proposed by not sleeping at all that night. Instead, she sat up, reading and rereading the review until she knew it by heart, smoking the entire pack of Player's Navy Cut that she had palmed when leaving his office, hating the slim counterparts that were marketed now toward women. In the morning, eyes red and puffy, she threw the review into the wastepaper bin, and made herself that suggested cup of tea.

It wasn't as though there weren't people who hadn't liked her books before. Her second had elicited a rather snippy review from one of the mainstream broadsheets, but, then, Frankie had known the reviewer, had known his disdain for anything that others loved, and so she had shrugged it off without much consequence to her ego. There was something different about this one. Something strangely intimate, personal, as if the writer of the piece knew her, so that she could feel their disapproval—no, it was something stronger than that—their *disappointment* pulsing in the words that swam on the page. She could feel that spool inside her give just a tiny bit more, could feel the panic harden and calcify, the embarrassment giving way to anger.

Perhaps if she were younger, she could have handled it better. But now everything seemed to hold so much more significance, so much more weight. There was more to lose now, so that it all felt precarious in a way that the naïveté of youth had always protected her from.

Several weeks later, she rang Harold. "Maybe," she told him when he picked up, "my next novel will be about the murder of a critic."

"Isn't that what Patricia Highsmith does?" he had responded.

Frankie didn't know but accepted that Harold was probably right and grumpily set the idea aside. After, she decided she was more like Steinbeck than Brontë. Like him, she wanted to meet the reviewer, to speak with them, to understand what it was that had cultivated such a dislike for her work. But all she had were the reviewer's initials, J.L., and the growing wall of silence that seemed to surround them. In response, she wrote missive after missive, planning to ask Harold to send them out to anyone he thought might know the identity of the reviewer, to the magazine itself even. In her most desperate moment she considered taking an ad out in the paper and printing both letter and review, embracing this public shame rather than hiding away from it, as she supposed the author of the review wanted.

In the end, she burned them all, one by one, sipping on whisky that tore at her throat, imagining that it was the flames she felt against her skin, hot and insistent. Forced to concede then that she would most likely never know the true identity of the mysterious J.L., she tried to temper it, tried to snuff it out—that feeling inside her that burned and twisted. At least, that's what she told herself, told her editor, at the frown settling between his eyebrows, told Jack, at the tight line that formed on her lips, every time they spoke.

In the end, what happened that night at the Savoy was unsurprising, seemed even somewhat inevitable, to both herself and those who knew her. As did her stay at Brimley House.

An establishment an hour outside London, Brimley House billed itself as a relaxation center, though anyone familiar with the institution knew it was far more than just that. Frankie hadn't wanted to go, but Jack as well as Harold had insisted, united in this one thing, arguing that the sanitorium was her best chance at avoiding being committed after what had happened at the Savoy. Frankie might have risked it, but in the end she hadn't been given a choice—not with the stories that had appeared in the papers. So instead of waiting for the men in white coats to come knocking, Frankie had turned herself in, as it were. She checked herself into the clinic under a false name, somewhat curious, despite her initial misgivings. Within a week she determined that it wasn't for her, that the treatments of exercise and painting were absolute rubbish and only made her angrier, more desperate. She had always been a solitary person, but confined within the creaky Victorian bones of Brimley House, she experienced a new type of isolation, and the totality of it terrified her.

She left in the middle of the night, nearly three weeks later, promising herself that she would never be so foolish again. At a hotel, she called Jack, told her about her plans for leaving England, not yet ready to go back to her old life, and it was then that her friend had first proposed Venice.

Frankie initially protested at the idea, but Jack had silenced her. "I know how you feel about Italy, Frankie, but just listen for once. Venice isn't even *really* Italy." At which point she had launched into a reasonable explanation for her choice—namely, money and space—ending with: "And, besides, all the great writers went there at one time or another."

And although Frankie hadn't intended to, although she had developed solid impressions of Italy over the years from things she had read, things she had overheard—too many leering men, too many stodgy dishes Italians wouldn't dare to eat themselves, dressed up in price—she was forced to concede that Jack's offer was rather appealing.

"There isn't anyone else staying there?" Frankie had asked, not daring to trust her luck.

"Not at the moment," Jack said. "It belongs to Mummy and Daddy, but they haven't been in ages. They've taken to renting it out over the years, mainly to local families, but there's been no one recently."

Frankie had taken a minute to consider. "What's the catch?"

"No catch at all, darling," Jack said, a slight hitch in her voice. "It is, technically, only half of the palazzo. The other part belongs to someone else, but they have their own entrance, so you'd never even see them. Never even hear them, if I remember correctly."

"That sounds perfectly reasonable," Frankie mused. "There must be something else, though. What aren't you telling me?"

"Nothing—only," Jack began, "I thought we might join you, help you settle in. We'd only stay for a few days, but we've been hoping to get out of London for a bit as well. Plus, to be honest, we've been thinking about selling recently. None of us have used the palazzo in ages, and I don't want the hassle of inheriting it. You being there would be such help. It would force me to make the trip and get the whole thing started. It's all a bit complicated over there—buying and selling in Italy is a difficult process, nothing is ever as easy as you wish it were."

"*We?*" Frankie asked, pressing a point she knew she should ignore but feeling somewhat irked by what she suspected was Jack checking up on her.

There was a pause. "Yes."

The word was spoken with a fair amount of courage mustered into it. If she hadn't been so annoyed, Frankie might have even laughed. The *we* Jack was referring to was Leonard, her husband. The decision to marry had surprised no one more than Jack, a woman who had long championed the independent, single woman but who had come around to Frankie's flat and confessed her contrary feelings one very drunken night two years earlier. Only a few weeks later Jack and Leonard had married. It was a small affair, just the two of them, and her parents, at a register office. Frankie was still smarting from not being invited. Since then, their relationship had been strained. It wasn't that Frankie disliked Leonard—no, he was perfectly fine, despite being a bit dull—it was more that she disliked what he had done to their friendship, how his presence had altered her own.

By the time of the incident at the Savoy, Frankie and Jack had spoken only rarely, had seen each other only a handful of times. At first, Frankie blamed it on her work, on her book, reassuring herself in those moments when she began to worry about the state of their friendship that it was only down to their busy lives. But that was not it and she knew the both of them realized it. With the introduction of Leonard into Jack's life, something had shifted, almost imperceptibly at first but still there, a crack that ran along the foundation of their friendship, that usurped Frankie. Change worried her in general but particularly so when it came to her friend. She had always thought that there might be a time when Jack might outgrow her or, worse yet, realize that theirs was a peculiar friendship, the heiress and the author, and decide it no longer suited. That night at the Savoy, Jack's had been the first name that came to mind when the police questioned her, despite the slight worry buried deep within that her friend would not come. Her fear, it turned out, was unwarranted. Jack arrived in an amount of time that defied all laws of London traffic.

And Leonard, to his credit, had been just as eager to offer help. Though Frankie was hesitant to involve him, Leonard had been instrumental in settling things afterward. He was, after all, the only solicitor that Frankie knew, and once Jack had insisted, both of them saw the added advantage of his involvement—his ensured silence on the matter.

But that was all in the past.

Frankie shuddered now and stood, leaving her glass of wine only half finished. Walking back into the market, she skirted the stalls, the sellers, anxious to be away from the crowds.

"*Vuoi comprare, signora?*" a seller called to her.

"*No, grazie,*" Frankie murmured. She moved away from the

market, toward the bridge. Determined to shake off this malaise, she reminded herself of how she had felt when Jack first told her about the palazzo, the vast structure sitting empty, waiting, it seemed, for her to fill it. After all her initial misgivings, after all her doubts, once she had decided that she would take the opportunity her friend had so graciously offered, Frankie was able to see it: the glimmer of hope as it began to take shape before her. A reminder of what she had once felt as a young girl, all those years ago. As she moved back toward the palazzo now, anxious to be inside, she tried to hold on to that same feeling.

In the courtyard, she paused.

The first time she had heard the neighbors was several days after her arrival. Frankie had returned home late, her steps echoing across the stone, when she paused to find her keys and was startled to hear the sound of footsteps continue. She had hastened up the stairs then, her fingers shaking as she undid the lock that led into the entrance hall, all the while wondering if an intruder had somehow managed to find their way in. But then a minute passed, and then another, and with it there came no further evidence of a stranger, nothing beyond the same interrupted pattern of footsteps on stone, so that at last she reasoned it must be from next door.

The way that the palazzo was divided, it made it possible to look across the courtyard from the entrance hall and into the stretch that must serve as a similar space in the neighboring apartment. Frankie had never seen anyone walk through the rooms, not even so much as a shadow, but there had been a night, not so long ago, when a light was turned on. Rather than feel alarmed, Frankie had found a certain measure of comfort in the warm glow, in the acknowledgment that she was not alone in what often seemed a giant mausoleum. For while she enjoyed the quiet of the streets during the day, night was another matter.

Now she paused on the foot of the stairs, searching for any sign of her mysterious neighbor. There was nothing. It was as if the palazzo, as if the city around her, were vacant except for her own presence, as if the nothingness stretched on for miles and miles around her.

The stillness of Venice reminded her of those years during the war when she had worked as an air-raid warden. She had been too young, but people then had looked the other way when it came to such things. She was willing, that was the important thing, and she was capable, an added advantage for the people in her section. While some air wardens were content to allow the more stubborn occupants to remain in their homes, swayed by pleading and earnest glances, once the yellow standby warning sounded, Frankie had made sure everyone in her domain was out and headed to the designated shelter, no excuses. She had even once carried an elderly man's birdcage when he refused to leave his beloved parakeet behind. Instead of wasting precious minutes arguing, she picked up the cage and made for the door, not waiting to see if the man was behind her.

Afterward, once all those under her watch were securely hidden below, she would stop, would look out at the changing landscape before her, at the city she no longer recognized, and be filled with the sharp feeling of panic that she was the only one left. It was nonsense—she could count on her hand the number of people who were only steps away from her, hidden beneath the ground. And yet still, standing on an abandoned street in the once-bustling city of her youth, she had felt nothing but desolation stretching in front of her, beside her, all around. In those moments, she worried that it would go on forever, that none of them would ever escape, not truly, not in any real way that mattered.

Now, Frankie forced herself to slowly inhale, a touch of sea and salt present on the edges of the air around her, reminding her once more where she was. In Venice—miles away from London and ghosts of the past. She let out a deep breath and hurried inside.

CHAPTER 2

The telephone had been ringing on and off for nearly an hour. Which was not in itself unusual, except for the fact that Frankie had not been aware of there actually being a telephone anywhere within the palazzo. The vast structure did not seem outfitted for such modern conveniences and so she had never thought to look upon her arrival, assuming the place would not be wired for a telephone.

The initial ring had woken Frankie early that morning. In response she had pulled the sheets over her head and returned to sleep, assuming that the ringing was from the neighboring palazzo, the sound muted and far away. Only fifteen minutes later she was awoken again, at which point she began to wonder whether it wasn't from somewhere within her side of the palazzo after all. With much regret, and a fair bit of grumbling, she pushed herself up and away from the bed, rubbing her eyes in an effort to dispel the fogginess and feeling as though she was still very much asleep. She grabbed her dressing gown, a silk kimono that Jack had given her one year for her birthday, the flower-patterned piece the only bit of color she had allowed into her wardrobe. Shivering as the cold material made contact with her skin, she descended the stairs to the first floor, determined to find the blasted thing before it drove her mad.

Which, considering the size of the place, was no mean feat.

The palazzo was a three-story structure, situated only a few minutes' walk from the Campo Santa Maria Formosa, looked after by an infallibly loyal housekeeper named Maria, whose near-constant scowl felt somehow appropriate given the atmosphere. The palace was enormous in scale, with a ground floor that featured an open-air courtyard with terra-cotta tiles and two staircases—one to the side in which she was staying and another for the owners of the other half. Frankie suspected that the palazzo had originally been intended for a single family but that economy had necessitated a change, resulting in a subsequent split and thus the twin set of stairs. Still, it appeared that this rearrangement had occurred fairly far back in history. Both the staircases—constructed of stone or marble, Frankie wasn't certain of the difference—were heavily embellished, the balustrade decorated with what appeared to be artichokes, and were supported by elaborate lancet arches that put her in mind of a Gothic novel. They had very clearly not been designed anytime within the twentieth century. As if in proof of such authenticity, the stairs themselves had a slight lean to them, so that on her first ascent Frankie had felt as if at any second the building could go toppling over and into the lagoon. It was at that precise moment that she had remembered once reading something about the whole city sinking, inch by determined inch. That first day she had shuddered as she made her way up and into the leaning palazzo, looking down at the courtyard, wondering why on earth she had ever allowed Jack to talk her into staying in this crumbling testimony to bygone decadence.

Even the name of the palazzo itself seemed to portend something dark and ominous.

"The name?" Jack had asked, the first time Frankie had inquired.

"Yes, aren't all these palaces named after the families who owned them or some such nonsense?" Frankie had read about the Golden families, those wealthy elite who had found their names recorded in the Golden Book, tangible proof of the titles and other riches conferred upon them throughout the ages. Like most things in Venice, they now belonged primarily to the past. "Jack?" Frankie prompted, when her friend remained silent.

"Yes," Jack finally began. "It's named after the family that first built it." There was an edge to her voice, as though she hesitated to speak the next set of words. "Only, no one really knows it by that name anymore."

"Oh? What do they know it by, then?" Frankie asked, suspicious of her friend's tone.

"It's silly—and the story behind it is probably not even true. In fact, part of me used to wonder, and still does, quite frankly, whether my father didn't make the whole thing up just so that he could keep us from playing too near the watergate. You know how rambunctious we all were as children," she said, referencing her two older brothers, both of whom had died in the war. "Isn't that what fairy tales are for? To warn children."

"And what exactly were they warning you against?" Frankie demanded.

Jack hesitated. "Drowning. My father used to say that his Venetian friends called the palazzo by the name Ca' de la Negà, or Ca' dea negà. I could never understand what the difference was exactly. They have their own dialect on the island, you know. It isn't at all the same." Jack gave a great sigh and began again with obvious reluctance. "The story is that the wife of the man who previously owned the palazzo drowned there. He found her floating in the canal, just outside the watergate. Whether it was accidental or otherwise, no one knows."

Frankie felt a sudden chill. "And the name of the palazzo. What your father and his friends called it. What does it actually mean?"

There was a long pause before Jack finally spoke again. "Palace of the Drowned." When Frankie let out a groan, Jack hastened to continue. "Listen, it's all just a bit of nonsense, I'm certain. You know my father. He has a wicked sense of humor, at least according to him. And besides, I can't imagine any person less inclined to believe in ghosts than you, Frankie."

Still, the tale real or not, there was something that made Frankie pause. Even now, whenever she passed by the watergate, she did her best to avoid looking too closely at the steps that descended into the lagoon. Instead, she steadied her gaze on the disused gondola that was moored just steps away—*the palazzo used to have its very own personal gondolier, if you can believe it,* Jack had once told her. Frankie had noticed the gondola, now affixed to a chain and covered in a heavy network of cobwebs, looked as though it hadn't been used in several decades. She doubted very much that the thing was still seaworthy.

Above the ground floor was the *piano nobile,* which Jack assured her was once the most important floor of the whole structure, providing, in its excess of windows, an opportunity to see and be seen by the rest of Venetian society. It contained a great hall in which to welcome guests, a sitting room with impossibly high ceilings supported by wooden beams, and the aforementioned windows, the outsides of which were embellished with ornate Gothic finishes consisting of more frills and details than Frankie had ever seen before. The windows themselves provided views of the canal below and gave on to a small balcony, a feature she suspected was more for show, so shallow was the depth that a single person would struggle to move except to step forward and then back again.

The first floor also housed the kitchen and two bedrooms, the latter of which looked out over the courtyard rather than the canal, a blessing given the stench that tended to rise up at various points of the day, no matter whether the window was fastened or not. On the second was another set of bedrooms, smaller and more intimate, and on top of all this, an attic, which Frankie had only ventured into that first day, noting, as she did, the division of smaller rooms for what she supposed was the staff's use. In one of them she had glimpsed an unmade bed and wondered if the housekeeper, Maria, slept there when the palazzo was unoccupied, despite living on one of the city's many other islands.

Jack hadn't mentioned how long the palazzo had sat empty, but it didn't seem like anyone had been there in some time. On Frankie's arrival, everything had been covered in stiff off-white sheets, and it had felt as though the rooms themselves were holding their breath as she placed one tentative foot in front of the other. The whole place felt empty, as though it had never been inhabited at all. Rather than be unsettled by this, Frankie had found a comfort in such absence, as if the place belonged to her and what she alone would make of it. Tying a handkerchief around her hair and pulling on a shirt and a pair of slacks, she had begun to tackle one room at a time. It wasn't that they needed cleaning so much as reinvigorating, a brushing off of the ghosts that seemed to lurk within the walls. They needed, she decided, shaking out the sheets, to be brought back to life.

With this in mind, she had told Maria, in what little Italian she knew, and with the aid of a well-thumbed English-to-Italian dictionary that she had discovered in one of the bedrooms, to take a holiday, that she would manage the cleaning of the palazzo on her own. Maria, however, had refused to listen. A widow over sixty years old, the housekeeper had been caring for the palazzo for nearly two decades. As such, an attachment seemed to have formed between herself and the palazzo, so that when Frankie first made the suggestion, Maria looked at her with something akin to horror. In fact, rather than accept Frankie's offer, she seemed determined to oppose the new tenant's suggestion in any way she could—by lingering in hallways, by arriving early in the morning and not disappearing until late into the night. Frankie never actually heard the housekeeper enter or exit the palazzo, she would simply turn a corner and find her standing there, always with her eyes narrowed or a scowl on her face, as though Frankie was the one who had been caught out, as if she was the intruder. So abrupt were these appearances and disappearances that Frankie was half-convinced the palazzo must contain hidden passageways as yet unknown to her—ones that she suspected Maria would be most unwilling to share.

Eventually, Frankie began to wonder exactly what the housekeeper got up to whenever she was just out of her range of sight—particularly when it came to the bedroom she had chosen for herself. She could never prove anything, but she could almost *feel it*—on certain days, at certain hours. When her room looked cleaner than it had before, despite her sweater being in the same place, crumpled on the floor by the side of the bed, her papers scattered across her desk. There was that sensation that made the hairs on her arms rise—the feeling that whispered to her that someone else had been there. On these days, whenever the two women passed each other in the hall, Frankie would stop and ask, "Were you in my room today, Maria?"

The response was always the same. The housekeeper would turn to her, head held high, eyes gleaming in the darkness, and respond tersely, *"No, signora."*

The telephone was still ringing.

On hands and knees, Frankie began a thorough exploration of the sitting area on the first floor, certain that the ringing was originating from somewhere within the ornate room. "Where the devil *are* you?" she cried in frustration, searching under the sofa, under the table, still finding no trace of it at all. She had nearly given up hope, had begun to move toward where her coat lay draped across a chaise longue, determined to leave the palazzo until the infernal ringing ceased, when she found herself with a cord between her fingers. Following the length of it as though it were a route on a treasure map, she was led directly to a closet, in which she uncovered its hiding place, behind a pair of wellies.

"At last," came a familiar voice. "I was beginning to think you would never answer."

Pressing the receiver against her ear, Frankie broke out in a grin at the sound of Jack's voice. "That's your fault entirely. It took me ages to find the blasted thing. Why on earth is there a telephone hidden away in a broom cupboard?"

"Maria hates the thing, if I remember correctly. She was probably hoping to avoid ever using it. But never mind that. It's been weeks since we last spoke. Tell me, how are you filling your days in the city of bridges?"

Frankie thought she could feel the real question, unspoken, lurking just beneath. "Well, you should know that I've attempted to give your Maria an extended holiday, though she refuses to take it. I swear, Jack, the woman is supernatural. I never see her come or go, never hear her at all except when she appears right before me." She paused to listen to the ring of Jack's laughter. "And to answer your question, most of my days are spent cleaning this enormous apartment, as you absurdly refer to it. The sitting room alone is nearly as large as my entire house."

"Well, at least your attire will be conducive to the task."

Jack often liked to joke about what she referred to as *Frankie's uniform*—a pair of black cigarette trousers and a crisp button-down dress shirt, eschewing the fanciful colors and patterns that her friend favored. The simplicity suited Frankie. She had always been straight as an arrow and taller than most of the boys in her class, although that didn't stop her from wearing heels—she wouldn't have given them the satisfaction. Simple clothes had always suited her body best, the embellishments that thrilled others looking only cheap and garish on her.

Jack, on the other hand, was everything Frankie had been taught a woman was supposed to look like—ample curves and a heart-shaped face, clothed in whatever dress was the height of fashion and that showed off her narrow waist to advantage. But her voice—deep and husky, entirely at odds with the rest of her, a surprising contradiction—was the reason that Frankie had leaned in rather than away the first time they met, at one of the society gatherings she had been sent to cover by the newspaper, back when she had tried her hand at reporting.

"You failed to warn me about this ghastly weather," Frankie chided, her eyes resting on the scene just outside the window, half of the glass already obscured with the day's rain.

Jack laughed. "I told you autumn wouldn't be Venice at its best."

"Yes, but nothing about it being the worst."

"No, my dear, the worst is the height of the summer, when San Marco is crawling with tourists." Jack paused for a beat, and when she spoke again, her voice was softer, more serious. "Promise me you're all right there on your own."

"Have I told you that I've just learned the Italian word for history is *storia*? I rather like that," Frankie said, ignoring her friend's question. And then, when Jack was still silent, she added, "I'm fine here, Jack. I promise."

A held breath and then: "Good. And I promise that I will do my best to be there by this weekend, at the very latest."

"I'll hold you to that."

There was the sound of a kettle from somewhere in the background, followed by the closing of a cupboard door. "I don't suppose there's a chance for any other company in the meantime?"

The truth was, at the beginning, Frankie had gone out for a drink or two, sipping on whisky and avoiding the eye contact of others around her, when a fellow Englishman, a photojournalist, had sidled up to the bar beside her and introduced himself. She had been intrigued at first, wondering how it all worked, how he managed to get his photographs to the newspapers in time despite being so far away. He had explained the process—how they sent the photograph by telephone, developing the film first and then running to the post office, where they used a scanner that somehow transmitted it to the receiving end. Frankie had been fascinated, had asked to know more, but then he slipped his hand onto her knee and she excused herself to the lavatory, where she promptly made a turn for the exit, the tedium of having to explain that it wasn't what she wanted, not really, making her more tired and irritable than she cared to admit. It was an anecdote she had no intention of sharing with Jack, however, and instead said, "Do the neighbors count?"

"The neighbors?" Jack asked, her voice betraying her surprise. "You've met them?"

"No, but I've heard them. Well, their footsteps, mostly," Frankie conceded. "Nearly scared me half to death the first time. I thought it was someone following me, but then I realized the noise was coming from above." She didn't tell Jack how relieved she had felt in that moment, how she had placed a hand on her chest and willed her heart to calm.

"But no sign of the actual occupants?" Jack asked. "That's peculiar."

"They could be elderly," Frankie suggested.

"Yes, maybe." Jack paused. "Still, it's a pity you're all alone there. I would feel better if I knew you weren't so isolated atop your castle."

"Actually," Frankie replied, speaking slowly, winding the coil of the telephone around her fingers, "I did happen to run into someone from home."

"Really? Anyone I know?"

"No, just the daughter of an acquaintance. Or at least she claimed she was." Frankie paused, wondering how Jack would respond if she told her how she had really felt upon meeting the girl. "I don't know why, but I had the strangest feeling that she was lying."

"About knowing you? Why on earth would she do that?" Jack asked, her voice a note sharper than before.

"I haven't the faintest idea."

When Jack spoke next, her voice was low but insistent. "Frankie."

She could hear the warning in just that one word. "Yes, I know," Frankie said, taking a deep breath. "Still, there was something so peculiar about her—"

"Shall I tell you what I think?" Jack interrupted. "I think that you've been alone for the past few weeks, wrapped tightly in your little blanket of solitude, and now, at the first sign of intrusion, you're seeing problems where there aren't any."

Her friend was probably right. She pushed the girl from her mind. "Enough about me, then. Tell me, what exactly has been keeping you so very busy in London?" She did her best approximation of what she hoped might sound like teasing, so that Jack would not know just how much her continued deflection on the subject injured her.

On the telephone there was a pause, and Frankie felt a different type of worry begin to take shape. Jack had always been the first one to abandon a day's responsibilities in favor of an outing, a party, anything at all that was enjoyable and skirted the realities of everyday mundane life. Frankie often teased her that she was the most frivolous human being she had ever met, to which Jack most often responded with a smile and thank-you. This avoidance of Venice was most unlike her.

When she spoke again, all traces of gaiety were gone from her friend's voice. "I'll be there soon," Jack said. And then, just before disconnecting: "I promise."

Leaning against the window, Frankie took a long sip of her drink and caught sight of her reflection in the glass. For a second, the face—pale and sharply contoured in the darkness—seemed unfamiliar, and she cast a glance over her shoulder to ensure that no one else was there with her. The room was empty, and yet she could not rid herself of the feeling that her reflection was not her own—that the woman in the glass before her was not simply an echo of herself but independent somehow.

She told herself it was only her nerves.

Over the past few weeks, the immediacy of London had been pushed away, so that at times Frankie could almost recall it with the indifference of a stranger, as if it was not a place that had ever belonged to her, nor she to it. Now, at the introduction of the girl, coupled with her friend's telephone call, Frankie felt her solitude further spoiled, felt the distance that she had worked so tirelessly to create begin to fall away, so that all at once the acridness of that city overwhelmed her. She closed her eyes, but it did nothing to shut it out. If anything, her senses seemed to heighten. She could smell the smoke from the chimneys and the grease from the chip shop, could see the lights of the city reflected in the rain-slicked streets beneath her feet and feel the flush of the heat against her cheeks as she pushed through those doors, into the Savoy, that night—could feel the eyes of the redheaded woman watching her.

She had tried to ignore it at first, the woman's stare, glancing away, pulling at the neckline of her dress, the material scraping against her throat. She was only imagining things, she told herself, tallying the glasses of champagne she had consumed since her arrival, the whisky before that, the missed supper and forgotten lunch. She had eyed the rest of the guests, peering at them through the insufferable cocktail talk and stale cigarette smoke, all the while knowing that she should never have come—should never have allowed her editor, who had conveniently disappeared from her side, to sway her into attending the extravagant gathering in honor of some talented new author he had managed to poach from another publisher. Most would have chosen a private celebration, considering the subterfuge that was no doubt involved in such a deal—but, then, Harold had never been like most people.

Frankie still smarted from his reaction upon seeing her that night. It had been evident when he approached her table that he had never really expected her to come in the first place. She couldn't fault him. It was always unusual for her to make such appearances, and, in truth, she hadn't planned to make that one either, but then she had opened a bottle of whisky at home—mixing it first with soda, before dropping the pretense of a mixer altogether—and then she was hailing a taxi, invitation in hand, and before she could so much as change her mind, the driver had pulled up outside the Savoy.

So, no, Frankie couldn't fault him his surprise. What she *could* fault, however, was the very discernible look of disappointment that had briefly flickered across his face after he noticed her presence that night.

"Are you certain you feel up to this, my dear?" Harold had asked, after bestowing on her a hasty kiss hello, his eyes locked on her hand as she accepted another glass of champagne from one of the waiters making their way around the room. He adjusted his gray silk cravat and she bit back the desire to tell him how ridiculous he looked, silently daring him to ask her what number drink she was on—not that she would have been able to answer by then. "It's just, well, you've been a bit fraught these days."

Fraught. She had almost laughed. The word didn't even begin to describe what she had been—and it had been longer than a few days. Weeks, by that time. Ever since the review.

"How's the new novel going?" Harold had asked then. "I would have thought you'd be at home, hard at work."

Frankie hadn't responded to his question—or his suggestion, she wasn't certain which it was meant to be—hadn't told him that she had yet to write a single word. It was not for lack of trying. Some days she sat for hours at a time, waiting, just in case, but the page continued to remain blank. She had had moments like that before, when the words refused to come no matter how much she pushed—but nothing so prolonged, and nothing that she wasn't able to make her way out of in the end. This had felt different, endless, in a way that made her mouth dry and her palms sweat.

"You'll see something soon," she had told him, looking for the waiter and his tray of sparkling glasses. Her editor had abandoned her not long after, waving to someone across the room and making his excuses, despite knowing full well how much she detested such functions.

She should have left then.

Instead, she turned back to her drink, took yet another pull of her champagne, emptying the glass—her fourth by that point, though most likely her fifth, certainly a bottle, at any rate. Her eyes had darted across the room to the other guests, and she wondered, as she often wondered by then, if they too had read the review, if they were thinking of it as they sipped on their glasses of champagne, if they were speaking of it as they dipped their heads closer together, exchanging whispered confidences, all while she stood at her solitary table, ostracized from the rest, and looked on. She had felt the anger vibrating inside her, those damned words clamoring for attention.

The clearing of a throat had broken through her thoughts then, and she noticed she was no longer alone, that there was someone standing just beside her, a young man dressed in a carefully pressed suit, hair swept to the side in a fashion that was becoming popular among the younger set. He was one of the waiters at the function, or at least she assumed so at the time, reaching for the glass of champagne he held in his hand. But instead of moving on, as the other waiters before him had done, the young man moved closer, dipping his head nearer to her own. She should have noted it—would have, on any other day.

"It's you," he whispered.

She remembered drawing back, remembered being offended by his closeness.

"I saw your name on the list, but I didn't believe you would be here." He had looked pleased with himself, she recalled thinking, as he straightened his narrow tie, before he continued: "I was such a fan of your first novel."

Frankie had opened her mouth to respond, a retort forming on her tongue, but paused when she noticed that the redheaded woman—her vermilion shade almost decidedly from a box—was looking her way again. Their eyes met, and the redhead turned to her companion and laughed. Frankie had stopped then, had wondered whether it was about her. Surely it was, she reasoned, for they were both looking at her, casting glances beneath their lacquered and hooded eyelids, the colors smeared across their skin, bright and crude. She had wanted to shout across the room, to demand what it was that they wanted—she had felt the words rising in her throat, had felt the blood in her face. She felt, she remembered, the pores of her skin contract and enlarge, her cheeks growing bright, like two large, imperfect circles of blush swiped by a child's hand. *Stop it*, she had commanded herself, *stop it, before*—

She turned away.

It took her several seconds to realize that the man next to her had been speaking the entire time. Later, she would wonder what exactly it was that he had said then, whether it would have changed the course of the night if she had not let her attention drift, if she had listened to him more closely.

"Your new novel—"

"Have you read it as well, then?" she interrupted.

"The novel?" he asked. "Yes, I—"

"No." Frankie waved her hand in dismissal. "The review."

The waiter had looked confused at her words. She remembered that later, wondering if he had even known about the review at all before she mentioned it. She hadn't waited for him to respond. "You did. You don't have to pretend otherwise." She paused to swallow more champagne. "Do you know they found Emily's locked away?"

"Emily?"

"Brontë," Frankie snapped, annoyed that the waiter was unable to follow the thread of conversation. "They found them in her dresser, after she died."

There was a pause and the waiter tilted his head, reached for her hand, stopping her from taking another sip of her drink. "And does it matter to you much?" he asked, holding her gaze. "What someone else writes?"

She had thought it was unusual even then, but through the blur and fog of the champagne she had pushed it aside, only managed to feel annoyed that he was stopping her from taking another sip, that he was touching her in a way that seemed altogether too familiar. "Of course it does. *Awkwardly and illogically constructed.* That's what they wrote."

"I don't think—"

"And I don't have someone to vouch for me, to wipe my name free of soil."

The waiter frowned again, but she didn't bother to explain. Something else had caught her attention. The woman across the room was still staring—still *laughing*. Her head thrown back, the curve of her mouth slightly askew from a smudge of red lipstick. Frankie noticed it as she drew closer to the table, her attention so focused on the detail that she stumbled slightly as she went, once or twice reaching out for the tables on either side of her in order to steady herself, the sound of breaking glass trailing her as she went.

The woman looked up at her approach, and as her face shifted—a sliver of fear, she remembered noting with satisfaction, emerging across her features—Frankie had felt a sudden thrill run through her body.

Now she felt that same heat rise up from her belly and she

leaned her forehead against the window, feeling the cool of it against her skin. She did not worry about the smudges it would leave, only pressed further, the chill of the glass helping to steady her, to remind her where she was, to keep her focused and in the present. Only after the flush lessened did she move again, though a quick glance in the glass revealed two bright spots of red, high on her cheeks.

She didn't remember hitting the woman, only the feel of the impact. She didn't remember the blood but had been reminded the next day by the stain on her white gloves. Afterward, she had disposed of them in the bin, had wondered, briefly, if it would count as tampering with evidence. She decided she didn't care and threw away the rest as well—a two-piece emerald column dress she had always loved and a black clutch that had once belonged to her mother. She couldn't stand to look at any of it—not ever again. The stark realization of what she had done, of the scene that she had caused—the shouts and accusations, the violence, her fury refusing to be spent until all around her there was nothing but silence and broken glass, along with that spark of certainty she had felt that everyone there, not just the redheaded woman, had known about the review, had been laughing at her, mocking her—left her breathless with fear.

She had been wrong—and not only about the woman.

It turned out that the waiter, the one she had chatted to without hesitation, without censure, wasn't a waiter at all. Rather, he was a writer—worse yet, a reporter, working for one of those tabloid rags that dressed themselves up as something smarter than they were. That was how it had all come out in the end. The only saving grace was that nothing had been captured in pictures. Instead, the publication had to settle for printing one of Frankie's older head-shots, a throwaway that she never worked out how they had found, her expression uneasy, her eyes dark, her mouth hardened. It had been the first time she had her photograph taken for anything official, and she had been uncomfortable at the attention. When the image ran alongside the sensational headlines, she knew what others no doubt saw: a woman who was mad.

She reached into her pocket now, touched the cold metal there. The feel of it always steadied her somehow, grounded her in a way that nothing else did. When the war ended, she had retired her ARP uniform with relief, glad to be rid of the stiff jacket and scratchy skirt—all except for the whistle, which she had slipped into her pocket upon hearing news of the war's end and kept on her ever since. In times of stress, she would reach for it, her fingers tracing the *ARP* letters inscribed on its surface. She had done the same when the bombs were at their worst, when the wail of the sirens and the racket of the planes above had created a deafening cacophony that at times she believed would never end. Now, in the silence that seemed just as overwhelming as that clatter of noise once had, Frankie gripped the small piece of metal, her fingers running across the groove of the letters.

The fallout from that night had been inevitable. A canceled book tour. Postponed interviews. Not that Frankie minded, always dreading that part of the process anyway, but she was smart enough to know it was necessary, to realize what the absence of such things might mean.

"It's only for now," Harold reassured her at the time.

She had always trusted her editor to tell her the truth, but she was no longer so certain.

Frankie turned away from the macabre reflection before her now. In the darkness, her face had been transformed, her eyes becoming sunken pools of black, her lips stained the color of blood. The memory of the thrill she had experienced that night at the Savoy was replaced with something sharp and icy, the coldness running through her veins, stretching up and down the length of her body. She tugged at the curtains, her reflection disappearing before her. Turning away, Frankie finished the last of her drink and headed upstairs to bed.

CHAPTER 3

Slowly, Frankie began to learn the rhythm of the city. She opened windows and closed them again, depending on the time of the day and stench from the canal. She learned that it was worse when the tide was low, when the seaweed peeked out from beneath the surface, and again nearly just as bad when the tide was high, when the water churned up and above the cobblestones, creeping first into San Marco and then slowly to the rest of the city. At those times, a sulfuric tang filled the air, one that caused Frankie to recoil, to hold her breath and back away.

For this reason alone, she had claimed one of the more modest rooms on the second floor. The space itself was plain, except for a large wooden desk that she had spent the better part of the first week shuffling across the floor, trying to avoid leaving scuff marks on the wood. Unable to decide where the best spot was, Frankie had at last decided to position the desk facing one of the room's bare walls, rather than the window, thereby ensuring minimal distractions from below. To the surface of the desk she added a sizable ashtray, an amber-colored piece of Murano glass she had discovered downstairs, in lieu of any real paperweight.

It was during this slight reorganization of the room that she discovered, just beside the bed, a speaking tube that jutted out of the wall and whose shape reminded her of a much smaller version of the horns one used to find on old gramophones. Frankie had placed her ear against the cold metal, listening to the howling that sounded from somewhere within its depths—the echoing of wind, she soon realized, like when one held up a shell to their ear. Curious, she had spent the better part of the day attempting to track down the other end, finding one in the *piano nobile* and another in the courtyard of the palazzo. An early version of the telephone.

Eventually tiring of such distractions—she refused to call them procrastinations—Frankie sat down at her desk and began to write again. It had felt unfamiliar at first, her hand hovering, faltering, as she searched for the right words, the right phrases, until she forced herself to cast such notions aside, the wall that she had built around her in London at last beginning to erode in the salty air of Venice. When she became certain that it was not just a fluke, that she had in fact found her way to the start of something at last, she began to visit the Biblioteca della Fondazione Querini Stampalia in the Campo Santa Maria Formosa. Frankie had been delighted to discover the reading rooms, all with parquet floors that squeaked under the slightest pressure, and which in turn caused every seated person in the library to look up in consternation. Most days Frankie was able to find a place at one of the half dozen wooden tables that were positioned in the room. Once in a while, when she didn't want to deal with the throat-clearing of one patron or the blowing of a nose by another, or even the curious habit the locals had of sitting right beside her, no matter if the rest of the table was empty, she claimed one of the leather chairs that were positioned in the corner of each room and did her best to write with pen and paper in her lap. Some days, the words came, but on others, she was content to sit and look up at the ceiling, the flourishes of which were beyond her knowledge of art but in which she could delight all the same.

Afterward, when she was spent, when no more words would come and her head felt fuzzy from being trapped inside it for too

long, she would head to the *bacaro* situated only steps away, beside
the Santa Maria Formosa church. There, she sat outside with a glass
of wine, despite the constant cold, despite the oft-persistent drizzle.
Her favorite spot was just to the side of the bar, despite the disadvantage of being near the canal and, even more disappointing, a
gondola station, so that every once in a while the stink of the water
reached her, followed closely by the gondolier's heavily accented offer for *a gondola, a gondola, anyone.* It gave her not only a clear view
of the church and all its visitors, devout Catholics and curious tourists alike, but a view of one of the more amusing gargoyles guarding
the church, which stared back at her with a lopsided mouth and
tongue, its expression both grotesque and comical. It was, she could
not help but think, a child's rendition of what a gargoyle should
look like. Often, after a second glass, she caught herself smiling, almost laughing in response to it, one time even sticking her tongue
out when no one was watching—at which point she felt certain
that she had had one too many drinks and been without company
for far too long.

At home, Frankie would pull out the pages she had produced
throughout the day, reading them carefully, critically, imagining
herself as their reader rather than writer, and in the end, she was
surprised to find that she did not hate what was there.

At the sound of the telephone, Frankie jumped. Glancing toward
the window, she estimated that it was still morning, though she
was uncertain as to the exact time. Unable to sleep, she had been
awake for several hours already, sitting at her desk, writing. Lost
in thought, only at this interruption did she realize that her room
was freezing—a sign she had loitered too long, as even the warm
embers in the copper pot that Maria had begun placing underneath
her bed each night had been reduced to nothing more than cold
ash. She reached for the sweater slung across the foot of her bed.

In truth, Frankie had learned to enjoy the oft-frigid air since her arrival, the warmth of the fireplace rarely reaching the second floor. There was something about it that seemed to jostle her mind, that made her reach for her pen, as if her previous lack of inspiration could be put down to the comforts of home alone. She found herself hoping it was that simple.

Pushing away from her desk now, she made her way along the landing and toward the iron spiral staircase that connected the first two floors. In the sitting room, Frankie had barely time to utter a greeting into the telephone before the person on the other end of the line cut in. "You might have told me sooner that you had a telephone out there, in the middle of nowhere, instead of leaving me to learn it from your little friend," came a hurried male voice. "Venice in the off-season. I still can't understand it."

Frankie smiled. "Hello to you too, Harold."

"Well," her editor responded. "I hope you're enjoying yourself, in your vast palazzo. It sounds frightfully grand." He paused. "Do I even dare ask about pages?"

"What pages, Harold?"

She could imagine her editor with his head between his hands, his favorite repose in moments of extreme frustration, a cigarette between his fingers. There was something vaguely gratifying in knowing just how much upset she often caused him. Though Harold was short and bald, with great big glasses that gave the impression that he was perpetually blinking, his diminutive size was by no means representative of his stature. He was known for his cunning among his colleagues, his ruthlessness, according to some. Frankie had long ago lost track of the arguments they had endured over the years—all of which had only further endeared him to her. They were family more than colleagues. Which meant that, at times, though she had no particular experience with siblings, she wanted to throttle him the way she supposed any older sister might want to do to a meddling brother.

"Any pages, Frankie."

She remained silent. She had been in Venice only a few weeks and they had both agreed this was supposed to be a break, a chance to relax, to restore—to leave the last year firmly behind.

"When can I come to visit?" he asked, changing tactics.

"It depends," she replied. "What exactly would the nature of your visit be?"

"To see you, my dear. To make sure that you're all right."

"I'm quite all right, Harold. I can tell you that without you having to board a plane and come all the way here." She narrowed her eyes. "What's the real reason you want to come?"

There was a pause on the other end of the line and for a moment she thought he might have hung up, as he often did during their more turbulent chats, but instead there came a great sigh of exasperation from the other end before he began, "If we could only talk about the next book." He hesitated then. "You do still owe us a look at one more, my dear."

Yes, she still had one more book and then after that—well, she was too afraid to ask, too afraid to know what she already suspected the answer might be. "I'll show you when I have something to show you, Harold. When it's done. When it's complete."

He let out a great sigh. "Frankie, the days of Emily Dickinson are over."

"What on earth does that mean?" she demanded.

"It means you can't simply sit in an attic all day, hoarding your work away and then declare it ready to be published. Let me help you."

But she didn't want his help, didn't need it, she told herself—not after what had happened the first time. She had taken his notes, his suggestions, had even, much to her regret, as Harold never failed to find an opportunity to remind her, taken his idea for the ending. At first she had been grateful, excited even, by their collaboration. But then they had gone to their first party together after the book was published and Harold had grinned and asked every person they met what they thought of the ending. When the person under interrogation assured them both that they had been thrilled by it, that it was the reason the book was so brilliant—which was what all the reviews had said as well, so they were only essentially parroting what had been said before—Harold had leaned forward, winked, and said, "That's mine."

There was always a moment then when the person before them seemed unsettled by this bit of confided news, or perhaps they were only unprepared for it, their romanticization of what it meant to write a novel so clearly defined in their own minds, so that their eyes widened as they looked between the two, between her and Harold, between author and editor, and tried to work out where the praise was due. As the situation threatened to grow awkward, Harold would always laugh and press his hand against Frankie's shoulder, insisting that she was the real artist. Frankie always thought then that his voice seemed raised, his words slightly thick, as though he had a toffee stuck between his teeth.

"Is there anything to see at all yet?"

"No," she lied.

Harold made a sort of begrudging noise—one Frankie had come to interpret as him backing down, surrendering, at least for the time being, as Harold's raised white flag never lasted too long. "Well, if you're not writing, tell me that you're at least looking after yourself."

"I am," Frankie said with a smile. "I promise."

"And Jack?" he asked, with a sarcasm that was difficult to ignore. "How is she?"

"You needn't pretend on my behalf, Harold," Frankie said, knowing full well how much the two disliked each other. She had always supposed it had something to do with them jostling for the top position in her life, but after the way Jack had swooped in after the Savoy, with Harold just beside her, she had imagined that a sort of truce had been formed in the face of the crisis. The armistice, it seemed, had run its course.

"Yes, well, my analyst says I need to be more understanding."

Frankie suppressed a smile, amused at the idea of Harold lying prostrate on a sofa, at someone else's mercy. "Listen, Harold, I'm off to the shop now." It was a half-truth, anyway. Frankie looked out the window—it was dark and the clouds were heavy, but it did not seem as though it would rain for another hour or so, if she was lucky. "Ring again soon." At her words, both of them laughed, knowing full well he would do exactly that—and whether she wanted him to or not. Frankie had only just put the telephone back on the cradle when it rang again. "Harold," she answered wearily, but with a smile as well.

There was a pause on the other end. "Hello?" the voice began, somewhat muffled. "Frances?"

"Yes," she replied, trying to place the caller.

"Oh good, it is you! I was worried I had the wrong number." There was a bit of static, so that Frankie held the receiver away from her. She returned it barely in time to hear the person on the other end say: "It's Gilly."

For a moment, Frankie couldn't place the name, but then she remembered the girl at the market, the feeling of unease that had followed, and it seemed absurd that she had somehow forgotten.

"I thought I'd ring about coffee."

"Coffee?" Frankie repeated, remembering only then that, *yes,* she *had* promised the girl that she would try to find time for them to meet. She wondered whether she might still be able to get out of it, claim a prior engagement that she had only just recalled. Somehow, though, she was certain that the girl would see through any such protestations and that inevitably it would only mean the outing would be postponed rather than canceled.

"Yes, I thought we could go to Florian's, in San Marco. Do you know it?"

Frankie didn't, but she also didn't want to make a fuss, worried that it would somehow prolong the whole thing. And so when the girl asked whether that would be a place she would like to meet, Frankie nodded and copied down the name of the coffee shop and directions, which didn't contain any actual street names, only *right* and *left* and such vague instructions as *turn right at the chemist, you know the one, with the large window display,* and promised to meet her at eleven the next morning.

"Till then," the girl said, and rang off.

Frankie hung up the telephone, pausing long enough to wonder how the girl had managed to get her number in the first place, when she hadn't known she was in possession of one until after they had met.

Frankie woke late the next morning and was forced to forgo her bath in order to meet the girl on time. For this reason, added to her initial misgivings about the meeting, she was in something of a foul temper by the time she arrived at the café.

It had taken double the time she had intended, Gilly's instructions leading her to a literal dead end on more than one occasion. She had been forced to ask a local, in her halting, terrible Italian, and only after much frantic pantomiming had she found the right path. Now, pushing past the steamed-up windows of the café, the heat of crowded bodies, Frankie was somewhat mollified to discover that she had, at the very least, managed to arrive first, allowing her to select a table and to hastily run her fingers through her uncombed hair. However, any such feelings of goodwill began to dissipate as the minutes passed. By a quarter past, Frankie had sent the waiter away for the third time, a regrettable fact that seemed to anger them both equally. At half past, she capitulated and ordered a cappuccino, which arrived lukewarm and far too milky. Fifteen minutes after that, she asked for the bill, determined not to waste another minute of her time waiting for someone who clearly had no possession of manners.

At the bill, Frankie blanched. The amount far exceeded anything she had ever before paid for something as simple as a cup of coffee. She had heard about the practice of charging for the privilege of using the house's table, of being able to sit and listen to the ever-present music of Venice, although today there were no musicians to be seen. It was, however, the first time she had experienced it, preferring those places that were hidden away and therefore immune to most tourists and thus the trappings that lay in wait for them. She cursed the girl for choosing such an ostentatious place, and then herself for agreeing to come. If only she had listened to her instincts, she could have avoided this—a morning wasted and her pocket emptied of lire she could have put to much better use elsewhere. Next time the girl telephoned her, she would hang up.

On her walk home, which was colder and rainier than it had been when she first set out, Frankie grew angrier still. Stepping over a puddle, she mused once more over the fact that she had been stood up, marveling at the impudence of the girl—dragging Frankie out all this way, when she hadn't even wanted to go in the first place, and then not bothering to turn up.

The whole thing defied belief.

She was just rounding the basilica when she felt the hairs on the back of her neck rise. Frankie stopped and glanced over her shoulder. A crowd milled behind her, just as it always did in San Marco. She scanned the faces quickly, a few remaining hidden beneath umbrellas. There was no one, or, rather, no one she recognized. It was only the damp, working its way underneath her coat and onto her skin. She chided herself for acting like a superstitious schoolgirl.

At home, she peeled off her wet clothes and climbed into the bath, into the scalding water, watching with satisfaction as her skin turned pink with warmth. She breathed deeply, working to empty her mind of the thoughts that had plagued her a moment before, thinking instead of the glass of wine that she would pour herself once she got out, and then something a bit stronger to ward off the chill.

By the time an hour passed, she had once again forgotten about Gilly altogether.

CHAPTER 4

Frankie stepped out of the apartment, closing the door behind her. Somewhere in the palazzo another door closed, the sound echoing throughout the courtyard. For a moment, she remained still, wondering whether she might be about to catch a glimpse of the neighbor. A minute passed and then another—but no one emerged from the door atop the staircase across the way. Disappointed, Frankie began to make her way to the ground floor, her heels against the tile echoing throughout the palazzo.

Only the night before, Jack had telephoned about the mysterious neighbors. "Listen," she had said, her voice so clear that it was as if they were in the same room. "I spoke with Maria."

"And, what's the matter?" Frankie asked, already hearing the note of concern in her friend's voice. She sneaked a glance around her, wondering where the housekeeper was currently lurking. It occurred to her then that Jack might have asked Maria to keep an eye on her, to keep track of Frankie's comings and goings, of her state of mind, even. Perhaps that had been part of the reason she had refused to relinquish control of the palazzo. Jack hesitated, and Frankie suspected she might be right.

"She said there's no one on the other side."

Frankie had let out a sharp laugh. "Don't be absurd. I've heard them. I told you as much last time we spoke."

"I know," she sighed. "And I don't know what it is you think you heard, but I can assure you it wasn't another tenant. It couldn't be. Maybe it was a rat? Not that that's much comfort, but they're huge there, you know. The Venetians even have a special name for them. *Pantegana.* It refers specifically to the sewer rat there. Regardless, Maria said that both of the apartments are usually empty over the winter."

Frankie let that settle. "Well," she said. "Be that as it may, I will have to respectfully disagree with your Maria. Unless rats can turn on lights, there is someone living next door."

Now, as she opened the door to the street, she could not stop herself from glancing once more over her shoulder. She paused, and in the entrance hall above, something seemed to shift. Frankie stepped away from the door. She could not be sure, but she was almost certain that someone was standing there, watching her. It was only a shadow, but the shape, she thought, was decidedly human.

Frankie was not a woman who believed in ghosts, nor was she a woman intimidated by shadows and bumps in the night. For this reason alone, she rushed over to the other side of the palazzo and knocked with a grim set of determination. "Hello, is anyone there?" There was no response. Frankie waited, just in case she was somehow right about them being elderly—it would take them a minute or two longer to make their way to the intercom and respond. She looked up into the entrance hall again, shielding her eyes from the sun. There was no one.

But there *had* been someone. Whatever Jack said, whatever Maria told her, Frankie was convinced that someone was there. She was less certain, however, of why they were hiding, when she had clearly spotted them. Perhaps they only valued their privacy, she reasoned, admitting that she would have been unlikely to answer the door to a stranger back in London. She tried to remind herself that *she* was the outsider here, the one who had only temporarily taken up residence in the palazzo, while they might very well be full-time residents, ones who had lived there for decades. It was only right that they be curious about the presence of their new neighbor.

Turning away, she decided that this continued anonymity between them was best. In London she had never wanted to know her neighbors, did not, in fact, know them now, despite living in the same flat for most of her adult life. She didn't know what it was about Venice that should make this different, that should make her behave so unlike herself.

Casting one last glance over her shoulder, she headed out.

That morning she visited the Doge's Palace.

Walking briskly through the vast structure, past countless halls and endless grand paintings, through the cavernous prisons etched with the words of those who had found their end there, she arrived at her favorite spot in the whole of the palace. Standing on the Bridge of Sighs, imagining all the prisoners that had passed along the same corridor on their way to the end, she was reminded of a Byron poem she had learned as a schoolgirl. Frankie had never been a fan of Byron, had found him a bit *too much,* just like the rest of the Romantics, that brooding group that always felt too indefinable, too ambiguous in their musings. Shelley, though, *she* was a different story. But while most other readers clamored for *Frankenstein,* its genesis as a ghost story told around a fireplace at Villa Diodati always lending it a certain superficial gloss, Frankie gravitated toward Shelley's lesser-known work—in particular, an apocalyptic tale that left Frankie wondering at the idea of what she would do were she the last woman on earth.

She stretched her arms now, touched the walls on either side of her, and whispered, *"I stood in Venice, on the Bridge of Sighs, A palace and a prison on each hand."* She tried to remember the rest, but it would not come. Something about the impermanence of the city, of how it had changed—its grandeur, its beauty, fading and diminishing as time went on. But—and she remembered this part clearly—the image that others carried of Venice was at least in one way preserved, through art, through the permanence of words. She sought to remember the line, looking down at the canal beneath her, trying to recall her lessons. *Her name in story.* That was it. The idea that this now doge-less city was not the same as it had once been, its celebrated past all but disappeared—*and yet,* through the words written about her, this image would always remain, captured, as it were, by the poetic musings of Shakespeare, of Otway, of all the artists that had been enthralled with the city throughout the centuries. Venice, as she once was, would never be truly lost, and though its visitors would continue to search for her, would continue to fail, those who understood where to find her would know she would always remain within the words, preserved against both time and the rising waters.

And perhaps it was for this reason that she had come to love it: the city's un-knowableness. The idea that visitors who came expecting one thing often turned away, bewildered, when faced with a city that so vastly differed from the romanticized ideal they had been taught to expect. Frankie had always disliked places that were too easy. Here, she suspected that to understand Venice, to understand Venetians, was something harder, more difficult. She could see it even in the layout of the city. If one were to walk by a *pasticceria* or a *bacaro* or an *osteria,* they might not know that such a space existed, so darkened and self-contained did it seem so as to prevent entry. Even the doors were smaller than what Frankie was used to—two half doors created to make one, with only one side ever in use. This too seemed to baffle most visitors, the look of confusion sweeping their faces as they attempted to make their way through the tiny door ultimately causing many of them to turn around, as if the smallness of the space warned them that this was not intended for them.

And then there were the streets themselves. Frankie had wondered more than once how long it would take to memorize the city, the endless series of bridges and *calli,* streets that narrowed and twisted, only to open again in *campi* or close in dead ends, wondered if even the inhabitants struggled to learn its every curve, if there were parts of the city that remained a mystery to them. Nights were more unsettling still, when the streets were emptied of residents, the darkness so entirely absorbing, absolute. For every day, at the onset of sunset, the hustle of only hours before seemed to evaporate into the air. Those first few nights Frankie had waited in vain for the rowdy men on their way home from the *bacari,* for the cry of children from the next palazzo, for the roar of the *vaporetto*—but there had been nothing. Nighttime in Venice was so quiet, so still— Frankie suspected that it was not for the faint of heart.

As she exited the palace, the fog that had been threatening to roll in since that morning began to steadily cover the island, parts of her own body swallowed by its thickness as she moved throughout the streets. Before Venice, Frankie had never seen fog so thick. Not even in London. Here, it rolled in discernible waves, curled around her ankles, so that she could feel it engulfing her. The Venetian fog seemed capable of obscuring everything—and she had found a peculiar type of comfort in it, in being wrapped up, swaddled, as though a cloak of invisibility had been draped around her shoulders. It wasn't only her sight that became affected—sound was muffled as well. Shapes no longer appeared rooted to anything. It was dizzying. She felt uncentered, unmoored, but rather than being panicked, she felt reassured, felt as though it was possible to forget the past and move forward, just as everyone around her kept insisting she must.

In London, she could do nothing but remember—but, then, London was sturdy, solid. She had only to look down and see the evidence in the pavement beneath her feet.

Here, there was no such solidity.

Which was why, on days like this, she preferred to roam— sometimes for hours on end, never certain of any particular destination even when she ended up there, content in the journey, in the mist of air and water that swallowed her as she moved, so that everything else fell away, including all her worries and anxieties.

In Venice, she was allowed to be someone else. Someone who was, she often thought, a version of her former self. She had read somewhere once that the fog in Venice obliterated all reflection, and while she knew they were talking about sight and images, she felt its other meaning was just as true.

In Venice, her mind stopped dwelling, stopped despairing.

In Venice, the past began to slip away from her, like a slow trickle of water.

Frankie took a *traghetto* home, standing up alongside the other locals as the gondola made its way down the canal. The first time she had tried it, her thighs had groaned, had protested, burning as she fought to stay upright and out of the dirty canal, a single trail of sweat snaking its way down her back as she fought to remain still. The second time had been easier, and then, after that, she began to feel a certain smugness in the way that she was able to hold herself, just as still as any Venetian, whether empty-handed or weighed down with the day's groceries.

Today, Frankie felt burdened by something else. She disembarked a stop too early, wanting to be alone, away from the push and shove of other bodies. It was as if all at once she could feel the silence she had built around herself start to crack, to dissolve. First that strange girl, and then Jack and Harold. Frankie knew that soon her solitude would be nothing more than useless shards lying at her feet.

She had made little progress in her walk home when she was stopped by a large crowd gathered by a canal, blocking her path.

At first, Frankie couldn't decide what all the fuss was about, only that they seemed to be intent upon staring into the murky waters. Then someone in front of her shifted and the obstructed view of the canal opened up. Frankie gasped. Two men in plain clothes—she didn't think they were *carabinieri*—were pulling a body from the water. A lifeless body, she could tell, by the way the crowd watched, solemn and silent.

It was a woman, she was surprised to see. Frankie noticed that one of her heels was missing and that her stockings were torn, the colors of her dress blurred and running from the water. It seemed uncanny somehow, to be so close to her, this stranger, to be privy to such a private moment. She was young. Much too young to have ended up in the canal, for Frankie was certain somehow that this had not been an accident. She felt a blaze of anger flare up in her core. *What a waste,* she wanted to declare, to walk away and leave the scene behind her, not caring whom she might offend in her haste. But she didn't. Instead, she thought the words, the taste of them bitter and hard on her tongue, but they did not make their way out, and she knew that she only half-believed them anyway.

She turned from the scene, desperate, wanting nothing more than to be able to touch someone, to be touched in return. The regret she felt at her loss of solitude seemed harder to grasp on to, as though she could no longer understand her former self. As she made her way back to the palazzo, Frankie felt something shift deep inside her—a hollowness she had never before experienced.

In the courtyard, she passed Maria as she was sweeping. Her step quickened at the sight of the watergate, reminded then of Jack's story about the previous owners and the woman who might have drowned there.

Just as Frankie was about to wish the housekeeper *buonanotte,* she heard it—the sound of footsteps overhead. She looked at

Maria, their eyes momentarily locked upon each other. The housekeeper had heard it too, Frankie knew. There could be no denying it now.

"You see, there is someone there," Frankie said, her words sharper than called for, shaped by her experience at the canal. "I know you heard them just now," she continued, pointing toward the other side of the palazzo, where the footsteps had come from.

But Maria only stared back, her expression dull and empty. "I hear nothing, *signora*."

Brushing past Frankie, the housekeeper headed toward the street entrance, closing the door to the courtyard without another word.

CHAPTER 5

The next day, the buzzer rang out.

Frankie, sitting at her desk, pen in hand, looked up as the shrill sound echoed throughout the rooms. It was almost as though the palazzo was empty and not filled with furniture and carpets and all manner of trinkets that should have absorbed the shock of the noise. It occurred to her that no one had ever rung the buzzer before, that, in fact, she knew no one in the city *to* ring the buzzer.

Her voice was tentative as she answered: "Yes?"

"Frances, it's me."

"Yes," Frankie responded, not bothering to correct the girl. "I'll be right down."

She could have sent the girl away, it would have been easy to lie. But, then, the day before seemed to have marked her somehow, like a chill she could not shrug off, and she realized that she had been truthful with herself when she acknowledged no longer wanting to be alone. Frankie had always taken comfort in her solitude, but during the last year or so, she had become aware of just how alone she was. If not for her friend, if not for her editor, days might stretch in which she had no one to interact with, to confide in, and the thought made her more miserable than she cared to admit.

Back in London, in the worst moments, alone with nothing but the words of that infernal review repeating in her mind, she had entertained the type of dark thoughts that she suspected led that woman to the canal.

She did not intend to go back there again.

Gilly stood outside the door, in the street. It was chill that morning, a sheen of damp on the cobblestones, and yet the girl was dressed in a skirt that seemed even shorter than the last time they had met, the hem just peeking out from underneath her coat. Frankie frowned. "What are you doing here?"

In response, Gilly gave a tentative smile. "I hope you're not too cross with me about the other day."

Frankie studied the girl and considered. "I'm less annoyed by you not coming and more so at the size of my bill."

"Then this next outing will be my treat."

"I'll be sure to hold you to that," Frankie said, having no intention of meeting the girl for a cup of coffee again, but enjoying the offer all the same.

Gilly looked at her expectantly. "Aren't you going to invite me in?" she asked, glancing into the courtyard behind her.

Frankie suspected that she should say no, should shoo the girl away like the child she was—but before she could consider her actions too thoroughly, she nodded, heading back into the courtyard of the palazzo, the girl following eagerly behind. Once inside, Frankie pulled her kimono tighter, aware that she was not yet dressed for the day. "It's rather early for a social call, isn't it?" Frankie asked, hating, even as she spoke the words, how prim she continued to sound around the girl. *Old*, she realized, with a sinking feeling.

"It's nearly noon," Gilly answered, leaving Frankie to wonder at the hour, surmising she must have been caught up with her writing. The girl's eyes roamed the sitting room, taking in her surroundings with such intensity that Frankie began to grow uneasy.

Gilly approached the windows in the *piano nobile*, gazing down below, her hands pressed against the glass. Frankie resisted the urge to lecture her about the smudges she would no doubt leave behind. "This is quite a view. I imagine you could see all the comings and goings of Venice from here."

Frankie struggled to hide her amusement at the awe evident in the girl's voice. Even as she did so she remembered how it felt when she first arrived, stepping from the water taxi and onto one of the city's bridges. For a moment, it was almost overwhelming: The splash of colors that comprised the city, made more moody still by the ever-present rain, the smell of the place, something old and musty and secretive, the smell of a promise to be fulfilled. She turned away. "Wait here," she instructed. "I'll just go and get dressed."

Upstairs in her bedroom, Frankie flung off her nightclothes, anxious at the thought of leaving the girl unattended for too long. There was something off about her—something too intense, she thought, recalling the way Gilly had taken in the sitting room. And she still could not shake the feeling that the girl had lied when they first met—that she was not, as Frankie had first suggested, the daughter of a colleague. Why she had let the girl in, and then left her alone downstairs, she couldn't decide. Her hands rushed to do up her shirt and, in her haste, she buttoned them wrong, so that she had to pause and start again.

"Your room's lovely."

Frankie glanced up, startled.

Gilly stood in the frame of the doorway, now taking in the space of Frankie's bedroom.

"What are you doing in here?" Frankie demanded, turning so that her back was to Gilly. She fumbled with another button. "Damn," she whispered. Looking back at the girl, she said, "I told you to wait downstairs."

The girl ignored her, glancing toward the desk, a jumble of papers obscuring its surface. "Are you working on something new?"

When Frankie did not respond, Gilly gave a small laugh. "You don't have to be afraid to say yes. I won't tell anyone, I promise."

Frankie stiffened. "I'm afraid I'm not in the habit of sharing my work with strangers."

Gilly tilted her head, leaning it against the doorframe, where she now lingered. "Has anyone ever told you that you're not especially friendly, Frances?"

Frankie marveled at the girl's nerve. "Only my friends."

Gilly smiled in response, then, noticing the book that lay just beside the papers, reached for it. "One of my favorites." She opened it, the spine making a small cracking noise, as if in protest. *"Her memory's your love. You want no other,"* she read.

Frankie narrowed her eyes. "I always hated that line."

"It's terribly romantic, though." Gilly placed the book back on the desk and began to make her way out the door and toward the staircase. "How did you manage to find this place?"

"A friend," she responded, following. "Why?"

From behind, she watched as Gilly gave a quick shrug. The wrought iron creaked under the combination of their weight, swaying precariously. Frankie grasped the banister, afraid for a moment that she might lose her balance. "I'm jealous, actually," Gilly confided, pausing on the stairs and glancing upward. "My own place leaves a lot to be desired."

"Oh?" Frankie held her breath then, waiting for the girl to move. Once she had, Frankie quickly followed, her own footsteps rushed in order to reach the bottom.

"Yes," Gilly said, moving into the sitting room. She cast a glance out the windows overlooking the canal, before turning to the fireplace. Staring down at the hearth, she poked one of the burnt logs with her shoe. "It's rather damp, with splotches all over the ceiling and no fireplace to remedy it. And it doesn't have nearly as much charm as this place." Gilly tilted her head, taking in the impressive ceiling height. "Don't you get scared, staying in a place like this all on your own? I don't think I could sleep, knowing that I was the only one here." She peered around her. "Every bump and creak in the night would force me under the covers."

"I'm not alone. There are neighbors," she said, pointing across the way.

"Venetians?" Gilly asked.

"I haven't met them yet," Frankie responded, hesitant to concede such information.

Gilly raised her eyebrows. "Mysterious neighbors? That would frighten me even more."

Frankie thought of the shadow she had seen the other day, felt a tremor of unease. "That is because you're a child. When you're all grown up, you'll realize that a few bumps in the night are hardly worth getting worked up about," she said, working the bravado into her voice, not wanting to admit that she had—that she did—have similar misgivings. "How did you know where to find me, by the way?"

Gilly glanced over at her. "What do you mean?"

Was she imagining it, or had there been a look of alarm on the girl's face when she asked the question just then? Frankie narrowed her eyes. "I mean here, at the palazzo."

"You told me where you were staying," Gilly replied, her face now a mask of indifference.

Frankie tried to remember. "Did I?"

"Yes. Off the Campo Santa Maria Formosa." She seemed to recognize the look of alarm on Frankie's face and gave a small laugh. "Venice is small, Frances. There aren't that many Englishwomen traveling on their own. It was easy enough to work out."

Frankie grew uncomfortable at the girl's words, wondering how many others had taken notice of the Englishwoman living alone in the palazzo. She felt exposed, knowing that this girl before her was able to find where she was staying with little more than the name of a nearby *campo*. Before Frankie could dwell further, Gilly said,

"You should take a day trip to Rome while you're here. Have you been before?"

"No," Frankie answered, struck by the shift in conversation. In truth, she had done very little sightseeing beyond the first few days of her arrival, except for the occasional trip to the Bridge of Sighs, tucking away the blue guidebook she had brought with her, unable to bear any more information about the mosaics of the basilica or the architectural wonders of the Doge's Palace. By the time she had read up to the eighteenth century of Venetian history—at which point, the author declared, the city was living off the grandeur of its past, the collection of islands a place where people came to admire what had already been done rather than any new developments—she had decided that was enough.

"I'm surprised," Gilly was saying now. "I suppose when I think of writers, I always imagine the Fitzgeralds on the Riviera or Hemingway in Spain and Africa." She gave what sounded like an embarrassed laugh. "Well, if you haven't been, then you should go while you're here."

"And what would I do there?"

"Oh, I don't know. Ride a scooter to the Colosseum. Throw coins into the Trevi Fountain. Eat gelato."

Frankie gave a short laugh. There was something about the girl—her optimism, her naïveté—that amused her, and she found herself warming, despite her best intentions. "That all sounds perfectly ghastly," she said, determined to at the very least still *sound* cross with her.

"Oh, Frances," Gilly sighed, looking delighted as she spoke. "I somehow just knew you would say that."

They headed to San Marco, Gilly talking the entire time, explaining to Frankie that they wouldn't be able to even dream of going there if it was the height of summer, which was why the off-season in

Venice was absolutely best. *No tourists,* Gilly said with a smile. They left the palazzo and followed one winding street after another—past the chemist and then the shop with the herbs—until they spilled out by the water, just next to the Danieli. From there, it was a quick hop across a bridge and then they were standing in the most tourist-filled area of the whole city, although the crowds, typically with breadcrumbs in hand as they fought to feed the pigeons outside the basilica, were mercifully absent.

That's the quickest way here, Gilly declared, tossing her words over her shoulder as they entered Venice's only piazza. Frankie noticed, with some surprise, that they were headed to the same café—only the route that Gilly had taken was completely different from the one she had embarked on the other day. But, then, it turned out that Gilly knew Italy, and Venice in particular, fairly well. She spoke about how her parents had taken her every year since she could remember, usually on summer holidays and, as she grew older, in winter as well. They had even owned a place in the city at one time but had sold it the year before, their focus shifting to warmer climes as they hurtled toward old age. This time around she was staying with a friend, more of an acquaintance, in a tiny apartment filled with four other girls her own age—two of them Italian, one British, and the other she had yet to meet. It was, she told Frankie, the reason she hadn't bothered giving her a number, as the telephone in the hall was occupied day and night, the other girls concerned with nothing so much as where they were going that evening and with whom.

She confided all of this unprompted.

Frankie was already regretting her decision to follow the talkative girl, already thinking of the solitude of the palazzo, of the café just off the *campo* where she had become a local in her own right, the owner nodding and beginning her order before she had even sat down.

As Caffè Florian came into view, Frankie realized how little attention she had paid it the other day, rushed as she was and then furious at the girl for not turning up. Now she marveled at her ability to so easily dismiss it, for the building in front of them was excessive in its opulence, even from the outside, its marbled floors and arched entryways out of another era altogether.

Few people sat outside the café now, the weather presumably too unpredictable in the off-season, the water from the lagoon already creeping slowly toward the center of the piazza. Inside, however, the place was near full, the dim lights casting a warm glow across its patrons, as they sat around steaming cups and lavish pastries, the chandeliers occasionally throwing a sparkle of light whenever it caught an earring or wristwatch. From where they stood, Frankie could see that the café was divided into a number of individual rooms, each one filled with the same red velvet cushions and gilded furniture, differing only in the subject matter of the large impressive paintings that hung as though they were affixed in a gallery. Frankie nodded at the waiter, dressed in an overly starched uniform, and moved toward the first room off the front, selecting a chair nearest to the entrance.

As she began to sit, however, Gilly reached over to stop her. "What on earth are you doing?" Frankie demanded, looking down at where the girl's hand gripped her arm.

"What on earth are *you* doing?" the young girl returned, staring at Frankie with a similarly aghast expression on her face. "Don't tell me you've been *sitting down* for coffee all this time, Frances. No wonder your bill was so large."

Gilly didn't wait for a response, only turned and marched out of the room, not bothering to see if Frankie was following. Ignoring the disappointed look on the waiter's face, Gilly led them toward a simple wooden counter situated at the back of the coffeehouse, just to the left and out of view from the rest of the rooms, where a group of local men were already crowded around a few plush stools, none of them sitting.

Frankie was grateful for the din inside, so that the girl could not see her blush in embarrassment—for the fact that she was blushing only made her blush harder. It was so unlike her, so dreadfully sentimental. So feminine, in a way that everyone still seemed to expect, no matter the year. Frankie remembered a comment that a columnist she had met early on in her career made at a party where she had been on her very best behavior. Jack had laughed for ages when she heard it, telling her friend, "You are many things, my dear Frankie, but you are most certainly not *sweet*." After, she had worn her friend's words like a badge.

"That's how they get tourists," Gilly was whispering now, leaning toward her with a conspiratorial smirk as they stood in front of the bar. "Sitting there," she said, pointing her finger in the direction of the room where Frankie had just tried to take a seat, "will cost you triple the amount."

"And so how exactly is one supposed to have a coffee?"

"You drink it *al banco*," Gilly replied, gripping the counter in front of her. "At the bar."

At that moment one of the waiters appeared before them. He raised his eyebrows expectantly. "Cappuccino," Frankie began, but Gilly shook her head and broke in with a different order, cancelling Frankie's own. Understanding a little of what the girl had said, she asked: "Isn't that just what I ordered, only with a few more words?"

"I ordered us a coffee *stained* with milk, Frances, not *drowned* in it." When the waiter had disappeared, she continued. "Never order that in a place like this, unless you're after a glass of warm milk."

Frankie could feel her blood rising. The first reprimand might have shamed her, taken aback as she was, but these additional lessons were beginning to grate. Frankie had never done well with being told what to do—and somehow it rankled more coming from a girl who was at least a decade younger than herself.

Frankie gritted her teeth. "Any other rules I should be aware of?"

Gilly considered, missing the rhetorical tone in Frankie's question altogether. "Only espressos after midday. That's another good one to live by here." She scrunched up her nose, as if the motion were imperative to thinking. "Oh, and never spend more than a few minutes drinking your coffee, except in a place like this," she said, indicating the elaborate interior around them. "This place is special, otherwise, coffee is a quick experience."

During this recital, Gilly appeared indifferent—or oblivious, rather—to the looks her presence was garnering from the men who crowded the bar on the other side. She was tall and thin and young, and that always counted for something in the world, Frankie knew. It was enough, at any rate, to ensure a casual glance, a roving eye. But this was something different, as was, it seemed, Gilly. There was the way that she spoke—loudly, not so much that it annoyed but enough so that it aroused interest—and there were the gestures that went along with her speech, wide and sweeping, without concern for the space of others around her. And behind it all, a confidence, a certainty, in the way she spoke, in the way she moved, that belied her youth. That was it, Frankie realized. She had never before met anyone so self-assured at her age—other than herself—and so she knew firsthand how it made one unique among peers, however unintentional.

Frankie stifled a smirk. It was strange to think of how differently these same attributes were viewed with age. Now, instead of confident, she was labeled stubborn. Instead of independent, she was a spinster. The most frustrating part was that she didn't feel any differently than she had at Gilly's age, only a bit less manic, a bit more calm, and yet the world insisted that she was entirely changed from her younger self.

When their order was placed in front of them—coffee *stained* with milk—Gilly gave the waiter another. "What was that?" Frankie asked, eyebrow arched.

"You'll have to wait," Gilly said, refusing to translate. "Do you know, Frances, at one point this was the only coffeehouse in Venice that allowed women? It's one of the reasons that I still love to come here, despite it being in San Marco."

Frankie was surprised by the solemnity that had encroached on the girl's words. "It's lovely," she conceded. Even at the bar, out of sight from the more elaborate rooms, there was something different here from the bars that Frankie had frequented, places without a sense of history, of architecture, the blandness that had always been a comfort to her displaced by the stirring she felt in this place that had existed for centuries.

A few minutes later the waiter returned, and with him a cup of thick hot chocolate, which Gilly promptly pushed toward Frankie. All the goodwill of a moment before disappeared. "You can't be serious." The words escaped her before she had time to consider. Frankie saw the evidence of hurt creep onto Gilly's face, blossoming right before her. And yet, rather than be ashamed for her tone, she felt herself moving toward livid. It was obscene, somehow, the coquettish pout on the girl's face. And what did she expect? Frankie hadn't been given hot chocolate since she was a child, and not even then. "Fine," Frankie snapped, imagining the dressing down that Jack would no doubt give her for such rudeness, were she here. Frankie sighed, making a great show of lifting the cup to her lips and taking a sip—only to find, much to her surprise, that it *was* rather delicious, much more so than anything she recalled having before tasted, the chalky cocoa of her youth always coating her tongue in a way that she found revolting.

Gilly's face broke out into a grin. "I knew you would like it. Now," she said, turning back to her own coffee, "you must tell me everything about yourself. I insist."

"I'm afraid I don't have much to tell," Frankie said, hoping that would be enough to dissuade the girl. "I live a rather solitary, and quiet, life."

"Oh, I don't believe that for a second," Gilly said, setting her now-emptied cup back onto the bar.

Frankie did her best not to smirk. "Is that so?"

The girl leaned in, until there were only inches between them. "Actually, I'm more familiar with the literary world than you know."

"Is that so?"

The girl seemed to hesitate for a moment, then said, "It is. Actually, my grandfather was a publisher."

"Was he?" Frankie asked, with real interest now. "Anything I might be familiar with?"

"No, it was a small operation. Mainly he printed poetry. I can still remember the smell of the ink and the paper—it was like burning but nice, if that makes sense. Almost like the smell of something caramelizing," she finished, giving a nervous-sounding laugh.

"It sounds wonderful," Frankie said, meaning the words and wishing that her own past could be made up of a lineage that boasted a family of letters—or even a family that was still alive.

"It's because of my grandfather that I grew up surrounded by books. Including yours. I can't tell you what *After the End* meant to me," Gilly said then, her eyes widening, becoming moist-looking, so that Frankie darted her own away. "Tell me about writing it."

"That was ages ago. I hardly remember it."

It was a lie. The truth was, Frankie remembered everything about the year her first novel was published. It was the year her life had begun again. Before she started to write it, in the years immediately after the war and the death of her parents, time had stood still. It was as though while everyone else was rejoicing around her, she remained lost, unable to push forward. Years passed, but to her it felt like days. By the time nearly a decade had gone by, she couldn't believe it, felt like someone was playing a cruel trick on her. All those years, gone, and what had she to show for it? A couple of lines in a few society magazines, casual observations of the comings and goings of the type of social strata that didn't really exist anymore, or at least not in the same way. She felt robbed, cheated, hollowed out. She wanted to scream, to rage, to demand back all those years she had so carelessly wasted, as if the war and all its sacrifices had taught her nothing about life, about living.

That was what her first novel had been about. All those things that she could not stop thinking, all the things that whirled inside her head so that she remained awake at night, unable to sleep, pondering, regretting, wondering what her life might be like if not for what had happened to her parents. It had been the real reason that she sat down in her kitchen, the thought of spending one more year in that miserable little bedsit forcing her to put pen to paper, writing out the whole bloody thing in one long exhausting week, her hand red and calloused and shaking by the end of it. She had felt possessed, as if something had caught hold of her and refused to let go until it had extracted each and every last word that had been circling around inside her since the start of the war. Her head swam, her vision blurred. There were moments in which she could not remember the one that came before. Time slipped away—but whether behind her, in front of her, to the side, she could not tell.

When she had finished, she addressed the manuscript to an editor that she had once heard her friend Jack mention and posted it off before she had time to change her mind. Within a fortnight, she was on the telephone with Harold, discussing plans to publish.

Frankie had been surprised to discover just how much being a novelist suited her. She had always been serious, even as a child, and there was something about the solitude, about the discipline that the work entailed—to make oneself sit, alone, for hours on end, even on those days when your mind seemed to scream in protest—that she found reassuring. And so she hadn't minded when the second novel didn't flow as easily as the first, viewing it as a challenge instead of a problem. When the third proved more difficult still, she had wavered only slightly, pushing ahead, telling herself that all writers went through it, but then, after the reviews for her fourth novel, she wondered whether she was still right, whether pushing ahead with words that refused to come was the correct way to go about things. Perhaps she should have ignored her own advice, the advice of others around her as well, and waited. Waited for that same feeling the first novel had elicited from her—that urgent need to write, to put pen to paper, as if she might burn up and disintegrate into dust if she didn't get it all down fast enough.

"Well," Gilly said, teasing her, "if you won't tell me about your life as a writer, then you must at least tell me about this novel you're working on now."

Frankie, still muddled in thoughts of the past, set her cup down with a clatter. "No, I don't think so."

"Why not?" Gilly asked, once more affecting a pout.

Frankie resisted the urge to tell her the gesture made her look a bit dim. "Because I don't like to talk about my work while I'm working on it."

"That's not true."

Frankie raised her eyebrows. "I beg your pardon?"

"I just mean, I've read something to the contrary. That you have a friend you always let read your initial drafts."

For a moment, Frankie didn't know how to respond. She had given many interviews over her career—far more than she could remember—and although this was not the first time she had had something quoted back to her, there was something unnerving in the way that the girl had relayed the information. She was struck, and not for the first time that day, with the certainty that she did not know the girl in front of her, that they had never been introduced, no matter what the girl had insisted the other day by the Rialto Bridge.

At Frankie's silence, Gilly pressed: "Is that wrong?"

"No," Frankie responded, a feeling of unease beginning to settle over her.

Gilly leaned forward. "So you *do* let someone read your work before it's finished?"

"Yes, I suppose so." Frankie wished that she could lie, not wanting to tell this girl anything about her life, the sense that something was

not right growing from somewhere deep within her. Frankie had always trusted her instincts, and there was something now that warned
against the girl watching her with an eagerness that continued to
unsettle her. Worried that the girl would proceed with an infinite
number of more-unnerving questions, she did her best to change the
subject. "What do you do, Gilly? Or are you still at university?"

"I finished university ages ago." Gilly laughed. "How old do you
think I am?"

Frankie narrowed her eyes. She hated questions like these, de-
spised the women who asked them, knowing that the real reason
such inquiries were posed was in hope—or, rather, in expectation—of
flattery. No one ever asked wanting to be told the truth. "Early twenties," she surmised, wishing she could truthfully answer older, just to
annoy the girl.

Gilly reached over and took a sip of the hot chocolate, leaving a
stain across her upper lip. "No, not even close." She waited, as if she
believed that Frankie would keep guessing. When no additional
one was offered, she added, "I'll be twenty-seven in the spring."

"So, twenty-six, then," Frankie observed drolly. She didn't feel
guilty about being rude this time, despite suspecting she should—it
was such a peculiar response, one that a child might give, declaring
they were nearly five when they had barely turned four. *What a
ludicrous response,* Frankie thought. She finished her coffee, hoping
that it would also bring a conclusion to their conversation and to
the outing itself. Already, in her mind, she had returned to the
palazzo, lit a fire in the sitting room, and collapsed onto the sofa with
a book.

But then, the coffee finished and the bill settled, as Frankie
prepared to say goodbye, the girl asked, "Do you have plans?" Her
words were spoken carelessly, in a way that seemed to imply she
already knew that Frankie did not, so that Frankie could only shake
her head and say, "No, I suppose I don't," as if this had just occurred
to her.

"Shall we go off on an adventure, then?"

Frankie scowled. "To where exactly?"

But that was all Gilly would say, in that odd breathy manner of speaking Frankie realized she had—her eyes opened wide, always too wide, as though it was an affectation. But because she had not thought of an excuse before, could not think of one now, Frankie allowed herself to be dragged through the city, blindfolded to their destination.

As they alighted from their gondola, Frankie turned to look at the girl. "Where are we?"

The structure in front of them was vast—larger in scale than Jack's so-called Palace of the Drowned, even, which was already ludicrously large—but it was also, Frankie could see, in far worse condition, as if it had spent many years vacant, without anyone to care for it. The outside was stained with centuries' worth of damage from the wind, the water, the sand, and part of the roof appeared to be caving in. Frankie couldn't believe that this was a place where anyone would live—not by choice, anyway.

"Don't look so worried, Frances," Gilly said, glancing over her shoulder. "A friend of the family lives here."

"And is she expecting us?" Frankie asked, already catching what she suspected were snippets of conversation from within. It seemed as though they weren't the only ones who had been invited.

"And a few others," Gilly said, confirming her suspicions. "We're in luck because she happens to be hosting one of her parties."

The inside of the palazzo was in worse condition than the outside. Surveying the ceilings as they entered, Frankie was appalled to find water stains that stretched nearly the expanse of the entire room, deep cracks running up and down the length of the walls. In another room, moss had crept into these crevices, creating a living garden. Frankie could smell the evidence of it—the stench of earth, of something dark and rank, permeating the space.

She turned to Gilly, expecting to see some of her own shock mirrored there, but instead found the girl's eyes widening in delight. First at the Murano glass chandelier that hung above them in the entryway, and then at the pieces of artwork that sat on the floor, leaning against the walls. The girl obviously hadn't noticed that a number of pieces were missing from the chandelier and that those remaining were shattered or half-torn off their hinges, as if someone had made a grab for them and failed, that the paintings rested precariously upon sodden walls that looked as though they were ready to collapse in on themselves.

Frankie caught only a fleeting glance of the host, Gilly pointing her out as they moved through the palazzo, whispering something about America, about a fortune. She was a woman around Frankie's own age, maybe older, dressed in a short shift meant for someone much younger, covered up with a fur coat that at times gave the unsettling illusion that it was all she was wearing. The coat itself was different from the ones favored by Venetian women—those carefully cared-for pieces, no doubt kept stored in the back of a closet during the warmer months of the year. This one seemed cheap in comparison, the fur faded and molting, as though the owner had taken it directly from whatever body had been sacrificed to make such a horrible-looking piece. There was a chill that hung about the palazzo, causing Frankie to shiver and pull her houndstooth coat closer to her body.

"How do you even know about this place?" she asked the girl.

"My parents used to come to her parties, but I was always too young to attend. Now I'm finally here on my own and able to come and see what all the fuss is about."

Frankie raised her eyebrows, taking in the scene around her.

She had seen the glamorous shots of stars and debutantes floating around Venice, playing to the camera in their tiny polka-dot and gingham-check bathing costumes and half-moon sunglasses, but for her that was not the reality of the city, not a place that she had experienced—or cared to, for that matter. Let them fly in and out for a day, scurrying on to Rome, to the Italian Riviera, as they searched for their illusory *dolce vita*, dancing in fountains and running wild through the city. At the end of the day in Venice, night still fell, and quiet continued to blanket the city, returning it to those who lived there. But this was different, Frankie thought, from those wild, hedonistic photographs she had seen. Despite the decadent display of wealth, there was a sadness to this particular gathering that she could not manage to ignore. The music was a touch too loud, the costumes everyone wore an approximation of what they assumed would be elegant but only felt out of place here, in this run-down palazzo that the owner could most obviously not afford to keep up.

Gilly disappeared to find them drinks—despite Frankie's assertion that she intended to leave once the agreed-upon fifteen minutes were up. At some point, as she moved between one chilled room and another—it appeared the heating in the palazzo was another thing that had been forgotten—Frankie began to realize that of all the conversations taking place around her, she could understand every single one. "Where are all the locals?" she asked Gilly when she returned, frowning as she cast her eyes over the patrons of the party.

Gilly shrugged. "Perhaps they're here but we don't see them."

Frankie nodded, suspecting the girl was wrong. She tried to imagine it—the grandeur and wealth of an outsider being brazenly shown around their town while others struggled to survive. She took a tentative sip. The champagne tasted bitter, as though it had gone off. This might have been the place to be only a decade before, the chicness evident even in the coupes, the delicate glass stained shades of soft pink and purple. They had no doubt cost their owner a small fortune but even they had seen their prime, with Frankie's own glass bearing a large crack that ran down the length of it and made her worry that the liquid it contained would come pouring forth at any minute.

Leaving Gilly to chat with one of the other guests—an over-exuberant man in his sixties, the bow tie and suit he wore too formal for the occasion at hand—Frankie found herself a corner from which to watch the spectacle. Leaning against the sharp corner of an end table, she glanced at the guests fawning over their host, their voices made brazen with drink, the laughter forced. It occurred to her then that she could have been anywhere in the world, could have still been at the Savoy that night—the same type of people, the same type of chatter rising up around her.

It happened quickly then. The feeling of something around her throat, the grip tightening so that she could not breathe. She set her glass of champagne down, ignoring the sharp clatter it made, the liquid spilling up and over the rim, staining her coat. She moved with haste toward the way they had come in, desperate for the open space, for the air, but she halted abruptly, realizing that only water would greet her there. For the first time, she cursed herself for choosing Venice as a place of refuge. How had she thought to find comfort in a place that was claustrophobic by its mere geography alone, she wondered.

Frankie headed toward the back of the palazzo. There had to be something that way, some little patch of land outside these unbearably crowded rooms, the stench of body odor overwhelming her in that moment. She needed an exit—a chance to catch her breath, to let her skin cool, for already she could feel it, the sharp pinpricks of heat as they crept across her skin, first on the inside of her elbows and toward her wrists, and then on her back, her chest, crawling up, reaching for her throat. Passing through one room and then another, she let out a strangled gasp, though she had not meant to. A pair of guests turned and eyed her skeptically—Frankie could see the judgment, could see the pronouncement settling in the man's eyes, the woman watching her coolly beneath heavily mascaraed eyelashes.

Over their shoulders, a sliver of fading light was visible. Frankie hurried toward it, relief overwhelming her as she stepped outside, releasing herself from that dungeon of a house, her heart slowing at the sight of a garden, dark and lush, green, even, in the ivy that covered the back of the house, that grew between and around the layered stone steps. She staggered slightly, moving toward an empty bench, collapsing onto its structure though it wobbled under even her weight, another crumbling piece of the façade. Minutes passed, the flush on her cheeks slowly draining, her breath becoming softer, steadier.

Eventually, she became conscious that she was not alone.

"What do you want?" she demanded, knowing who it was that stood behind her. She could feel the gaze of the girl burning into the back of her neck. Her temper flared and she fought to hold on to it, knowing it would distract her from the other.

"I—I just wondered where you had gone to, that's all. I saw you leaving."

"I needed a moment to myself." She stood, ignoring the girl, and headed back into the party, the inside now rendered more grotesque by the quiet of the last few minutes. Bodies pressed up against her as she struggled to make her way to the terrace. The smell of alcohol, sweet and cloying, flooded the rooms, along with the sharp tang of perfume. It was enough to make Frankie retch. She moved faster.

"Frances, wait," Gilly called behind her, prompting Frankie to increase her pace.

She headed toward the front door, toward the terrace and gondola.

"I'm sorry, Frances." Gilly was practically running now, trying to keep up with Frankie's determined stride, her breath coming short and labored. "I thought you would like it."

Frankie paused at the door's entrance, curious. "Why on earth would you think that?"

Gilly looked lost for words. "I thought—I don't know what I thought."

Frankie considered. The panic had subsided now, and she felt foolish for the way she had acted, embarrassed further still that the girl had been witness to it. "You're entirely too romantic for your own good. Has anyone ever told you that?"

A tentative smile broke over her face. "I'm sorry, Frances. I only wanted to impress you."

"Impress me?"

Gilly answered her question with one of her own. "Are you hungry, Frances?"

Frankie once more marveled at the girl's nerve. "Starving, actually."

The evening turned to night, and before long the sun had set and the city fell quiet, enveloped by the darkness. During this time, they made not one, not two, but three stops for *cicchetti,* which turned out to be those savory little bites displayed atop counters as though they were sweets in a pastry shop. Frankie had seen them before, in the bars she frequented, but had never dared try them herself. The ones that Frankie liked best were the slices of toasted bread with a variety of toppings, some with heaps of bright-orange *zucca* on top of ricotta, dotted with balls of red pepper, others with marinated radicchio and *pesce spada,* a streak of balsamic vinegar running over and down the sides. She tried *baccalà mantecato,* which tasted of the ocean, and *acciughe marinate,* which made her mouth pucker from the vinegar, and other dishes that Frankie didn't know the meaning of and couldn't remember later, but she thought the smell and the taste would remain with her forever.

"Won't your friends wonder where you are?" Frankie asked at

one point, as they stood leaning against a wooden counter, cocktail picks from the consumed *cicchetti* gathering on their plates. She peered at Gilly's face, trying to read her expression.

"I don't know the girls I'm staying with so well." For a moment, Gilly looked uncomfortable. "And I don't have many friends, not even back home," she admitted. Frankie thought she could see the effort behind the gesture, thought she could hear it in the words as well.

"No?" Frankie asked, doing her best to sound neutral. She was surprised by the admission—at the readiness with which she had confessed it and at the idea that it could be true. She wasn't certain what type of image she had built of the girl in her mind, but not one of a loner, surely. "Well," she pronounced, after Gilly had given a shake of her head, the tips of her ears running a girlish pink, "friends are overrated."

The girl seemed somewhat mollified by Frankie's statement. "Do you not have any?"

"One," Frankie answered. "But I had only just met her when I was your age." She took a sip of her wine. "So you see, there's still time."

Gilly rewarded her with a smile large enough that Frankie turned away and busied herself with her drink, hardly protesting when the bartender replaced her first with a second. She did not know if it was the alcohol, but she felt a softening, a yielding, as she stood across from this girl and listened to her talk on and on. Frankie had been teetering throughout the stretch of the day between amusement and annoyance, but now she landed firmly on the former. Afterward, they stopped at one of the cafés in the Campo Santa Margherita and sipped hot wine in glass tumblers so that they could enjoy them outside—on a bench, despite the cold weather, despite the fog—and people-watch. Gilly quizzed Frankie on the places she had been and lectured her on the places she should still go. And then, after promising that they would meet again soon and reasserting once more that, *no,* she did not need a chaperone home, Frankie began her way back to the palazzo, the image stuck in her mind of Gilly from earlier that night, sitting on the bench, a stain of red wine on her upper lip as she threw back her head, as she laughed and exclaimed, "Oh, Frances, what have you been doing in Venice all this time!"

CHAPTER 6

Frankie woke to the sharp smell of cigarettes. At first she assumed she had been only dreaming, and then, once she was fully awake, that the smoke had drifted in from the window. But a quick glance reminded her that she had secured the latch before retiring the previous night. Stumbling from bed, she grabbed her discarded dressing gown and padded down the stairs to the *piano nobile*. "Maria?" she called out as she went. There was no response as she rubbed her eyes against the back of her hands, trying to brush away the bits of sleep that still clung, making her vision distorted and blurred. Perhaps she had imagined the smoke, she allowed. But at the bottom of the stairs she inhaled, and the familiar scent hit her once again—and stronger than before. More alert now, she cast her eyes over the sitting room, trying to find the source, wondering as she did so whether Maria was somewhere in the palazzo, in some hidden passage, smoking in secret. She almost smiled at the thought, but then her eyes caught on the fireplace— and the figure standing just there.

Frankie blinked, wondering if she was still asleep, even gave herself a small pinch on the back of the hand to be sure. But, no, she was awake, was standing in the sitting room of the palazzo, as was the stranger before her. It was a man, she could decipher that much, his back angled toward her as he stood in front of the mantelpiece, the embers of the fire glowing a deep red—a cigarette dangling from his fingertips.

For a moment Frankie stood, lost for words, for any idea at all of what she was supposed to do. She took a step closer to the man. He didn't look like a burglar. He was dressed in a suit, expensive by the look of it, a silver watch of obvious value secured on his wrist. Perhaps this was how burglars looked in Venice, Frankie reasoned. What other possible excuse could there be for his presence in the palazzo. Unless he was a reporter. The thought struck her, shifting something, unsettling something, deep within. The thought decided her.

"Don't move an inch or I'll scream," Frankie said, the words leaving her mouth before she could decide whether it was the right way to handle the situation, whether she should have slunk off before he noticed her rather than speaking. But if she could just get him to remain where he was, she might be able to make it to the telephone, to ring the *carabinieri*—surely that was a better plan than hiding out in the palazzo, waiting for the stranger to find her. As she stood there, trying to hold her stance, she began to wonder what the number for the *carabinieri* was—surely not 999, it couldn't be as easy as that.

At any rate, it didn't matter. The man was already turning before she had time to move toward the telephone, already starting to walk toward her, a string of Italian rushing from his mouth. "Stop," Frankie cried, moving backward, clutching her kimono to her neck—a gesture, she realized, that was vaguely idiotic. What did she think that would help? A madman—albeit a very nicely dressed one, she surmised, noting his slim black tie, the tailored waist of his suit, the deep-red pocket square that sat just so—had broken into the palazzo, and she was concerned with flashing her nightclothes at him. "Stop right there or I'll scream," she said again, trying to get across her meaning through tone alone, uncertain whether he understood a word she had said.

The man kept talking, only now he was using his hands as well, gesturing to her, to the walls, to the door, to every corner of the palazzo, it seemed. He paused, ground out the cigarette in one of the room's many ashtrays.

"I don't understand," Frankie responded, backing up slowly in the direction of the staircase. The man continued to advance on her. "Please don't move. Please stay where you are."

She felt her foot hit the beginning of the step, and then she heard it. The unmistakable sound of a door creaking open—the entrance hall, she thought—and then the quick scuffling of footsteps, and suddenly Maria was there, standing in the sitting room. The housekeeper stopped, looking first at Frankie and then the stranger. For one wild moment Frankie wondered if they were in on it together—though what *it* was, she didn't know.

"Maria!" Frankie exclaimed, deciding the housekeeper was her best chance out of this mess. "Call the *carabinieri*. Call them and tell them we have an intruder."

But rather than do as she said, the housekeeper only folded her arms and turned to the man, saying something in Italian.

"No, don't speak to him," Frankie hissed. "Why are you just standing here?" she protested, even as the man's response drowned out her own words. She wondered then whether she had been right, whether the two were in cahoots. Perhaps the housekeeper had got the wrong end of the stick, had thought Frankie was as well off as her friend and had decided to stage a heist. If that was the case, she would be sorely disappointed, Frankie mused. But then the man dug in his pocket and produced a set of skeleton keys, and Frankie could not help but note how similar they looked to the pair that she herself had been given. Frankie looked back toward the housekeeper. "What's he saying?"

"He is not intruding," Maria responded. "He is *geometra*."

"He's what?"

"*Geometra.*" Maria indicated the walls around them. "He checks the house."

Frankie remembered the conversation that she had had with Jack before she arrived, about her desire to sell the palazzo. A ragged breath escaped her, and she silently cursed her absentminded friend. "Do you mean he's a surveyor?"

Maria gave a shrug.

Frankie shook her head in disbelief, her heart still hammering. She intended to make Jack grovel for forgiveness on this one. "Well," she said, the word clipped. She lowered her shoulders, tried to ignore the pounding of her heart. She took a few steps toward the unannounced guest. "Maria, would you ask the gentleman if he wouldn't mind sharing one those cigarettes?" The housekeeper obliged and the man smiled, producing a small silver case from his pocket. Frankie accepted with a curt nod, bending her head to the proffered light, trying to calm her shaking hands. "Now, would anyone like a cup of coffee?"

The *geometra* was only just leaving when Jack finally rang. It had been a long day, interspersed with numerous cigarette and coffee breaks, and while Frankie was surprised to find herself comforted by the presence of another person in the palazzo, she was close to inquiring whether the *geometra* intended to spend the night before he finally packed up his things and wished her a *buonanotte*.

Picking up the telephone, Frankie expected to find a contrite Jack on the other end of the line. Much to Frankie's displeasure, however, it soon became apparent that her friend was entirely unaware of the encounter she had had with the unexpected guest that morning.

"Unexpected guest?" Jack echoed. "What do you mean?"

"I mean the *geometra*," Frankie replied, using the word that Maria had. "The one with a set of keys who was standing in the sitting room this morning when I came down in my dressing gown."

"Oh, God," Jack murmured.

"Yes, oh, God," Frankie repeated. "Jack, I nearly died of fright." In fact, Frankie thought, she was beginning to feel as though she were a heroine in some Gothic ghost story, what with the mysterious comings and goings next door and now with strangers appearing in the palazzo. She glanced around the sitting room, to confirm she was indeed its sole occupant.

"Oh, Frankie, I feel absolutely awful. Someone contacted me the other week, someone interested in purchasing the palazzo. They wanted to send a surveyor before making a deposit. And a *geometra*, you're right. That's what they call them there. It's all part of the transaction."

"You might have told me, Jack."

"You're absolutely right. I don't know where my head has been at these days." There was a pause. "I am sorry, you know. And not just about the *geometra*."

It was unlike Jack to apologize. The words put Frankie on edge. "I'm still surprised you're selling," she said, desperate to change the subject. "How on earth did your family ever find this in the first place?"

"Oh, a friend of a friend," Jack replied, her voice garbled so that it was all at once apparent how far away she was. "You know how these things are."

Frankie didn't. She had never had many friends, and never a friend of a friend, people she could rely on for favors such as this. She thought again of the girl, of her admission over drinks. Perhaps they were not so different from each other, she mused.

"I'll be there soon."

"I can take care of myself, Jack."

"I know, Frankie."
They both fell silent.
"Night, Jack."
"Night, Frankie."

CHAPTER 7

They stood outside the Teatro La Fenice, heads tilted back, mouths agape, taking in the vastness of the structure. Neoclassical columns stood on either side of them, the theater's emblem, a golden phoenix rising from the flames, affixed in the air above. In that moment, with the darkness creeping around and the lights from the theater spilling out and into Campo San Fantin, Frankie thought she had never seen anything so beautiful before.

Only hours earlier, she had sat at the desk in her room, pen poised above the empty sheets of paper, and found herself unable to commit anything to the page. It had been like this ever since the intrusion of the *geometra*—the words had refused to come. It worried her, this block. It reminded her too much of London and how the words had similarly evaporated, leaving the pages beneath her blank. A part of her blamed Jack—the insistence of her phone calls, the refusal to explain her prolonged absence from Venice. It was causing her to worry just what it was that was keeping her friend away. Never mind the rest. Lost in such thoughts, Frankie was startled when the buzzer rang through the palazzo.

"Gilly?" she spoke into the intercom, knowing it would be the girl.

"Frances," came the girl's voice. "What are you doing tonight?"

Despite herself, Frankie had suppressed a smile. "No plans to speak of. Why?"

"I've got two tickets to the opera and absolutely no one to go with me."

It had been years since Frankie had been to an opera—not since, she realized with a start, her time in Paris as a young girl. She had a dim memory of a lush, tiny box—all rich gold and dark-red velvet, with narrow, unforgiving chairs that squawked in protest at the slightest movement. And then there was the opera itself—she thought maybe *La Bohème*, but she couldn't manage to recall. There was only an impression of colors, violent reds and sorrowful blues, and that smell of the theater, so rich and deep, filled with dust and smoke and something full and heavy, something that filled her, head to toe, with promise. She had intended to decline whatever offer Gilly was about to make, but standing in the vast emptiness of the palazzo, she found that the idea of dressing up for a night out, sitting in the hushed audience of a theater, was exactly what she wanted to do.

"They're playing *Macbeth*," Gilly told her as they approached the building now, her face relaying more than just those words, exclaiming, it seemed, *Aren't we lucky, isn't this the perfect opera, the perfect night*, and Frankie had a vague impression that this was how Gilly's life often was. Filled with luck, filled with perfect moments by being somewhere at just the perfect time, by being the type of person to always say the absolute perfect things.

Frankie tried to remember whether she even liked *Macbeth*, with all its blood and gore and premonitions. She wished that it had been *Aida* or *Carmen*, or something similar that dealt with a lovers' struggle, something that she could watch and enjoy but that would never touch her in the same way as Lady Macbeth and her rapturous doomed ascent.

"All the girls were scandalized that I was giving up a Friday night to spend at the opera," Gilly said, evidently proud of herself for appearing at the cultural institution rather than following the rest of her flock to the local *bacaro*. She had dressed for the occasion. The cut of her costume was simple, with a defined waist and full skirt, but the fabric was of a floral print that sparkled and shone under the light. Despite the chill, she had forgone a coat. Frankie felt rather dull in her own black sleeveless shift by comparison, grateful she had thought to pair it with gloves, which she hoped added something to the effect.

Frankie frowned. "What do you mean?"

"They're on the hunt," Gilly replied, with an insinuating smile. She linked her arm with Frankie's own, her voice tinged with a delighted kind of exasperation, as she explained, "For a man, Frances!"

"And so why on earth aren't you out with them?" Frankie asked as they ascended the steps together, the question that she had been wanting to ask ever since they met hidden just beneath.

Gilly turned to her. "Instead of spending time with you, you mean?"

"Yes, that is exactly what I mean." Frankie eyed her, noting that the girl had done up her face that evening. The effect was disorienting. She looked older, shrewder. Her eyes were made somehow more narrow by the wing-tipped eyeliner, and the huge false eyelashes gave them a mean appearance, rendering the near-permanent grin on her face garish, macabre. She could have no doubt joined the company onstage, looking as she did.

Gilly failed to notice she was being observed. Instead, she cocked her head to the side and said, "You're a bit funny, aren't you?"

Frankie noticed the way the girl had avoided answering the question. "Sorry to disappoint."

"Not at all," Gilly began, missing the sarcastic note in Frankie's voice. "In some ways, you're everything I imagined a writer would be," she replied in earnest.

Frankie did not know how to respond, and so they pushed

through the front doors silently, their arms still linked, one entwined with the other.

Their seats were better than Frankie expected. The girl had managed to swing a private box, although admittedly part of that was down to luck. It was designed for four, but it seemed their fellow attendees had decided not to make an appearance, and so Frankie and Gilly settled onto the plush red velvet seats in the front, closest to the ledge. Together, in the minutes before the production began, they watched as all of Venetian society emerged from the cold and made their way into the gilded cage of the Teatro La Fenice. *It's burned down twice already,* Gilly whispered to her as they watched women draped in furs and ballroom-length gowns, their necks and arms adorned with jewels, swan into their orchestra seats, the men walking stoically behind them, clutching at opera glasses. *Look there,* Gilly urged, pointing toward the back of the theater, where a distinguished-looking woman in a kimono was making her way solemnly to her seat.

The orchestra began to tune up, and there was a perceptible shift in the crowd.

Conversations dropped to a murmur, most falling silent altogether, and then the lights dimmed and a hush fell over the place. There was something Frankie always loved about that moment—the sound of anticipation, of preparing to embark on a journey. And then it began: the real thing, the deep melodic tones sweeping through, around, enveloping one entirely. Frankie had missed that feeling— of being swallowed, consumed, overwhelmed. She struggled to remember the last time she had felt anything like that at all. It was, she realized, sitting up straighter in her chair, during the time when she had written her first novel.

Now she prepared to let it wash over her—the music, the ability to escape, even for a short time, from the corporeal ties that bound her. In the darkness, she turned to find Gilly watching her, a look of curiosity settled there. She seemed to contemplate Frankie with a measured inquisitiveness that Frankie herself had experienced on occasion, when something crossed her path that both fascinated and puzzled her in equal terms. Frankie gave a small smile and turned back to the production. After a minute, she could sense the girl's attention shift as well.

The curtain went up then, and they were plunged into darkness. There was nothing else after that but the light in front of them and the actors and musicians who filled it.

During the interval, Frankie was hesitant to leave her seat.

"Come on, let's grab a glass of champagne before the lights dim," Gilly murmured, reaching for her arm. So enraptured had Frankie become during the last hour and a half, her fingers clutching the ledge in front of her, that the thought of standing up, of leaving the private box that had become their own, was somehow distasteful to her. She wanted nothing more in that moment than to remain in the world that they had been invited to inhabit, the world of smoke and swords and the promise of blood.

Reluctantly, Frankie allowed herself to be led out of the privacy of their box and into the chaos of operagoers now all destined for the same place. At the bar, Gilly leaned against the counter, holding her champagne glass so that the bubbles tilted dangerously to one side, as if she would let them spill over and onto the floor. Hordes of others were still calling out to the bartender in the hope of ordering a final drink before they were ushered back to their seat, but Gilly, in her typical fashion, had managed to order them each a glass without even noticing the fracas around her.

"Why aren't you married, Frances?" she asked, leaning against the bar's wooden ledge.

It was a question that Frankie had been asked before. A question that made her almost glad that her parents were gone—not really, of course, for she missed both of them with an intensity of emotion that was still aching and raw—only so that they would not have to endure the unpardonable offense of having an unwed daughter. Frankie herself was not embarrassed, only tired of the question, which had grown more and more tedious, her patience diminishing as the years passed. She looked at the girl in front of her, took a sip of her champagne, and sighed.

"I've bored you," Gilly guessed, a slight frown forming.

"No, it's not you," Frankie said, uncertain why she felt the need to reassure the girl. She took another sip, felt the zing of the bubbles as they descended into her stomach, warming her against the damp that could be felt even here, in the heart of the opera. "It's the question."

"The question," Gilly repeated. "The question is boring?"

"Yes," Frankie replied. "Immensely so."

"Ah," Gilly said, as if that cleared things up, and perhaps it did, Frankie found herself thinking. For as much as the girl's comments rankled her, there were still those times when Frankie was reminded of herself at that age. Not in the openness or the optimism, the constant grin that reasserted life would only ever be good. None of that, no. But the streak of independence, the determination. Such attributes often spelled a lonely road, unless you were like Jack, who seemed able to exist in multiple worlds. Frankie had never been good at juggling, had never felt the desire to learn. She was a cynic and she was stubborn, and both of those things made her happier than they should have. No matter if it made the world more difficult to share, particularly with a partner—she had long ago found herself company enough.

"But do you never get lonely?" Gilly pressed.

Frankie wondered whether she was asking out of curiosity or for some other, more personal reason. "Don't be daft," she replied, with a smile. She downed the last of her champagne. "Besides, how could I be, with the likes of you pestering me?"

Gilly laughed. "Do you have many fans, then?"

Frankie thought of the dwindling sales, of the review, before pushing it all resolutely out of her mind. Tonight, she would not let herself think of such things. To Gilly's question, she gave only a careless shrug in response.

"I bet you do," Gilly said, just as the lights dimmed.

"No time to answer," Frankie said, laughing, the drink working, lightening her, so that all at once she felt she could shed her body completely. Champagne had always done that. *Liquid magic,* her mother had called it, during some holiday season back when Frankie was still a child. She worked to dispel the tears gathering. Champagne had always done that to her as well. The lights above them dimmed again. "Back to our seats," she managed, turning abruptly.

The second half passed quickly. Lady Macbeth's famous sleep-walking scene was Frankie's favorite moment, the deep timbre of her voice resonating throughout the theater, the sense of a collective breath held as she finished her final note. It felt like a cliché to love Lady Macbeth, but she did, reverently, and she found herself leaning toward the stage as the actress concluded the scene, as if she would be able to understand the words, or, rather, *feel them more,* if only she could get a tiny bit closer. The opera singer was clothed in a simple black dress, her arms encased in long bloodred sleeves that ran from wrist to floor. The result was striking. Frankie thought it was an image that would stay with her for a very long time.

Afterward, Gilly was surprisingly silent as they made their way home, both of them, Frankie supposed, lost in their own private reveries. Her new friend insisted on walking her back to the palazzo, despite Frankie's assertion that she could find her way perfectly well on her own. In truth, she was grateful for the girl's presence. The streets of Venice became more menacing in the darkness of night, and she found herself filled with the absurd fear that it was possible to turn a corner and see a collective of witches beckoning to her. Stealing a quick glance at the silent girl beside her, Frankie found herself no longer quite as bothered by the suspicion that they had never met before. Maybe it had only been an honest mistake—maybe the girl had recognized her from London or the back of her book jacket or something equally innocuous but bothersome to explain.

At the door, Frankie paused and wondered whether she should invite the girl in, her mind already casting back to that moment when the lifeless body of that poor woman had been pulled from the canal. But then she shook off such dark thoughts, telling herself not to spoil the evening.

"Good night, Gilly," she said, turning to the courtyard behind her. "Thank you for tonight."

"Good night, Frances," the girl called out after her.

That night, Frankie fell into bed happy and still more than a little drunk from the whisky she poured herself before retiring. For the first time in a long while, she felt content, felt as though something sharp and tight had been loosened inside her.

CHAPTER 8

I t was nearly midnight when she heard it. The sound of a door opening, followed by a great crash. Frankie sat bolt upright in bed. Surely it was not the *geometra,* unless he had drunkenly arrived at the palazzo's door instead of his own by mistake. Somehow she didn't think so. And this time, Maria was far away, in her own home somewhere on the Burano island, she had since learned, and Frankie still hadn't the faintest idea what the number for emergencies was in Italy.

She blinked against the darkness. Sitting up, Frankie took in the room around her, assessing it for anything she could use as a weapon—when another sound crashed from below.

This one was closer.

Lowering herself from the bed, she cursed the wooden floors, aware of every creak and groan as she made her way over to the fireplace and, more important, to the ancient poker she had spotted resting on its ash-stained tiles.

There were voices now—hushed but audible, and coming closer.

Frankie gripped the poker, raising it in front of her as she drew nearer the door.

They were almost at her bedroom—she could hear the rattle of the iron staircase, could hear footsteps alighting.

And then, before she was ready, before she had time to truly prepare, the door swung open and a silhouette filled the doorway—

And burst into laughter.

The light came on, leaving Frankie momentarily blinded.

"I know you find me rather tiresome at times, Frankie—but murder?"

And then another laugh, a laugh that was deep and rich and familiar, so familiar that Frankie's heart thrummed at the sound of it.

Jack stood in the doorway, arms crossed, an amused expression on her face.

"You scared me half to death," Frankie snapped, her face stretched into a grin. They were sitting on the bed now, Frankie in her night-clothes, still shaking, gripping the poker with both hands as though she might still be called upon to use it. As for Jack, she was dressed more or less as she always was—which was to say, impeccably so, in a checkered skirt suit without a single wrinkle, her hands still encased within her brown leather gloves. She looked as though she had just stepped from the pages of a fashion magazine, rather than the cramped interior of an airplane.

An airplane, Frankie thought with as much disdain as she could manage, that Jack had not bothered to tell her she would be on.

"We did try to be quiet, but getting off a gondola in the middle of the night isn't exactly the easiest of tasks," Jack laughed. "Nor is finding a gondola, come to that."

"We?" Frankie questioned, deciding in that moment that she *would* be angry with her friend. First for scaring her half to death, and second for not having the decency to at least come alone.

Jack's lips pursed. "Yes, *we*."

"I didn't realize *he* was coming as well," Frankie lied.

"Give me that," Jack said, taking the fire poker from her hands, looking ready for a fight. "And, yes, you bloody well did."

Frankie relented at that. Jack was the only person who could get away with speaking to her like that and they both knew it. She gave a great sigh. "All right, so where is he?"

Jack placed the poker back in its rightful place next to the fire. "Leonard? Probably fixing a drink, knowing he has to deal with the likes of you."

Frankie leaned against the pillow behind her. "Am I really so bad?"

"Darling, you're horrible and you know it." Jack smiled. "But it's also why I love you. Now, put on a dressing gown and come downstairs for a drink."

"It's the middle of the night," Frankie protested.

"Don't be silly," Jack said, already turning and heading toward the door. "It's just the start. And besides, I know you. If you don't say hello straightaway, you'll spend the rest of the week sulking, trying to hide from us both."

"I told her we should have waited until the morning," Leonard said as they stepped into the sitting room.

Jack threw him a glare. "Traitor. You did no such thing."

"How did you even get in?" Frankie asked, collapsing onto one of the sofas and tucking her feet up underneath her. She ignored the pointed look this remark earned her from Jack.

"Hello to you too, Frankie," Leonard said, placing a drink on the side table beside her.

"Thank you, Leonard," she said, exaggeration in each word, so that Jack made a noise of annoyance, at which Frankie gave Leonard a quick wink.

"Oh, you two," Jack exclaimed, claiming the other sofa. She kicked off her heels. "I swear you'll be the death of me."

"Ah, but what an adventure." Frankie laughed, taking a sip of her drink. Leonard was the only one capable of making a negroni exactly the way she liked them—heavy on vermouth and light on everything else. He asked her once why she didn't just drink the vermouth alone, to which she fixed him with a disappointed stare. Secretly, though, she thought the idea didn't sound too terrible.

Leonard's and hers was a complicated relationship, one born of their mutual love for Jack. She accepted him more easily than she once had, although she still cringed at his preference for cardigans—tonight's choice was a prime example, chevron-patterned and suede in material. Still, Leonard loved Jack, anyone could see that, and for reasons Frankie could never understand—particularly when she saw them in plain view, Jack standing a good several inches taller than her husband—Jack felt the same way about him. It had stung at first to find herself displaced—and by such a small, silly man, at that—but in the end, even she could not help but be swayed by his obvious devotion to her friend.

"So." Jack was staring at her now with that expression that felt as if it could burn a hole clean through her.

Frankie only raised her eyebrows in response. "Yes?"

"Don't make me beg, Frankie. Tell me how you are."

Frankie noticed that Leonard had casually turned his back toward them, his way of providing at least some curtain of privacy, however unrealistic. "I'm fine. Honest," she added, at Jack's disbelieving stare. "Or I was, until you two traipsed in here during the middle of the night, scaring me half to death." Frankie laughed, but there was something in it that sounded hollow and feigned.

"It is hardly the middle of the night," Jack said, in her usual bantering tone. "But I *am* sorry," she said, voice lowered, eyes intent, "if we frightened you." Jack held her gaze then, searching, but Frankie turned away.

"And how was your journey over?" Frankie asked, to cover the moment.

Jack paused, just long enough to let her know she wasn't fooled. "Dull," she responded. "And nothing you want to hear about, I suspect."

"Oh, on the contrary," Frankie replied, with a smile. "I love a good dull story to put me to sleep." Jack laughed, and Frankie watched as some of the worry etched into her friend's face began to give. She hesitated, afraid that her next words would be too much, would change the atmosphere in the room, but she pushed ahead before she could talk herself out of it. "You could finally tell me what kept you in London for so long."

Jack and Leonard exchanged a look. *There,* Frankie thought. She knew something had been amiss, something that could not be explained away by her friend's usual excuse of charity work or a family emergency—no, there was something else this time. Leonard cleared his throat then. "Frankie, dear, when you have a minute, the two of us should have a chat."

"All right," she said carefully. "But aren't we chatting now?"

He seemed to hesitate. "Alone, I mean. It's about that business in London, I'm afraid."

"Oh," she replied, taken aback.

"Don't worry yourself," he said, bestowing her with what she assumed he thought was a reassuring smile. "It's nothing terribly important, I promise."

Afterward, Frankie had trouble following the conversation. She knew that Leonard had not been truthful just then, knew that whatever it was, it must be important if he needed to speak with her alone, something she suspected they were both hesitant to do. Never mind, she told herself, glancing toward where her friend sat. Jack was here now. She would not let her mood be spoiled. She took another sip, raised her empty glass to signal for another, and rejoined the conversation.

Later, once Leonard had gone to bed and Jack had promised to follow him shortly, Frankie and Jack sat, nursing a final whisky, huddled together under a cashmere blanket Frankie had unearthed during one of her cleaning sprees.

"God, I can't believe how freezing it is in here," Jack complained, despite the fire that had been lit by Leonard before he retired for the night. "I'd forgotten how cold Venice can be." She burrowed further under the blanket. "So, how do you like it?"

"Venice? I've been to the Continent before, you know. When I was younger."

"Yes, but everything is beautiful when you're young. I've had the most wonderful memories of places I traveled to as a child, only to go back to them later as an adult and be disappointed. Heartbroken, in some cases."

"Well," Frankie said, draining the last of her drink, "I'm quite impressed so far."

"Brava!" Jack exclaimed. "Do you know, I've always loved Venice, despite getting older, and particularly in the autumn, regardless of the wretched cold and the even more wretched chilblains. I blame Henry James, in part, for that."

"I loved *The Wings of the Dove* as a child," Frankie said with a sigh.

"Of course you did." Jack's eyes narrowed. "Though something tells me it wasn't poor old Milly you commiserated with."

"Absolutely not," Frankie cried. "Kate risked everything for the man she loved, and in the end it was all ruined because he was a foolish sentimentalist, in love with ghosts. I can't even remember his name, that's how much I disliked him."

"We shall never be as we were!" Jack pronounced with exaggeration, flinging one hand out and the other to her heart. "That was the line, wasn't it?"

"Near enough." Frankie laughed.

In bed, Frankie smiled, grateful for the sound of her friends below. There was a comfort in it, knowing that they were here and she was no longer alone. Though she supposed she hadn't been entirely alone, thinking of Gilly. Her presence these past few days had, however hesitant she was to admit it, at the very least kept her occupied. If she allowed, she had very much enjoyed herself that evening, despite the girl's tendency toward the dramatic and her own curmudgeonly ways.

It wasn't just the city of Venice that she had been surprised by that autumn, she found.

It was also herself.

CHAPTER 9

The next morning, Frankie came down to find an assortment of brioche, S-shaped *buranei* biscuits, and a half dozen *krapfen* spread on the kitchen table, and Jack standing beside it all, apron wrapped around her waist as though she had just taken them out of the oven.

"Is this your doing?" Frankie asked, raising her eyebrows in surprise. "Have you actually gone to a bakery so early in the morning?"

"Yes," Jack responded somewhat tersely, taking off the apron and smoothing out an invisible line on her pencil skirt. "I *am* capable, you know."

"Oh, I don't doubt it," Frankie said, taking a seat and reaching for a piece of brioche. "Which is why I suspect you must know something of why your husband seems so eager to speak with me." It was abrupt, she knew, but, then, it wasn't always easy to get Jack alone. She had been up the better part of the night thinking about it, wondering what it was that they needed to discuss, when the thing was supposed to be over and done with. She was confident that her friend would not keep such a secret from her if pressed.

Jack handed her a cup of coffee. "I haven't a clue, honest. He doesn't ever discuss his clients with me."

"Even when they're your closest friend?"

"Especially then," Jack said, leveling a gaze at Frankie. "Talk to him, Frankie. You'll only make yourself sick with worry if you carry on like this."

"I know."

"Promise me, Frankie."

"I promise."

Jack pointed at Frankie's arm. "You ought to put something on those, you know."

"I have," Frankie said, pulling down the sleeve of her kimono to cover the red welts left over from the mosquito bites that first week. "The damn things won't go away."

"I didn't know you were so allergic."

"I'm not, usually, but in Venice they seem extra fond of me."

"You're lucky they drained all the marshes after the war or malaria would still be a concern."

They fell into what should have been a companionable silence then, but Frankie could feel it hanging in the air around them, a reminder of that terrible night in London. A part of Frankie resented Leonard for bringing it all to light again, after she had done her best to lay it to rest. It wasn't his fault, she knew that. If something had happened, some new development, it was his job to tell her. Was it possible that the woman had changed her mind, had decided to make a complaint against her? She felt herself pale.

"Frankie?"

She looked up to find Jack watching her. "I'm fine," she said, doing her best to smile. "I know you worry about me, but I've been absolutely fine here in your absence, Jack. In fact, before your unannounced arrival, I was at the opera last night," she said, offering the bit of information in the hopes of distracting her friend.

Jack took a sip of her coffee. "On your own?"

"No, with that girl I told you about. Gilly."

"The one you weren't certain if you knew?"

"That's the one. In fact, I had only just returned home about an hour before you two barged in. You know, for a moment I wondered whether the neighbors hadn't decided to come around and introduce themselves."

She had meant it in jest, but Jack look troubled at the mention. "Frankie, I told you—"

"Yes, well, despite that," she interrupted, "I must argue that your Maria is wrong, as there is most definitely someone living next door. You'll see, soon enough. And then you'll be forced to admit that I was right." Frankie stood, reaching for the cupboard. "Now, let me show you a little trick I've learned from the Italians." She grabbed a bottle of sambuca she had stored there and tipped a measure each into their coffees.

Jack took a sip, looking skeptical at the addition. "Aniseed," she pronounced after a few minutes. "Do you know, I think I could get used to that." She took another sip, less tentative this time. "Have you been writing?"

For a second or two, Frankie wavered whether or not to tell her friend the truth, thinking of the growing pile of pages that even now sat on her desk. In the end she only shrugged, hating to lie to Jack but unwilling to share, all the same. It seemed too soon, too tenuous. "Now you sound like Harold."

"Don't worry, it'll come," Jack said, reaching for one of the S-shaped pastries. She dipped it into her coffee. "You just need time."

Frankie gritted her teeth. "That's what everyone says, in between asking me if I've already had enough."

Jack made a face. "It's only because we love you and we're concerned."

"And Harold?" Frankie asked of her editor.

"The two of you have been together for years now. I'm certain he only wants to make sure that you recover from this. That you don't feel intimidated about jumping back into it all again."

She was right, Frankie knew. "Still, I wish he would have the decency to leave me alone for a while. I wish everyone would just leave me alone." Jack was silent then, and to anyone else it might have appeared as though she was only deep in thought, as though she was considering her friend's words. Frankie, however, had known her long enough to interpret the expression otherwise. "What?" she snapped.

"I'm worried this wasn't such a good idea," Jack said, her features collapsing into a frown as she laid both pastry and coffee on the table.

"What wasn't a good idea?" Frankie asked, suspecting she knew already what her friend's answer might be.

"This," Jack said. "You, here, on your own. I should have told you to stay in London, or anywhere that wasn't so isolated, that wouldn't allow you to get lost in that dangerous mind of yours, in that frustrating way you always do."

Frankie was relieved to see a smirk on her friend's face, despite the gloom that had settled there. "Yes, well, I suppose I never was very good on my own."

She had meant it as a laugh, had imagined Jack would do just that, tilting her head to the side and smiling, as always, before letting out that throaty laugh that always reminded her of the past, of London, of their days before life had somehow become so achingly serious.

But Jack only shook her head and said, "No, you weren't."

A silence settled over them then—but it was a different silence from days past, one that made Frankie sit up and frown, made her look around and wonder what it was that seemed to be in the room with them now.

"Where on earth are we going, Frankie?"

Frankie didn't respond, only directed them out of the palazzo and toward the Campo Santa Maria Formosa, an empty glass bottle clutched in her right hand. As they walked across the open stretch, Jack complained about her heels, about the soreness of her feet in the heels, about the cold, about the damp, so that Frankie wanted to both laugh and shout in exasperation. "Here," Frankie announced, once they had made their way through the *campo* and over a bridge, indicating to Jack that she should follow her into one of the shops that lined the small alleyway.

In the darkness of the *sfuso,* Frankie's eyes struggled to adjust.

"Buongiorno," the man behind the counter murmured as they entered.

Frankie had been to the shop several times already, but not trusting her Italian in front of her friend, she only nodded in recognition. Her eyes flickered to the row of wine casks that ran the length of the wall behind the man. She placed the empty bottle she had been carrying onto the counter between them. "Pinot nero," she pronounced, followed by a *grazie.*

"Well, look at you," Jack said, clearly amused. "You're turning into a proper little Venetian."

The shopkeeper went over to a cask in the corner, holding up the empty bottle to the tap and turning its wooden valve. A dark-purple liquid began to fill the bottle. Once finished, the shopkeeper grabbed a cloth, gave the outside a quick wipe, and handed over the bottle of wine to the customers.

"I am, actually," Frankie said, a smile settling on her lips as she paid the lire owed.

Afterward, they walked toward a little park that Frankie had discovered her first week, which sat on what seemed to her the edge of Venice, or at least the edge of the Castello neighborhood, the water stretching out in front of them rather than ending abruptly in another building, another bridge. It was a place she had come to visit whenever she needed reassuring that there was something outside the Venetian bubble that encapsulated all its occupants. Frankie located the spot she had been searching for—a wide, tree-lined street with a row of benches, a glass conservatory hovering in the background, the park and lagoon just a dozen or so paces away.

"God, it's cold," Jack complained, sitting on the bench that Frankie indicated.

"I told you," Frankie laughed.

Jack reached over for the bottle and took a deep pull. "But it's also beautiful. Thank you for bringing me here." They sat quietly, passing the bottle back and forth, staring out at the water. Jack was the first one to break the silence. "I'm glad you've managed to do so well here, Frankie. I know I keep pestering you, asking the same questions over and over again, but after everything that happened, I wasn't sure. And yet here you are—on your own, going out, meeting people. I can't remember the last time you went out with someone who wasn't me or Harold. I don't know whether to be happy or a bit jealous."

"There's nothing to be jealous of," Frankie assured her. "I can only half-stand the girl, as it turns out. She's no replacement for you."

"Glad to hear it." Jack took another sip of the wine. "In all seriousness, though, Frankie, I'm proud of you."

"Stop it," Frankie said, knocking her shoulder against her friend's own.

Jack continued tentatively, "What happened that night—"

"It doesn't bear repeating. I talked and talked about it at Brimley House and now—" She took a deep breath, felt the richness of the Venetian air fill her lungs. "Now I just want to forget."

"Forget?"

"Move on," Frankie clarified, seeing the look of concern on her friend's face. "I want to leave it all behind me, in the past."

"I just worry."

"What about?" Frankie asked, knowing full well what she meant.

"You, going—" She paused, as if unable to speak the words.

"Mad?" Frankie supplied.

"Well, yes," Jack conceded. "I wouldn't use that word."

"Why not? It's accurate, no matter how insulting. And, anyway, you know me. Thick skin." She gave her friend a grin.

It took Jack a moment before she returned the expression. "The thickest." Jack pulled her attention away from her friend then, looking first to the water and then turning to take in the full expanse of the park. "I don't think I ever realized that Venice was so green," Jack said, reaching for the bottle again.

On their way back, in the darkness—the sun setting earlier now that winter was just around the corner—they paused and looked up at the Church of Santa Maria Formosa, its bells chiming loudly, announcing the late hour. The *campo* was nearly empty save for the café workers stacking chairs against the building, closing up for the evening, and an older man who had paused with his dog at the *fontanella*, the animal lapping at the day's accumulation of spilled water.

Jack pointed to the church. "Do you know how it got its name?" she asked, playfully leaning over and placing her head on Frankie's shoulder.

"No, but I expect something wicked and scandalous."

Jack laughed. "Well, I suppose it is in a way. A priest, sometime long ago—I'm terrible with dates, you know that—said that a woman, Mary, of course," at which Frankie chimed in with an *of course,* "came to him and told him to build the church."

Frankie cocked her eyebrow. "And?"

"And he described her in a very particular way." Jack indicated the church in front of them. "Santa Maria Formosa."

Frankie frowned. "I'm missing something."

"Italian lessons, apparently," Jack said. "*Formosa.* It's the word for, ahem, *buxom* in Italian."

Frankie nodded solemnly. "A buxom Mary. How very interesting."

Jack let out a great laugh then, one that startled the few others who stood in the *campo,* causing inquisitive glances and an occasional glare to be thrown their way. Neither of the women paid them any mind. Instead, they continued laughing and, with linked arms, made their way happily back to the palazzo, where Leonard was waiting with dinner, a feast of fresh spaghetti tossed in olive oil and anchovies and garlic and chili pepper spread before him, the warmth of the kitchen welcoming them home.

CHAPTER 10

A few days later, as Frankie and Jack stood together in the kitchen, Leonard lying on the sofa, and the housekeeper hovering just a few steps away, Frankie realized that it had been some time since she had last heard the neighbors. "Maria," Frankie said, turning to the housekeeper, "will you please tell Jack about that time we both heard the neighbors—you know, that day in the courtyard?"

Maria shrugged her shoulders, murmuring something in Italian that Frankie could not understand.

"Oh, God," Jack said, tearing off a piece of brioche, although typically Frankie's friend avoided any food that threatened one's waistline—a product of having been raised by a woman who believed her sex's worth could be measured by the numbers on a tape measure. "I hope we haven't got rats."

"Unless rats have learned how to open and close doors, you haven't," Frankie huffed, irked at her friend's dismissal.

"I once had a tabby cat that could," Leonard interjected from his place on the sofa.

"Could what, dear?" Jack asked, pressing the brioche into dense pieces of dough and then dropping them into a napkin.

"Open doors."

"No, it couldn't," she admonished.

Frankie grabbed the pieces of bread from Jack and pointedly placed them in her mouth. "Leonard's tabby is beside the point. What you have is not a rodent or any other type of animal problem. You have neighbors."

Maria mumbled something under her breath.

"What's that?" Frankie demanded.

But Maria refused to answer, only shook her head and left the room.

"You're making too much of this, Frankie," Jack warned, watching the housekeeper's departure.

"I'm not," Frankie protested, like a child being told off for telling tall tales. "There is someone next door, Jack. I have heard them." She gestured in the direction where Maria had disappeared. "And so has your housekeeper, even if she denies it."

Jack was squinting at her, as if measuring her words, weighing them. "All right," she eventually said. "Follow me."

Leonard sat up. "What are we doing?"

"We are settling this once and for all," Jack declared.

Together, the three of them descended the stairs of the palazzo and crossed the courtyard to the other side. Frankie could not help but feel that Jack was behaving like a mother forcing her child to look under the bed, in the closet, in order to prove that no monsters were hiding there. She wanted to tell her that she wasn't a child, that she knew the difference between real and imaginary, but suspected that Jack would only ignore her.

On the other side of the palazzo, Jack knocked on the door.

"I've done that before," Frankie said from behind her shoulder, still feeling slightly irked by the whole affair. "No one will answer."

Jack ignored her, knocked again, and when this still did not produce the desired effect, banged on the door.

"Jack," Frankie began again. "No one is going to answer."

Jack reached for the doorknob, at which point Leonard cleared his throat and asked, in a somewhat tentative voice, "My dear, should you be doing that?"

Jack tossed a look over her shoulder before continuing. "Anyone got a hairpin?" she asked, after she failed in her attempt to jostle the thing open with force alone.

Frankie reached into her own hair and offered up a tiny silver pin.

"Thank you, Frankie," she said curtly, returning to her task.

For a minute or two, Frankie believed that her friend might be able to break open the door, such was her faith in Jack and her abilities. But as that minute or two passed and another went by and then another, Frankie grew less sure. She shot a look over to Leonard, who was watching his wife with evident concern. Once or twice he opened his mouth as if to say something, but then he seemed to think better of it, closing it again without uttering a single word.

The hairpin snapped in half. "Damn," Jack muttered.

"Well, that's that, then," Leonard offered.

"That's nothing, Leonard," Jack snapped, obviously flummoxed by her inability to open the door. "I know there's a key around here somewhere. There has to be. I'll ask Maria about it and we'll see then."

"See what, darling?" Leonard asked, as they moved together across the courtyard.

She looked at him as if the answer was obvious. "Whether we've got rats or humans, Leonard."

In what Frankie later put down to unfortunate luck, Gilly chose to ring the palazzo when all three of them—she, Leonard, and Jack—were lounging in the sitting room that night, several glasses in, commiserating over their failed mission next door. To make matters worse, Jack had only just been teasing her about her new friendship, declaring to Leonard that she felt so proud, to which her husband had only laughed and shaken his head, while Frankie had uttered a number of obscenities at her needling comments.

Jack's smile turned predatory when she realized who was on the phone. *"That's her,"* she pronounced in a poorly executed stage whisper, turning to Leonard even before Frankie had spoken more than a word or two into the receiver. "Frankie's new friend. I know it."

Frankie pushed her off, as Jack was now trying to take the phone from her. "Invite her to lunch," Jack was saying. "Invite the little sprite over so that we can meet her properly."

Frankie ignored her. "Sorry, I couldn't hear," she said into the telephone, and not for the first time. She thought Gilly had said something about dinner with friends, but she wasn't certain.

Jack grabbed the telephone from her. "Is this Gilly?" Her smile widened into a grin. "Yes, this is Jack, one of Frankie's closest friends. Listen, my husband and I are in for a few days and we'd love to meet some of the friends that Frankie's made here. Would you be able to come to lunch tomorrow? That's perfect. Well, we shall see you then. Yes. Looking forward to it as well."

"You sound ridiculous," Frankie hissed at her.

"Well, ridiculous or not, I've just arranged for us all to have lunch tomorrow," Jack said, putting down the telephone. A sudden frown crossed her face.

"What is it, darling?" Leonard asked.

"Nothing," she said. "Only, do you think it's too late to ring Maria?"

There was no way out of it, no matter how hard Frankie tried, the thought of such a formal gathering making her skin itch. It was the type of afternoon activity where Jack shone best—ladies out to lunch, taking tea, hosting various charity events that made Frankie want to scream in boredom. But no matter: When Jack set her mind to something, it was often impossible to change it. And Jack was resolute that it would happen—had even managed to get hold of Maria early the next morning to arrange for some lunch to be brought in—and Frankie was very much expected to attend. Leonard, however, had managed to find a way out, claiming an errand that had to be looked after with the utmost urgency. A visit to a hat shop, it seemed. Frankie had struggled to contain her smile as Jack fussed and demanded to know whether it wasn't something that could be put off for another day, to which Leonard assured her it was not, that the man in question was only open one day a week. Frankie thought it sounded like a lie, but she didn't blame him, only wished she could think of a reason to go with him.

Gilly was on time, down to the minute.

Jack ushered her in as if they were old friends, while Frankie watched from a distance. Gilly, for her part, made all the appropriate remarks, exclaiming over the chandelier that hung in the *piano nobile*—*it's eighteenth century,* Jack told her—and the spectacular view—*if only it was warmer so we could open the windows,* Jack offered—as though Gilly had never set foot in the palazzo before. Frankie tried to remember whether she had told Jack that Gilly had already visited once but then dismissed it with a shrug, deciding it was better to let the hostess have her moment.

"Frankie tells me you've been to Venice before," Jack said, as they took their seats on the sofas in the sitting room, Jack and Frankie on one and Gilly on the smaller settee.

"Yes," she answered, smoothing her skirt, which was, Frankie noted with amusement, longer than normal. In fact, everything about the girl's outfit seemed unusually conservative, based on what Frankie had already seen of her wardrobe, from the full skirt to the demure sweater with a high neckline. The effect was unsettling, somehow. "My parents were always so fond of the city, but they come less now that they're older. They find the walking that the city requires a bit too difficult."

"It's nice that you've carried on the tradition for them," Jack reassured her. "Do you have your own place here?"

"No, unfortunately my parents recently sold their property in Venice."

"Are you staying at a hotel, then?"

"Yes."

At the girl's response, Frankie recalled one of their recent conversations. "What happened to the apartment with that group of girls who hog the telephone?"

"It was becoming rather chaotic," Gilly said, reaching for the cup of tea that Jack was offering. "The telephone was impossible, and the queue for the bath took ages. In the end I decided it was too much, so I moved on to the Danieli."

Frankie let out a low whistle. "That's an improvement."

"I suppose, though I don't particularly care for hotels. I'd much prefer a place like this, where I could be on my own instead of surrounded by strangers."

"Agreed," Jack said, taking a sip of her tea. "I wanted to thank you, Gilly, for taking such good care of Frankie in my absence. I'm so glad you happened to run into each other again, that she's had a friend to spend time with. Though I know she can be rather tiresome when she puts her mind to it." Frankie only laughed in response, but Gilly, strangely enough, looked almost troubled by the kind words, prompting Jack to set down her cup and ask, "What is it, dear?"

In response, Gilly placed her own teacup gently on the table before them. "I have a confession to make." She darted a quick glance in Frankie's direction. "Though I suspect Frankie might have already guessed by now. The truth is, the first time we met was that day by the Rialto Bridge."

"I don't understand," Jack said, turning to her friend, clearly startled by the admission.

Frankie found herself similarly taken aback by the girl's words—not by the actual revelation itself, for she had long suspected that the girl's words about an introduction in London were false, but rather by the fact that the girl had actually decided to admit to the lie. At the confession, Frankie felt whatever had been tightening in her stomach since they first met begin to ease. "I did wonder," she said.

"But why?" Jack pressed, clearly still taken aback.

"Frances is one of my absolute favorite authors," Gilly began. "I couldn't believe my luck that day when I saw her standing by the Rialto Bridge. It just seemed too good an opportunity to pass up. And so I invented a connection in order to introduce myself." She turned to Frankie. "I hope you won't be too cross with me."

Frankie considered but found, to her surprise, that she was not. Why should she mind if the girl had recognized her and decided to tell a little white lie in order to introduce herself—it was something she herself might have done in her younger years, something she most certainly *had* done while working as a writer for a newspaper, on the hunt for any opportunity, any connection that might help her out. "It's water under the bridge, as they say," Frankie said, meaning it.

"Well, now that's been cleared up," Jack said, an expression of relief sweeping across her features at Frankie's words, the tension that had filled the room, however briefly, now dissipating in light of the truth, "what other sorts of things do you read, Gilly? Besides Frankie's work, I mean."

Frankie was impressed by her friend's question, testimony to the many years she had spent fielding situations no doubt more fraught than this. She took a sip of her tea, the liquid still hot enough to scald the tip of her tongue. She inhaled, the comforting scent of bergamot flooding her senses. She felt herself relax.

"There are a lot of contemporary writers that I'm fond of. And I particularly love continental writers at the moment," Gilly began eagerly. "All the experimental writing they're doing. There's a real interrogation into narrative, into what it means, what purpose it serves, and how it can be played with."

Whatever Frankie had expected as a response, it was not this. Her friend appeared equally taken aback. "Right," Jack replied, nodding, although it was clear she hadn't a clue what the girl was talking about. Despite her encouragement of Frankie, her willingness—no, eagerness—to read her friend's work, Jack had never been what one would describe as a reader. Jack's intake of words was limited to the weekly magazines, to a novel every few months or so that Frankie begged her, then practically forced her, to read. Now, at the girl's words, she looked slightly out of her depth. "Well, that sounds nice. What do you think about all that, Frankie?"

Frankie laughed, uninterested in carrying the conversation further. If there was one thing she hated more than talking about her own work, it was talking about others'. Let readers decide for themselves what they felt, what they took away from the text. Let them wrestle within their own minds over such ambiguous things as meaning. She had never understood the idea of reading—an undeniably solitary act—as a collective experience. She shifted in her seat, ready to be done with the conversation. "I rather think I prefer traditional literature to experiments," she said, hoping that would bring an end to it.

"That's not surprising," Gilly said.

Frankie raised her eyebrows in surprise. "Oh?"

"I only mean to say, it's evident in your writing," Gilly explained.

At the mention of her work, Frankie stiffened. This was not what she had expected when Jack proposed lunch. A few polite inquiries, a few tiresome anecdotes—not an interrogation into literature, into her own work.

"By your tone, I can only assume that's a defect of mine." Frankie turned to Jack for help, but her friend offered only a tentative smile, concentrating on the task of pouring tea, refusing to be drawn into the argument that seemed to be looming. Frankie was uncertain why it bothered her so much, but in Gilly's choice of reading material she found herself realizing how wrong she had got it all, the image she had created of the girl who only a few days before delighted in viewing *Macbeth*, invariably involved her curled up around a book by Virginia Woolf, gazing out of the window.

"Not exactly," Gilly said. "But I do think there's a danger in always looking behind, into the past."

Frankie fought to find the words to prove that the girl was wrong—for she was, clearly. Frankie felt the certainty just there, beating beneath her chest. She opened her mouth, retort ready on the tip of her tongue, argument prepared, when Jack interjected: "I don't think Frankie ever told me what it is that you do, Gilly."

Frankie fell silent, recalling the way the girl had deflected the question the time she had asked at the coffeehouse, interested to see whether she would answer now.

The girl looked slightly uncomfortable, Frankie thought, or perhaps she was only misreading her again, for already Gilly seemed to be sitting upright at the question, lengthening, her spine straight, her shoulders back. She looked at them both and said, in a measured tone, "I'm a writer."

At the admission, Frankie was incredulous. "You never mentioned it before," she observed wryly.

"I didn't want you to think—"

"What? That you had an ulterior motive?" Frankie gave a brusque laugh.

"Frankie." Jack shot her friend a sharp glance. "Have you been published yet, Gilly?"

"Just a few lines here and there. Nothing too impressive yet."

Frankie swiped a pastry that Jack had set out alongside the tea and began to take pointed bites. She felt stung, in a way she couldn't quite explain. She had not been lying a moment ago when she said she was not bothered by the girl's fib. If anything she was flattered by it, but the other—hiding an apparent disdain for Frankie's work, for she had heard it, hadn't she, the disapproval underneath her words, and then announcing herself as a writer—those revelations she was having a more difficult time accepting.

"What have you got in your pocket there?"

Frankie looked over at the girl, startled. "What?" she asked, thinking she had misheard.

Gilly was smiling, as though the gesture might expunge all traces of the growing animosity that Frankie could feel starting to burn within her. "In your pocket. You're always reaching for something there whenever you're lost in thought."

"Am I?" she stalled, unnerved that the girl was watching her so closely. She thought that she might deny it, let the girl think she was mistaken. Instead, after a moment of hesitation, she produced her ARP whistle.

"I didn't know you still had that," Jack cut in, something stealing across her face.

In lieu of response, Frankie only shrugged. There was something uncomfortable about having it on display, an artifact of her life from before she had known either of these women, and them both watching her in a manner that put her teeth on edge.

Gilly reached out. "May I?" she asked, hesitating at the last minute.

Frankie nodded, although part of her wondered whether she shouldn't have stuffed the thing back in her pocket. The afternoon, and its turn in conversation, had thrown her off-balance. "It's nothing," she rushed to explain, embarrassed. "Just a bit of my uniform from before, in the war. I don't know why I still carry it around."

Gilly was turning the piece over in her hand. "It's a talisman."

"I'm sorry?" Frankie asked, wondering whether she had misheard.

"A good-luck charm. Something to ward off evil and keep you safe."

"Don't be daft," Frankie laughed. "I don't believe a bit in that type of nonsense."

"But you do," Gilly protested. "This is proof of it," she said, holding up the whistle. "You made it through the war, safe and sound. And now you carry this around with you for that same reason, because of how it makes you feel. Safe and protected. Don't you see?"

Frankie did not answer, not right away. She didn't go in for such stuff—séances were the work of charlatans and nothing more, she firmly believed—but there was something in the girl's observation of how it made her feel. Frankie glanced quickly at Jack, who was still staring at her with that same queer expression. She shifted uneasily, turning back to the girl. "Stop being so insufferable," she rebuked.

Following this last exchange, conversation stalled, so that awkward pauses transformed into stretches of time that not even a sip of tea or a polite nibble of sandwich could cover. Frankie wasn't certain what had happened, but she could feel it in the way she held her tongue, reluctant to offer any more of herself among the present company, and what was more, she could see it in Jack, her usual effervescent mask as hostess having slipped more than Frankie could ever recall witnessing before. After another half hour or so of this, even Gilly seemed to pick up on this shift, for she stood and began to make her excuses.

"Frankie," Jack said, rising, "why don't you see our guest out?"

The journey downstairs was silent, punctuated only by the sound of their shoes against the tiled floor. At the door, Gilly turned and looked at her. "You're not angry about before, are you, Frances? I am sorry, you know."

"I'm not angry." Frankie sighed wearily, although she did wonder in that moment which indiscretion the girl was apologizing for. She had already forgiven her for the first, and could she really be that upset that it turned out she was an aspiring writer as well—who else but an ardent fan or future scribe would have recognized her among a sea of other faces? As for the snipes about her writing— well, there was a chance she had only imagined it, thrown off-balance by the other. "Don't apologize. Just because we're friends doesn't mean we have to agree on every little thing. Life would be rather dull if we did. Agreed?"

"Agreed, Frances. And I'm glad."

"Glad?"

"That you think of us as friends."

Frankie paused, taken aback by the girl's earnest tone. "Yes, well," she said.

The girl hesitated. "Do you know, it wasn't entirely a lie."

"What?"

"We have met once, though I don't suppose it counts. It was at a reading that my father took me to. I asked for your signature."

An image came to Frankie then—a young girl in plaits, standing defiantly at the start of a line, watching her with an intense gaze. "I don't remember."

Frankie stood at the door, leaving it open a crack, watching until Gilly slipped around the corner and out of sight. She couldn't explain why, but she stood there a few minutes longer, just to ensure the girl did not return.

CHAPTER 11

At some point during her walk home from the market the next day, Frankie became aware that she was lost. She wasn't certain how it happened or when she even became aware of it, but, as she hoisted the canvas bag over her shoulder, the straps straining under the weight of the fish and vegetables she had purchased for dinner that night—refusing to subject herself to another round of Maria's bland concoctions—Frankie realized that she did not recognize her surroundings.

She reached inside her pocket.

It was empty. For a moment she stopped in the street, certain that she had just missed it. She felt around for a second before turning out her pocket, convinced that she was only mistaken. But, no, it soon became clear that her suspicion was right—her whistle was missing.

No matter, she would find it later. For now she needed to find her way home.

The thing to do was to stop and assess where she had gone wrong. To stop proceeding in the direction she was now, a direction that was taking her farther and farther away from the Campo Santa Maria Formosa and everything she recognized. Frankie realized this and yet she could not bring herself to do so, strangely embarrassed at the idea of having to turn around, for it meant that she had become susceptible to Venice's many twists and turns—as though she were a mere tourist. And so she pressed on, cheeks burning, from cold, from embarrassment, she didn't know or care to find out. She only wanted to find her way home. To quell the panic that was snaking its way through her. She crossed a bridge and then turned left. She went up one set of stairs and then down another, emerging in a *campo* that was vast and altogether unfamiliar. A few times she was certain a local turned her way and glowered, as if they could read her confusion and embarrassment.

She began to wonder whether she might ever find her way home, began to wonder whether she wasn't in some sort of purgatory, forced to wander paths that looked familiar but for which she had no real memory, the bag on her shoulder growing more and more heavy.

But then, after about an hour of wandering, she found herself on the right path, without any idea of how it happened or what she had done to right herself. Bursting into the entrance hall, she pre-pared herself for Jack and Leonard, for the onslaught of concern, of demands for where she had been, the hours slipping away since she had first left. The story of her humiliating defeat was ready on her lips.

But no one rushed to greet her.

In fact, no one came at all.

Dropping the bags onto the parquet floor, she walked farther into the palazzo, wondering whether they weren't already out searching for her—what a mess that would be, she thought with an inward grimace, and what an embarrassment. Getting lost was a sign of weakness that Frankie dreaded to betray, even to her closest friends.

She turned the corner—and there they sat, in the sitting room, lounging on the sofa.

Jack half-raised herself up when Frankie walked into the room. "Frankie, doesn't it still feel like ice in here? I was just telling Leonard the Venetians need to sort out something about the heat, otherwise I'm never coming to Venice in the winter again." She paused, taking in Frankie, who was still wearing her overcoat. "Have you already been out and about today?"

Frankie opened her mouth, ready to relay it all—her trip to the market, her misadventure back home, but then something stayed her. "Just a quick trip to the market."

"Brilliant," Jack declared. "Anything we might be able to cook up for ourselves?"

"Yes," Leonard cut in. "I don't think I can stomach another night of Maria's cooking."

"Agreed." Jack looked to Frankie. "Everything all right, Frankie?"

"Yes." Frankie nodded. "I'll go and get the groceries from the hall." She paused. "Have either of you seen a whistle lying around?"

"A whistle?" Leonard asked, while Jack only looked pensive. They both agreed that neither of them had seen it.

"No matter," Frankie said, trying her best to smile. "I'm certain it will turn up."

She exited the room quickly.

Harold rang the next day.

Frankie had come home to find the palazzo empty, Jack and Leonard out exploring. She had tried to revel in the quietness of the place, pouring herself a drink and standing at the windows, looking out at the canal, watching as the traffic of gondolas made its way, slowly, languorously, but determinedly all the same. She would miss it, she decided. The quiet of the city, the hush that fell across it and that she could feel, settling her, calming her, a balm to soothe her frayed nerves. But she was ready to head back, she realized, to jump back into the work that she had been ignoring for so long. Thinking of the pages that now sat on her desk, she knew that she had found her way to the start of something. No, it was more than that. Since the arrival of her friends, she had begun writing again, although in shorter increments. In the morning, when she woke early and her mind refused to calm, to go back to sleep, and in the evenings, listening to Jack and Leonard as they moved below her, these interruptions a surprising encouragement rather than the deterrent she had always supposed the presence of others would be. What had started as a few hastily scrawled ideas, the possibility for something bigger, had now transformed into a real, tangible something. A nearly completed novel, although she was too nervous to admit it to herself yet.

"Harold," she said, once she realized who was on the other end of the line. "I was just thinking of you."

"Really?" He sounded doubtful.

"Yes. I was thinking that it might be time to start back for London soon."

"That's wonderful news, my dear," Harold said, with a greater amount of solemnity than seemed necessary. "I'm so pleased to hear it." He paused then—and she could sense it, whatever it was, the real reason that he had called, filling the silence on the telephone, the emptiness of the palazzo.

"What's happened?" she demanded over the sudden ringing in her ears.

"Listen, Frankie," he began, hesitating over the words. "Has Leonard spoken to you yet?"

"He hasn't had a chance. Why don't you tell me now," she suggested, frightened of what he might say but knowing that she could not wait another moment. If she had to receive bad news, she almost preferred it to be from her editor rather than Leonard, the latter somehow too close, too personal for such revelations to be comfortable.

She heard a grumble on the other end of the line, something along the lines of, *That's the problem with solicitors,* before Harold cleared his throat and said, "It's that woman. There's been, well, a bit of a development."

Frankie had been expecting as much. Still, the news startled her. "I don't understand, that's been ages now. I thought you said it was over and done with."

"It was—it is."

"But then—" Frankie stopped, not understanding.

"She's given an interview."

Frankie felt the blood drain from her face. "About that night?"

"Yes. It doesn't name you, but it will be obvious to anyone within our little circle."

"But she signed something—"

"She *did* and Leonard is on it, there's no need to worry. We just wanted to let you know."

"If there's no need to worry, then why are you telling me this?" He knew Frankie, the way her mind worked. He had to have realized that she would not be able to stop worrying now that she knew. Why the blazes had he told her?

"In case it goes any further, darling."

"Further how, Harold?"

He hesitated. "To court."

Frankie let out an exhale. To court. It wouldn't ruin her, not financially anyway, but her reputation would take a serious dent, one that she could very much not afford.

"It will be fine, Frankie. I promise. Speak with Leonard, he knows the details."

Frankie was suddenly desperate to be away. "I've got to go, Harold," she said, her voice louder than she intended.

"All right, my dear," he replied, his voice cautious. "But, listen, let me know when you book your tickets. I'll pick you up at the train station, no need to call for a taxi."

Frankie didn't remember hanging up the telephone, didn't

remember whether or not she had bothered to say goodbye. Instead, she stood there for a long while, wondering how it was that she was right back to where she had started, all those months before. She wasn't certain how much time passed, but eventually she became aware of the cold, of the stiffness that had settled into her bones and joints. From downstairs, she heard the sounds of Jack and Leonard returning home.

"Frankie?" Jack's voice rang out.

Frankie cast one last hurried look at the telephone, as if Harold were still there, waiting for her response. "Just a minute," she called back. She scurried out of the room, toward the warmth and comfort of her friends.

CHAPTER 12

Frankie did her best to follow her own advice. A day passed and then another, and instead of sitting around the palazzo, thinking about what Harold had said, she visited the Museo Correr and the Ca' Rezzonico with Jack and Leonard, sipped *vino rosso* in the *bacari*, and enjoyed Venice in the presence of her friends.

Frankie also agreed to see Gilly again. For while she would have preferred to spend her days in the company of Jack, she suspected that her friend was anxious to spend time alone with her husband. Jack never said as much, but Frankie could see it—in the furtive glances they would shoot each other when they thought she was not looking, in the way they would disappear for hours on errands that should only take a matter of minutes. And so Frankie deferred to Gilly, allowing herself to be led to the Ca' Pesaro one rainy day when she would have preferred to stay inside by the fire, going from one vast, chilly room to the next, being lectured on the extensive Asian collection that filled the space, as if she were some great student of art and Gilly the lecturer. Most of the time she ignored what the girl was saying, as her gaze swept past one decorative kimono and then another. It still rankled her at times, the girl's bossiness—and yet she continued to find herself charmed by it as well. Charmed by *her*.

Later, at Harry's Bar, known for its Bellini cocktails, Gilly ordered them each a spritz, as if in defiance, instructing the bartender to use Campari in Frankie's and Aperol in her own. When the strikingly orange concoctions, each with a pierced green olive, were set on the counter before them, Gilly lifted hers and toasted. "To second chances and new beginnings."

Frankie raised her eyebrows in place of a response, clinking her glass against Gilly's own. Perched on barstools, legs facing each other, they drank quietly, Frankie still unsure as to what she should make of the girl opposite her.

"Can I tell you a secret?" Gilly asked, the pit of the olive rolling in her mouth.

"Only if you spit that thing out first," Frankie instructed, the sight somehow grotesque.

The girl obeyed, placing the pit into the napkin beside her drink. "Do you know that day when we were supposed to meet at Florian's?"

"Yes. What about it?"

Gilly drew in a deep breath. "I was there."

"You were where?" Frankie asked, not understanding.

"At Florian's. I was waiting just around the corner."

Frankie narrowed her eyes. "Explain, please."

"I was nervous," Gilly began, undeterred, it seemed, by the steeliness that had crept into Frankie's tone. "And for a moment I thought maybe it would be best if I didn't show, if we didn't meet. I had built it up so much in my head already—what I would say, how you would respond. The way we would become firm friends. Before I could decide either way, it was too late. You were standing up and leaving. All I could do was watch. The only reason I was able to muster up enough courage to try again was because of that terrible party, which at the time I hoped would impress you."

Frankie considered the girl's words. "Why are you telling me this?"

"Because I want you to understand why I lied about us knowing each other when we first met. I desperately wanted to meet you and couldn't think of a proper way to introduce myself without seeming like, well, an overeager fan."

Frankie paused. Gilly was dressed once more like the girl she had first met at the Rialto market, her skirt rising up her thighs as she shifted uneasily on the barstool, and there was, at the very least, a measure of comfort in this reversion. "You mean, exactly what you are?" she teased.

Gilly gave a soft laugh. "What brought you to Venice, Frances? When we first met, you implied that it was sightseeing, but knowing you now, I don't think that's probably very true."

Frankie was slow to answer. "I needed a break from London."

"Because of what happened." Gilly took a sip of her spritz. "I remember reading about it in the papers."

So the girl had known all along, then. Frankie took a sip of her drink, let the bitterness fall across her tongue. "Oh?"

"They said you vanished into thin air afterward. That it was like Agatha Christie all over again."

"What nonsense," Frankie said, secretly pleased by the comparison.

"Was it for the reason he said?"

Frankie looked up, startled. "What?"

"The reporter. I forget his name. He said what happened at the Savoy was all because of something someone had written." Gilly paused. "A review."

Frankie faltered then. "It doesn't matter now."

"But, Frances—"

"No, let's not speak of it anymore." She rearranged her features into something sterner, something made of harder stuff than what she felt like in that moment. "Promise me, Gilly."

"All right, Frances. I promise." The girl started to speak, then stopped.

"What?" Frankie demanded, exasperated.

"I was just going to say that you're not the first author to receive a bad review. Dostoevsky. Hemingway. Did you know Virginia Woolf was terribly affected by criticism? She didn't even like to read what others wrote about her fellow authors. She said that *no creative writer can swallow another contemporary.*"

"Yes, but how did she deal with it?"

They were silent for a minute.

"And one more thing," Gilly pressed.

"What's that?"

"Stop thinking so hard, Frances, or that line will become permanent." Before Frankie could stop her, Gilly reached out and pressed her finger against the space between her eyebrows. "My mother would make you wear one of those beauty strips pasted between your eyes all night long to correct that."

"Well, I rather like my lines."

"Which I like about you. And which tells me that you don't care what other people think." She held Frankie's gaze. "So stop letting one review upend your entire life."

Frankie studied the girl. Perhaps this was the real reason that their paths had crossed. The girl was there to shake her of the malaise that had gripped her for so long—something only a stranger, who did not know the ins and outs of her life, of her past, could do. Frankie had spent so long, most of her life, in the shadows that she wondered whether it had affected the way she saw others. Maybe there had never been anything unusual about the girl at all, maybe it had always been in her own mind, her own doing, her own making. She finished her drink, pushing it toward the bar, signaling the waiter for another. "All right. So you know why I'm here. Now tell me why *you're* here. Surely sightseeing in Venice during the winter can't be high on a young girl's list."

"Oh, I don't know," Gilly said with a smile. "I rather like places when they're off-season."

"I don't believe you. A girl like you, you're made for sunshine and parties and being shown about on the heir-of-something-or-other's arm." Her eyes narrowed. "What are you *really* doing here?" Frankie raised her eyebrows in expectation, wondering what dark secrets the girl might be harboring—and which ones she would be willing to reveal.

A glint shone in Gilly's eye. "I'm working on a novel."

Frankie told herself she should not be surprised. "Are you?"

"Or finishing one, rather. I'm almost done."

"I see."

Gilly averted her eyes, color rising to her cheeks. "Maybe you could look at it for me? Give me your opinion?"

Frankie thought there was nothing she would like to do less. She had never enjoyed reading the work of people she knew, didn't understand how others didn't feel the same. The idea of Jack, of other acquaintances, reading her work set her on edge. After the publication of a book, she always spent a fortnight or so wondering what they might read into her words, whether they saw themselves reflected, however unintentional, in the characters she portrayed. It was like letting her closest friends read her diary. She dreaded to think what she might find reflected in Gilly's.

Their spritzes finished, they paid and made their way to leave. Standing in the doorway for a moment, Gilly let out a great sigh. "Don't you just love it?"

"What?"

"This," Gilly said. "Venice."

Frankie looked around her, at the shimmering green of the water, its sulfurous tang stronger than it had been an hour before, at the grand architecture surrounding them, crumbling and fading. It was a study in contrasts.

"Well?" Gilly pressed.

The girl was impossible. Frankie shook her head at such optimism, even smiling, despite herself. "We'll see," she said.

"You and Gilly seem to be getting on," Jack said one afternoon, as they lay sprawled out on the sofa, her eyebrow crooked with amusement. It was raining, and neither of them had managed to gather up enough strength to do more than light a fire and pour a measure or two of whisky from the bar trolley, both still clad in their dressing gowns. Eventually, even that had required too much effort, and on her last trip Jack returned bottle in hand, the pair of them content to sit and watch the window overlooking the canal, just as the Venetians must have done years and years before them.

"You can take that expression off your face right now," Frankie snapped. "The only reason I've endured her presence is because of how scarce your own has been."

"I'm sorry," Jack responded, not looking it one bit. "But to the casual observer, you two seem thick as thieves."

Frankie gave a short laugh. "Don't be absurd."

But Jack persisted. "I'm not. It seems like every time I turn around the pair of you are together." When Frankie didn't reply, she said, "Am I to interpret that you no longer find her so insufferable, then?"

Frankie only rolled her eyes.

"Well, I like her," Jack said, shaking her head. "I think she's fun. And *young*."

"Young?" Frankie asked, squinting her eyes to take a closer look at her friend. "Are you jealous, Jack?" she asked, only half joking, based on the expression on her friend's face.

"Don't be ridiculous," Jack retorted, shaking her head. "Have a drink. Relax."

"I don't want to," Frankie responded, irked that her friend had ignored the question.

"What? Drink or relax?"

"Either," Frankie answered, just to be contrary.

Jack let out a cackle of laughter as Frankie reached for her whisky. "You are absolutely impossible, Frankie, darling, do you know that?"

"By the way"—Frankie propped herself up on her elbows in order to see her friend better—"Gilly wants to take us all out."

Jack pulled a face.

Frankie laughed. "You only just said you liked her."

"Yes—for you," Jack said, reaching for her drink. "But you're already quite a bit older than her, and I'm a bit older still, and Leonard is, well, he's ancient," she said, beginning to laugh.

At that moment, Leonard walked into the sitting room. "I'm what, now?" he asked, reaching for his wife's glass.

"Leonard," Frankie said, speaking over Jack's already growing protests, "my dear friend Gilly wants to take us all out, show us a good time, but your wife is very rudely objecting. Will you please talk some sense into her?"

"Gilly?" he asked. "That little redheaded thing that popped round before?" He took a sip of his drink. "She's rather intense by the sound of it, isn't she?"

Jack nodded. "Yes, yes, she is."

"Only because she's *young*, Jack," Frankie teased. "Regardless, she's invited us out, and it would be rude not to accept her invitation."

Leonard nodded. "That's very true."

Jack let out a groan.

"Don't worry, darling," Leonard said, taking a spot on the sofa. "You're very youthful, you know."

"Not me," Jack sputtered. "Heaven knows I'm far too old to

know whatever the children get up to nowadays." She placed a hand on Leonard's face. "But it's rather kind of you to say so, my dear."

Feeling as though she was intruding, Frankie drained the last of her whisky and looked away.

The next morning, Frankie sought out the housekeeper.

"Maria, have you seen a whistle lying around, by any chance?" When the woman standing in front of her did not respond but only deepened her frown, Frankie assumed it was an issue of translation. "You know—a small metal object. You blow into it, like this," she said, completing the pantomime. "It makes a sound." She pursed her lips and did her best to make a low, steady whistle. It took her several attempts before she succeeded.

The housekeeper shifted her weight. "No, *signora*. I have found no whistle."

CHAPTER 13

That Saturday, Gilly took them to an *osteria* buried in the heart of the Jewish ghetto for a leisurely afternoon lunch.

Frankie had yet to venture to that side of the Cannaregio, and as they neared the restaurant, she thought she detected a marked difference between this area and the Venice that she had come to know, as though one could feel the history of it etched into the stones. At one time, Frankie knew, this was how the city of Venice had kept the Jewish population sequestered from the rest, closing the gates in the evening, guards patrolling the canals to ensure that no one escaped, essentially cutting off those who lived on the island from the rest of Venice, locking them into a makeshift prison each night. The thought made Frankie shudder now, as her footsteps fell across the cobblestones beneath her.

At the restaurant, her gloom began to dissipate, the desolate *campo* they had crossed forgotten in light of the crowds before them that pulsed and throbbed despite the early hour, patrons spilling from inside the establishment, tables and chairs pushed up against the very edge of the canal. Laughter and the clinking of glasses filled the air. Despite the drizzle, a stray couple or two sat outside on the ground, legs dangling above the water.

Together, their party of four squeezed their way inside the

restaurant, brushing past patrons who stood, glasses of *vino rosso* in one hand, *cicchetti* in the other, the smell of the salt water, of fish, rising in the air around them. The crowd was not what Frankie had been expecting. A vibrant backsplash, at least compared to the dreary colors that she had become accustomed to seeing on most Venetians, herself included, greeted them as they elbowed their way to their table, positioned just slightly too close to the band that was already performing, despite the early hour. Frankie watched with amusement as girls in lime-colored dresses with pink tights, some with honeycomb patterns, others with flowers, but all of them loud and unapologetic, verging on garish, moved around the restaurant. Their male counterparts were equally flamboyant, in striped and brightly colored shirts. When she mentioned this to Gilly, raising her voice to be heard, the girl laughed and said, "Artists," the single word seemingly explanation enough.

"Oh, dear," Jack said, as they took their seats. "We are by far the oldest people here."

Leonard peered over her shoulder. "By at least a decade, it seems."

Frankie stifled a laugh. It was true, but she wasn't bothered by it, not in the way Jack often was. Gilly had been right when she surmised that Frankie had never cared a bit for other people's opinions and she didn't intend to start now. Jack, on the other hand, had always been sensitive when it came to the way others perceived her. Still, even Frankie had to confess that they did not belong in this tiny smoke-filled den, the sounds of unfamiliar music playing at an unbearable volume. Everyone was so *hip*. Frankie herself was dressed in her trademark cigarette trousers and shirt, so she wasn't too badly out of place, but poor Leonard looked as though he was off to church, and Jack had chosen a stiff cocktail dress—sleeveless, yes, but one that covered her knees and was decidedly too prim in the current company. The strand of pearls around her neck only made it worse. It was as though somebody had invited their auntie to tea, Frankie realized. She wished then that she were twenty years younger, imagining what it might be like to come of age in such a time, at once envying those around her and resenting them for the opportunity they no doubt failed to realize they were being afforded.

"Well, now," Leonard said, burying himself behind the menu. Jack was already inspecting the cleanliness of the cutlery, having moved on from wobbling her chair back and forth, at last giving up on it ever being level. "Let's see what we have."

But before Leonard, or anyone else at the table, could determine what exactly that was, Gilly leapt up and pulled the menu from each of their hands. A cry of protest went up from Leonard and Jack, but Frankie grinned, smug in her immunity to the girl's theatrics.

"There's only one thing here worth ordering," Gilly said with a coy smile. Without divulging more, she pushed her way through the crowd, over to the waiter at the back of the restaurant.

"I did warn you," Frankie laughed.

"She certainly is enthusiastic," Jack offered.

"That's one word for it," Leonard murmured.

In that moment, Frankie worried that it had all been a horrible mistake, bringing them here together, and that the four of them were doomed to endure an insufferably awkward meal—much like that day at the palazzo. But then, mercifully, the waiter arrived with wine. Ordered by Gilly, the wine was full-bodied and dry and good enough all around that even Jack admitted so with a bit of surprise. After that, time sped past. Conversation became loud and impassioned, hand gestures correspondingly so. At one point, Jack and Leonard drifted outside, drinks in hand, to stare at the canal, leaving Frankie and Gilly on their own.

"I still can't believe just how short some of these dresses are," Frankie said, their conversation having turned to observances of the crowd. "How do these girls even manage to sit down?"

Gilly peered at her. "You're strangely old-fashioned, do you know that?"

Frankie's eyes narrowed. "Why strangely?"

"Well, because you're so liberal elsewhere." Gilly motioned toward her, as if the evidence were writ on her own body. "Single. Independent. A writer."

Frankie bristled. "And sexless, by the sound of it."

"Oh, I didn't mean—" Gilly began.

But Frankie quieted her. "I'm only teasing."

Just then, Jack and Leonard returned, glasses empty. "And what are we discussing?" Jack asked.

"The rest of the clientele," Frankie replied, signaling to the waiter for a new bottle.

Jack looked around them, smoothing out her dress and shaking her head. "I don't think I would manage well with the latest fashions. Something about wearing nightclothes in public makes me rather nervous," she said with a shudder, referring to the trend for palazzo pajamas, which were being worn by several of the young women present. "And the noise."

"The music?" Gilly asked.

"Darling," Jack responded, "is this music?"

Gilly laughed at that.

"The only word I understand is *bang*, and I don't have any desire to know what else they're saying." Jack surveyed the room. "I thought Sinatra was supposed to be popular in Italy. Why can't we have him?"

The waiter returned with another bottle, prosecco this time, and for a few moments they were occupied with idle chitchat as glasses were filled and tentative sips were taken, no one wanting to be the first in need of a refill.

"I hear you're a writer, Gilly," Leonard said.

Gilly beamed, evidently overjoyed at the attention such a question promised. "Yes, I am."

"And so what type of things do you write?" Leonard asked.

Frankie hid a smile. His tone was that of a father asking about his daughter's day, so paternal and out of place with the atmosphere. She sneaked a quick glance at Jack, who only glared in response.

Gilly, however, didn't seem to mind. "Beautiful things, Leonard," she answered, clearly affected by both the wine and prosecco. It became near impossible for Frankie not to laugh or at least roll her eyes. Not even Gilly talked in so embarrassing a manner normally, so that it was clear the bubbles had gone straight to her head. Frankie felt a small kick under the table, knew it was Jack, and did her best to remain composed. Gilly was still talking. "I want to write poetry," she said, her voice earnest.

"Oh," Leonard said, reaching for his drink. "So, you're a poet, then?"

"No, I write novels," she replied, frowning, as if she couldn't understand the confusion. "Only, well, you see, I love poetry so much that I want to infuse it *into* my prose."

"Oh. Golly," Leonard replied again, clearly at a loss for words. He turned to Frankie. "What do you think about all this?"

Frankie considered. "I think it rather sounds like Gilly writes poetry." This earned her another swift kick under the table.

"You've written something, then?" Jack asked. "Or are you talking in theory?"

"Well, I do have a manuscript," Gilly confessed, eyes averted. "In fact, I just finished it the other day."

"Oh, God, of course you have," Frankie laughed.

Their conversation was interrupted as one of the waiters, pushing a large trolley bearing an enormous wheel of cheese, stopped at their table.

"What on earth?" Jack leaned over to get a better view.

The waiter started to speak then, in a steady stream of Italian that none of them could understand except Gilly, who responded loudly, exuberantly, never bothering to translate for the rest for the group. And so they could only watch, spectators to a sort of theater, as the man added great, bouncing tubes of pasta to the wheel of cheese, as the heat of the pasta caused the cheese itself to grow soft and begin to melt. He produced a mortar and pestle filled with peppercorns, the spicy notes of which greeted them only seconds later. Leonard descended into a sneezing fit, causing the waiter to pause and laugh and Gilly to shake her head and Jack to go digging into her handbag for a handkerchief.

All this Frankie watched with amusement, as the prosecco unwound itself within her, making her feel warm and comforted but distant. She laughed, loudly, but no one seemed to notice.

And then plates were put in front of them and they were eating, the salty tang of the pecorino, the pepper, all of it combining into something she had never before tasted.

"I had this the very first time I came to Italy, and even though that was in Rome, I thought it would be perfect for tonight." At this, Leonard gave an enthusiastic clap, which earned a rueful smile from both Jack and Frankie.

For a few minutes, no one spoke, concentrated as they were on eating, on filling up what had been left empty and hollow by the wine and prosecco. Frankie felt as though she had never before been so hungry, as she placed forkful after forkful into her mouth. Glancing up, Frankie became aware of a crowd moving outside, chairs in hand, gathering on one of the bridges that she could just make out from her vantage point. "What are they doing?" Frankie asked, her mouth full.

Gilly leaned nearer, looking over to where she had gestured. "Hoping to catch sight of the elusive golden hour," she said with a nod, before turning back to her pasta. "But if it does happen, it won't be for another hour or so at least. They're far too early."

"The golden hour?"

"You've never heard of it?"

Frankie laughed, surprised at the lack of sharp retort ready on her own tongue. Instead, she reached for the newly uncorked bottle of wine, filling her cup and letting the deep berries, the slight tang of tobacco, fall over her tongue. "No, tell me."

"It's the time right before sunset, when the city is bathed in a golden light. Venice is supposed to be at its most beautiful in the golden hour, according to painters, to photographers, to just about anyone you might ask."

Frankie noted her tone. "You don't agree?"

Gilly shrugged. "I prefer the blue hour."

"Did you make that up?" Frankie couldn't stop herself from asking.

Gilly laughed, finishing the rest of her wine in one easy gulp. "I'll show you sometime. And then you'll see."

Jack and Leonard left soon after, claiming exhaustion. Frankie stayed only an hour or so more, then excused herself, Gilly having taken up a conversation with a group of other twentysomethings at the next table, Italians and a few Spaniards, who were even now doing their best to understand one another through broken sentences and frenzied gestures. For a moment or two, Frankie was content to watch, to revel in the enthusiasm of youth, to re-member a time when she might have been the same, although she didn't think she had ever been so carefree, so hopeful as the group in front of her. A consequence, she often thought, of com-ing of age during the war. It marked you somehow, as though you could see the difference. Frankie shivered. It was then—the fresh flood of alcohol having already leached from her bloodstream and the dull, sullen restlessness she often experienced once the initial high was over—that she decided to make her exit. She turned to Gilly to tell her, but the girl was deep in conversation, her cheeks bright pink as she accepted another glass from the boy next to her. Frankie stood from the table and made her way out into the evening, alone.

The sun had begun to set. Frankie found herself hurrying her footsteps, anxious to be inside, to be back home in the palazzo before nightfall. She paused, standing on a bridge she didn't recognize, watching as the light receded. Her hands gripped the railing beneath her, her skin aching with cold.

"Frances! Wait!"

Frankie turned and saw Gilly running toward her, heels in hand. "Put your shoes back on," she admonished the girl, thinking of nothing in that moment but the cold and the filth of the streets.

"Wait!" Gilly cried again, despite the fact that Frankie was standing still.

"What is it?" Frankie asked, wanting nothing so much as a bath and a hot-water bottle in her bed.

"Oh, don't be so moody," Gilly said as she approached, grabbing Frankie's hand and leading her in the same direction in which Frankie had been heading. "I'll have you home before your bedtime, I promise. I just want to show you something first."

"What?"

Gilly did not respond, only led her forward, one hand holding Frankie's own and the other still clasping her discarded heels. "Only a little farther," she murmured, repeating the promise every minute or so as they continued on, over one bridge and then another. Frankie surrendered to the girl's lead then, allowing herself to be pulled through the streets, down ones that were vaguely familiar and others that were still unknown to her.

Eventually they came to a stop on a bridge, its wooden curve rising up and over the water in a steeper incline than most. It was situated on one of the city's wider canals, providing an unobstructed view of the water and buildings in front of them. Frankie wondered that she had never noticed this particular spot before.

"There," Gilly said. "Look."

Frankie made a noise of annoyance. "At what?"

But Gilly didn't respond, and Frankie didn't need her to, not when she saw what was in front of her. Everything was bathed in a deep blue from the lights of the buildings, from the lampposts sparkling with an intensity that made them look otherworldly. Frankie was reminded of her mother then, of her insistence that as a child she had once seen a fairy as it flew by her, its light bright and shining and unlike anything she had ever seen before. At the time, Frankie had only rolled her eyes, had wished her mother wouldn't say things like that—but now, now she could understand the human inclination to believe in magic, to believe in the things that could not always be seen by the naked eye. A hush fell over them as they stood, taking it all in.

Frankie wasn't certain how much time passed as they stood and watched the hues of blue transform before them, gradually growing a shade or two darker, but when Gilly spoke again, it was with a softer tone than before. "They're even more special at this time of year, you know."

Frankie glanced over to her. "How's that?"

"Usually it's too foggy to see the blue hour, it's all obscured." Gilly turned to her. "You're good luck, Frances."

Frankie stopped herself from making a disparaging remark, tempted as she was, and in response Gilly smiled, as if she knew how difficult it was for Frankie to remain quiet in the presence of such sentimentalism. They stood together, their shoulders touching, watching, waiting, until gradually, with the passage of time, the blue deepened, turned to black, and then was gone, as if it had never been there at all.

Frankie's breath caught.

"Well," Gilly said. "What about now?"

Frankie looked at her. "What?"

"Venice." Gilly spread out her arms. "Do you love it now?"

Frankie did not respond, finding no words that would be sufficient to convey what she was feeling, so she only nodded, and together they began to make their way home.

She had not extended a verbal invitation to the girl—words were not needed. Perhaps it was the drink, or the view, but there seemed to exist between them in that moment a sort of understanding that she had rarely experienced with others in her life.

Once inside the palazzo, Frankie went to work making a fire, aware of just how chilled she had grown from standing outside, her toes now burning with the cold, her clothes a bit dampened from the light rain, from the wind that had started to blow on their way back. Gilly headed straight to the bar trolley, pouring them each a generous finger of whisky. They were silent as they settled onto the sofa, the rain sounding loudly now against the vast windows. Gilly reached for a blanket, arranging it so that both of them were covered.

"Frances?"

"Yes."

"This is one of my favorite nights, I think."

"Don't be absurd."

They were quiet then, but there was a comfort in it, so that all at once Frankie's limbs grew heavy and her eyelids drooped. At Gilly's heavy breathing, Frankie forced her eyes open long enough to take both their still nearly full whisky glasses and place them on the coffee table.

"Do you know," Frankie began, but only when she was certain the girl was half asleep, "I wish I would have been more like you when I was young."

"Mmm," came the sleepy response.

"Fearless," Frankie whispered.

Gilly's eyes opened then, although there was still the look of sleep behind them, so that Frankie was uncertain whether or not she was awake. "Really, Frances? Do you think so?" she murmured.

"Of course, I do, you silly girl. Now go to sleep."

CHAPTER 14

When Frankie woke late that morning, it was with the uncanny sensation that something was wrong. It was the silence, she thought, opening her eyes. It was off somehow, too overwhelming in its totality, so that her ears rang as though she had come down with a case of tinnitus, her skin prickling in the absolute stillness. Standing, she cast a look around the room, at the girl, her form rising and falling gently with sleep, at the fire, now entirely burnt out. Frankie could find nothing amiss.

Making her way to her bedroom, she paused as a loud groan sounded from somewhere within the palazzo, cutting through the stillness of only moments before. The wind, she realized, glancing toward the windows, where the rain beat against the panes. Perhaps that was what had woken her. In the doorway to her bedroom, Frankie glanced toward her desk. Over the last few days, she had all but finished the novel that she had started when she arrived, the novel that she had never intended to write. She had already decided to tell Jack, to have her read it before she took it to Harold, just to make sure that she was on the right path, that she wasn't deluding herself into thinking she had written something worth saving.

Her attention shifted then, as a gust of wind tore through the room. Someone had opened the window. Frankie didn't know how long it had been raining, but already water pooled on the wooden flooring, the wind causing the curtains to billow out, filling nearly the length of their room with their volume. She moved hurriedly to shut the window, the glass rattling under the force of her movement. Turning back to her desk, she searched for any traces of damage to her work. Frankie stared at the stack of papers, at the heavy Murano glass obscuring the words and she began to feel it again, that same sensation of dread from when she first woke, its fingers snaking through her.

Frankie moved aside the paperweight and felt the breath catch in her throat as she read one sentence, and then another.

The words did not belong to her.

Frankie wondered, for one mad moment, whether she hadn't imagined it all, whether the novel she had only just now been thinking of had ever existed, except in her mind. How else to explain this changeling here before her? But no—she was not mad. Frankie quickly dispelled the thought and set to searching the room. She looked in drawers, under the bed, between the sheets, tearing apart everything before her sight finally landed on the now closed window. Walking slowly toward it, her heart beating faster, she pressed her forehead against the glass as she gazed out onto the canal.

Her manuscript floated in the water below.

For a moment, she was unable to breathe. For a moment, she could sense everything around her, including the beat of the currents as they lapped up and over her pages, devouring her words. For a moment, Frankie felt as though she were drowning.

Frankie tore from her room, her heart beating wildly.

Downstairs, the girl was awake—although no longer alone. Jack and Leonard sat beside her, as Maria placed a tray of tea and cakes before them. It all looked so normal, as if everything were the same as it had been only moments before. The scene provoked something in Frankie, and she could feel it—the rage that even now burned within—rising, fighting to find its way out, so that by the time she descended the final step, she was nearly breathless with it.

"Finally," Jack exclaimed at the sound of her friend's approach. "We were just about to send up an expedition in search of you." Her face stilled upon seeing her friend's own. "What's happened?"

Frankie ignored her friend. Instead, she rounded on the girl, brandishing the pages in front of her face. For in those moments as she had stood at the window, watching her own pages sink into the canal, she had begun to realize who the author of the pages that she now held clutched between her fingers was. "Do these belong to you?" she asked, her voice shaking with anger. She heard someone—Leonard, she thought—gasp.

"Yes," Gilly stammered, looking up at Frankie, then over at her friends with a look of bewilderment.

Feigned, Frankie could not help but think.

"It's my novel," Gilly explained. "The one you promised to read."

"I don't remember making any such promise."

At that, Gilly only frowned, only shook her head and looked around at the others as though in distress. "But you said so, the other day at Harry's."

She should never have allowed herself to trust the girl. "And yet, rather than hand the manuscript to me yourself, you waited until I fell asleep before you crept up to my room—"

"No, Frances, I—"

"—and replaced my manuscript with your own."

The girl appeared stunned. "I didn't replace anything, Frances."

Frankie didn't believe her. The girl was lying. She took a step forward—

"Frankie, stop," Jack called out. Leonard stood. "You're frightening the girl—and you're frightening me."

A silence fell over the group, and she saw herself from their perspective. The way she looked, how she sounded. She cringed, the anger beginning to ebb, to leach out of her, so that she felt herself go cold and quiet with embarrassment in its absence. But then the housekeeper muttered, *"Questa donna è pazza,"* and all at once it returned, white and searing, threatening to consume her. Frankie might not have been able to translate the words, but she understood them well enough. The housekeeper was accusing her of the same thing that everyone else had this past year, she knew, what Jack continued to accuse her of with all of her endless questions and lingering gazes. At least, Frankie thought, Maria had the temerity to say it to her face.

"Let's everyone calm down," Jack was saying now, rising from her seat. "Frankie, why don't you sit here and I'll pour us some tea. Then you can tell us what's happened."

But Frankie didn't want any tea, didn't want to calm down. It was too late for that. "What's happened is that I went to my bedroom this morning and found this manuscript in place of my own."

"I'm not sure I understand." Jack's tone was gentle, placating. "You've misplaced your manuscript?"

Frankie bit back a laugh. "Oh, I know where my manuscript is." She turned back to Gilly. "It's in the canal because someone opened the window."

At this, Gilly began to protest: "Frances, I didn't—"

"Of course you didn't." Jack's heels clicked against the tile as she made her way to the girl's side. "You'll have to excuse Frankie. Sometimes she lacks even the most rudimentary of social graces."

Frankie watched her friend in disbelief. "You're siding with her."

"I'm not siding with anyone, Frankie, but—"

Frankie did not stay long enough to hear the rest of her friend's words.

She had had enough of their lies—of Gilly's, even of Jack's, pretending to be on her side, to believe her, when the truth was clearly written across her face. Jack, for all her talents, had never been a very good liar. Turning from her friend now, all she could think of, all she could see, were those pages, floating, drowning, the water erasing everything she had worked on since her arrival. She could not lose them.

In the courtyard, she looked around for anything that might aid her retrieval. She caught sight of the old gondola, the one that lay propped up, unused, next to the steps that descended into the lagoon. If she could manage to push it into the water, then she could try to steer herself out of the palazzo and around the corner to where the pages had scattered. It would be difficult but maybe not impossible. Reaching for it, Frankie felt someone grab her by the elbow—firmly enough that she stumbled backward, her body colliding into Jack's own. "Frankie, what on earth are you doing?"

Frankie ignored the look on Jack's face—fear, she could not help but note—as she shook herself out of her grip. "My pages!" Frankie exclaimed, pointing toward the water.

"And you're going to do what? Take a swim in the canal?" Jack moved her body in front of her friend's own. "Listen to me, Frankie. That water is dangerous, it's filthy. And that gondola hasn't been used in decades—you'll sink right to the bottom."

Frankie tried to circumvent her friend, her hands reaching out. "I don't care. My novel."

"You can rewrite it." Jack's eyes flitted to her face and then away. "I don't understand, Frankie. I thought you weren't even writing yet."

"I lied," Frankie said, exasperated by her friend's endless questions.

Jack's hand reached out again. "I didn't see any pages, Frankie. I looked out the window, after you went barreling out of the room. I didn't see anything. Neither did Leonard."

It was too late. "They're gone, then," Frankie whispered. "Lost."

It was in her friend's ensuing silence that Frankie understood what Jack actually meant by her words. She wasn't breaking the news that the manuscript was already gone, already devoured by the Venetian canals—no, she was suggesting that they were no longer there because they had never existed in the first place. Frankie broke from her friend's hold. She let out a noise—of hurt, of rage, she wasn't certain. She only knew that she didn't recognize it, would never have even known it had come from herself if she had not felt it welling inside, escaping her throat.

"We all know how difficult things have been—"

But Frankie wasn't listening, was tired of Jack's platitudes, tired of Jack's refusal to believe that she was capable of taking care of herself. She had been doing fine on her own. Her manuscript had been there, finished, a sparkling new hope for the future, and now it had been thrown out, cast aside into the muddied lagoon below. There was no dispute over who was responsible. *Gilly.* She had been wary of the girl from the beginning, had felt the prickling of something at the nape of her neck telling her that the girl's presence did not make sense. She thought of what Harold had once said to her, about love and hate being muddled, and she remembered the way that the girl had bolstered her, encouraged her, urging her to forget the review and move past it all. What was that the girl herself had said about Woolf? "Don't you think it's strange," Frankie said, "Gilly turning up in Venice?"

At first, Jack looked only bewildered by the apparent change in conversation, but then something hardened in her expression. "Oh, Frankie," she said, shaking her head. "One day you can't stand the girl, the next she's your closest friend, and now you're accusing her, of what I don't know. I don't think you even know. The whole thing is mad, you sound—"

"Mad?" Frankie challenged.

"I didn't mean—"

But she did, and they both knew it.

"Why did you offer to let me stay here?" Frankie asked. "Why did you even bother to come that night if you think I'm just some madwoman who needs to be locked away?"

"I didn't say that, Frankie. You're putting words into my mouth." Jack shook her head. "And I came that night because I *missed* you. I missed *us*," Jack said, thrusting her hands in the air. "And part of me thought it was your way of avoiding an apology but holding out an olive branch."

"Apology?" Frankie laughed, and the noise echoed in the emptiness of the courtyard. "Apology for what?"

Jack made a noise of disbelief. "For your behavior."

"My behavior?"

"Yes, for being so absolutely rotten to everyone," Jack said, her voice nearly a shout.

Frankie tried to respond, to answer, but nothing came out. She *had been* rotten, that was true, and they had avoided each other for months, not calling, not visiting, as if daring the other one to make the first move. After that night, after the incident at the Savoy, they'd somehow managed to put it behind them, to avoid the fight that both of them knew was brewing, building, long before Leonard appeared on the scene. He had been the catalyst, yes, but he was not the cause. Frankie saw that plainly now, something acrid sitting on her tongue. She could taste it, bitter and choking. She looked at the woman standing before her, her only friend, her only family. They had fought before, had said terrible things to each other, flung angrily in the heat of the moment, both of them ruthless when it came to such things. But this—this was different. These words were not hot, smoldering to the touch. These were deliberate, carefully planned. Frankie felt them as a physical sensation, a lump that had traveled to the pit of her stomach, where they sat, a heavy stone that would never completely work its way out.

Frankie looked at her friend, at her one trusted ally throughout the years. They loved each other, were closer than sisters, but something had not been right between them for some time now. Frankie's eyes narrowed. "You're the one who dropped me when Leonard came along."

"That isn't fair, Frankie," Jack warned.

"Isn't it? I suppose it was all rubbish anyway."

"What was?"

"All that talk about growing old together, buying a house in the Shetlands, having a herd of cats."

Jack let out a breath. "Oh, Frankie." At first it seemed as if there would be more, but then that was it—the simplicity of two words standing in for everything they held between them. "It's clowder, by the way," Jack said.

"What?"

"The collective noun you're looking for. Herd is for cattle. For cats, it's clowder," Jack finished.

Frankie could sense it, could feel it, the two of them growing ever closer to the precipice. A part of her wanted to rush over it, to have out what they had been avoiding for months. Instead, she asked the question that had been nagging at her ever since Jack's arrival, the answer to which she had both imagined and avoided, fearing that it would only confirm what she knew about their friendship. "Why were you so late coming to Venice?"

"What?" Jack stammered, clearly taken aback by the question.

"You heard me. Why were you so late? You never gave a reason, never gave an explanation. Why on earth couldn't you be here? What was so important that you left your supposedly closest friend stranded on her own?" she asked, the words slow, steady.

Jack refused to meet her eye.

"Where were you?" Frankie demanded, petrified to hear the truth. She didn't know what to think, but she could tell, in that moment, that her friend had hidden something from her, was *still* hiding something from her.

"I had an appointment that I couldn't miss."

"A charity function?" Frankie laughed. "A fashion show? What was it this time?"

Jack broke her gaze. "An appointment with my physician."

Frankie felt her anger stumble. Of all the excuses that she had imagined, this had not been one of them. She tried to steady herself, her thoughts. "Is everything—"

"I'm fine, Frankie," her friend snapped in response, red creeping up her cheeks. "Just too old to have children, according to the doctor."

Frankie stopped, startled by the admission. Jack had always been so adamantly against children, had sworn that she would never have a pack of brats overtaking her home, her life, as she had seen happen to her mother, to others around her. Their shrugging off domesticity had been one of the things that initially drew them to each other, their steadfast declaration that they would not marry, would not have children, despite society's great expectations. But, then, Jack had already broken one of those vows, Frankie realized. "But you said you never—" she began, sensing immediately that it was the wrong thing to say.

"I said a lot of things when I was younger," Jack retorted. "But things change, Frankie, people change. Not everything is so damn permanent."

Frankie did not have a chance to respond, to form a rebuttal to her friend's words, a version of the same thing that they had been circling around these past few years. Jack turned and headed back up the steps, into the palazzo, her shoulders shaking as she went. Frankie remained, numb, unable to decide what to do. She turned to her left, to the pages, which were gone, she knew, and then back again, to the right, to where Jack had just been. It was an impossible decision. And so she did nothing at all, simply stood and waited for the moment to pass.

CHAPTER 15

Frankie spent the rest of the day trying to sleep, to forget what Jack had said and the truth of what it meant for the two of them, for their friendship, but the dull pulsing in the back of her head made such oblivion impossible. She wasn't certain when, or even if, the girl had left the palazzo. After standing in the court-yard, indecisive, she had stormed back upstairs, not bothering to stop and speak to any of them. Now she wondered whether the three of them were still downstairs, heads bent toward one another as they whispered about her, about her outburst, about how instead of Venice she should be locked away in a place like Brimley House again. Her head ached. For God's sake, why had she drunk so much the night before?

Groaning, she turned over in bed. The light falling through her window warned her it was already late afternoon. Surely she had waited long enough—her editor should be awake by now.

In the hours that she had been hiding in her room, she had come up with a plan. She needed more information in order to answer the questions she had about Gilly, to prove to the others that her suspicions about the girl were right—and there was only one person she could think of who was capable of providing such answers.

Now, creeping down the stairs, she paused to listen for the fall of footsteps, for the hum of conversation. There was nothing. In the sitting room, Frankie lifted the telephone, her anxiety making it feel as though every turn of the dial was taking longer than it should.

"Yes?" His voice came through strong and—she couldn't help but note—slightly irritated, once they had been connected. It was also more gravelly than she had anticipated, and she worried for a moment that she had miscalculated, worried that he might still have been fast asleep when the first shrill cry of the telephone had sounded. It was the weekend, and Harold was notoriously unattainable until a certain hour on his days of respite.

"Harold, I need you to look into something for me," she said in a rush, not bothering with preamble. "I need you to ask around, see if anyone has ever heard of a girl called Gilly."

"Frankie? Is that you?"

"Who else would it be," she responded, trying her hardest not to show her irritation. "Now listen, this is urgent. She might also go by her full name. I assume it's Gillian."

"You assume?" he repeated.

"Yes," she said, pushing brusquely back against his confusion. "Have you written that down, so you don't forget?" she asked.

"Frankie, what's wrong? Has something happened?" He didn't sound worried, she thought, only suspicious. There was a pause. "Frances, are you all right?"

Harold never called her by her proper name unless he was angry or worried. Frankie bristled, hoping in this instance it was the former, not wanting to deal with the implications of the latter. "Have you written the name down or not?"

There was another pause, and then: "Is Jack with you?"

"Why?" Frankie countered, the mention making her angrier than it should have. "What have the two of you got to do with each other?"

"It's nothing, only—" He paused. "You sound a bit, well, *addled,* my dear."

"I'm perfectly fine, Harold."

"Frankie, I've had a bit of a late night, so I'm just confused. Why on earth do you want me to ask around about some Gilly person? What has she got to do with you?"

Frankie hesitated, wondering how much she could tell him. She thought of Jack, of her reaction. "Don't concern yourself with the details, Harold. Just know that this is important."

"What is, Frankie?"

"That I find out who she is, so that I can understand why she's here—" She broke off, realizing that she had already said too much.

"Frankie. I thought, based on our last conversation, that you were coming home soon."

She brushed off his comment, his gentle tone that she had heard him use before. *Placating.* That's what he was doing. Handling her. Managing her. As if she was a problem, something that needed to be dealt with. She allowed herself to think of his words. *Home.* How could she think of returning now, with everything as it was?

"Frankie," Harold began again, his tone lower than before. "Frankie, we can't have another repeat of the Savoy. There are only so many favors I can call in, my dear." He paused. "And only so many—"

Frankie didn't bother to listen to the rest. She placed the telephone down onto the cradle and headed back up the stairs.

Standing in the kitchen later that evening, she heard Jack's footsteps behind her.

"We're leaving tomorrow," Jack said, her voice firm. "We're going on to Ljubljana for a few days as planned and from there back home." She paused. "I think you should come with us."

"Why?" Frankie asked, not turning around. "Have you found

another particularly good sanitarium you were hoping to introduce me to?"

It was cruel, but that was the point. Jack ignored the barb. There was a silence, and for a moment Frankie thought that she had gone too far, that Jack had left without bothering to respond, but then she said, "I'm going to bed early," her words clipped. It was something she always did whenever she was angry. Usually Frankie would tease her about it, but not this time.

"I'll see you in the morning, then," Frankie replied. She waited for a minute or two, enough time to make sure that Jack had truly gone, before throwing away the sandwich that she had started. Instead, she went into the sitting room to fix herself a whisky, which was where she found Leonard, standing next to the bar trolley. By the expression on his face, it was clear that he had overheard their exchange.

"Well," he said, taking a deep breath. "Why don't we have that chat now, Frankie?"

She nodded. "I should warn you that I already know what it's about. Harold called."

"In that case, what would you say to a stiff drink?"

Frankie let out a sigh and gave him a small smile. "Yes, please."

They were silent then, as Leonard began mixing a negroni for her and whisky and soda for himself. She took a seat on the sofa and watched, content to remain silent. "There we are," he said after a while, handing her the drink. "Excuse the lack of orange peel. It seems Maria didn't go to the market today."

At his wink, Frankie let out a laugh. "I knew it wasn't Jack."

He laughed. "Our girl isn't one to do those things herself, is she? A delegator rather than a doer." The laughter died. "Which is why, I suspect, she finds it so difficult when people refuse to listen."

"Ah," Frankie said, sipping the drink in her hand.

"Yes, *ah*." He sat down onto the sofa, next to her. "You didn't think I could let you get away without any sort of lecture, did you?"

"I had rather hoped."

"I don't think I need to remind you just how worried Jack has been since that night, hence her sometimes admittedly short temper." He held up his hands. "That's it, I promise."

"Thank you, Leonard," she said, finding that she meant it.

"It won't come to anything, you know."

"What won't?"

"That business with the woman."

"Harold said as much." She paused, trailing her finger around the rim of her glass. "He also mentioned the possibility of it going to court."

"Yes, that's true. But only if she ignores the cease-and-desist letter, and which I highly doubt she'll do, given our rather impressive letterhead." When Frankie did not laugh, he said, "Don't worry. It won't come to that."

"And if it does?" she asked. "I don't think I could bear it, Leonard."

"We'd win."

"That isn't the point, though, is it?"

"No, I suppose not." Leonard shifted in his seat. "Look, Frankie, I hope you don't mind my asking, but what exactly happened that night? I know what the papers wrote, what Harold told me in order to take care of the situation, but I'd prefer to hear it from you, if that's possible."

Frankie turned to him in surprise. "Jack didn't tell you anything?"

He let out a low laugh. "You know that one, silent as the grave when she wants to be."

Frankie considered this. "Still, aren't there supposed to be no secrets between a husband and wife?"

He gave her a look. "You of all people know how unconventional Jack can be."

She did. Still, the idea that Jack had not relayed to her husband everything that had happened that night at the Savoy surprised her—and touched her as well. In a way, it meant more than any protestation of friendship ever could. "It started with that damn review." She paused then, shaking her head and giving a small laugh.

Leonard leaned in closer. "What is it?"

"Nothing, it just seems silly now, saying it aloud." Frankie sat up. "Do you have any cigarettes?" she asked. "I don't normally, but, well."

"Yes." Leonard nodded and extracted a pack from the pocket of his cardigan. He handed her one, followed by the striking of a match.

Frankie inhaled, fighting back the urge to cough. "I hadn't been sleeping."

"Because of the review?"

"Yes—well, the review and other things. I was worried about my next book. I still am. I've only got the one left on my contract, a first look, not a promise to publish, and sales haven't been the best. When I read that review, it was as if someone had printed all my worst fears, all my deepest secrets, for everyone to read. I was frantic after that. Trying to work out who had written the review, as if that would make a difference, trying to hold it all together, but not managing at all. That night, I couldn't stay in the flat. It's hard to explain, but I felt like I was burning from the inside out, and I couldn't sit still, no matter how much I tried to dull it. And I did, Leonard. I drank and I drank, and eventually I had enough to convince myself that the Savoy was a good idea.

"There was a party that Harold was hosting there, at the American Bar, something for a debut writer they were ecstatic about. Harold had been pestering me to go and I had been adamantly refusing. I shouldn't have gone, but I was beyond thinking straight, too busy trying to prove to myself that I was fine. That the review hadn't managed to get to me. Which was rubbish. I was nearly out of my mind by then. Maybe that's why I went. To prove that I could.

"And then, right when things were starting to seem a bit muddled, I realized there was someone watching me. A woman. I didn't recognize her and I did my best to look away, but—Leonard, she just kept *staring*. I was already so unsettled, so convinced that everyone knew about the review and was talking about it, about me." Frankie paused, wishing she hadn't finished her drink. She was slightly dizzy, so that she was reminded of that night, of the kaleidoscope quality it held for her now, her memories fractured and split, no matter how often she tried to push them back together. "I had another drink. Maybe two. I don't know. But at some point I decided I couldn't stand it anymore."

"What?" Leonard asked.

Frankie tried to recapture that moment in her mind. "I'd never felt so small in my life. And so I decided to do something about it." That was when she had started toward the woman, unsteadily, she recalled, but resolutely. Frankie shifted uncomfortably. "Turns out she was a nobody. She wasn't even staying at the hotel, only stopping in to meet a friend." The next bit was harder to admit. "While she was there, an anonymous gentleman had bought them a round, and she and her friend were giddy from it, laughing, trying to discover the identity of their mysterious admirer." She looked at Leonard. "She wasn't staring at me at all. They were looking at a man just over my shoulder."

Leonard closed his eyes. "Oh, Frankie."

"I know."

It was the first time she had ever spoken about it to anyone other than the police. Not even Jack had heard the entire version. Frankie had refused to talk about it. It had been too hideous, too embarrassing to voice aloud. "The police were called then." She gave a slight nod, placing the empty glass onto the table. "I managed to give them a telephone number for Jack. Harold was already there, but it took him a minute or two to find out what had happened. Together they contained the situation, as it were, and then

I was off to Brimley House for an extended stay. I stayed there as long as I could, I did, but it only made things worse. All I could do was dwell on what I had done. All day, all night. I'd wake up in the morning and be sick about it. I'd turn a corner in the hallway and there she was, red hair shining in the sun." She cast a glance around the palazzo. "I couldn't stay there a minute longer or I would have gone mad. So here we are."

Leonard was watching her now—but not with the disgust or hatred she had anticipated. Instead, it seemed as though he was considering, or, rather, puzzling over something that had piqued his interest. "And so today," he said.

She let out a breath. "Yes, today."

He took her empty glass and went back to the bar trolley. "It explains Jack's concern."

She watched him begin to measure the Campari. "About a relapse, you mean." She looked at him, a frown settling between her features. "Aren't you going to ask me?"

He eyed her. "What?"

"Whether I did it myself—the pages, I mean. Whether I didn't toss them out into the canal. Whether they even existed in the first place."

He studied her briefly and then headed back toward her, handing over a fresh drink. "No, I don't think so."

She nodded, grateful. "Thank you, Leonard," she said.

"I don't think you're mad, Frankie." He shot her a pointed look. "And I don't believe that you would ever sabotage yourself that way. You're too damn smart."

"Thank you," she said once more. "What I can't stop wondering is whether it was an accident. I mentioned as much to Jack, but she didn't take it too well."

He nodded. "I see."

"It doesn't matter in the end, though, does it? The novel is gone." She looked away. "There's no getting it back."

"You wrote it once, you could write it again."

She gave him a small smile, knowing he only meant to be helpful. "It doesn't work like that, I'm afraid."

"No, I don't suppose I expected it to." He waited a moment before asking his next question. "So, what will you do now?"

Frankie considered. She could leave with them in the morning, tag along and follow them to Ljubljana. The simplicity of it was appealing, as was the idea of not remaining in the palazzo on her own. She had confessed now, confessed to the very worst thing that she had ever done in her life, and the man before her, who had every reason in the world to dislike her, had not turned away. Instead, he had listened and nodded and, yes, grimaced too, but at the end he looked at her with compassion, with pity. He did not see her as the monster she had supposed herself since that night. There was a sort of lightening that accompanied such an unburdening. A feeling that allowed her to imagine what it might be like to pack her bags and follow Jack and Leonard out the doors of the palazzo together.

Still, she knew that she wouldn't do it.

Not only would it spoil their holiday, but it would make things worse for her and Jack. No, what they needed was some time apart—time for Jack to forgive her, and time for Frankie to reassemble that sense of calm she had first experienced upon arriving in Venice.

The question was how.

She leaned back into the sofa. "Do you know, Leonard, for once in my life I haven't the foggiest."

"Some space might do you good. Room to breathe, and all that."

Space. There had been a time not so long ago when she thought she had more of it than she could bear. "Oh, but I'm not alone. You forget. There's still the mysterious neighbor next door," she teased, trying to lighten the mood.

At this suggestion, he looked troubled.

"What is it?" Frankie asked.

"Well," he began, "I did look into the whole matter with Maria, about the neighbors. Even went to speak to the property manager myself one afternoon while you and Jack were off. Got to try out my Italian, which it turns out, is rather worse than I remembered."

Her heart stopped. "And?"

"And I'm afraid the apartment next door is very much empty, my dear. It has been for a long time now. The family who owned it disappeared during the war, and the new landlord has rented it out a few times over the years but never did find a buyer."

"You're certain?"

"Yes, quite."

Frankie frowned. "I must have been mistaken," she allowed, wondering if faulty wiring had been to blame for the lights, and the palazzo's acoustics for the footsteps. But then she remembered the shadow and shivered. "Let's speak of something else," she said. Instead, Frankie and Leonard finished their drinks in a companionable silence before each retired to bed.

Alone in her room, Frankie waited for sleep, eager to leave the day behind—the argument between her and Jack, the loss of her manuscript. She feared that in both instances what had been lost could never fully be recovered. She pulled the sheets closer to her body and willed her mind to quiet.

That night Frankie dreamt of her manuscript floating in the canal, arms reaching up from below to claim them.

By the next morning, the rain had begun to fall in sheets.

Frankie looked out of her bedroom window, bleary from all the drink she had imbibed with Leonard, and could not help but think it was a bad omen. The skies were darker than they had been the day before, and the rain seemed somehow different, more threatening. For a moment, Frankie carried a dull hope that it might delay

Jack's determination to leave, if only for a day. But, then, she knew Jack, and so she knew that a few drops of rain would not deter her, not if her mind was set. With a sigh, Frankie pushed herself out of bed and grabbed her dressing gown.

Downstairs, it became apparent that not only was their departure still taking place, despite the nasty weather outside, but that it was imminent. They were both already dressed for the outdoors, complete with wellies and raincoats, two suitcases sitting at their feet.

"Won't you come?" Jack asked, as Frankie made her way down the spiral staircase to the *piano nobile*.

The stairs seemed to be wobbling even more than normal, at least to her own ears. She gripped the banister. "To Ljubljana?" Frankie pretended to shudder. "Don't be daft."

"I don't think you should stay here on your own." The expression on Jack's face was not as cross as the night before, but there was still something of anger held there, and Frankie knew only too well that it could not be righted within the space of a few minutes.

"I'll be fine," Frankie said, knowing there was nothing else she could say just then to mend what was fractured. "Unless you want to kick me out."

"Don't be so dramatic," Jack said, her face set in stone. "Still, I don't think it's wise."

Frankie dared to crack a smile. "When have I ever done anything that's wise?"

Jack did not laugh.

"You needn't worry, I'll be absolutely fine on my own."

Jack started to respond, but Leonard intervened. "She's a big girl, Jack. She can take care of herself."

The statement earned both of them a sharp look. "Fine, then," Jack said, running her hand over her hair. For a moment, it looked as though she planned to say more, but then she turned and began to make her way toward the hall.

"Do you think *she'll* be all right?" Frankie asked, staring at the space where her friend had stood.

Leonard sighed, grasping the two suitcases. "You two. I know Jack says we'll be the death of her, but sometimes I think it's the other way around." He leaned over and pressed a kiss against Frankie's cheek. "Don't worry, she'll be fine. You know her, she just needs a day or two to cool off and then everything will be right as rain."

Frankie nodded. "Make sure she rings."

"I will."

Frankie stood in the middle of the room, long after Leonard had disappeared down the stairs after his wife. She did not rush to the window to watch their retreating figures, did not look to see if Jack cast one last anxious glance behind her, both hoping she had and fearing she had not. Instead, she waited until a chill settled over her, until the cold of the palazzo had crept in through her feet and wound its way up through her body, until she was shaking. Only then did she retreat upstairs to the second-floor bathroom, where she ran the water until it steamed and fogged the entire room, her skin a violent red and then a softer pink as the heat cooled.

Frankie spent the remainder of the day in a sort of gloom, matched only by the increasing rain outside and the thick fog that swept through the city, intent, it seemed, on devouring it whole. The wind beat against the building, against anyone brave enough to venture outside. Moving despondently from room to room, she was surprised to find that by afternoon she could scarcely see anything at all when she peered out, all traces of gondolas, of life itself, extinguished.

Frankie felt very much alone.

CHAPTER 16

She was standing in the entrance hall, the near absence of light from outside making it feel later in the day than it actually was, when she saw it: a flicker of movement in the corner of her eye.

Frankie wasn't certain what had brought her there—most likely boredom, she surmised, the palazzo achingly empty with the departure of her friends, with the absence of her novel. Desperate to keep her mind occupied, to keep herself from dwelling, she had drifted toward the hall, standing at the window and placing her feet the way she had under Madame Dumont's tutelage as a child, testing her turnout. It was with her arms out and angled slightly forward in second position that she had first detected the movement. She froze, waiting only a moment before dropping her arms and rushing to the window.

A figure stood in the other half of the palazzo, *watching* her. Frankie ran her hand across the beveled glass, a futile attempt, as the surface, worn by both time and lack of maintenance, continued to warp her vision. Despite this, she was certain. There was no mistaking the figure across the way for anything other than what it was: a person, standing behind the glass, watching the rain, watching *her*.

Without a second thought, Frankie ran down the stairs and into the courtyard, over to the other half of the palazzo. Raising her fist, she pounded, the thuds falling heavy and loud. When there was no response, she shouted: "I see you!" Her voice was lost amid the clatter of the rain. "I see you up there!" she called again. There was no response—but, then, she hadn't expected one. She fell back, chest heaving. And then, although she knew she shouldn't, although something whispered that she should walk away, Frankie placed her hand on the doorknob and turned.

The door clicked open—unlocked.

Inside, the palazzo was a mirror image to the other. Its twin in every way, and yet somehow not. She thought of Alice and the Looking-Glass. The same sitting room on both sides, but one completely different from the other. The same formation, the same type of furniture, but the pieces in this one covered by ghostly rags that had not been moved in many years, the edges stiff with dust and age. Frankie recalled just how much the threat of the Jabberwocky, his entry foretold by darkness, had frightened her as a child, and she paused for a moment, overcome by fear, her legs refusing to take her any farther.

She called out but heard nothing in response. She became aware of the sound of her own feet—still bare and now leaving traces of water behind her as she moved farther inside. After a while, Frankie's voice fell more softly, and then, silent. For as she moved deeper into the palazzo, first into the sitting room and then through the rooms at the back, her feet echoing on the tiles beneath her, one thing became very clear to Frankie: There was no one living here. No one that *should* be living here, she thought.

The second floor was similarly silent. She wasn't certain what she had expected—the bogeyman to emerge from behind a curtain and rattle his chains? Instead, there was no one and nothing.

She almost left the attic alone. Frankie was hesitant enough to spend time in the attic within her own palazzo, the idea of exploring this one was even less appealing. Still, she pushed herself up one step and then another, knowing that she would not be able to rest comfortably until she had explored the whole of the apartments.

Once there, she glanced into each of the small rooms, her eyes taking in the emptiness. Approaching the final one, she prepared to breathe a sigh of relief, to head back down the stairs and out of the palazzo, content in the conclusion that she had only imagined it all—when she saw it. There, in the corner, where all the other rooms had been empty, was a tangle of rolled blankets, arranged as though to create a makeshift bed.

She could be wrong. It could simply be a bundle of rags that the owners forgot, or a pair of blankets thrown off some furniture and left behind when whoever had once claimed this place as home left. But she didn't think so. Instead, something beat in the core of her. Whatever she had been imagining all these weeks—an elderly couple ensconced within an aging relic, a similarly lonely woman who spent her days moving through the fractured rooms—she realized in that moment that none of it had ever existed. That there was nothing in this space but dust and cobwebs, the water stains stretching far and wide over the ceiling and creeping outward, toward the walls. She could smell the damage they had wrought, the stink of damp almost unbearable. She took the scarf from her hair and pressed it to her mouth and nose. Frankie turned and fled to the staircase then, desperate to be back outside and away from this place, the inside a sarcophagus from which she might never escape. She was not a woman to be afraid of ghosts—but this, this was something else.

At the bottom of the stairs, Frankie threw open the door, grateful for the rain, for the rush of wind that greeted her. She gulped eagerly, trying to still her beating heart.

Once inside her own palazzo, Frankie set to packing.

She would not stay in Venice another minute.

CHAPTER 17

The water taxis weren't running, the gondolas covered and abandoned by their gondoliers. No matter—she would walk.

Downstairs, the courtyard was flooding. The water from the canals was surging in through the watergate, the old, ornate gondola floating, desperately tugging at its chain, as though begging to be freed. It made a loud clanging that echoed throughout the courtyard. She shuddered—at the noise, at the rain, she didn't know, but with that movement came a trembling that she could not stop, so that her body shook, her teeth clattering together. Her hands were like ice as she stood there, temporarily unable to move.

Thankfully, Frankie had thought to put on a pair of wellies that had been left by either Maria or the former tenant, despite them being a size or two too large. Still, the presence of the water unnerved her, the pooling around her ankles somehow more threatening than it had been in the past, so that her need to escape felt all the more urgent. She stumbled forward, one hand grasping her battered leather suitcase, the other covering her mouth, her nose, trying but failing to shield herself from the stench. It was the sulfuric tang that she had come to associate with Venice, the one that could be found in the water, in the glasses, even on her own body, but that was now also somehow sharper, richer. She pulled her scarf over her nose, trying not to inhale. There was something animal about it, something close to rotting, so that her stomach heaved as she moved farther down the street.

Without the help of the water taxi, it took ages to reach the train station. Down one path and then another, avoiding the dead ends that she could remember and working her way out of the ones she could not. There were a few moments where she found herself ready to cast aside the suitcase, which seemed to pull her down into the water that continued to creep higher and higher still, but she pushed through, feeling throughout it all that white-hot urgency tugging her forward, out of Venice. She went up and over the Rialto Bridge, her body shaking under the weight of her suitcase, under the pelting of the rain, under the gusting of the wind. She found herself in one *campo* and then another, recognizing only some, the others familiar but different in the onslaught of water. A cry of frustration rose in her throat when she realized once, twice, a third time that she was lost, that she hadn't a clue where she was in this twisting maze of a city. Still, she pressed on, knowing that she needed to get out, that she needed to get out *now*, before it was too late.

Frankie moved as swiftly as she could with the heavy suitcase. She tried not to think about the contents, certain that she would find them ruined by the time she arrived at the station, for the rain, along with the wind, had increased in ferocity. Her head down, eyes squinted, she felt a dim wave of panic roll through her at the thought that this was not normal, that this was not supposed to be happening.

When she finally arrived at the train station, wet and shivering, she found it empty save for a few of the workers. All traces of passengers had disappeared. Despite the temporary break from the rain it promised, she found herself hesitating at its threshold, as though she were trespassing. The stillness of the place was overwhelming. Her footsteps seemed to echo across the vast concourse, despite the thunderous rain hammering against the ceiling above.

At the ticket counter, the man shook his head at her request. "*Signora,* there are no more trains."

Frankie had expected this response, had known, she supposed, somewhere deep down, refusing to acknowledge it. The realization hit her now, the panic rising. She was trapped.

The man motioned outside, where Frankie could see the rain coming down in a torrent, the winds kicking up at a surprising rate. "The water is not retreat."

She didn't understand.

He appeared to search for words. "Wireless?" he asked.

"No, I don't have a radio," she said, her voice shaking. "And I don't speak Italian."

He gave a small nod of his head at this, as if in commiseration, and Frankie was tempted to ask what he felt sorrier for—the fact that she did not have a radio or that she did not speak the language.

"This," he said, pointing up to the ceiling, "is no normal."

She looked upward to where he indicated, and she found herself flinching. Her gaze returned to him. "What am I supposed to do?"

It was unsettling to Frankie to find herself in such a situation. She had years of experience taking care of herself, and she was proud of them, of her ability not to rely on anyone else. There were times when she had *wanted* someone else there, like the night she had called Jack, but she had not *needed* her. Not in any practical way. But now she found that she did not know what to do or where to go. She only knew that she did not want to return to the palazzo. She thought of the figure in the window and clutched her suitcase tighter.

"*Signora,*" the man said, reaching out an arm through the railing of the counter in an apparent attempt to steady her.

Frankie hadn't known she needed steadying.

Just then, the lights cut out, plunging the station into darkness.

"Get somewhere safe, *signora.*"

CHAPTER 18

At half past six, the buzzer rang.

Frankie considered ignoring it. She reached for her glass, letting the wine numb her tongue, her mind. Only for a moment did she wonder whether she had fastened the locks, but then she remembered the turning of the key, the satisfying click, and the dull hope that it would be enough to keep out whatever was lurking in the next palazzo over. The wine had helped assuage any lingering worries.

Now the palazzo sat in darkness—she hadn't bothered to turn on any lights when she returned, the gloom appropriate, she felt, to her mood—and so she knew she could fool the caller down below into thinking the place was abandoned. In fact, the only source of light she had allowed herself was the fire she had built.

The caller.

Frankie gave a snort.

As if she didn't know who was ringing the buzzer. As if there was a chance it could be anyone other than *her*. Frankie took a long, contemplative sip of her wine. She would have preferred something stronger, but the wine was all that had been left in the bar trolley once she and Leonard were through with it, and all the shops she had passed on her way home were shuttered because of the storm.

The buzzer rang out across the palazzo again, and she was achingly aware of how empty the palazzo was, how alone *she* was. Despite this, she was still of two minds about whether or not she should answer. She did not want to be alone, and yet she did not want to be in the company of the girl either. The buzzer sounded for a third time.

God, the girl was relentless.

Later, she would wonder whether she would have answered if she hadn't already consumed more than half a bottle of wine on her own. More likely she would have sauntered to the bathroom, run another long, hot bath, and ignored the wailing of the buzzer. That would have been the sensible thing.

But that night, Frankie didn't feel like being sensible.

Downstairs, Gilly stood, shivering in the cold, the rain and wind lashing behind her. The weather had grown worse since Frankie's failed flight, the water reaching up to her calves, and though she was protected in wellies, the girl wore nothing but a pair of flats. Rather than feel sympathetic, a frown settled deeper between Frankie's brows. "What are you doing here?"

"I came to apologize," Gilly began, shaking slightly as she spoke the words. Sensing Frankie's hesitation, she added, "Please, Frances. Don't turn me away. It's absolutely ghastly out." She paused. "And I don't want to be stuck in some cold hotel with a bunch of strangers. I'd much rather be with a friend tonight."

Frankie started slightly at her choice of words. After what had happened, after the accusations she had flung at the girl, she would not have thought *friend* was a word Gilly would care to use.

Gilly reached into her bag. "And in case that is still not enough to allow me entrance"—she produced a bottle of whisky—"I noticed the bar was rather empty."

Frankie hesitated, then moved aside to allow the girl in.

Together they dashed across the courtyard, hands above their heads, a useless attempt to keep away the rain.

Inside, Gilly moved quickly toward the fire. "Where are your friends?"

"You've just missed them, I'm afraid. They've gone off to Ljubljana for a few days."

"I suspect they're in for much better weather than us."

"Yes," Frankie said, watching the girl shuck off her shoes and stockings. Gilly collapsed onto the sofa, tucking her damp legs underneath her as if there was nothing unusual about her presence here in the palazzo, despite the scene that had taken place in this same room only the day before. "So," Frankie began, crossing her arms. "You wanted to say something to me?"

"A riddle for you first, Frances." Gilly began, apparently deciding to ignore the question. "How many times do you think the word *blood* appears in *Macbeth*?"

"Gilly."

"The answer is forty-two."

The wine had made Frankie a bit light-headed, a bit confused. As she stood, she tried to remember why she had opened the door below, why she had permitted the girl entry into this place she had come to think of as home. "Gilly," she said again. Frankie didn't know if she believed anything could intimidate the girl before her, but judging by the wretched expression on her face, she figured her feelings of guilt were at least honest. "You said you wanted to apologize."

Gilly nodded, as if preparing herself. "I've thought and thought about it, and I don't remember the window being open, Frances. I'm forever sorry if it was. I truly am. You know I'm your absolute biggest fan and I would never do anything to damage your work. I feel miserable now, thinking that you've lost the whole thing." She hesitated. "How far along were you?"

Frankie narrowed her eyes. "Nearly finished."

Gilly placed both hands over her face. "Oh, God. Frances, I

don't even know how I can begin to apologize, to ask for your forgiveness."

Frankie looked away from the girl, toward the window. She thought of her pages, at the bottom of the lagoon, if they still existed in any form at all. The thought made her ill. She shook her head, trying to clear the wine from her mind. "Why didn't you say all this from the very beginning?" she demanded.

"You make me nervous, Frances. I feel as though I never know what to say."

Frankie studied her then, for the first time, it seemed, and realized just how *young* the girl was, and for a moment her heart ached with something she couldn't quite define. She moved to speak but stopped, embarrassed as well for getting lost in her own head, as Jack had so aptly noted the other day, for her determination to turn the girl into a villain, despite the fact that the role had never quite fit. How she had managed to convince herself that the act was intentional, that it was anything other than an accident, she could not understand now.

"Let me fix you a drink, Frances," Gilly said, her voice wavering slightly. She reached out her hand. "Oh, please, let's forget all this, shall we? We've had such a wonderful time in Venice, I would hate for this to muddle everything. Please let me fix you a drink."

An hour ago, Frankie would have said there was nothing she was less likely to do than have a drink with Gilly, but already she felt herself softening, wavering, as she always did in the girl's presence. What was it about this insufferable girl that made her change her mind so many times? It seemed that she couldn't make up her mind about her—something that was unusual for Frankie, who was steadfast in her beliefs, unwavering. She nodded, taking a seat on one of the sofas and watching as the girl poured them a whisky, and then a little bit more.

"Will you miss them?"

Frankie looked up, realizing that Gilly had asked her a question. "Miss who?"

"Your friends. Jack and what's-his-name."

"Leonard," Frankie replied, realizing as she spoke his name that she did so with a fondness that had never been there before. "It's not as if they've gone forever."

Gilly shrugged. "I'd be glum if my friends abandoned me."

"They haven't abandoned me, you nitwit," Frankie said, not unkindly. "They've gone on to Ljubljana, which was always the plan."

Gilly seemed to consider this, then handed Frankie the drink, flopping onto the sofa and drawing her legs up underneath her once again. "I suppose that means now I have you all to myself." Her eyes darted to the corner of the room, where Frankie's suitcase still sat. "Unless you're leaving as well?"

"I tried. Hauled the blasted thing there and back to the station, but there were no trains running, because of the damned weather."

"But why?"

"Why did I want to leave?" Frankie thought of Jack, of the figure next door, of the quiet that had continued to settle over the palazzo these last few hours, the quality somehow false, tentative. "I suppose I thought it was time."

"I'll be sorry to see you go," Gilly said. "It's been like our own little world here, hasn't it? I hate the idea of going back and having it all disrupted by London. Does that make sense?"

Frankie nodded—it did, more so than she could ever express to the girl.

Afterward, they spoke of nothing, of everything, Gilly entertaining her with tales of her family, of her life back home. She was an only child, as it turned out, something that Frankie did not have to stretch her imagination too far in order to believe. Her father—Larson, it turned out was his, and by extension, her, surname—owned a magazine, carrying on the tradition of his father before him, and her mother had been one of his senior editors before exchanging it all for marriage and a child.

"She sounds interesting," Frankie said.

"She's the one who encouraged me to write, when I was younger. I don't expect she thought I'd take to it like I did." Gilly looked toward the fire. "Now she tends to agree with my father, who would rather I chose something sturdier. Like a husband."

Frankie gave a laugh.

"Father's fine with me writing a piece or two under a pseudonym. Thinks it's a phase that I'll grow out of. But he's not entirely enthusiastic about the novel." She pulled a face. "He thinks it'll spoil my marriage chances."

"And what do you say?"

"That he's terribly old-fashioned and that I don't want to just be someone's wife." She looked stunned by her own admission. "It's one of the reasons that I've never got along with them, even my mother. I can't understand how she could have given up her whole life, all of her ambitions, for someone else's. I wish I could have met her when she was younger, before she became so prim and correct and concerned with the fact that I am very much none of those things." She turned to Frankie. "I don't know what she would make of you."

"Why is that?"

"Because you're all of those things and none of them, I guess. Prim, but not in a prudish way like her, in a way that's frightening and terribly clever."

They were silent for a minute or two, watching the fire flicker before them. Talk turned to Frankie's own career then and, although she didn't like to speak about it, to her parents and the time during the war. How both her parents had survived nearly all of it, the constant air raids that shrilled in the night, that lit up the sky, only to be killed just a few weeks before it all ended.

"Were they killed in London or abroad?" Gilly asked, her voice a whisper then.

"At home, in London." Frankie gave a rueful laugh. "They didn't die *in* the war, you see, even though that's what most people assume. Just *during*. A driving accident. They died instantly, according to the doctors, so at least they didn't suffer, I suppose. But it was so sense-less," Frankie said. "That's what I can never manage to get past. How absolutely senseless their deaths were."

That was when the clock had stopped for Frankie, in many ways. The moment the police had appeared at her door, her heart seemed to skip a beat, before stopping altogether. She had known, even before, that something was wrong. Gone all night, she had arrived at home once her shift ended and, bleary-eyed, her head full of the sound of sirens, stood in the doorway, listening. There had been nothing. Only the absence of sound. No scraping of a spatula against a pan, break-fast waiting for her, no rustling of a newspaper as her father sat, wait-ing to discuss her night. She had, they later told her, frozen at the news, her hand held midway between her own body and the officer's, as if she could prevent him from voicing the words she already knew he would speak. In many ways she felt like she had never left that moment, as if, somehow, she would always be there, stuck on that doorstep, listening to the news repeated again and again.

Gilly placed her hand over Frankie's. "I'm so sorry, Frances. I honestly can't imagine it."

Frankie nodded, not trusting her own voice. It was, she even-tually confessed, once her voice steadied, the reason that she had started writing. It was the only way she had found to grieve that felt real, that felt as though it mattered.

At that, Gilly sat up on the sofa, more serious than normal. "Listen, Frances, I know I went about it the wrong way, which I often do—I can't seem to help myself—but will you read it?" she asked, eyes wide. "My novel, I mean. You'd be the first one to look at it, no one has read so much as a word yet. And your work has been so important to me, the idea that you might have a look at something I've written, that you might tell me what you think of it—well, it would mean so much, Frances."

"Would it?"

"Yes. It's only the carbon copy, so it's a bit difficult to read because the letters aren't quite as clear, but I couldn't bear the thought of typing a second one. I'm a terrible typist. Do you know, my parents once threatened me with secretarial college, and the only way they relented was when the teacher confirmed that I was indeed hopeless. Oh, say you'll look at it, Frances, please."

"How can my work mean that much to you?" Frankie asked, curious. "Something tells me you don't care for my more recent novels."

"Why do you say that?"

"You said as much yourself that one day, didn't you?"

Gilly shook her head. "Your first novel meant so much to me, more than any other book, that it doesn't matter about the rest. I'll always read your work, hoping and waiting for something like that first one again."

Something tightened in Frankie's chest. *Yes,* she thought, *you and the rest of the world.* It took a few minutes more of cajoling after that, but at last she conceded. It was the least she could do, she supposed, after everything she had accused the girl of, although to be fair, Gilly had been guilty of a fair number of things herself—was no doubt still guilty of more. Frankie pushed it from her mind. She was tired of keeping score, keeping track. The girl sprang from the sofa and began to make her way across the room, heading toward the stairs. "Where are you going?" Frankie asked, watching her with amusement.

"To get the manuscript," she cried over her shoulder. "Did you put it back in your room?"

Frankie nodded, but then added, "What, now?"

"Why not?" Gilly threw her arms out, indicating their surroundings. "It's not as though we have anywhere to go."

With that, as if it was all sorted, all decided, she bounded up the stairs and out of sight. Frankie drained the last of her drink. She got up and walked to the bar trolley, poured herself another measure of whisky. She sipped, eyeing the darkness outside and the rain battering the windows. Looking down, she realized just how swollen the canal was. She had experienced versions of flooding ever since her arrival, but they had amounted to little more than an inch or two, the water creeping up over the edges of Venice and making its way into San Marco, into the shops and cafés that surrounded the area. A nuisance more than anything else. But this—this seemed like something different. She remembered the words of the man at the station. Even if the tidal outflow were to take away most of it, Frankie suspected it would be dangerous for anyone to be outside tonight. She supposed she should offer Gilly a bed.

And Frankie didn't particularly feel like being alone.

It wasn't only the strangeness with the mysterious figure next door. It was something more. The girl had been wrong about her friends abandoning her—they would have left anyway, argument or not—but there was something about going back to the stillness, to the emptiness of the weeks prior, that did not sit as easily with Frankie as she had thought it would. The past days had been filled with people, with friends and laughter, and Frankie had begun to realize just how lonely she had been as of late, how truly cut off she had allowed herself to become from those around her. So while the girl often needled her, she was not ungrateful for her presence in that moment.

Frankie looked up, as if she could see through the ceiling to the second floor. What was the girl doing up there, she wondered. Perhaps she had gone to the lavatory, had become lost. It was at this point that Frankie realized they hadn't bothered to turn on any of the lights, that they were still sitting in darkness, in the small amount of light that the fire cast.

Frankie crossed the room, part of her hesitant to break the somewhat cheerful gloom that had settled. All the same, if the girl was going to insist that she read her manuscript, she would need the light. She flipped the switch.

Nothing happened.

Frowning, Frankie flipped it down again and then back up. Still nothing. She remembered the station then, how they had been plunged into darkness.

The electricity must be out.

Frankie looked once more out the window, and through a patch of clouds, caught a glimpse of a full moon. Something ran through her then, a shiver, one that crept across the expanse of her collarbone. She heard the girl's footsteps sound behind her. "I think something might be wrong," she said, still peering up at the moon. "The man at the station—" She stopped and turned. There was no one behind her. "Gilly?" she called out. She began to walk toward the stairs, her gait faster than intended. She cast a hasty glance over her shoulder. There was no one there, and yet she could not stop herself from checking, could not stop the rising panic. "Gilly?" she called again, her voice, even to her own ears, sounding strained. Frankie cleared her throat. She stood at the bottom of the stairs, peering into the darkness above her. She placed a tentative foot on the first step, and then the second.

Just then a creak sounded overhead.

Frankie stepped back quickly—too quickly—and stumbled. Before she could right herself, she had lost her balance, falling to the floor, her ankle smarting in pain.

"Frances!" a voice overhead cried, followed by the quick sound of footsteps. Gilly appeared at the top of the stairs, her face a white orb floating in the darkness. "Frances!" she exclaimed again, her gaze falling on Frankie's crumpled form. "What's happened?"

"Nothing." Frankie stood but, unable to place the entirety of her weight on the injured ankle, found herself lurching forward to grab the banister for support.

Gilly rushed down the stairs. "Let me help you."

Frankie resisted the girl's offer. "Where were you? I was calling just now." She was angry and embarrassed, the fall causing two bright-red spots to bloom on her face.

Gilly took Frankie's arm and placed it around her neck. "I forgot which room was yours and then I lost my way in the dark," she explained. "I tried the lights, but they wouldn't work."

They moved slowly back into the sitting room, Frankie at a shuffling pace. "What do you need?" Gilly asked, helping Frankie onto the sofa. "Is there ice?"

"Never mind that. Just pour me another drink," she said, pointing to the bar trolley.

Gilly worked swiftly. "I am sorry, Frances," she said, handing her a refreshed glass. "You only fell because you were looking for me."

"You apologize far too much." Frankie let the warmth of the whisky spread through her.

"But look," Gilly said, lifting her shirt. The manuscript was tucked into her waistband. "When I heard you cry out, I put it there and rushed to the stairs," she said, sitting on the sofa and placing the manuscript next to her.

A pain just behind Frankie's eye began to throb. "I'm tired, Gilly."

"Oh, please, Frances. You don't have to like it, I promise. I won't mind."

Frankie flinched at the desperation in the girl's words. Her head was swimming from the drink. The rain pounded against the windows, louder now, and all at once Frankie felt confused, lightheaded. She remained silent, listening to the heavy thud of precipitation pelting the glass.

"Frances?"

"Hmm?" Frankie turned back to the girl. "Oh, why not?" She suspected that it would be far easier to acquiesce, to at least attempt to read the thing, rather than argue with the girl over it. And if she fell asleep only a page or two in, well, no one could blame her for that, could they?

Gilly erupted in a delighted gasp that made Frankie fight the urge to cover her ears.

"And what will you be doing while I read?" Frankie asked, staring down at the pages she now held in her hand, noting the inscription that Gilly had scrawled for her on the front page.

"I'll be at your service, your beck and call." Gilly gave a little mock salute. "I will be in charge of drinks and all refills. And if you need ice or anything else, anything at all, I'll get it." Gilly paused. "And, Frances?"

"Yes?"

"I do want you to know how much it means to me," she said, all seriousness now.

Frankie gave a laugh, shaking her head. And then she sat back into the sofa, raised the first page to her eyes, so that the fire hit it with just enough light, and began to read.

The stiffness in her neck told her where she was before she opened her eyes.

For a moment, Frankie thought she had been asleep for only a few minutes, that it was still evening, or a little later, perhaps the dead of night, and that no time at all had passed. But then she noticed that the fire had burned down, so that even the warm red glow of the last dying embers had disappeared. She shivered. It must be morning, but the room was still cast in darkness, the windows covered with a splattering of rain so thick that she could barely see out.

Rising from the sofa, limping slightly as she went, she rubbed her eyes and surveyed the room. There was no sign of Gilly. She moved closer to the window, cast an appraising look below. It was still raining, that much was obvious, and the wind was still blowing just as fiercely, perhaps more so. The water in the canal was swollen—the word *pregnant* came to mind—and although she couldn't be certain, she thought it was raised much higher than she had ever seen it before. Frankie leaned forward and squinted. Yes, it appeared as though the water level was now above the bottom door of the palazzo across the way. She was moving to get a closer look when she heard footsteps behind her.

"Morning," Gilly exclaimed, carrying in one hand a carton of orange juice and two teacups in the other. "I tried to make us coffee,

but nothing will work. Have you seen outside yet? It's apocalyptic."
She paused to take a breath. "Well, what did you think?" she asked,
her face filled with expectation.

At first, Frankie couldn't fathom what the girl was talking about.
And then she saw it, the pages strewn across the cushions of the
sofa. The manuscript. Frankie paused, her mind still addled with
sleep. She reached for the cup, waited impatiently for Gilly to pour,
her mind racing. Frankie thought about lying. It wasn't something
she would have done normally, and were someone else to suggest
it, she would have admonished them for being so weak—but there
was something in the girl's face, something so open, so genuine and
excited, that she wondered whether the truth was even possible,
whether she was capable of such cruelty. In the end, Frankie never
got the chance to figure out what she might have done, as her silence
seemed to fill in everything that she had not yet managed to say.

"You didn't like it," Gilly said—not asked, Frankie noted.

"No, it isn't that," she countered, taking a sip of her juice. It
tasted too sour, as though it had gone off, and she placed it down
onto the coffee table.

"No," Gilly protested. "I can tell by the look on your face. You
didn't like it at all."

Frankie opened her mouth, searched for something to say, some
sort of lie to appease the young girl's suffering, but came up empty.
She had finished only about half the manuscript and sat there,
taken aback by what the girl had written. More than that, she was
baffled why the girl had chosen *her*, in particular, as the reader of
the manuscript. Their styles were nothing alike. How on earth had
the girl convinced herself that she, Frankie, would have anything
positive to contribute, for truth be told, Frankie wasn't even sure
what she had written. The novel began with a young woman sitting
underneath a tree, described from what first appeared to be a lover's
gaze—but as the descriptions became more urgent, violent almost,
Frankie experienced a sense of discomfort, realizing soon enough

that it wasn't a lover at all. Although no dialogue, no interaction, existed between the two, it soon became apparent that the watcher was another woman, older, envious of the girl sitting underneath the tree. At this revelation, Frankie had cut an anxious glance in the direction of the girl on the sofa and drained the last of her whisky.

From there, it had only grown stranger still. Gilly seemed to do away with all conventions of the novel itself: characters, plot, setting. Instead, it read as a mix of observations, not in any complete sentences or logical pattern that she could decipher. At times, it devolved into a mere listing of words. There were half-finished sentences, the words left dangling on the page, as if the author intended to return and finish them at a later date. Apostrophes were often ignored, commas were avoided altogether. There were times when Frankie allowed that it might *sound* pretty, if one were to read it aloud, in front of an audience, but she suspected that beyond this flowery rhythm of the words, there was nothing more. And then there were the blank pages—a slew of them, inserted every once in a while—without any explanation or warning. The first time she encountered them, Frankie thought it was a mistake, had moved to toss the page aside, until she realized there was another one just behind it, and another just beyond that. As she turned the pages, as Frankie began to recognize Gilly's style, she could see that it—all of it—was deliberate.

Now she looked Gilly in the eye, squaring her shoulders. "No," she admitted. "No, I didn't like it."

Gilly sat down on the couch, not bothering to move the pages first. They crinkled underneath her. "Why not?"

Frankie hesitated. The girl was staring at her, with such a wide-eyed peculiarity that it was somehow more off-putting than if she had thrown a tantrum, had started crying and screaming in response. Frankie would have preferred it—anything to this strangely hollow expression that seemed to bore into her. "There was no narrative, for starters. And the prose, it was broken and scattered and difficult to follow. I'm not even certain there was anything *to* follow." Frankie stopped, taking a pause for breath, searching for something to say, searching for the type of writerly advice that Harold was always encouraging her to give. "It was well written. If you spend some time on revisions, I think that, with a bit of hard work, you could get there."

"There?"

"Yes," Frankie said, gathering her thoughts. Gilly was still staring at her, her face expressionless, her body motionless. "Yes, I think you could get it to the point where someone might want to publish it." And she meant it—even though she had detested every page, she could tell that there was something hidden behind all the flourishes and frills. A potential that could be made into something great, if only the girl would apply some discipline to her work.

There was a beat, and then Gilly looked up at where Frankie stood. "But somebody *does* want to publish it."

Frankie wondered whether the girl hadn't gone mad, whether her words had so upset her, this bright little thing that had likely had never heard *no* in her entire life, that she had completely lost her senses. "You're not making any sense," Frankie said.

Gilly blinked, and her smile returned. "It's just what I said, Frances. Somebody *does* want to publish it."

"Who?" Frankie asked, wondering whether some editor who had taken kindly to the way the girl looked had gone on to promise her something he was not capable of delivering. She felt for her in that moment, despite her near-constant irritation with the girl. Gilly had been taken in, her head filled with promises that would no doubt never come to fruition. "Are you certain they were in earnest?" she asked, her voice more gentle than usual.

"Sometimes you're so old-fashioned, Frances," Gilly laughed. "I think you might even know my editor. John Bailey? He's a friend of my father's. They go back ages. He's at the same publishing house as your own editor. It's one of the reasons I was so excited to have you read this."

Frankie blinked in surprise. "Bailey?" She knew who he was, could picture the aging editor easily, his narrow, slim-waisted build, his tall stature. Conversation between them had always been limited, but he had seemed an intelligent person. She couldn't imagine him being the sort to promise a contract only in order to gain some advantage with the girl. "And you've already signed?"

"Yes," Gilly said, nodding her head. "He was so enthusiastic when I told him about the idea I had for the novel. I thought Venice would be the perfect place to write it."

"So he hasn't read it yet?" Frankie asked, massaging her temples. "But he's agreed to publish it?"

"Well," Gilly said sheepishly, "he said he owes our family a favor. And it's not as if he hasn't ever seen anything from me. We had a meeting just the other month, and I showed him some poems I've written recently and a few short stories that won awards."

"Awards?"

"Yes, when I was at school. So, you see, he's confident from those. And besides, he said the publishing company has been looking for new authors. Something about shifting attention and allowing room for new voices."

"That doesn't make any sense." Frankie was bewildered by the whole thing, speechless. It was unlike anything that she had ever heard of, unlike anything she herself would have done—the thought of relying on one's connections for publication was appalling. She was embarrassed for the girl and, more than that, angry that the girl was *not*. On the contrary, Gilly seemed content, satisfied, almost smug, at the revelation of how she had procured her contract.

Frankie shook her head, still puzzled by the whole affair. "But then why on earth did you ask me to read it, if you already knew it was going to be published?"

"You know I've always admired you, Frances. *After the End* was written with such—such plain, honest language. I thought you might like this." Gilly gave a tiny shrug, her smile still in place. "And because we'll be at the same publishing house now."

Somewhere in the distance, a wail started up. For a minute Frankie thought she was only imagining it, but her body trembled at the familiar sound, despite the years since she had last heard it.

"It's an alarm for the *acqua alta*," Gilly said, breaking through her thoughts. She gestured outside. "They use the air-raid sirens left over from the war. That's all. Nothing to be frightened of, Frances."

Nothing to be frightened of. Was it her imagination or had there been the slightest bit of derision in the girl's tone just now? In that moment, Frankie felt her fear begin to turn into something else, something larger, wilder, something she could not contain. What did this girl know of fear, *real fear,* she wanted to demand. Not the type of fear that came with things that went bump in the night, but the kind of heart-stopping, breath-stealing fear. The type of stomach-churning fear that came with surviving something so indescribable that those who were not a part of it would never understand, surviving only to be left alone, to have the comfort of home torn away, so that hunger and cold became a part of everyday life, so that days when you woke up and breathed frigid air and saw frost gathering on the inside of the window were not ones that called for alarm but rather signaled a particularly difficult week where there hadn't been enough left over to pay the meter for heat. This girl knew nothing of such hardships— would never know. The breach between them was impossible, *gaping.* It was one that could never be crossed. She could see that now.

Frankie felt tired. A type of tired that she had never before experienced, not even during everything that had happened in London, not even during the war. It was a tiredness that crept inside, filling her up from the inside out. Frankie could never make sense of the strangeness that she had always sensed when it came to Gilly, perhaps built on the revelations that seemed to slip from her tongue each time they met, the idea, the image, the portrait that Frankie had made of her always shifting and changing, refusing to stay the same. Now, she realized with a start, she wanted nothing more than to be finished with her, with this place, wanted nothing more than her flat in London, with the leaky tap and the bed that creaked, with the doors that did not properly shut whenever the damp set in.

Frankie looked at the girl standing there, skin smooth and glowing and luminous in the dark. "I think I'd like you to leave," she whispered.

It was clear that Gilly thought she had misheard. "Frances?"

"It's Frankie," she snapped, placing fingers to her temples. "And I said I'd like you to leave," she repeated, her voice stronger.

Gilly turned toward the window. "But it's still raining cats and dogs out there."

Frankie didn't care. She needed the girl out of the palazzo— she wouldn't spend another moment with this entitled child, she couldn't. "I said *get out.*"

The girl flinched, but still she stood there, hesitating, as though she doubted the words that Frankie had spoken. And then, all at once, she set to hurriedly collecting her things. Frankie followed the girl's frantic movements, first with her eyes and then, as the girl began to make her way through the hallway, Frankie followed in her footsteps. She had to make certain the girl was gone, had to lock the door between them, once and for all.

Outside, halfway down the steps, Gilly stopped and turned to her. The rain was already soaking them both and the girl, Frankie noticed, was shaking from the cold. "Frances, I know you're upset with me. I don't know if I understand why, but I know that you are. Please, please let's go back upstairs and talk."

A part of her wanted to—to be able to deny her anger, to be able to tell herself and Gilly that she didn't give a damn about what the girl wrote and who was interested in publishing her novel. But the fact that the girl had been given a contract on nothing more than her connections—the truth of it burned in her when she thought of the nights she had spent writing and editing in the darkness, too poor, too hungry to use the money for a bit of electricity. That this girl had been given everything, that she always would, made something inside Frankie crack, just a tiny bit, so that whatever had held back her rage and fury the day before threatened to overwhelm her now.

"Frances, please let's not end things this way," the girl pleaded. "Not after I came all this way to find you."

For a second Frankie thought she must have misheard, that the rain and wind had folded and bent the girl's words into something other than what she had actually said, or that she had only misunderstood, that the girl was talking about her journey through the rain last night to reach the palazzo. But then she looked at the girl's face, at the expression creeping over her at this unintended admission, and she knew.

"That day," Frankie began. "By the market—"

Gilly took a step backward. "I was waiting for you," the girl confessed.

The air escaped from her. "Why?" she cried, the word vibrating within her, whether because of cold or something else, Frankie didn't know. She grasped on to the balustrade to steady herself.

"Let me explain, Frances."

"Tell me why," she demanded.

"It isn't what it seems, Frances. I promise." She gave a laugh, the sound brittle and forced. "I was here for days before we met, you know, waiting to catch sight of you. I thought maybe I had got it wrong at first, the address or even the dates. That maybe you had decided on another palazzo, or that you weren't here at all." The girl's words were rushed, hasty, tumbling from her as though she could not stop. "I was so worried at first, Frances, but then there you were. Standing next to the Rialto Bridge. And I couldn't believe for a moment how similar you were to your photograph. It was the oddest sensation, finally seeing you there, just steps away from me."

She looked at Frankie and smiled. "And then Venice wasn't such a waste and I wasn't such a little fool for coming. It all seemed like fate."

"Fate," Frankie repeated dully, wondering if the girl understood the meaning of the word.

"Frances," Gilly said, taking a step closer.

Frankie stepped back. "Why are you here?" she asked again, no longer believing the girl would ever answer the question. She had to get away from her—*now*. Frankie cast a hurried look around her. If she tried to make it inside, up onto the second floor, to her bedroom, it would take too long, she would be too slow in her wellies, with her injured ankle. Gilly was likely to overtake her. It would be better if she continued down the stairs and into the courtyard, the element of surprise gaining her a minute or two in order to work out a plan.

"Frances," Gilly was saying. "Listen to me, let me explain."

No, she was done listening. She didn't believe a damned word that came out of the girl's mouth—how could she? The girl had done nothing but lie, dissemble, tell her one story after another, from the time they had first met until now. And yet here she remained, staring at her, eyes wide, asking for more.

Frankie bolted. Down the stairs, her ankle throbbing, but she did not bother to pause, to slacken her pace, the sound of Gilly right behind her.

"Frances," the girl shouted. "Where are you going?"

It took only seconds for them to reach the bottom of the stairs, and just a few steps for Gilly to overtake her, so that she stood blocking the door—the one that led to the street, to safety. Frankie glanced frantically in the direction of the watergate, her eyes landing on the floating gondola.

"Stay where you are," Frankie cried, her voice shaking despite her best attempts to remain calm. She began to move toward the watergate, the water surging around her, over her knees, making it harder for her to move in that direction, but she was unwilling to take her eyes from the girl, who even now was slowly inching her way toward her. Frankie could feel the cold.

"Frances, what's happening?"

Frankie was nearly there. She descended the steps, the water above her waist, and leaned forward to wrench it open—no easy feat in the face of the wind, of the swelling water. "You should leave, Gilly," she cried, her voice drowned out by the noise around them. She didn't expect the girl to listen, but she thought she would give her one more chance, just in case. The gondola floated a few feet from where she stood. Frankie was dimly aware that she was shaking even harder now. She wondered how she would unchain it, whether it was locked or whether it would come away, undone by time and erosion. She wondered how she would prevent the girl from following her, from stopping her. She did not think about afterward, about where she would go and how—about whether, as Jack had surmised, the boat was even seaworthy.

"Frances," Gilly began. "Frances, you're frightening me."

Something threatened to break in Frankie then—she could feel it swelling, could feel it pressing up against her. She moved closer to the gondola's lock, the fetid water swelling around her. Her teeth chattered and she felt as though she might never be warm again. The girl followed, reaching over, grasping Frankie's wrist—just as she had done that first day in the market. Gilly's skin was hot to the touch, feverish nearly, and Frankie recoiled, casting her hand aside.

Gilly stumbled, her balance thrown by the water.

Frankie had used more force than she realized, and she could see that it had startled the girl. Gilly reached toward her once more, and Frankie pushed, so that their positions were reversed, Gilly on the lower step and Frankie standing above her. *No, Frances*, Gilly kept repeating, as if it would change things, would save her, would save them both. But Frankie was beyond listening, beyond reason as they each struggled to remain upright. In that moment she was aware of nothing but the insistent, clawing need to expel the girl from the palazzo, from her sight. She reached for the gondola again, but Gilly was still trying to grab her, to hold her. A scuffle took place then, a macabre dance in which Frankie pulled and Gilly pushed, leading the two of them farther into the water, the rain bearing down on them.

"Frances," Gilly gasped. But whatever she said after was lost in the rain and the wind, all of it swelling around them. "Frances," Gilly cried again, and this time Frankie could see that it was a plea, a cry for mercy, and instinctively she paused. Then Gilly sprang to life, her hands finding purchase, her nails digging into Frankie's skin, into her forearm, into the mosquito bites that had refused to heal from those first few days. Her lips moved against Frankie's ear, her words muffled by the rain, but Frankie could not focus, could only let out a surprised shout of pain at the girl's nails, and found herself pushing harder, more forcibly. Only for a tiny second did Frances wonder whether she had misread things, whether Gilly was no longer fighting but grasping, whether her pull wasn't to knock Frankie from her place but to keep herself upright—because suddenly Gilly was falling. Falling back and into the churning water below. The both of them seemed to realize it at the same time, the look of shock, of horror, that crowded Frankie's features mirrored in Gilly's own.

And then she was gone.

CHAPTER 19

Time moved, but the rain did not stop.

Frankie, entombed in the palazzo, sat and watched as the skies grew darker. The water below had taken on a metallic sheen—oil, she realized, though at first she thought she was only imagining it. Various bits of debris floated by. A sofa, a suitcase. Planks of wood. Bolts of fabric. Each time they emerged, for one heart-pounding moment she thought it was Gilly.

Frankie went to the bar, finished the rest of the whisky that the girl had brought over. After, she managed to locate a quarter-full bottle of gin hidden at the back of a cupboard. She drank eagerly, greedily, anxious to be transported. In the bathroom, she found several plasters and placed them on her arm, over her gouges, now red and swollen, dry rivulets of blood staining her skin.

By late afternoon she was left with nothing but her thoughts and the image of Gilly—as Ophelia, as the Lady of Shalott, as a body, bloated and blue. Only once did she try to make her way into the courtyard, but she was stopped halfway down the stairs by the rising tide of water, pinning her in. She guessed that it would reach her shoulders by now. By the time she crawled back up the steps, pushing against the water, she was shaking, her fingers numb, her teeth chattering, her body stumbling every now and then. In the hall, she bent over double and was sick, the bile burning her throat. She looked at her hands, at the paleness of them, her fingers puckered from both the salt and the water.

Inside, she could not settle, could not decide what she should do. She picked up the telephone, as if she intended to ring someone, except that she knew there was no one she could call. No one she could tell. A whisper sounded in her mind: *You're alone.* She did her best to ignore it, to shake it away, but it remained, steady and insistent, a beat she could not push aside. Frankie registered the absence of a ringtone at the same time she realized the sound of something else—a foghorn, loud and insistent, somewhere in the distance.

She imagined it then, the scene that would no doubt follow were she to inform the *carabinieri*—the way she would look, hands shaking, cheeks flushed, the marks on her arm. She imagined the way things would unfold, the misunderstandings, the mistranslations. They would accuse her. They would say that it was deliberate, that she had murdered the girl. They would put handcuffs on her, throw her into a cell, and she would never make her way out again.

Or she could tell no one.

Frankie placed the telephone back onto the cradle. She could feel her heart pounding and set a sweating palm against her skin, as if she might be able to will it to stop. She was sick again, but this time she made it to the toilet in time. She wiped away the spittle with a determined motion. No, she would not tell anyone. She would wait for the rain to stop and then she would leave. Where she would go from there, she was less certain. She tried to estimate how long it would take them to find the body. Frankie caught sight of herself in the mirror then. She looked worse than she had imagined—hair plastered to her face, the hollows underneath her eyes large and sunken. She looked monstrous. But, then, that's what she was, wasn't she?

They had fought, together, but had she pushed Gilly, or had she attempted to save her in those final moments? She tried to remember, as though it were a simple matter of forgetting, but just when she thought she had made sense of it, just when she thought she had determined what had and had not happened, it changed, shifting in her mind once more, until she was no longer certain of anything but her uncertainty.

Her forearm throbbed where the girl had grabbed at her. She retched again and thought she could smell it—the water, Venice, spewing up from inside her.

Later, Frankie moved to the second floor, worried that the first would disappear like the courtyard. It wasn't so much drowning that frightened her but rather the thought of being trapped below with Gilly. In her bedroom, she thought at first that it was only the water, only the wind, that howled against the speaking tube downstairs, that made the noise she heard emerging from the fluted piping by her bed—but soon she became certain it was something else. Trapped inside the room, with nothing but her thoughts to occupy her, she became convinced that there was something—*someone*— down there in the courtyard. That they were making a repeated *gasping* noise, as though they couldn't catch their breath or, worse yet, were struggling to breathe.

Frankie left her place on the bed, moving slowly toward the tube. The piece was cold against her skin, achingly so. She pressed her ear close and listened, sure that she would be met with the sound of a voice begging for help. Frankie turned her head, placing her mouth against the tube, the coppery taste of blood filling her mouth. "Gilly?" she whispered, her voice hoarse, her lips cracked. "Gilly, is that you?"

For a moment, all was silent, and then a rush of sound emanated from the tube—a *whistling*, she realized with growing horror—and she pulled away, too quickly, falling, her injured ankle smarting from the motion of it. She cursed, feeling the strain in her tendons, but crawled back to the tube. The fear that she had felt, the trepidation, was replaced by something else now—a certainty that there was something real, whether visceral or otherwise, awaiting her in the courtyard below. A phantasm. An echo. For she knew that it was not truly Gilly. No, that girl had been swallowed up by the murky water below, never to return. Still, something had remained. The violence of it was writ across her arm, in the gouges that the girl's fingernails had left. She thought of the *moeche,* made soft in the water, and she paled, thinking of Gilly, of her body, made soft and swollen by the icy touch of the lagoon.

Frankie descended the stairs to the *piano nobile.* In the kitchen, she found a dishcloth in one of the cupboards and, returning to her room, stuffed it into the opening of the tube. Still she could hear it—the wind, the water, whatever else was down there in the depths, calling out to her. She placed her hands over her ears and gave a wail, a keening, so loud that she was certain it could be heard throughout the whole of the drowning island.

CHAPTER 20

The next day, the rain stopped.

On the streets, she learned from passersby, from *carabinieri,* from whomever could spare an explanation, a few words in English, that the water had retreated late the night before. A strong surge had withdrawn the waters at last, leaving behind a Venice unlike the one that had existed before. The walls were streaked with black. On every corner there was debris: chairs, mattresses, dead rats, pigeons even. Frankie wondered at the latter, wondered why they hadn't been able to fly away, wondered what good it was to have wings if they were useless when you needed them most. Shops were ruined, buildings destroyed. Anything that had been on the ground floor was no longer functional. The electricity was still out. The city was aching, injured.

Frankie had left the palazzo that morning, walking for several hours, not knowing where she was going, not knowing what she was supposed to do. There had been no body in the courtyard. She searched every corner, descended the steps by the watergate to look, her ankles submerged in the stinking, filthy water. Standing there, she had closed her eyes and breathed a sigh of relief and for one small moment allowed herself to think that she had imagined it all. That it had been a terrible dream. But then, opening her eyes, she glanced down at her forearm, where Gilly had grabbed at her. At the angry, torn skin that refused to remain covered, the plasters having fallen away. Evidence that would not be ignored.

Afterward, she continued walking. She turned down one passageway and then another, anxious to be around people, to be around life, if only to reassure herself that she had not died as well, had not drowned under the rising waters of the Venetian lagoon.

After two hours spent roaming the city, Frankie found herself standing in front of the Danieli. Now that the shock had subsided, the panic had begun to set in—about what she had done, about what would happen. She was not fool enough to believe that she could get away with it, but perhaps she could avoid it, even if only for a little while.

Inside, the hotel was deserted. Without the aid of electricity, it was dim, the red plush carpets and golden flourishes turned ordinary and mundane. As if a spell had been broken. A stench filled the lobby, the water having claimed every inch of space during the flood. Frankie approached the counter and rang the bell—surprised that it was still there, wondering if it was affixed onto the desk. It gave a tinny ring, and after a moment or two, a harassed-looking bellhop stuck his head out from the back. "*Sì?*"

Frankie did her best to smile when she asked if he spoke English. He shook his head but then also said, "Yes, maybe a little." She sighed in relief, grateful that the concierge was nowhere to be seen, that the bellhop was young and had a look of frightened bewilderment across his face, as had most of the people she had encountered that morning.

"Brilliant," she began. "You see, I've lost my key. During the flood, I was—" She let her voice trail off, tried to appear wide-eyed and innocent. The bellhop stared at her with concern. Perhaps it was the catastrophe they had all just survived, together, no matter that they were strangers. In any case, he hesitated only briefly, turning toward the hanging keys, as if he knew how much trouble it would earn him to touch the glittering objects. But, then, this was not a normal day, and that very thought seemed to occur to him as well, so that he reached his hand toward the board. "Your room number?" he asked her.

She had worried about this. "Room 304," she said without hesitation. "Or, no, wait, that's not right." She gave a small grimace. "I'm horrible at remembering things." It was the type of thing that she supposed Gilly would say—if she were still alive to say it.

The bellhop looked troubled at this complication. "Your name?" he asked.

Now all she could do was hope. That this place was big enough that Gilly would not be remembered, if, in fact, this was where she was staying at all. Frankie still did not fully believe it—the girl had told her so many half-truths. "Gilly," she said, followed by a hasty "Gilly Larson."

The bellhop nodded, opening the large book in front of him. It was waterlogged, but somehow the ink was still legible. "Ah, yes, here. *Signorina* Larson. Room 307." He glanced up and smiled. "You were close."

Frankie blushed, surprised that the room was something about which Gilly had not lied. "Yes."

He turned to the board again. The spot for 307 was empty. "A moment," he said. "I will retrieve the master key."

The bellhop disappeared behind the wall, and while he was gone, Frankie's gaze settled on a box with cards in it. Another minute passed and she began to think. About the box, about what it held within. Registration cards, she realized. Before she could change her mind, she leaned over, flipping through them, her fingers stumbling over the thick card stock, one sticking to another, until there—there it was. *Miss Jillian Larson.* Her name, her nationality, her passport number. Before she could consider the ramifications of the action, before she asked herself of the necessity for such deception, she placed the registration card into her pocket.

The man reappeared a moment later.

"Here you are," he said, placing a key, large and heavy, into her hand. Frankie was aware of the heat of his skin against her own. It took everything within her not to flinch. "Please, if you need help. With anything. Anything at all. Tell us, please." His gaze lingered on her arm. "Madam—you are injured?"

Frankie looked down at the marks on her arm, red and angry. She did not respond. Instead, she turned, headed to the stairs, and made her ascent, barely pausing to take a breath.

Gilly's room was sparse, the overpowering stench of mildew causing Frankie to pause at the door. Inside, there was only a small suitcase with a few items of clothes—there were no luggage tags, no names scrawled anywhere. She checked the pockets thoroughly but found no sign of her passport. The girl might have had it on her, she supposed, in her handbag, or the hotel might have held it, as was sometimes policy. In the bathroom she found a bar of soap, half-used, which smelled of Gilly, of cloves and cinnamon and nutmeg. She tossed the bar into the bin.

Only as she was preparing to leave did she see it.

A stack of pages, set just inside the wardrobe. The girl's original manuscript, Frankie realized with a start. She tucked it into her coat, grabbed the suitcase, and headed toward the door.

As Frankie exited the Danieli, a light-headedness swept over her, so that she grasped at the stone to steady herself. A dull ache was beginning behind her eye. She could feel it in her bones as well, a type of restlessness in her arms, in her legs, that made her want to stretch, to flex, if only to shake the pain that had settled there.

She did her best to ignore it as she headed toward the docks, where she hired a gondolier—no less than a magical feat given the state of the city—and ordered him to row them out into the open water, to the edge.

As they pushed off, she clung to the suitcase that had once belonged to Gilly, feeling the wooden boat as it rocked them back and forth, wondering if she was about to be seasick for the first time in her life.

When they were far enough away that Venice seemed only a hazy portrait, she instructed the gondolier to stop, and turning wildly one way and then the other, making sure that there was not a soul but her and him, she stood and upturned the suitcase, along with its contents, into the water. This prompted an explosion of shouting from the gondolier, peppered with threats and dramatic hand gestures, which Frankie ignored. Eventually, the gondolier abandoned his protestations, sitting back into the boat and glaring at her when words failed to do otherwise. She leaned farther out into the water, as much as she dared, pushing the floating contents under, willing them to sink faster, deeper, her hands turning icy and blue. She watched, sitting in the boat, shaking now from the cold, from everything that had happened, as Gilly's things followed their owner. Once or twice already the gondolier had picked up his wooden oar, had tried to begin the row back to the city, but Frankie had stopped him, laying her hand across his own, making sure that they waited until the last of the things were submerged, until no trace remained. At the last minute she remembered the pages she had tucked into her coat, and though she meant for them to meet the same fate, her hand stilled as she held them over the watery grave. Frankie's teeth chattered and her face burned, so that she could imagine the red vivid flush even now staining her cheeks. She placed the pages back into her coat. It seemed the gondolier sensed something of her turmoil, her grief, for he handed her a blanket on the journey back to the island, making sure that she had wrapped it tightly around herself before picking up his oar again.

Once onshore, she pressed a large amount of lire into the gondolier's hand and walked away. She heard him call out, his words leached of their earlier anger. She did not turn around.

CHAPTER 21

F rankie boarded a train to Rome.

It had been the first train running that morning, and standing in the freezing station, shaking from something colder than the temperature, Frankie had known that she would take it, that she wouldn't go home, wouldn't resume her life. That she couldn't—for the *carabinieri* would come for her eventually. She didn't want it to happen there, in her flat, in her garden, where her neighbors, where Jack, would see. In Rome, she would be a stranger. And so she purchased a ticket, one-way, and boarded the train along with the other shell-shocked passengers. At least she was not out of place, she thought, a similarly fevered look upon their countenances, their eyes wide and shining with emotion as the train sped out of Venice, across the water, and back toward Italy.

At some point during the journey, she fell asleep, woke to find Gilly beside her, smiling, assuring her that she would love Rome. Frankie woke with a great start, gasping for breath. Frightened glances were cast in her direction. A sheen of sweat settled across her features, and she wiped a hand over her face and assured those around her that she was fine, that she was not in need of help. She disembarked quickly, clutching her suitcase to her side. Walking through the halls of the train station, she kept her gaze lowered to the floor.

Outside the Roma Termini station, she came to an abrupt halt.

Frankie wandered the streets before settling on a hotel in the heart of the Monti neighborhood, near the Colosseum. It was a former convent, centuries old, the concierge behind the desk told her with far too much cheer, pointing to the original wooden beam work above them. Frankie nodded and smiled, pretending the information was of interest. The concierge clicked his tongue when he heard where she had traveled from, inquiring if she was well, if Venice was coping, if it was as bad as the newspapers claimed. Frankie did her best to respond, to try to act as though she were there, in the present, listening to the conversation between them, even though her mind and her body, she thought, were somewhere far away, still trapped in the stench of the lagoon. The concierge seemed to understand, insisting she take a hot bath while he had tea sent up to her room. His kindness smarted.

Later, as Frankie stared at the wooden beams from where she lay on the bed, she wondered if she too could lock herself away within these walls for the rest of her life. Whether it would offer her sanctuary, just as it had to the women who came before her.

As if in answer, she raised her arm, looking at the angry marks left there.

Soon, Frankie became aware of the smell.

She assumed, at first, that Rome, like Venice, struggled with the management of their sewers. But then she realized that the same rich, unsettling odor that had marked her days in Venice was found only within the confines of her hotel room. If she stepped outside, the smell vanished. If she locked herself inside the room, windows closed, it flooded the space, the presence of it so ripe and overpowering that she gagged from the stench of it. She searched the room, trying to locate its origins, finding only herself and the single suitcase she had brought with her.

She headed to the front desk, clothes bundled in her arms, and requested that they be laundered, not caring that it would cost her a fortune. The man behind the desk nodded, took the clothes, promising their return later that evening. She wondered that he did not grimace at their smell.

Frankie left the hotel, grateful for the fresh air.

She went to the Trevi Fountain, stared at the shine of coins coating the bottom, at the one or two tourists who had braved the cold to throw in another in exchange for a wish. She went to the temple where Caesar was murdered and tried to remember how many times he was stabbed—twenty-three, she recalled. She walked to a number of other monuments and museums, up one cobbled hill and down another, not understanding what it was that she was looking at, the places leaving no lasting impression on her. Nothing seemed real. It was as if her former self, her former life, was still left behind in Venice and she was now only a shadow, unable to absorb anything around her.

At one point, she stumbled upon a tour in English and paused to listen. The guide was lecturing the group of tourists that swelled around him about the layered history of the city, how one thing was never only that alone. The streets themselves were evidence, those from the medieval era sitting yards below the more recent cobblestones. Even the buildings were not exempt from this layering, for what appeared to the layman as Baroque or Renaissance was often hiding something older, more ancient. The tourists were delighted by these revelations, but Frankie found herself affected by the idea of such concealment. She hurried away, her eyes glancing at the street beneath her, wondering in which time period she was walking just now.

Her legs ached as she continued, protesting against the growing distance and sharp inclines that she had already traveled, when she became aware of a sound. At first she thought she must be mistaken, that her mind was playing tricks on her, tormenting her—but, no, as she walked down one street and then another, through one piazza and then the next, she could hear it: *water*, and it seemed to follow everywhere she went. Somewhere in the hilly neighborhood of Monti, lost among the winding streets that carried her up and down but never to where she wanted to go, she found one of the sources. A *nasone*—similar to the *fontanelle* in Venice, although those had not constantly run—the water here pouring out into the streets and down into the gutters below.

As she drew nearer, an elderly woman paused in front of the spout. Frankie knew she was staring, but she could not look away. Noticing her presence, the old woman indicated a spot on the tap—not the main one, where the water was pouring from, but a smaller hole, which sat just inches above. She placed a thumb on the main spout, blocking it, and a thin stream erupted from the smaller hole, from which she took a long sip. When the older woman had finished, she reached out, holding Frankie by the wrist, beckoning her closer.

Frankie tried to break from the woman's grip without insulting her. She couldn't explain it, she knew that it made no rational sense, but she was petrified of getting too close, as though the water would scald rather than refresh. The old woman's hand clenched the open wound on Frankie's arm, and she exclaimed in pain. Instantly, the old woman reared back. A torrent of words followed, angry this time, the encouraging tone of a moment before dissipated. Frankie wrenched her arm free. She was certain others were looking now, watching her, for she was aware enough to concede how odd she must appear, yet there was nothing she could do, not until she was away from the well, from the water. She turned and began to walk, to run, and as she did so, she became more aware of it than before—this background noise to a landlocked city, as if the water had followed her only in order to drive her mad.

By the time she reached the hotel, her head was reeling.

Once inside, Frankie found that her room smelled just as terrible as before, despite the neatly folded clothes at the foot of her bed.

She waited until the guise of night to leave the hotel. Gathering the freshly laundered clothes into her arms, regretting only for a moment the undoing of their perfectly creased lines, she could once again smell it—the rancid evidence causing her to turn away in disgust.

She deposited them all, still reeking of the Venetian lagoons, in one of the large dustbins she had seen lining the streets and returned to her room.

Back inside, she waited. For a telephone call. A banging on the door. A stern voice speaking in Italian. A command, followed by the binding of her hands, and then the hard, cold metal of prison between her and everything she had ever known. For surely they would know soon. Surely they would find her—*Gilly*, she reminded herself, as though she were in danger of forgetting the girl's name— and they would know what had happened. They would find proof of her guilt.

Frankie did not sleep, only sat huddled in the corner of the room, the image of Gilly as the water closed in around her and over her, sealing her in, just there, before her eyes. Frankie felt her—her lips against her ear, the pressure of her hand against her arm, reaching, pulling, pushing, she didn't know any longer. *I didn't mean to*, Frankie whispered, quietly at first, so that no one would hear her, and then louder, almost hoping that someone would. Looking in the mirror above the tiny half basin in her hotel room, she told herself: *You can't run forever.* And she didn't want to—she was guilty. It was her hand, her palm, that pushed, that pulled, that condemned or failed to save the girl. Even now, the simplicity of it all startled her. How easily she had slipped under the water. How quickly it was over.

It couldn't end there. Nothing was ever that easy.

The next day she could not muster enough strength to leave the hotel. Instead, she spent the day lying prostrate in the dips and curves of her bed. During that time, she did not eat, barely drank, only cupping the water from the tap when she managed to lift herself from the bed and toward the toilet. She knew that she must be imagining it, but the water burned her throat. Eventually, she returned to her bed, shivering, her arms and legs aching from the exertion.

Time became difficult to catch—but, no, she reminded herself, it was not something to *catch* but to *tell*, to *watch*. Either way, she had lost sense of it. Instead, she marked the progression of time by the state of her body. At first she felt hot and feverish, the sheets around her gradually growing damp with sweat. But after a while they seemed to cool, until a deep chill settled itself on her body, her bones aching from the change. She struggled to stay still in those moments, turning one way and then another, unable to find any respite from the painful ache that pulsed through her body.

At some point, there was an insistent rapping on her door, followed by a stern voice calling out in Italian. A part of her softened then, relieved that they had come at last. She could not remember who *they* were exactly, only that she would know them when they arrived. And that the wretched feeling she was experiencing now would soon cease as a result. That now everything would begin to right itself.

Despite this, she could not summon the strength to leave her bed and allow them entry or even to cry out. *Never mind,* a voice told her, *they will come.* She nodded dully at this, trusting in the whisper. And so she lay, the voices outside the door growing more insistent, until at last there was a great banging and the two doors were thrust open.

Frankie stayed awake long enough to realize that the intruders were not whom she had supposed they would be, nor, in fact, whom she had *wanted* them to be. It was only the man who had handed her the key, along with what looked like a chambermaid, standing above her, concern deepening their brows.

The woman moved closer, lying a cool, dry palm across her forehead.

Frankie sighed with the relief of it, of her touch, and with that, closed her eyes, where sleep claimed her at last.

When she awoke, it was with the certainty that time had passed—not simply hours but days. The room in which she lay was blinding in its brightness, and for a moment she could not remember where she was. She turned her head from the window, from the sun pouring into the room, hurting her eyes. Then she remembered, all of it—Venice, the girl, Rome—and she let out a soft groan. She shifted in the sheets, slowly conscious that the clothes she was wearing were not her own. Glancing down at her forearm, she could see that it had been freshly bandaged.

"It was infected," a voice said. "You're lucky it wasn't worse." The accent was English—West Country, she thought, by the pronunciation of his *r*'s, although it seemed a surprising thing to find in Rome. Maybe she was still dreaming.

Her eyes cut to the unfamiliar man who was rising from a chair—a doctor, she supposed from his appearance. He looked real enough. She tried to speak.

"Don't," he said, holding up his hand. "You'll strain yourself."

"How long?" she managed, pointing first to herself and then the bed.

"Three days." Frankie gave a start, but he held up his hand once again to indicate that she should relax. "It's surprising it wasn't more. You were feverish. Delirious by the time I was called. And, as I mentioned, that wound on your arm was infected. You're lucky it didn't turn septic." He paused. "The man behind the desk said you were in the flood, in Venice. I would assume the water is to blame for that."

According to the doctor, Frankie had not left her room for a day or two, had not responded to the insistent knocking of the chambermaid. When the same maid found Frankie's laundered clothes in the dustbin outside, she decided to report her behavior to the concierge. Together, they had forced the doors and discovered Frankie delirious with fever.

Frankie noticed then that the chambermaid in question was standing beside the door, almost half-hidden, as if afraid to reveal herself. *"Grazie mille,"* she said, feeling the dryness on her lips pull as she spoke. "I must have given you a fright," she added, holding the young woman's gaze.

The maid took a step into the room. "I am glad to see *signora* is well again," she murmured, her English heavily accented.

But there was something else, Frankie guessed. It was in the way the maid would not meet her eye, in the high blush that had appeared on both of her cheeks. Had she said something in her delirium? Revealed something that she ought not to? She wanted to ask, but the question stilled on her lips. Instead, she thanked them all again, promising the doctor she would make as quick a recovery as possible.

The maid, she could not help but note, settled an appraising look on her—as if she knew something that the others did not.

"I almost forgot," the doctor said. "The concierge gave me this to return to you once you woke. The laundress discovered it but didn't know what it was. She set it aside in lost property, and only after a few days did it occur to the concierge that he knew exactly to whom it belonged."

Frankie accepted it in her outstretched hand, closing her fingers around the familiar cold.

Her ARP whistle.

Frankie closed her eyes and exhaled.

Frankie returned to London in the middle of the night, nearly a fortnight later. After she recovered, she had been hesitant to remain in Rome, consumed only with thoughts of home. The *carabinieri* were not coming, she had realized, her fear of them seeming to dissipate along with her fever, so that she wondered whether the one had only ever been present because of the other. But the doctor had forbidden her to travel, and so, much to her unease, she had been forced to remain in the hotel, avoiding the maid and her inquisitive looks, thanking the concierge over and over again, every chance she saw him, until they were all, in the end, relieved to be rid of one another.

From there, she should have gone back to Venice and then through Milan or Turin—that would have been the easiest, most direct route to Paris and then onward to Dover and London—but she couldn't do it. The thought of returning to Venice was unfathomable. Instead, she reconciled herself to a longer journey and went from Rome upward, adding time and additional connections but content in the knowledge that it would not bring her anywhere near the watery grave that Venice had become.

Walking down the high street now, she was grateful for the absence of people, for the absence of cars. It was what she liked most about Crouch End, the way that it was able to transform, a bustling outcrop of the city during the day and the quietness of a small town at night.

Inside her flat, there was the smell of disuse.

For a moment it took her right back to Italy, to her first day in Venice, when she had walked among the sheet-covered furniture, wondering whether anything would dispel the staleness in the air. She could not recall at what point she stopped noticing it, at what point her presence and that of her friends had displaced the smell of emptiness and filled the rooms with orange blossom and tobacco, with whisky and sweat.

She made herself a cup of Earl Grey, which she did not drink but left sitting on her bedside table, cooling, the scent of bergamot filling the room. She was home at last, but it still did not feel real, even at the touch of the creaking wooden floors beneath her feet. She had the lingering sense that she had only to turn in order to find the palazzo rising before her.

That night, for what felt like the first time since the flood, she slept with no dreams or nightmares, so that when she awoke, for one long, glorious moment she believed it had never happened. That she had never gone to Venice, that she had never met Gilly. But then the truth of it hit her and she ran to the bathroom, retching. Kneeling against the toilet, she looked down at her forearm, still bandaged, and suspected that she would never be able to forget. That it would haunt her, always.

CHAPTER 22

She woke to a loud, insistent rapping on her front door.

At first Frankie thought that she was only dreaming, had pulled the blankets over her head, shivering, wishing she had lit a fire the night before. She hadn't even remembered to throw a few coins in the gas meter. She exhaled slowly and saw a little cloud of breath expand in the air before her.

The knocking persisted.

Throwing back her covers, Frankie reached for her dressing gown. Her head was aching as though she had drunk her way through a bottle of gin, and she knew the damp was to blame.

Jack stood outside her front door. They stared at each other in the wintry sunlight. "You're here," Jack said. It wasn't a question, and yet she sounded incredulous.

"Yes."

Jack blinked. "How long have you been here?"

"Just since last night." Frankie wrapped her arms around herself. "Come in already, it's freezing out there."

They moved from the hall to the sitting room, and Frankie went to work until the fire was lit, although in its typical way, it put out less heat than it should have. A moment passed and then another, and still neither of the women spoke. Frankie felt herself grow fearful—of what, she didn't know, but certainly the look on Jack's face was one reason to tremble. She was staring at her now with such intensity that Frankie worried that somehow her friend knew everything.

"You do know that we thought you were dead," Jack eventually began. "That we've been searching everywhere for you, Frankie. Everywhere. I was ready to hop on an airplane to Venice, but I was told it would be a waste of time, that it's chaos there and everything is impossible. Not that it would have stopped me. But then I had this feeling, a niggling at the back of my mind, that told me I had better check your flat again, just in case, before I went flying off in the middle of the night. I suppose I'm glad I did."

Frankie could not bring herself to look up at Jack. "I'm sorry," she managed at last.

"I was worried sick," Jack said, sounding less angry. "Where's the whisky?" she asked, which meant, Frankie knew, that she had been forgiven. Frankie offered to help, but Jack refused, ordering her to sit on the sofa, to warm herself by the fire, while she busied herself in the kitchen. At one point, Jack picked up the telephone, made a quick call, presumably to Leonard, saying, "She's here. Yes. Yes, I will," before hanging up. "I couldn't find glasses," she said, returning with two chipped teacups, into which she poured a measure each. "Cheers," she murmured, before swallowing it in one go and then pouring them each another. "God, I wish you would move. Sometimes I can't sleep thinking about you here, on your own. Do you know how many robberies, how many murders, take place around here?"

"No, do you?" Frankie asked, genuinely surprised.

"Well, no," Jack conceded, "but I can imagine."

Jack fell silent then, and Frankie knew what was expected of her. It was what she had been dreading on the train journey back to England, as she planned in her mind what she would say and how it should be said. The truth, as much as she could, for wasn't that always how people got caught out in novels, in films, by spinning such elaborate deceptions? "I'm sorry I didn't telephone," she began. "I was trapped in the palazzo for several days, the electricity was out, the water was rising. I panicked."

Jack nodded. "Yes, but where have you been, Frankie? They're calling it the storm of the century, you know. This was no ordinary flood."

"No, I suspected as much," Frankie said, trying to make her friend laugh.

Jack remained stony-faced. "I sent Maria round, once everything calmed down a bit. She went and said there was no sign of you anywhere."

"I went to Rome."

Jack frowned. "Rome?"

"Yes." Frankie paused. She had known this bit would be harder to explain, that Jack wouldn't accept anything less than a complete answer—but how could she tell her that she had fled to Rome believing it was only a matter of time before the *carabinieri* arrested her? And so she decided the best way, the easiest way, was to indicate that she hadn't been in her right mind—and, after all, that was at least partly true. "I didn't know what else to do, Jack. I just left. I couldn't stay there any longer, so I took the first train out. I'm sorry I didn't ring, didn't let you know I was all right. I don't know what I was thinking. I don't think I *was* thinking. I had a fever— the doctor thought it was brought on by an infection I might have developed because of the floodwater, and so then I couldn't leave, not until I was better."

Jack downed another shot of whisky. "Leonard was ready to ring Scotland Yard, you know."

Frankie smiled. "My knight in shining armor."

Jack gave a short nod, not quite smiling yet. "Well, if there's one thing that comes out of this whole mess, then I guess it's that the two of you seem to be getting along." Jack paused. "I'm sorry, you know. That we argued before."

Frankie waved her hand. "It's already forgotten. And besides, I'm sorry as well. About everything," she said, thinking of the news that Jack had received from the doctor.

Jack nodded and turned toward the fire. "God, I'm ready for spring."

Frankie reached across the sofa and squeezed her friend's hand. For one moment, one glittering, wonderful moment, she allowed herself to imagine how things might move forward. There would be more days like this, confidences over drinks and the roaring fire, and sometimes Leonard would join them, but it wouldn't change anything, not in any way that mattered, wouldn't make a difference to their friendship—not anymore. She would forget Venice, forget about the girl. It was some time before Frankie could speak, before the roaring in her ears began to subside.

Jack's grip tightened. "Frankie, I want you to know that I'm sorry about this past year."

Frankie felt suddenly ill.

"No, listen," she continued. "I know I'm guilty of neglecting you, of putting Leonard before our friendship." She pulled Frankie in closer. "I promise, I won't ever take you for granted again."

"So you're not angry with me?" Frankie was compelled to ask. "For disappearing?"

"I'm absolutely furious," Jack responded, although she was smiling as she spoke. "Don't ever pull that sort of thing again."

"I promise. I'm sorry too, Jack. For the way I acted, toward both you and Leonard."

Jack nodded, taking a sip from her teacup. "God, what a mess. Did I tell you, the buyers have pulled out now."

"What?" Frankie asked. "Wasn't there a deposit?"

"There was, and we'll keep that, but still, the thought of going through it all again." Jack grimaced. "There's just so much damage now from the floods. They don't want to take on such a major renovation, and I can't say I blame them."

"Is it that bad?"

"Horrendous." Jack snuck a glance at her. "There's something else."

"What?"

"The owners of the other half of the palazzo hired someone to stop by and check their property for any damage from the flood." Jack exhaled, as if bracing herself for what was to come. "It turns out you were right."

For a moment, Frankie couldn't figure out what she was referring to. "About what?"

Jack looked at her. "There *was* someone living next door."

Frankie felt the blood drain from her face.

"Apparently the door was unlocked. The owners keep a spare key on the property, just in case, and they assume it must have been found by whoever had been staying there. They said there was water and mud tracked all up and down the stairs."

"Oh?" Frankie remembered her own exploration of the place, how she had come from outside, dripping with water and grime. "Are they certain it wasn't from the flood?"

"It might have been—except that they found someone there. Gave them a real fright too, by the sound of it. They went running out of the palazzo, shouting for help. As luck would have it, there were some *carabinieri* only steps away, and they were able to grab the man before he made a run for it."

"How extraordinary," Frankie mused, her mind all the while trying to keep up, trying to decide what it meant for her, for Gilly, and what had unfolded between them. It occurred to Frankie then—if she had seen *him* from the courtyard that night, might he not have seen *her* from above? The thought stopped her cold.

"I feel so guilty."

"What for?" Frankie asked, still distracted by the news.

"All those times I laughed when you said you had seen someone next door. I should have listened. Who knows who the man might turn out to be—some madman who could have murdered you in your sleep."

"I'm sure that's an exaggeration."

"Well, the authorities will soon find out."

"Will they?" she asked, turning to Jack.

'Yes." Jack watched her. "Are you all right?"

Frankie nodded, doing her best to act as if this discussion were the most natural thing in the world, as if her life, her future, did not hang on the question of whether or not this man, whoever he was, had happened to be in the palazzo on the day of the storm, had happened to see what transpired.

Jack took another sip of her whisky. "I wonder if we should ring the girl?"

Frankie started. "Who?"

Jack made a face. "Gilly."

"No." The word left Frankie before she could help herself. "I mean, I'm sure she's absolutely fine."

"Did you see her again? After we left?"

"No," Frankie replied, her voice tight. "Why do you ask?"

"No reason, I just hope she managed to stay safe."

"I'm sure she did. I'm sure she's already back in London. I would check, but we didn't exchange details, didn't think we were in any rush to at the time."

"Well," Jack said, seeming to consider. "I suppose she's a grown woman."

"Yes," Frankie said.

Jack gave a shudder. "I don't know about you, Frankie, but I've had my fill of Venice. At this point I'd pay someone to take that damned palazzo off my hands. I'd offer it to you, but something tells me you're probably just as glad as I am to see the back end of it." She pushed further into the sofa. "Let's talk of something else. Tell me what you're going to do with yourself today."

Frankie considered, the thought of returning to *before* a notion she had never fully entertained until that moment. "I hadn't thought. I suppose I should go to the market, and then—"

Jack looked up. "And then?"

"I thought I would go to the library and start writing."

Jack was silent, still, and then a smile broke across her face. "I think that sounds wonderful, Frankie. Just promise me one thing."

"Anything."

"I'm sick to death of stories where anyone over thirty is ancient, and forty extinct. Do you know I read a novel the other day and was convinced for about three-quarters of it that the protagonist was a woman of at least seventy, before the author got around to declaring her thirty-eight." Jack paused. "Thirty-eight. Has the world gone mad in their obsession with youth? Should I pack it all in now?"

Frankie allowed herself a genuine laugh then, although its edges felt sharper than normal, the image of the ghostly figure standing in the window of the palazzo lurking somewhere just before her.

Instead of catching the bus to the library, Frankie headed to the King's Head.

It wasn't *her* local, since she had never so much as been there before, but if she were the type to spend a night out in a pub, then by its mere location, this would be hers. There was a comfort in the realization, that this was a place in which she was meant to belong. It created a sense of the familiar, despite the smoky room being unknown to her.

It had just gone noon and already the pub was full, mainly with men on their lunch break or older men meeting friends. In the corner there was a group of elderly women, sitting over their sweet sherries. The food was just starting to be brought out from the kitchen, the comforting smell of fried food wafting throughout the tiny establishment. For the first time in days, Frankie felt her stomach rumble.

She settled into a seat hidden in the corner, a pint of Guinness growing warm before her. She hadn't wanted anything to drink, not after the whisky with Jack. She had only wanted to be somewhere where she could sit, her mind could wander, and she did not have to think about how close she had come to destroying the life she had worked so hard to create.

She took a sip of her beer. It was a good pour, rich and creamy, and only slightly metallic, and for a moment she let her eyes wander the bar, her mind blank.

Through the din, she began to hear a voice, low and interrupted by static. It was the wireless—the news, she realized, just as she heard the word *Venice* spoken aloud. She looked around the bar, expecting them all to be listening, to be turning with interest. No one moved. Instead, the clinking of glasses, the murmur of conversation, continued. Frankie strained to hear: *Venice . . . the worst flood in history . . . destroyed.* She tilted her head to one side and then the other, trying to pick up the words in between. A body. That was what she was waiting for. The announcement of a body found, an unexplained death, the search for the culprit.

Frankie looked up and felt her heart stop.

It was her. Standing at the bar, her long red hair hanging down her back, slightly wavy, as though she hadn't had time to comb it properly. It was improbable that she should be here, in this dingy bar, in Crouch End, but there was no doubt in her mind. It was Gilly.

She was alive.

That was the first thought that caught her, that trapped her, that pinned her to the seat so that she could not move, could not speak, from the shock. How on earth was it possible, she wondered. But, then—she had never seen her body. No, she had turned around and headed back upstairs, had hid. Gilly must have still been alive when she left her, must have still had enough fight to struggle to the surface, to claw her way out of the salty lagoon, eyes stinging, lungs burning. And it was no wonder that she had not knocked on Frankie's door for help, not after what had happened. Frankie started to stand, her knees trembling. How would she react to seeing her?

The girl handed over a few coins and Frankie moved toward her, feeling as though she were back in Venice, pushing against the flood, the current stronger than her body. She opened her mouth, the words right there, ready to speak—but then the girl turned, and it wasn't her at all. Just a plain-looking girl with unremarkable features and a heavy scattering of freckles. Nothing about the girl resembled Gilly at all. Her hair was too frizzy and the wrong shade entirely—and she was larger than Gilly had ever been, broader, particularly in the shoulders. How could she ever have mistaken the two?

The barman looked at her. "You all right there, love?"

Frankie nodded, unable to find the words to reassure him, then turned and pushed through the pub's front door, desperate to be outside. Her face was hot and covered with sweat. She felt as though she were on fire, despite the cold swirling around her.

Frankie walked home, head down, eyes focused on her leather oxfords, tarnished now by the sludgy mess that tried to pass itself off as snow. Christmas was only a few weeks away. She had spent it alone last year, and she supposed this year would be no different. Instead of feeling depressed at the prospect, she felt only relief, a sense of ease, knowing that she would not have to smile and nod, have to pull Christmas crackers and place a paper crown on her head, have to laugh at the idiotic jokes tucked inside and pretend that everything was as it should be, that absolutely nothing had changed.

She would be alone, and it was fine with her.

It was, perhaps, the way things were meant to be after all.

But, then, that wasn't what happened.

Jack and Leonard appeared on her doorstep early on Christmas Eve morning and insisted on taking her out. Refusing to tell her where they were going, they shuffled her from shop to shop, stopping at Fortnum & Mason for chocolates and half a dozen bottles of champagne that made Frankie gasp at the price, at a butcher for a last-minute goose with all the trimmings, at a greengrocer for all the rest, and then at an outdoor market selling the last of the year's Christmas trees. They all retired home, and Jack made them hot sloe gin as they dressed the tree and then later put together some sort of festive punch, which tasted mainly of gin and which caused a few cooking disasters, which Leonard avoided by sorting out Frankie's leaky tap in the bathroom, and then at last supper was served, and they all sat round with a glass full of bubbling champagne and wished one another a Happy Christmas.

Frankie could imagine what they must look like to an outsider—a merry group of three, with not a single care or worry in the world. And it was true, for two-thirds of them, anyway. It was only Frankie who was not like the rest, she thought, knowing that beneath the exterior a darker something beat, steadily and without fail.

Leonard and Jack left late that night, promising to call soon, and Frankie waved them away with a smile and a sadness that she had never before experienced. She was grateful in that moment, so grateful for the friends that she had, and so heartbreakingly sad for what had happened in order to make her appreciate them.

As she closed the door behind them, Frankie realized that no one had mentioned Gilly or the man that had been discovered hiding in the palazzo. It was as if Venice, the flood, none of it, had ever happened at all.

And then life resumed.

Frankie would wake early in the morning, grabbing the 91 to the British Museum and back up again to Crouch End by late afternoon, before the sun set too low. Some days she treated herself to breakfast before she began work. There was a small café just a few steps from the reading room, and although the woman was from Sorrento, not England, she was the only one who cooked eggs the way Frankie liked them—poached, but not with vinegar, and set in a circular mold, fluffy and white around the edges, none of the burnt crispy wisps that other cafés produced, the middle runny and accompanied by tea, strong, with only a dash of milk.

The familiar lilt of the woman's voice as she greeted each of her customers with the same salutation—*hello, darling*—made Frankie's heart constrict the first time she entered the café that winter, the familiarity of it making her realize that she had missed it more than she had suspected. More than that. It made her realize, for the first time: *She was home.*

Venice became a distant memory, and as the days passed, she allowed herself to think of it less and less. Frankie burrowed back into her old life, inhabiting the couple of miles that surrounded her home, her whole world. Some days Jack and Leonard came by, while on others, Jack came alone. Often, they met for tea, for a slice of Victoria sponge in a cafeteria around the corner from the British Museum, the cream and raspberry jam a comfort that Frankie had only ever taken for granted before. But never again, she promised herself. Things were good. *No,* Frankie told herself, rushing to meet her friend after a fruitful day of writing, late in January, things were *better than before.*

CHAPTER 23

J ack was knocking on her door. "Have you heard the news?" she
asked, not waiting to be invited in but barreling past her friend,
into the hall of her flat. "God, I'm frozen to the bone. Can we put
the kettle on?" Again, she did not wait for an invitation but moved
down the hall and into the kitchen.

Frankie typically delighted in watching the way her friend made
herself at home, rummaging through the cabinets after a hasty attempt at permission first. Now, however, Frankie felt nothing but
dread at Jack's mention of news. "What's happened?" she asked,
coming up behind Jack as she filled the kettle with water and set it
onto the burner.

"Where are your matches?" Jack asked in response, still clothed
in her coat and gloves, her hat bearing traces of sleet.

"Here," Frankie said, handing her the tiny box she had absently
placed between the sugar and flour canisters. "What's happened?"
she asked again.

"What?" Jack asked, her voice muffled as she bent over the stovetop. "Oh," she said, straightening up, leaning against the counter,
near enough to the flame that Frankie worried she might go up in
a blaze. "The girl from Italy. She's dead."

Frankie's reaction was not feigned—she visibly paled at her

friend's words, her legs going weak. She had been awaiting this moment, had been dreaming of it, dreading it, for so long that now that it had arrived, it seemed somehow false and far away. She could hear the words, but they didn't mean anything at all. It took a minute before it felt that life had started up again, until she felt it at last, crushing against her chest, so that she struggled to breathe.

"Oh, darling," Jack said, rushing to her side. "I shouldn't have said it like that, I'm sorry. I think I'm in a bit of a shock still myself, that's all."

"Dead?" Frankie murmured, pushing aside Jack's attempts to help her. "How do you know?"

"It was on the wireless." Jack reached for cups and saucers, once she had made certain her friend could stand on her own. "Where's the Earl Grey, dear?"

"Here." Frankie crossed her arms. "On the wireless? What did they say?"

"Nothing much, only that they found her body in Venice. Found it a while ago, it's just taken this long to identify her. Isn't that terrible?"

Frankie brought her fingers to her temples, a headache beginning to twinge. "But what did they say happened?"

"Drowned." Jack dropped several tablespoons of tea leaves into a pot and shuddered. "It seems she never did return home."

At that moment, the kettle let out a piercing shrill.

Frankie, despite herself, jumped.

"Such a shame, she was such a bright young thing. I feel awfully guilty now for not checking on her." Jack paused, mid-pour, and looked up to examine Frankie. "Will you be all right?"

Frankie fixed a smile onto her face, knowing such pretense was made only in vain—the only person who could read her better than herself was Jack. "Of course."

"It's unbelievable to think we were all together not so very long ago," Jack mused. "And you never saw her again? After we left, I mean."

"No, I've already told you that," Frankie said, her voice more defensive than she had intended.

"All right," Jack replied, with a raise of her eyebrows. "I didn't mean anything by it. I'm only surprised."

"Why?" Frankie knew her tone was still too short, but she found she couldn't stop, couldn't manage to control it, the thought that Jack might suspect something causing her stomach to curl into knots.

Jack gave her a questioning look. "You could barely keep her away when we were there. I would have thought she would have jumped at the chance to have you all to herself."

The girl had said something similar that last night—hadn't she? Frankie saw Gilly's face, felt her hand—pushing, pulling. She gave a small shudder.

"Oh, Frankie." Jack reached over. "I'm sorry, I shouldn't talk about her like that. Not now that she's, well, that she's gone."

"It's fine, Jack. I'm fine."

"I feel dreadful for her family." Jack's eyes widened. "Apparently I know them, did I tell you that? The Larsons. I don't know them well, but they're acquaintances at the very least, someone I run into every now and again. I've heard they're a wreck. Though I suppose at least now they have some answers. They've been unable to contact her for weeks, it turns out." Jack shifted. "I'm sure I'll run into them again at some point, and I'm torn about whether or not I should mention seeing their daughter there. It would only make things frightfully awkward, I think, and besides which any connection would only draw the type of attention that neither of my parents would appreciate. I don't want any reporters hounding them. Do you think that's awful?"

"No," Frankie said, too eagerly. "No, I think it's best. Besides, it might only hurt her family more to know."

"Yes, I thought so too." She paused. "It's odd, though, isn't it?"

Frankie inhaled sharply. "What is?"

"This whole thing. It's like something from one of your stories, not something that happens in real life."

"Oh," Frankie said, nodding her head in agreement. They drank their tea, standing in the tiny alcove of the kitchen.

"Well, darling," Jack said, cup still half-full, "I should dash. Dinner tomorrow?"

Frankie nodded, watching her friend take one last sip of tea and then disappear out the door. She looked down at Jack's cup, a bright-red stain of lipstick on the rim. Reaching out her hand, Frankie wiped it away with her fingers.

Frankie had bought her place in Crouch End, a maisonette on Wolseley Road, after the publication of her first novel. At the time, it had stood next to a row of houses that still had wooden boards instead of actual doors, shattered glass instead of windowpanes—the enduring reminders of what they were all trying so desperately to forget. But the sight hadn't bothered Frankie the way that it had others. It was a testimony to the fact that she had endured, that they all had, that although she might not be the same as before, she had been made into something stronger, sturdier, just like that tiny little corner of the world into which she had been born. Bombs may have fallen all around them, homes may have been destroyed, part of Wilson's department store reduced to no more than smoldering ash—but other parts had survived. Like the clock tower, that stalwart structure of the nineteenth century had been an unwavering mark in her younger years, and after the war Frankie had found a solace in its presence, her North Star of sorts, for whenever she was too lost. It was there that she had made the decision to remain in Crouch End, days after the war had ended, standing in the deserted high street late into the night.

By then Crouch End was no longer the same area as the one

she had known in her childhood, not after the havoc wreaked by the war. Gone were the larger, well-to-do families that she remembered gracing the high street on the weekends—although a few did manage to hold on, despite time and circumstance—replaced instead with a younger, more creative set, attracted to the area by the bedsits that dubious landlords had carved out of the once-palatial houses in the chaos of postwar London. During Frankie's childhood, her parents had rented a house on Nelson Road, and although she rarely passed by anymore, once in a while she allowed herself the indulgence of recalling her childhood, of playing knock down ginger around Priory Park with the rest of the children in the neighborhood. She remembered warm summer nights, the darkness of evening settling in, the smell of dew on the grass. She realized that most nights were probably not so idyllic as her memory allowed, that they were probably filled with quarrels over such innocuous things as tea or bedtime, but in the intervening years, in the absence of family, of friends, of any sort of collective memory, she had arranged within her mind a set of instances that may or may not have existed but that she was ultimately content with.

Yes, the Crouch End of her childhood was not the same—if it had ever existed at all—but, then, neither was Frankie.

Now the neighborhood had begun to change once again. Families had started to move back in, with larger properties becoming available as landlords did away with bedsits, once they realized the higher prices they would be able to charge as their clientele shifted. Frankie found she missed it a bit, the air of recklessness she felt walking home late at night, her scowl daring anyone to try something.

Still, she knew her friends disliked visiting her—Jack tolerated it, but Harold avoided it whenever he could. When he made his way to her first flat, back when she was still renting one of those terrible bedsits, she had shared a toilet, not to mention a telephone, with she didn't know how many people, the majority of whom came and went at all hours of the day and night, new faces emerging and then disappearing before she had time to learn them. Harold had been horrified, declaring that there were to be no more meetings at hers until she sorted herself out properly. When Frankie rang to inform him of her purchase, he had been dismayed to find that while her number had changed, her postcode had not—which was why Frankie was startled to find him standing on her doorstep one wintry day in February, looking somewhere between amused and angry.

For a moment, Frankie hovered in the frame of the door, the look on Harold's face already telling her why he was there. Despite being back for some time now, she had not yet managed a visit to her editor's offices in Piccadilly. Although there were times when she felt guilty at her avoidance, she felt mainly justified, knowing that what she needed was time, was space.

"Oh, move over and let me in," Harold said and laughed now, when Frankie still hadn't stepped aside.

"You have to promise first," Frankie said, blocking the doorway. "No talk about the book."

He glared. "What book?"

"*Any* book, Harold."

He let out an exasperated sigh but held his hand to his heart. "Fine. I swear."

Frankie moved aside to let the diminutive figure past, not believing for one second that he would be silenced. "Tea?" she asked, throwing the question over her shoulder.

"Black," he responded. "My dear, I passed some extremely suspicious young men outside—"

She headed into the kitchen. "Those are the neighbors, Harold."

"Well," he said, not at all pacified by this explanation. "If those were my neighbors, I would look into moving."

She smiled. He had been saying a version of this ever since they met. As she placed the kettle on the stove, she listened to the sounds of Harold in her sitting room. Even through the wall, she knew what he was doing: rummaging through her bookcase, picking out one edition and then another, riffling through a few pages, not pausing to read but unable to stop. It was one of his most infuriating and endearing qualities, his inability, his refusal, to stay still. She dropped some tea leaves into a pot, wondered whether she shouldn't break her own resolve and tell him about what she had been working on. She may have lost her manuscript in Venice, but the ideas remained, and since she had been home she had been resurrecting them, feeling as though she were some great anthropologist rather than just a writer.

She poured the water over the tea leaves, watching as they steeped in the water, turning it first lightly brown and then a deep, dark black that she knew only Harold would truly appreciate. Frankie raised her head and listened, realizing that she had not heard him for some time now.

She grabbed a cup for Harold and a tin of biscuits. "I'm worried what it means that you've managed to stay quiet for so long," she called out, turning the corner.

She stopped, spilling some of the pot's contents onto the floor.

Harold had indeed found a book that he was enjoying. She blinked, not trusting her own eyes, not believing that she could have been so utterly, completely careless. She must have left it out, must have placed it somewhere on the sofa or the coffee table. *The manuscript.* Not her own, but Gilly's.

"I knew it," he cried, looking up at her.

Frankie stood, frozen, still holding the tray out in front of her. "Knew what exactly?" Her voice was hoarse, the words sounding strained and damaged, so that she wondered whether Harold could hear it too—the panic that had crept into her voice.

He flashed her a smile. "That you were writing."

Frankie felt as though the blood had left her face. Or, no, she felt as though everything else was gone and she was nothing *but* blood. Thunderous, rushing blood that caused her ears to sing, to roar, so that she couldn't hear anything but a buzzing. She struggled to compose herself, setting the tray onto the coffee table with a slight crash that sent more of the pot's contents spilling up and over the rim.

Harold held the manuscript between his hands as if it were a serving plate, as if it were something precious that could not be touched. She resisted the urge to reach over and snatch it back. To throw the damn thing in the bin, just as she should have done weeks ago.

"Don't be silly," she said, attempting a lightheartedness that she did not feel, that she suspected she would never feel again so long as those pages remained between his hands.

"I'm not," Harold protested. "This is *good*, Frankie."

She did not respond.

"It's *great*, in fact. So different from your other work. The perfect direction to take after—" He paused, finishing his sentence with an awkward clearing of his throat.

She let out a shuddering breath. "Harold—" she began. Now was the time to tell him that it wasn't hers, that she hadn't written it. It could be no real secret that she had known the girl, that they had been friends while in Italy—Jack and Leonard rendered that lie impossible. It was normal that this manuscript should have passed between them, between budding writer and established author. And yet all she could see when she looked at it was evidence. Evidence of guilt, of the act itself, of everything she had done afterward. The words were there on her lips—*it isn't mine, it's hers*—but she could not will them to come. Saying those words would mean mentioning her, Gilly, and letting in everything that she had worked at forgetting. No, she couldn't do it—wouldn't do it. And so she crossed the length of the sitting room, prying the pages from Harold's grasping hands, despite his sputtering protests, and, doing her best to seem casual, to seem undisturbed, she marched into the other room and tossed it onto the kitchen counter.

"What are you doing?" Harold cried, confusion and something else—*hurt*, she thought—crowding his features.

"I don't want to publish it," she said, hoping that the stern tone in her voice would put an end to it. "It was just an experiment I was trying in Italy, but it isn't me, it isn't my voice." That at least was the truth. "I've got some other ideas that I want to pursue instead."

Harold blinked. "Well, pursue them, then, but let's publish this in the meantime."

"No, Harold." She worked into her voice as much strength and finality as she could muster in that moment, hoping it would be enough. Frankie had always trusted Harold's judgment, had always agreed, at least for the most part, on the suggestions that he made for her own and her fellow writers' works, able to recognize his magic touch within a dozen or more books. But this—what did he see in this? She could not find the answer to the riddle on his face. "And besides," she continued, hoping to appeal to his pragmatic side, "no one would believe it."

"Believe what, my dear?"

"That I wrote it."

He studied her. "And why ever not?"

"Because it sounds nothing like me, Harold."

For a minute it seemed like Harold might not respond, but then he shook his head and smiled, saying, "My dear, people will believe anything, so long as you believe it too."

A part of her wanted to ask him exactly what he meant by that, but she was too nervous to continue the conversation for much longer. "I won't change my mind on this," she finished.

Harold was sullen after that, although she could hardly blame him. He drank his tea in silence, thanked her curtly, and then excused himself first to the toilet and then from her flat. "I'll be in touch," he said wearily at the doorstep.

Frankie gave him a short nod, caught between annoyance and guilt, not knowing which to let win. In the end, she regretted the coldness with which they parted and resolved to call him and apologize. She might even tell him about the novel she had begun to reconstruct and that would soon be ready. That thought gave her a small measure of comfort, made her feel less guilty, as she turned away from him, shutting the door with a thud.

It took Frankie an hour to realize that the manuscript was missing.

At first she thought she was imagining things. Her heart beating, her palms sweating, she told herself to calm down, whispering the words, until they grew louder, until at last they were a shout as she ran through the flat, lifting up cushions and pillows, opening drawers and dragging away pieces of furniture, finding nothing despite her frantic search.

The flat, when she was finished with it, looked like it had been ransacked.

Standing in the doorway of her kitchen, she looked around in disbelief. She had put it just there, on the counter. It was an action so recent that she could still recall it: the heft of the pages, the way her wrist had twinged ever so slightly as she tossed it, casually, as casually as possible, onto the surface of the counter. She closed her eyes slowly, hoping that it might reappear when she reopened them, despite the fact that she did not believe, had never believed, even as a child, in magic. The faucet dripped, the sound echoing alongside her breathing. She opened her eyes.

The counter was still empty.

She stood in the middle of the kitchen, her bare feet growing cold against the wooden floors. And then she realized. *Harold.* When he had disappeared to the toilet. It would be just like him to do something like this, to use those moments in subterfuge, disappearing not to the bathroom but to the kitchen, slipping the manuscript underneath his coat like some sort of spy.

She placed a hand against her heart, willing it to slow.

He had taken the manuscript and now it was out there. Gilly's words, disguised as her own. The thought made her ill.

She reached for the telephone.

"Don't be cross," he said, as soon as his secretary connected them, confirming all her fears. "I wanted to read it properly, here at the office. That's all."

"Harold—" she began.

"Nothing more, I promise."

"Harold, I told you. This isn't to publish." She was out of breath, as though she had been running. She fought to control it, to control herself, her body, her heart now beating at an uncomfortably fast pace, her hands perspiring so that she clutched the telephone, afraid it might slip between her fingers.

"I know, Frankie."

"I want it back, Harold. *Now.* Bring it yourself or, if you're too frightened, have your secretary do it."

There was a pause on the other end. "Suit yourself, Frances."

They hung up, Frankie feeling decidedly less magnanimous toward her editor.

Frankie spent the rest of the afternoon pacing back and forth, waiting for the knock on her door. In the interim, she continued to berate herself for allowing it to have happened in the first place. As she put her flat back together, bit by bit, trying to ignore the sound of the tap dripping once again, loath to call the plumber, she scolded herself for not standing up to her editor. The moment she saw Harold with his paws on the manuscript, she should have pried it away. She did her best not to think of him as he sat in his office, poring over the words, tried not to imagine what would happen if a certain editor were to walk by and inquire what he was reading. Would Gilly's editor recognize the words? Gilly had claimed that he had never seen it, that she had never showed so much as a single page to him, not even a sentence, but could she be believed? Frankie gripped her stomach and willed herself not to be sick.

It wasn't until evening that there was a knock at her door.

Harold's latest secretary—they never lasted long—stood there, an embarrassed expression on her face. She had no doubt been informed of the situation and more than likely warned about Frankie's infamous temper. *Well, let her be scared,* Frankie thought, reaching over and grabbing the bundled manuscript from her.

There was a note scrawled across the top: *Don't be cross, but I've made a copy.*

Frankie looked up, but the secretary was gone, disappeared into the dark, chilly night of London. She didn't blame her. She closed the door and her heart dropped. Leaning her head against the wall, Frankie wondered at what a fool she had been. To think that it was all over, to think that she could forget. In many ways, she thought, it made a perfect sort of sense that Harold had stumbled across Gilly's manuscript, that he had claimed it for his own.

This was her punishment.

Frankie couldn't stay in the flat—her skin itched, and she knew that nothing would cure it but a cold, brisk walk. She grabbed her wellies and headed for the door. The weather had been edging toward warmer weather over the past few days, but now the skies were dark, covered in billowing clouds that seemed to mirror her own mood.

Frankie made her way to the high street, purchasing a pack of cigarettes at the newsagent when she could think of nowhere else to go. As she queued to pay the shopkeeper, her eyes fell on a stack of tabloids. She thought of the woman then, the interview that Harold had mentioned all those weeks before. Just one more thing that had once worried her and had now fallen away, a speck in a sea of her own misdeeds. She stifled a laugh, the clerk eyeing her with suspicion.

Outside, she felt a sensation at the back of her neck—but it wasn't the cold. She raised her umbrella, her eyes scanning up and down the street. Across the way, the lights of a chip shop blinked, casting the otherwise darkened street in a warm yellow glow. No one else was there. She wondered then, as she left the Broadway behind, whether it wasn't only a trick of the light against the drizzle that was causing the shadow that fell against the pavement in front of her, behind her, creating the flicker of movement that she continued to catch out of the corner of her eye, the rain obscuring it all. She was sweating underneath her coat now, and her skin began to itch again.

Her footsteps quickened as she made her way home, every tree, every rhododendron bush, seeming to transform in the darkness. Unused to the bulk of the wellies, Frankie tripped. She righted herself and cursed the lack of light, which now came only from the indoor lights of the neighbors still awake, streetlamps nonexistent this far from the high street. And then, just steps away from her flat—her mind already inside the warmth of her home, her hands cupped around a steaming mug of tea—she saw it: a figure, distorted and misshapen by the rain, standing in the middle of the pavement ahead. She stopped, held her breath, aware of all the noise that she had been making stomping along the street. She blinked, trying to convince herself that it was only a bush or a bag of rubbish. That it was only her mind playing tricks on her.

But then she saw the glint of red.

Frankie let out a breath and it expanded in front of her in the now rapidly cooling air. She took one step forward, resolute, and then another. *Don't be a fool,* she told herself, not daring to whisper the words aloud. She was mistaken. Between the rain, between the limited light. It was only one of the local lads. She often saw them lurking outside, smoking late into the night. Insomnia a bygone conclusion of youth.

Frankie peered through the darkness, searching for any familiar signs of cigarette smoke—as if that would prove her case—but there was nothing, just the scent of earth and damp. She felt something brush against her: fear, she realized, cold and unrelenting. The figure moved then, the rain now coming down hard enough that the movement was somewhat obscured, somewhat difficult to follow, but she could see it nonetheless as it descended, as it folded—*down onto all fours.* Frankie stumbled, her rubber heel catching on the pavement. "Gilly?" she gasped, the name sticking in her throat so that it came out wrong, garbled—like someone drowning.

She fell, and then everything seemed to come into focus, all at once.

Only several feet away from her stood a fox, eyes glowing in the darkness. She searched the rest of the street, but there was nothing else, no one else. The fox moved and its coat caught in the lights of one of the houses, a reddish tint glowing in the darkness. That was what she had seen, then. Not a dead girl, only a fox, the vermin having increased their presence in the neighborhood so that mothers were warned not to leave their babies unattended in the garden.

Lifting herself from the pavement, her hands scraped and bleeding, Frankie shooed the thing away with a dismissive wave of her hand. It held her gaze for a second longer, then turned and ran off.

Inside her flat, Frankie slammed the door, bolting it behind her, and let out a deep breath. Her fingers shaking, she pushed away a stray hair, feeling the sweat that had gathered on her forehead. Frankie did not bother undressing that night. Instead, she crawled under the blanket thrown across her bed, pulling the heavy weight of it up and over her head, until there was nothing but the ceaseless, stuffy darkness that it created. She lay there, eyes open, listening to the unfamiliar sounds of her flat. When she awoke, hours later, drenched in sweat, the sun streaming in through her bedroom window, she realized that she had not remembered to turn off the lights.

CHAPTER 24

Jack came bustling in through the front door later that morning. "I've come to take you out to breakfast," she announced. She stopped when she saw her friend. "You look wretched."

"I had a late night." Frankie flinched.

"Sorry. I thought we could both do with a bit of cheering up. And I wanted to make sure that you were coping, after the news about the girl." She stared pointedly at Frankie's rumpled clothes. "Which it seems you're not."

"I'm fine, Jack," she hastened to say. "It's just—" Frankie searched for something to explain her unkempt appearance. "It's just that Harold stopped by."

Jack groaned. "Oh, God, what did the little pest want?"

"A novel."

Jack watched her. "And?"

"And." Here Frankie paused, wondering what she should say, whether she should claim to have sent him away empty-handed or whether he and Jack might be likely to run into each other, at which point Harold might mention the manuscript and Jack would question why Frankie lied to her. "And he stumbled upon a manuscript I had stashed away. Not something that I ever intended to publish, just an exercise."

Jack's face split into a wide grin. "Why didn't you tell me?" she gasped, delight evident on her face.

"It's something I had written a while ago," Frankie said now, the lie nearly catching in her throat. "I'd honestly forgotten about it until Harold found it again, snooping through my bookshelves." That at least was the truth.

Jack beamed. "I'm so proud of you, Frankie. When can I read it?"

"What?"

"The manuscript. When can I read it?"

In the past, Frankie had always shared her work with Jack. First drafts, revisions—her friend had seen them all, and yet she knew that she could never let Jack see this one. "It was never meant for anyone to see, Jack."

"But if Harold thinks it might be something, then it must be. I don't care for the man, as you well know, but I can't fault his taste. So, come on, let me see it." She started to take her overcoat off, then paused. "Oh, I forgot."

"What's that?" Frankie asked, watching her reach into her pocket.

"Your post. I picked it up on the way in. Honestly, Frankie, sometimes I don't know how you manage," Jack said, sorting through the stack of letters that had accumulated over the last few days, obviously forgotten. "Looks like there's something here from the court. Forget to pay your wireless license, maybe?" she teased.

Frankie took the letter from her, running her hand against the envelope, which seemed thicker somehow than the standard fare, the print announcing her name in a richer type of ink. It was clearly not something as simple as a bill. "That's odd," she murmured, trying to guess what the contents might contain. She stepped into the sitting room, reaching for the envelope opener on one of the bookshelves, and ripped it open.

It was a letter, fairly brief, and as she took in the words and then sentences, as she put them together and realized what they all meant, she felt that same sense of dread from the night before filling her stomach.

"What is it?" Jack asked, coming to stand beside her. When Frankie gave no response, Jack reached over and plucked the letter from her friend's hands, beginning to read aloud for herself.

"It's a summons from the court," Frankie said, hearing the words as though someone else were speaking them. "To appear at the inquest into Jillian Larson's death."

"I don't understand," Jack said, puzzled, turning the letter over and then back again, as if she had missed something. "Why on earth are they holding an inquest?"

That was exactly what Frankie wanted to know as well. "Someone isn't happy with the story they've been told," she said quietly.

"What story?" Jack asked. "The girl drowned. It's sad and tragic, but there's no mystery."

"Oh, I don't know," Frankie said, moving toward the fire, the room filled with a cold, ghastly air that she could have sworn was not there only a moment before. "A pretty young thing dies on her own in Venice. That's bound to raise a few eyebrows."

"Yes, normally, maybe, but this was during a disaster," Jack argued, joining her friend by the fire.

"Yes, well."

They stood together in silence, Jack still holding the letter, the flames from the fire illuminating it from behind, so that the missive seemed to glow within the tiny confines of the darkened room.

"But, listen," Jack began. "How on earth do they even know that you were acquainted? I haven't received anything from them, which means they must not realize I knew her as well, so how do they know about *you*? I haven't said a peep to anyone about Venice, and you know Leonard hasn't either."

There were records. Of the trains Frankie had taken, of the bank that she had visited and the money she had withdrawn. Still, it did not explain how they had drawn the connection, whoever *they* were. Surely she and Gilly had not been the only two Englishwomen who happened to be in Venice? No, there must have been dozens, if not more. There had to be something else beyond nationality that linked them.

Someone must have known. A shiver ran through her, and she thought once more of the stranger in the palazzo. She wanted to ask Jack if they had found out anything else, if he had spoken of her, of Gilly, but she worried that any mention of him now would only look damning.

"How can they not tell you anything more?" Jack was asking, moving back to the sofa and burying herself underneath a blanket. "About why they want you there, I mean."

Frankie followed her, plucking the letter lightly from her friend's hand. She scanned the typewritten words again. "There's nothing like that here. Just that my presence is requested."

"I can't make sense of it. Couldn't you decline?"

"I don't think that's possible," Frankie said, wishing that it were.

Jack looked worried. "Maybe you could write a letter? To be read to the court, I mean? In lieu of attending. Isn't that always possible? I could ask Leonard."

It sounded like a good idea and one that Frankie was tempted to try—but then she thought about how unusual it might seem, declining to help the girl's family. And writing a letter—wasn't that always for those who were too upset, too traumatized? It would seem peculiar, surely, if she were to appear so affected by the girl's death, given their brief time together. Frankie glanced at Jack, saw the concern there. "I think perhaps it would be best to go," she said, surprising even herself with the resolve. "It can't be too bad, can it?"

Jack opened her mouth as if to speak, and then shut it again. The gesture did little to reassure Frankie.

Several weeks passed before she heard from Harold again.

During that time, Frankie allowed herself to indulge in the fantasy that her editor had forgotten about the manuscript, or, better still, that something far more interesting had piqued his interest since they had last spoken. Harold liked shiny things, after all. Her only hope, she knew, was that he had found something shinier, something brighter than Gilly's manuscript.

"Can you come into the office?" he asked, after his secretary had connected them.

Frankie thought she could practically feel his excitement traveling down the line, reaching out and threatening to engulf her. She resisted. "What, today?"

"Yes. I thought we could have a quick chat. Talk about some notes."

"Notes?"

"Yes, for the book."

"What book, Harold?"

He was silent for a moment—cursing her, no doubt, for ruining his good mood. "I'll see you in an hour."

Frankie heard a click on the other end.

She stood in the kitchen, cradling the receiver. He was moving ahead with the novel, then, despite her protestations, despite his promises. She had always known that they would be useless against Harold's determination. Still, she had allowed herself to hope.

She dressed slowly, in no rush to leave the flat.

Her mood was downcast as she made the journey into town and to her publisher's, her mind filled with arguments that she meant to articulate to him—with threats, if it came to that. And yet, standing in the doorway of his office, all such rhetoric left her, so that she could only growl, "Harold," hoping that her voice would serve as enough of a warning.

He held up his hand, a command to be silent. Frankie hesitated in the doorframe. "Well," he said, exasperation etched on his face. "Come in, my dear, I haven't seen you in ages."

"It's been three weeks, Harold," she said, walking in and taking the seat in front of his desk. "Since you came and stole that manuscript from my flat," she finished, indicating the pile of papers that sat before him and that she recognized, even now, from her vantage point. The pages were, she could see, covered in ink, Harold's distinctive scrawl running along the margins.

He made a tsk-ing sound with his tongue. "*Stole* is such a strong word, Frankie."

"And yet somehow surprisingly apt." She paused. "You said you wanted to speak to me, Harold—what about?"

He looked at her with incredulity. "About publishing your book."

"I've already told you. I don't want this published."

He sighed. "I don't understand you, Frankie. You owe the house a first look, why not make it this one? With just a few revisions, it's done, ready to be published."

"Listen, Harold," she said, launching into the speech she had practiced on the bus on the way down. "I want to tell you about the book I've been working on."

"Another book?" His eyes lit up. "It's always good to be prepared with the next one in hand. Especially if it's like this one. Excellent work, Frankie."

"No." She hurried to explain. "I mean something for now." She pointed to the manuscript in front of him. "Instead of that."

Harold lowered his eyes then, as if examining the contents. Frankie suspected that he was trying to buy himself time. "Listen, Frankie," he began, in that tone she knew so well. "This is the one I'm interested in, the one that I very much think we should move ahead with."

"Yes, but—"

"Frankie—"

"If you would only just look at it, Harold, I think you'll see what I mean."

Harold seemed to be watching her with something like unease—she could see the panic glazing his eyes. "Frankie, you know I'll look at anything you've written."

Yes, he would look at it—but would he accept it in place of the manuscript that he now held? She didn't know. "And if it's as good, if it's better, you'll consider it?"

He raised his eyebrows. "Consider what, dear?"

"Publishing it. Instead of that one," she said, indicating the pages between them.

"Oh, well," he said, starting to fidget in his chair. "Let's not get ahead of ourselves, Frankie. Let's concentrate on one thing at a time." He pushed a slip of paper toward her. "If you'll just sign here."

She hesitated. If she signed the paper in front of her, there would be no turning back. Her hand hovered above the pen that he had slid across the table. "Shouldn't we wait?" she asked, her eyes scanning the contract, taking in the words but not the meaning.

"For what?"

"For you to read the novel I just mentioned." She picked up the pen. "What if you prefer it to this?"

He waved his hand. "Don't worry about that, Frankie. This is all standard, you know that by now. It's the same thing you've signed each time."

"Yes, but—" She sought the words to explain that this wasn't like the other times, that this was something different.

Harold leaned forward in his chair. "Is something the matter, Frankie?"

She met his lean, opening her mouth to explain, but the words would not come. She picked up the pen and signed. It was a formality, she told herself, giving a nod. Once he read what she was working on, once he saw the finished thing, then he would understand. They would make a quick switch then, exchanging one for the other. It would not impact the contract, she told herself. As long as there was a book—and there was. She had only to finish it, to show Harold and convince him.

Frankie pushed the signed papers back across the table.

"Now that that's settled . . ." Harold moved the contract out of sight and began to sift through the manuscript pages in front of him.

Frankie felt a pang of alarm—surely he didn't mean for them to do the edits right now, together in his office? The thought struck her that he might very well ask a question that she could not answer. "Wouldn't you prefer to send me your notes?" she asked, trying to buy time. That was all she needed, she told herself—time to correct the situation in which she had found herself.

Harold gave her a bewildered look. "Nonsense. You're here now, and I have a few questions. It won't take more than a few minutes."

She was silent then—after all, what could she say without it seeming too suspicious?

Harold once again turned his attention to the papers before him. "Now, I want to make certain some of these choices are deliberate."

Frankie waited, but he didn't explain further. "Choices?"

"Well, it's just there are a number of blank pages," Harold said, holding them out to her as if in proof. "I wasn't sure whether or not that was intentional."

"Oh." Frankie paused, remembering all the stylistic choices that she had puzzled over while reading it, how she too had wondered whether the pages he was referring to were in fact meant to be that way. She realized then that she had never asked the girl, had just assumed. She felt a fleeting sensation of panic as she answered, "Yes, it was." When he did not respond, she continued, "Deliberate, I mean. But—would it be possible to take them out? I think I've changed my mind." It was, she told herself, a bit like what Charlotte did for Emily. She was changing it to make it better, to ensure that the world would be kind, that the world would understand. She didn't know what possessed her to begin making changes where she had intended to make none, but the meeting had solidified something for her, had made her realize that the publication of the manuscript was possible, the inclusion of her name a therefore unavoidable feature. She would be damned if such a frivolous addition was ascribed to her name.

"Oh, good. That'll make things easier." Harold dipped his head back to the pages, scribbling with his furious and typically illegible scrawl. He stopped and glanced up at Frankie. "I have to admit, it was rather unsettling."

Frankie breathed in. "What was?"

Harold gave a small smile. "Reading this. It was almost like—" He stopped, looked around, as though searching for the rest of his sentence somewhere in the room.

"Like what?" Frankie asked.

His eyes returned to her. "Like it was a different person who wrote it," he finished, the smile still in place.

She felt herself begin to tremble. "Oh?"

"Yes, the structure, the syntax. You become used to the way a person writes after a while. And this—" He paused. "It's like you sat down and said, *I'm going to write completely different than the way that I normally do. I'm going to write as though I'm someone else.*" A silence hung between them. "Is that what you did?"

Frankie struggled to find her voice. "Yes, that's just what I did."

He held her gaze, apparently pleased with her answer. "I thought so."

A moment passed, and then another. Frankie wondered what it was that he was waiting for—whether he was testing her, waiting to see how she would respond. Was it possible that Harold knew the work did not belong to her? That he was willing to publish it despite that fact? Was this his way of letting her know? She waited for something—a wink, a tilt of the head, a conspiratorial smile that would let her know he was in on the deception.

"Well," Frankie began, "was there anything else?"

He paused, then shook his head. "No, I suppose that's it for now. I'll send over my suggestions soon." She stood, walked to the door and was about to shut it when Harold called again, "Oh, I almost forgot. The name you asked me to look up when you were in Venice."

Frankie inhaled sharply.

"I hadn't realized at the time. Gilly Larson. That's who you were asking about, wasn't it? I don't think you mentioned a surname then." He paused. "She had recently signed as an author here. Did you know?"

"I did." She paused, willing her voice to sound natural. "Though she claimed her editor had never even seen the novel she was working on. I wasn't certain I believed her. The girl said a lot of things during our brief acquaintance."

Harold shook his head. "I heard the same. Apparently, he promised her a contract based on some writing sample she gave him. It was reckless, no question, but he's getting old and rather sentimental in his age. I gather he was close friends with her parents as well. Still, it's a shame, after all that's happened. Funny, though, isn't it?"

"What?"

"You meeting her in Venice."

"Yes," she replied.

"Why did you ask, by the way?"

"What?"

"When you called. You asked me to look into her, to find out anything I could about why she was in Venice."

"Oh," Frankie said, giving a little laugh, trying to stall for time. She fought the urge to be sick right then and there. "It was only that. The bit about the contract. I was curious as to whether it was true."

"Why not just ask that?"

"I didn't want to sound like I was accusing her, just in case."

Harold nodded, as if her explanation made perfect sense. Once again, she was struck by the notion that he knew far more than he was letting on. She waited, needing him to make the acknowledgment. "Well," he said, "I'll be in touch."

Outside, Frankie rushed down the hallway and toward the staircase, not bothering to wait for the lift, anxious to be back outside.

CHAPTER 25

There was still time to turn it all around.

That was what Frankie told herself in the morning, when she looked in the mirror, and again at night, when she went to bed. She still had time.

And so once more she began her old routine. She woke at seven, queued for the bus, and descended on the gates of the British Museum. Some mornings she ate breakfast at the café run by the woman from Sorrento, others she waited until her stomach grumbled loud enough for the entirety of the reading room to hear before treating herself to a cup of Earl Grey in a cafeteria down the street. She wrote faster and with more ferocity than she ever had before. She wrote, knowing that it was working, that the words were flowing, that the story was more captivating, more compelling, than anything she had ever written.

This was it, she told herself. In her new work, Frankie wrote about Venice, about grief. She wrote about a woman buried away in a palazzo, interred, just as a mummy in a sarcophagus. She wrote about the city as dying instead of thriving, she wrote about the crumbling palaces that had no one left to care for them, either financially or emotionally. She wrote about this woman as though she were the core, the exemplification of everything the writers who had been drawn to this isolated place had at last been repulsed by. It was rougher than her previous work, considerably more raw, but the story seemed to require it, as if the price she had been asked to give was greater than anything before.

And she could feel it—the rightness of it, pulsing away as she wrote, as she scribbled one page after the other, her hands trembling, cramping, the callus on her middle finger growing larger, rougher, than it had ever been. This was it, she told herself, falling into bed at night.

At some point she realized that she had experienced this same feeling before—when she wrote her first novel. The intensity of the feeling, the need to pour herself onto the page. She had been missing that, ever since those first words tumbled out, years before, leaving her empty and hollow.

It was back now, she could feel it again.

This was it.

In the moments when she wasn't working on her novel, she forced herself to respond to Harold's notes on the other manuscript, the one that was not her own but that now belonged to no one but herself. Frankie tried to think of herself as a translator, as doing her best to ensure that Gilly's words and ideas would come across to the readers who one day would grasp the pages between their hands. But even so, she could feel the trace that she left behind, could feel the displacement of the original author, so that there seemed an estrangement between Gilly and the text in certain places, while in others her own was apparent.

She had worried, in the beginning, how Harold would respond to her new additions, had half-hoped that she would be caught out before things went too far. But then Harold had been ecstatic on the telephone, had declared the revisions *brilliant*, saying, "It's perfect. A reflection on time, on aging."

Frankie looked down at the pages she held between her hands.

"Is that what it's about?" she asked, forgetting, for a moment, that Harold didn't know the book's true authorship.

"You tell me, my dear," Harold laughed. "You're the one who wrote it."

She had looked down at the novel and wondered, when Harold praised it, when he insisted on his love for the words, whether it was her work or Gilly's or even his own that he had been speaking of. But, then—perhaps it didn't matter.

Only late at night did Frankie truly allow herself to think about what she had done, what combining her words with the girl's own meant. She thought of history, of literature, of the books that society went back to time and again, pulling them from their places on the shelves, unearthing their words and the lives of the people who wrote them. It seemed self-assured, indulgent even, to presume that hundreds of years from now there might still be someone reaching for her own work, and yet *what if,* she wondered. What if they did and they grasped not her first or the few after but her fifth, the one book that she had not written, that had not come from whatever well her words poured from, and they used that to re-create her life, to ascribe it meaning. She shuddered at the thought.

The truth, she knew, was that women occupied a liminal space within the history of literature—within history itself, when it came to it—and she did not want herself further marginalized by her mistake. She wanted to be able to claim her own name, her own story, for her volume to sit among those of other men, other women, and to know that, wherever she was, ephemera or otherwise, she would be able to stand by those words and phrases that made up her work, that made up *her.* For that's what they were, in the end, pieces of herself, bits of her, the inner workings of her mind that would otherwise empty themselves out day after day.

No, she could not give that up, not when it meant so much to her. She would not lose control of her own narrative, would not allow herself to be erased by this other voice. She was still here, still mattered to someone, surely. *I still matter,* she told herself, the reassuring words washing over her—no, skipping over her—so that she did not feel them. They were a tease, a taunt, one she could not grasp within her hands.

Gilly was a subject rarely mentioned now, and yet it was strange, she often thought, just how much space the girl had come to occupy in her life—even more so since her death. Perhaps it was down to the novel, to the act of channeling her voice day after day. How could she ever expect to bury the girl when she was tasked with bringing her back to life?

Frankie was reminded of her every time she glanced toward her writing desk, where the letter from the court lay, alongside her growing manuscript. She did not attempt to separate the two, the deadline for the inquest and the deadline for her manuscript becoming fixed in her mind, for she knew, if she were to have a chance, it would have to be somewhere around that same time— before anything could be printed. She worked at a furious pace, canceling lunches with Jack, postponing promised dinners at hers and Leonard's. "I don't understand," Jack said on the telephone one day. "I thought the manuscript was already finished." *It was,* Frankie lied, only there were edits, changes that she wanted to make after Harold had taken the first draft from her. She didn't tell her friend that she was working on two separate novels. It would only be a little bit longer, she reassured her, and then things would go back to normal. She promised.

The day before the inquest, Frankie finished her manuscript.

It had been a strange day to start. She had missed her bus into town, arriving a few minutes too late after realizing she had left the kettle on the stove, which had meant running back to the flat and then once again to the bus stop. At the reading room, she could see right away that the initial crowd had already claimed the best seats, the one that she always gravitated toward—number 402—already occupied by an elderly gentleman buried behind a stack of books. Luck continued to elude her later in the day as well, when, her stomach rumbling loudly through the quiet, she had made the short journey over to the café run by the woman from Sorrento, only to find it closed, a notice posted on the door thanking customers for their many years of patronage and announcing the owner's early retirement. After that, Frankie had taken an earlier bus back to Crouch End, the day's events making her feel too off-kilter to think of returning.

Once at home, she sat back in her chair, let out a sigh, and began to bundle the pages together so that she could post them to Harold in time for their scheduled meeting in a few days' time. Her mind was dulled and frayed, tired out after so many days of editing, of staring at the pages in front of her, of existing within the world of her own mind.

That night she went to bed without bothering to change out of her clothes, her eyes weighted with exhaustion, so that she did not open them again at the sound of the tap dripping. *I'll go to court tomorrow and I'll tell the truth,* she whispered to herself with confidence. *And then, then it will all be over at last.*

The truth.

Eyes still fixed shut, Frankie stayed awake long into the night, wondering just what the truth actually was and whether or not she would ever know herself.

CHAPTER 26

⁓

The day of the inquest, Jack met her at the flat and together they made their way to the St. Pancras Coroner's Court, arms linked. "I haven't a clue why I'm so nervous," Jack said as they approached the building, "but I've been shaking ever since last night. Leonard was determined to call the doctor around or, at the very least, persuade me to let him come today. I told him, no, it would look too strange. Besides, what if someone here recognizes us from Italy? Wouldn't it look odd that we haven't come forward already to say that we were there, that we knew Gilly, that we met her in the days before she died? I mean, what if they read it wrong, if they started to suspect something? I didn't want them to start on anything that was untrue."

Jack stopped, gasping.

"Just breathe." Frankie understood her friend's anxiety. Death made people do funny things. Only earlier that morning, for a brief moment, staring into the mirror, Frankie had considered telling the truth. Considered what it would feel like, and what would happen, if she were to stand in front of them all today and confess that she had been with Gilly during her last seconds on earth. If she admitted out loud, in front of them all, that she wasn't certain what had happened, whether it had all been a terrible accident or something worse.

Now, standing in front of the redbrick building, Frankie felt all
her resolve crumble. The truth was impossible, she knew, reaching
for the door that would allow them inside. For all that she might
think of turning herself over, of confessing, what stopped her was the
thought of how Jack would look at her afterward, how the woman
beside her would turn away, unable to think of her in the same way
ever again. She was the only real family that Frankie had, and the
thought of relinquishing that, of allowing Jack and all that they had
built to slip through her fingers, was impossible.

And so Frankie bowed her head and pushed into the hot, stuffy
hallway of the court, determined to do whatever she had to in order
to survive, to protect the life that she had created. A life that, no
matter how small, how inconsequential, was hers all the same.

"Good morning," the coroner began. "My name is Robert Wil-
liams, and we are here today to inquire into the death of Jillian
Larson, which took place in Venice, Italy, somewhere between the
early or middle days in the month of November, in the year 1966."

Frankie was trembling, her whole body seeming to hum and
vibrate within the chair, her teeth chattering. The courtroom was
more filled than she had imagined it would be, with not only friends
and family in attendance but even a few members of the press. The
latter were marked first and foremost by the notebooks they held
low in their hands, as if hoping to blend in among the crowd. But
they were easy to distinguish, Frankie thought. For while friends
and family sat rigid and alert, as if frightened of what might be
revealed, the press sat with slackened expressions, immune to the
talk of death, the details only logistics that had long become part
of their everyday lives. She felt Jack shift beside her. She looked
over and did her best to smile, although the corners of her mouth
were shaking. It was ridiculous to be this nervous. As part of the
proceedings she had submitted a statement which would form the

basis of the questions she was asked today, thereby eliminating any real chance of surprise. Despite this, she found herself unable to calm her nerves, remembering what had happened last time she had spoken in front of a member of the press.

Jack reached out, covering her friend's hand with her own. "You'll be fine," she whispered.

Frankie nodded, not daring to trust her own voice.

In truth, it was not the only thing that Frankie did not trust. She felt as though if she was asked to stand, her legs would crumple beneath her. She had never experienced this sensation before—her heart was beating both too fast and too slow. Frankie took a shaky breath. She wondered what would happen if she passed out, how guilty it would make her appear.

Her only consolation was the discovery that she would not be the first one called. In fact, she appeared fairly late on the list, a number of medical experts and Gilly's friends and colleagues scheduled to appear before her. It made sense. They were the ones who knew her best.

As Frankie listened to them recount their time with the girl, her stomach still roiling, her heart still thundering in her chest, she became aware of the very peculiar fact that they all seemed to be describing a different person. In each of their responses, she struggled to locate the Gilly that she had known. Indeed, in all of their responses, she struggled to create a portrait of one distinct and cohesive person. It unnerved her, somehow, as the memories she had of Gilly were already beginning to slip through her fingers, and now these disparate portraits only further dismantled the image she had created.

Eventually, it was Frankie's turn.

She rose slowly, feeling Jack's hands helping her, supporting her. She fought the urge to brush them aside, knowing that while Jack was only there to provide her with support, in that moment she wished that her friend was far away, convinced that this would all somehow be easier had she not attended. As if her comforting presence only made things more difficult, siphoning from Frankie the strength that she needed in order to make it through. She had always thought that she was stronger on her own. Love, friendship, all of those things that people spent their entire lives craving and searching for, only made her somehow weaker. And she had never been more aware of it than now, as she made her way toward the front of the courtroom, her legs protesting with each step.

She flinched when they closed the door of the witness box.

"Thank you for appearing today, Miss Frances Croy."

Frankie inclined her head.

"From your statement, I understand that you only recently became acquainted with Miss Jillian Larson."

It was not spoken as a question, and Frankie was briefly uncertain whether she should proceed or whether there was still an actual question forming. "Yes," she said. "I met Gilly while I was staying in Venice."

"Gilly. This is what you referred to her as?"

"Yes, that was how she introduced herself." It occurred to her then that none of the others had used that name. What was more, they all seemed to be using a "*j*" rather than the hard "*g*" that the girl had impressed upon her. She wondered how it would seem, the fact that she had barely known the girl but was somehow privy to such an intimate abbreviation.

"And under what circumstances were you introduced?"

Frankie paused, wondering how to explain. "Gilly approached me, introducing herself as the daughter of an acquaintance." She looked to Jack, who was nodding with encouragement. "Or, rather, I assumed she was the daughter of an acquaintance."

The coroner paused. "I'm not sure I understand."

Of course he didn't, Frankie thought. That was because the way that they had met, the whole thing, had been ludicrous, just like the girl. She scanned the courtroom, her eyes falling on Gilly's father.

Adam Larson was exactly as Frankie had pictured him. Tall, lean, still good-looking despite his years. And yet there was something that made her ill at ease, something that made her feel as if she understood Gilly a little bit more. It was nonsense—the man had never spoken so much as a word to Frankie—and yet there was something there, his gaze hard and unrelenting, that told her he was a man used to being listened to, a man used to giving commands, a man used to being obeyed. The observation made her uneasy.

"You see," she continued, her fingers beginning to pick at her skirt, "she claimed to know me, and so I assumed her to be someone I knew—mistakenly, I later learned."

"She *claimed* to know you. So, did she, in fact, *not* know you, then?"

"No," Frankie said, hearing a rush of whispering in the court, no doubt further bewildered by this admission. She took a shaky breath. "This is sounding more complicated than the situation was, I think. You see, it turned out that Gilly was familiar with my work."

"Ah, yes," he interjected. "You're a novelist, I see?"

"Yes."

"And so Miss Jillian Larson approached you in the streets after recognizing you, claiming a former acquaintanceship."

"Yes, that's it, but—" Frankie paused, already wishing she had not said anything.

"Yes?" he prompted her.

"It turns out we *did* know each other. Or, at least, she claimed we did."

"Yes, you've just told us that." The coroner was starting to look not only confused but also vaguely irked—a fact that somehow made Frankie herself feel irritated.

"No," she said, trying not to sound too stern. "I mean, not that, not what I said before. It turns out I signed a book for her at a reading, or at least I might have."

"You're not sure?"

Frankie paused. "No."

The coroner glanced down, consulting the notes that he had in front of him. Frankie suspected it was only to put an end to this line of tedious questioning. She took the time to exhale a tiny, shaky breath. She was making such a muddle of it already, she knew, and yet she couldn't see her way out of it. What would happen when they arrived at questions regarding that day?

The coroner looked back up. "Let's move on, shall we? How well did you come to know Miss Larson, following your introduction?"

"Fairly well, I would say."

"Fairly well? After just a few meetings?" He raised his eyebrows.

"Well," Frankie said, shifting her weight from one foot to the other.

"On how many occasions did you meet with Miss Larson?" He gave a shrug. "Twice? Maybe three times?"

Frankie tried to remember. "More than that, I think. We met once for coffee and then another time to go to the opera. She came to the palazzo where I was staying once for lunch, and then we had drinks another time after that." Frankie searched her memory. "And then there was a night out." She did not mention that final night and day, when Gilly had come to the palazzo during the storm. Even so, without these, Frankie realized, they had met only a handful of times. She shook her head in disbelief, feeling like a fool for having claimed to know the girl well at all. Everyone in the court must be thinking the same. How on earth was it possible to know anyone well over such a short period of time?

And yet, she wanted to protest—to the court, to herself—she *had* known her, hadn't she? Or at least parts of her. Yes, the girl had been peculiar, always telling half-truths or allowing omissions to unsettle something between them. Despite this, Frankie had a sense of who the girl was, or who she had been: eager, impetuous, daring. But, she thought, staring at the coroner's disbelieving face now, perhaps she was wrong—perhaps that had only been the front the girl had put up, the face that she had shown her. *It's Gilly,* she had told her that first day, in the market, insisting on a name that she had never used with anyone else. Was it possible the rest had been the same?

"Miss Croy?"

Frankie looked up, finding the coroner staring at her with obvious irritation and a sea of frowning faces before her. She glanced at Jack, who was watching her with a line of worry etched across her forehead. She wondered how many times he had repeated himself already. "I'm sorry, I don't know where my mind went just then. Could you repeat the question?"

"Certainly," he agreed, any attempt at civility undermined by the slight clip at the end of his words. "I had asked, when was the last time you saw Miss Larson?"

Frankie hesitated only a fraction of a second—she wondered how that appeared to those watching: a stumble, a lie, or only a woman sorting through her memory, trying to process everything she had been through? "It was the morning after we all went out together," she responded.

The coroner's eyebrows went up. "*We?*"

"Yes, some other acquaintances that I made in Venice," Frankie said, trying her best not to look in her friend's direction. "They never met Gilly, except for that night."

"I see." He paused. "And the name of these friends?"

Frankie hesitated again. "I'm afraid I don't remember."

"You don't remember the name of your friends?" he asked, confused.

Frankie attempted a placating smile. "I'm afraid I'm hopeless with names. I could tell you their given ones, but surnames I'm absolutely rubbish with. I don't think I even ever knew them, to be honest."

"I see," the coroner said. It was apparent that he had been thrown by this unexpected admission. "But they only met Miss Larson the once, according to you?"

"Yes," she answered in a rush, eager to leave her misstep behind.

"And they barely spoke, just a few minutes at dinner. It was mainly toward me that her attention was directed."

He returned to his papers. "And what was Miss Larson's state of mind, during the time that you were acquainted with her?"

They all looked to her at that, but Frankie only stared, feeling as though someone had forgotten to feed her the next line. "I'm sorry?" She tried to remember whether she had addressed anything like the question put before her now in her statement. She couldn't seem to recall.

"Her state of mind." He paused. "How did she seem to you in those days? Upset? Distraught?"

The coroner was watching her now with something she could not interpret—frustration, anger, even. But, no, that was not it. She took a breath, tried to slow her speeding heart. And then she realized. "Oh," she murmured. Suddenly it was so clear. Frankie wondered how she had ever been such a fool. She had been so worried, so caught up in her own mind these past few weeks, her anxiety mounting as the number of days before the inquest dwindled, imagining what they might say, what they might ask, *what they might suspect*. But in that moment, as she gazed up at the coroner, she realized how terribly wrong she had got it—*all of it*.

The man looming before her wasn't threatening, she could see that now. And he wasn't looking at her with anything like suspicion, wasn't trying to catch her in a lie. No, his questions were only in aid of creating a timeline, a portrait of the girl in the last days of her life. They did not believe *her* guilty of anything at all—no, it was *Gilly* who they thought responsible.

That was what this whole thing was really about.

"Her state of mind," she repeated, while she adjusted to this new line of thinking. The coroner nodded. "She was, well, she was worried."

Immediately the man's eyebrows went up. "Worried, you say?"

Frankie shifted. "Yes."

"And what was she worried *about*, Miss Croy?"

"Her novel," Frankie began, thinking. "She knew that the date was approaching when she had to submit her manuscript, and she was struggling."

"With?"

"With finishing."

"I see," he said, nodding. "And as a professional writer yourself, is this something that you are familiar with? The stress that such a task can have on oneself?"

Frankie nodded. "Absolutely." Her mind was racing, considering. *This* was the story. *This* was the way to explain what had happened in a way that others would accept, could understand. The unstable artist. It was a trope as old as any and one that she could see the audience in front of her grasping at—for that's what they were, wasn't it, an audience, come to be entertained by the tragic tale of a pretty young thing who died full of promise.

They went on like this, back and forth and back again, the man inquiring what her own schedule was like, what the demands of the job of a writer were exactly, how she felt in moments when inspiration would not come.

Despair was the word that she landed upon.

"You see, I've struggled myself with writing recently," she said, although she had not meant to, had not planned to speak of it beforehand. "It's something that I'd never experienced before in my career. But, well, this past year was different. I had a book published and it wasn't very well received, and then there were some stories in the press, and even though I told myself that it didn't matter, that I wouldn't let such things bother me, the truth is that it did. The idea of other people reading what you've written, of other people, complete strangers, judging your every word, your every thought—it can be terrifying. Absolutely terrifying. And I'd never thought about it, not until recently. And that terror, it just sat there. It settled in. Right here, on my chest." Tears pricked at the corners of Frankie's eyes. The room was quiet—*so quiet,* she realized. She gave a slight cough. "What I mean to say," she said, trying to compose herself, trying to shake the tremor in her words, "is that it can be paralyzing, that kind of fear. And sitting there in front of a blank page, unable to write the words, it can be—well, you can *despair* in those moments. There's no other word for it," she concluded.

The coroner was silent, and then he nodded, repeating the word out loud, *despair,* letting the tenor of his voice settle on the now-silent, attentive faces before him. Frankie could feel something inside her shift, could feel it in the room as well, and knew that somehow they had arrived there at last, arrived at the very heart of the matter.

The examination did not last long after that.

"Miss Croy," the coroner asked, his tone indicating that this would be his last question, "do you have any idea what might have happened to Miss Larson?"

It was a fair question, a good question, and Frankie wondered then: *Did she?* If she was asked, in the blink of an eye, to decide, to say one way or another whether she had had a hand in Gilly's death, whether hers had been the one to push her into those murky, churning waters, what would she say? Frankie opened her mouth, closed it. She didn't know—whether because she wouldn't allow herself to know or because she honestly did not, she couldn't say. Would never be able to say, not with any real finality.

Frankie looked down. "I don't know, I'm afraid. I honestly can't say what happened to Jillian Larson."

When she looked up again, Frankie was not surprised to see Gilly standing at the back of the room, arms folded. She tried to read the expression on the girl's face, but it was impossible, whether from a distance or otherwise.

Outside the courtroom, Frankie took a deep breath.

Her armpits were clammy, her gloves damp with perspiration—*but she had done it.* She had survived the coroner's questions, and now it was over. There was still an official ruling to be made, but she had little doubt what the coroner would decide. It was only a matter of waiting.

"You never told me any of that."

Frankie turned, surprised to find Jack standing behind her. In her haste to leave the courtroom, she had forgotten her friend's presence, concerned as she was with the door at the back of the room, with the promise of fresh air, of freedom, upon her descent from the stand. She had worried that it might draw attention, rushing out of the courtroom, but as she had made her way down the aisle, she had seen only expressions of sympathy and understanding written on the faces she passed—the realization of which had made her need to leave the room all the more urgent.

Jack's tone, she realized now, while accusatory, held no malice. Instead, she looked at Frankie with sadness at the idea that her friend had kept something so important from her. "I had no idea the girl was having so many difficulties."

Frankie shrugged, sick with guilt. "I suppose I hadn't thought about it. My mind never connected it all—with the girl's death, I mean. I suppose that seems absurd."

"No," Jack rushed to say, reaching out a hand to lay on her shoulder. "No, not at all. You were in shock. You couldn't have known what was on her mind."

Frankie caught the expression on her friend's face then and knew she was wondering. "What I said back there, it was all true, but—it was before, Jack. I don't feel that, not now."

Jack nodded, giving her a weak smile. "That was good of you not to mention me, by the way. Is it wrong that I'm glad not to have had to get up there, in front of all those people?"

"No," Frankie assured her.

"Come on," Jack said, looping her arm through Frankie's. "Let's go home and have ourselves a drink. I think we both of us need one after that."

Frankie felt the warmth of her friend's hand pressed against her own. It felt wrong to be so content in that moment, but she couldn't stop herself. It was as if something had been loosened a bit and now she wanted nothing so much as to toast with her friend, at home, in her quaint little flat that she never wanted to leave again. They headed toward the door, the word *home* so close that Frankie could taste it, soft and sweet on her tongue—when her name echoed in the entry hall of the courtroom.

They both turned and found a woman of around fifty striding toward them.

Jack's grip on Frankie's arm tightened. "Gilly's mother," she murmured.

Frankie had failed to notice Saskia Larson inside the courtroom, and it was because of this that Frankie had allowed herself to imagine that Gilly's mother might be something closer to the girl she had known, a woman who was whimsical, just as her daughter had been. She had imagined someone tall and willowy, someone who favored bold colors and current trends, maybe even a scarf done up in her hair. But, no, that wasn't at all how Gilly had described her, she recalled, and as the woman approached them, Frankie was startled to realize in her sharp, unrelenting movements just how different Gilly's mother was from her daughter—a mirror to her husband, rather than a complement. Saskia Larson's silver hair was pulled back in a severe bun, the only ornamentation to her somber black dress a rope of pearls that were wound tightly round her neck. She was shorter than Frankie had imagined, but as she neared Frankie and Jack, her austerity caused them to wilt, and it seemed all at once that Saskia was the largest of the three.

"Saskia," Jack said, reaching forward and planting a kiss on either side of her face. "I'm so sorry, my dear. Leonard too. He sends his condolences."

"Thank you," Saskia responded, sniffling demurely. She turned toward Frankie. "And thank you—may I call you Frances?"

Frankie nodded.

"And thank you, Frances, for everything. I'm so grateful that you spoke at the inquest. My daughter was such a fan of your work. I'm glad she got to meet you before—" She paused. "I can imagine just how much it meant to her."

"Of course." Frankie hesitated over her next words. "May I ask something?" When Saskia raised her eyebrows, Frankie decided to take this as consent, and hurried on: "I've been wondering how the court even knew about our connection. I mean, how did they know that Gilly and I had become acquainted in Venice?"

Saskia did not immediately reply. "The Danieli. They found her passport some days after the flood. There was little else they could tell us, unfortunately. Her suitcase and all her belongings had disappeared by then. But it was later discovered that she had placed several telephone calls while she was there, and the name the concierge had recorded was your own." Saskia seemed to hesitate. "It was strange, when we spoke to the Danieli."

"Oh?"

"Yes." Saskia glanced between the two women. "There was a bellhop who swears that Gilly came asking for her key—sometime in the days after the flood."

"How curious," Jack interjected.

"Yes, we thought so too." Her eyes flickered to Frankie. "What was stranger still was his description of her—it sounded almost as though he was describing someone else."

Frankie's mind raced. "He might have been describing me," she offered.

Saskia's eyebrows raised. "You?"

"Yes, you see, I had visited there once, with Gilly. We had drinks on the terrace. Perhaps he confused us. Everything was so muddled in those days after," she said, turning from Saskia to Jack, an appeal, she could not help but think.

Saskia was quiet for a moment. "Yes," she conceded. "You didn't mention that encounter, in your testimony."

"I must have forgotten." Frankie placed a hand to her temple. "My memories from that time, well, they're difficult to recall. I'm sure you understand."

Saskia gave a silent nod, her gaze lingering on Frankie. "I *am* thankful that Gilly got to meet you. She was always so enamored with you—with your books, I mean. And she was so excited to go to Italy, to finish her own novel. We were against the idea at first, the thought of a young girl alone in a foreign country, but she was adamant that Venice was the only place she would be able to write it. My daughter was hard to say no to, as you may have discovered for yourself." She paused. "Do you know, I've often wondered since if the reason she was so set on Venice was because of you."

"Because of me?" Frankie asked, hoping the tremor in her voice could not be detected by either of the women standing beside her. "How could she possibly have known I would be there?"

Saskia smiled. "It's a small world sometimes," she said, shrugging her shoulders as she spoke.

For the first time, Frankie saw her resemblance to her daughter. She smoothed a piece of flyaway hair behind her ear, struggling to compose herself. "How true," she said, trying to swallow. There seemed to be something hard, immovable, in the center of her throat.

Saskia indicated the doors to the courtroom just behind them. "Well, I had better."

"Yes," Frankie agreed.

"Before I forget." Saskia reached into the handbag that hung from her wrist. "I brought this, hoping I would run into you. I thought you might like to have it. There's a mistake, with the spelling of her name, but she never did seem to mind."

Frankie and Jack left after that, both women silent as they walked toward the door leading out of the court. As they stepped from the building, a light bulb of a camera flashed. Frankie turned away. Once in the cab, she looked down at what Saskia Larson had handed her. Frankie recognized it immediately. A first edition of her novel *After the End*. It had been years since she had seen one. She ran her hands over the cover, lingering there before opening the book, searching for the title page, already knowing what she would find.

> *To Gilly,*
> *My youngest fan. May we meet again one day.*
> *All the best,*
> *Frances*

Back at Frankie's flat, holding their coats tight against their bodies, desperate to keep out the cold, Jack asked, "Shall we light the fire?" Frankie nodded, and in silence they began to stack the logs together, pushing a bit of crumpled newspaper underneath the little triangle they had formed. Once finished, they retreated to the kitchen, placing the kettle on the stovetop. Not a word passed between them as they waited for it to come to a boil.

"Well," Jack said, breaking the silence. "That was depressing."

"It was an inquest, Jack."

"Yes, but still. I feel even more sorry for the girl now. She was quite the enigma, it seems."

"Yes," Frankie mused. "To be honest, I sometimes don't trust half of the things she said, in the end." Then they were quiet again, each of them locked within their own memories. Frankie wondered what Jack's were like—whether she remembered much about Gilly at all, or only the little things that often came to define acquaintances. Was it her red hair that stuck out, or that terrible pout she affected whenever she fancied herself the center of attention? Just then, Jack's face crumbled.

"What is it?" Frankie asked.

"I can't help feeling guilty."

"What on earth for?"

"This," her friend cried, waving her arms. "I'm the one who bullied you into going to Italy. If I had never mentioned it, none of this would have happened."

"Jack," Frankie began. "The flood would still have taken place and Gilly still would have died, despite whether or not I was there." She didn't believe the last bit, though she could never place such blame at her friend's feet. What had unfolded in Venice was her fault and hers alone.

"I know you're right," Jack said, managing a smile. "I just can't see it that way now." Her friend wiped away the tears on her face. "It's all turned out to be such a mess. And now Maria has lost her job."

"What do you mean?"

"Didn't I tell you?" When Frankie shook her head, Jack continued, "Remember the man, the one living in the palazzo next door? It turns out that he was Maria's cousin."

"Her cousin?" Frankie repeated.

"Yes, or at least some sort of relative. I understand he had come up from one of the islands—Pantelleria, which I'd never even heard of until the other day—without a penny to his name or a single prospect."

"But why on earth did she let him stay there?"

"Well, that's the thing. Apparently he had been staying at the palazzo, in one of the attic rooms. When I mentioned you would be coming, she found a key to next door and moved him there. It was only ever supposed to be temporary. She didn't think anyone would be any the wiser."

Frankie remembered the rumpled bed she had noticed on her first day exploring the house, how she had assumed that Maria was the one who had been sleeping there. And the time she had run into Maria and they had both heard the sound of footsteps above. She thought it was malice that she had seen in the other woman's eyes then, but now she wondered if it had been something else—fear. She had got it all so horribly wrong.

"Mummy and Daddy insisted that Maria be let go." Jack gave a little shake of her head. "I can't say that I disagree with their decision, but still, it's such a pity things have turned out the way they have."

"Yes," Frankie agreed. She waited until a moment passed before asking, "What about her cousin?"

Jack shrugged. "He's disappeared, it seems. Maria claims she doesn't know where he is, and because nothing was broken or stolen, the owners aren't interested in pursuing any charges. I don't suppose they'll ever hear from him again."

"So it's over, then?" Frankie asked, stunned at the conclusion, at the quietness of it all.

Jack nodded and gave a small sigh. "Yes, I suppose it is."

After Jack left, Frankie moved closer to the fire, holding out her fingers so that they were stretched mere inches in front of the flames. She glanced at the book that Gilly's mother had given her, which now lay discarded on her sofa. Reaching for it, she tossed it into the hearth, before she could change her mind. She sat there for hours, watching the fire as it raged, as it wore itself out, tired and spent, until there was nothing more than a glowing ember left in the grate.

CHAPTER 27

Frankie sat across from Harold, her manuscript laid out on the table between them.

When she had arrived, minutes earlier, Harold held up his hand, indicating the pages in front of him. He still had about twenty or so left. To pass the time, she had lit a cigarette, content to exist in that suspended state for as long as possible, walking aimlessly around his room, stopping only to pause at the window. From this high up, she couldn't make out any particular faces, could only see the movement of bodies as they crossed from one point to another. It was a relief, somehow, not to be too close, not to know enough about the people below to become entwined in their daily dramas.

She had her own.

The night before had been restless, her mind consumed with thoughts of her manuscript, of Gilly. Somewhere in the dead of night she thought of those words that Gilly's mother had spoken, of the idea that Gilly had come to Venice only in order to find her, and she had rushed to the bathroom, certain she was going to be sick.

She glanced over at Harold—about five more pages, she estimated.

Frankie reached across the table, stubbing out her cigarette. She drew another one from his case, hoping it would steady the trembling of her hands. She waited until he had turned the last page before she asked, "Well, what do you think?"

Harold let out a great puff of air, placing his hands on either side of the pages. "Frankie, dear." He raised his eyes, away from the manuscript in front of him and toward her own. She knew then that she would not like what he had to say. "I know you're frightened."

"Frightened?"

"Yes," Harold said, easing back into his chair. "The manuscript you turned in earlier this year is something new, something completely different from what you've done before." He leaned forward, eager. "But that's what makes it brilliant."

"Brilliant?" Frankie was dimly aware that she was only parroting what he was saying, but in that moment she could do nothing but grasp at the words that she wanted to say, the ones she had spent all morning preparing, just in case Harold's response was exactly the one he was now expressing.

"Yes. A work that absolutely no one will be expecting."

Frankie pointed to the manuscript before him. "And this?"

He looked down again. "It's good, Frankie. It's just—"

"What?" she prompted, when he did not continue.

He seemed to weigh his words. "Familiar."

"And the other manuscript?"

"It's exciting, Frankie. Fresh."

Out with the old, she thought grimly. That was what this was about, though Harold was too kind to say so. And perhaps that's where his enthusiasm for the manuscript came from—his devotion to her, his attempt to save her from whatever upcoming cull must be right around the corner. If only she could let him do it. If only she could nod, could smile, could pretend without guilt, without remorse, that this was something she had written. If only she could forget the girl and everything they had shared in Venice. But she couldn't—wouldn't.

"No, Harold."

"No?" he asked, confusion sweeping his features.

"*This* is the one I want to publish," she said, indicating the pages in his hand.

"And maybe we will, Frankie. With some revisions, with some time, maybe—"

"No, Harold. You're not listening."

"No, Frankie, dear. *You're* not listening." Something in Harold's voice shifted, became harder than anything she had heard from him in some time. "I won't publish it. Not now."

She had expected him to say as much, but it was the tone he used that momentarily shook her. "I'm sorry, Harold, but that's not going to work for me."

He sighed. "I'm sorry to hear that, Frankie."

She started toward the door.

"One more thing, my dear. There's still the matter of the title." Harold was already shaking his head at her protest. "Don't, Frankie. You owe us a book. You're under contract. And this is the one you submitted."

"I didn't submit anything," she argued. "You took it from me, from my flat."

He waved his hands, dismissing her comment. "We've been working on it for some time now. Time has been spent. *Money* has been spent. You signed a contract, right here in this office. There is no turning back." He paused. "And if you try to, it won't just be this house that refuses to work with you any longer."

"Harold," she began, her voice wavering. "Please."

It felt strange to be asking for his help, that thing he had always offered to her with such quickness, with such ease, and that she had turned away from time and again, never fully listening to him. Now Harold only stared as if he had not heard her. "I hate for it to be like this, Frankie, but you've left me no choice. You must see that." He cleared his throat. "Now, the title."

All business, she noted dimly. It was just like Harold. She

admonished herself for being so naïve, for allowing herself to forget who the man in front of her truly was and what he would always be willing to do for the job. She reached across the table for a pen.

He peered at the two words she had written. "I don't get it."

But she did, and for the first time. Frankie was surprised she had not realized it before. "It's all a trick," she said, looking at her former editor. "There never was a second woman."

Harold was still frowning when she walked out of the door, but she did not stop to explain. She pushed ahead, knowing, in that moment, that it was all coming to an end at last.

She was supposed to meet Jack for lunch after her meeting with Harold.

Instead, she rang her house from a telephone box, leaving a message with Leonard, asking him to pass along her apologies, and then making excuses when he began to ask her in a somewhat suspicious tone whether anything was the matter.

As Frankie sat on the bus now, on the way back to Crouch End, a laugh escaped from her. It didn't matter that she was not alone, that she was in a public place, sitting among a bus full of strangers. She could not have contained herself, her emotions, even had she wanted to do so. Frankie reached for the cord, the bus screeching to a halt. She didn't know where she was, didn't know how far away from Crouch End, but she didn't care. Frankie descended the steps, feeling the stares of strangers on her back. For one ridiculous minute she wondered whether she should close her eyes and click her heels. Perhaps that was what would bring a close to this.

Instead, Frankie walked.

It was spring, but there had been a bit of frost earlier that morning and Frankie knew that she should head home, that walking through the icy rain wouldn't do her any good, but the thought was unappealing, loathsome even. She turned in to a nearby park, anxious to be away from the throngs of people and umbrellas that had begun to congest the pavement. It was empty there, the wind, the occasional lashing of rain, no doubt keeping everyone else away. Head pushed down, eyes on the ground, she endured it all in silence. She walked for an hour, and then another, darkness falling around her. She looked up and searched for any trace of stars, remembering a warm summer night long ago, when her mother had dragged a telescope into the garden and they had stood together, munching on custard creams, watching for shooting stars. She was not aware of time passing, only that her hands were shaking, her lips numb, her clothing drenched, when at last she headed home.

The tube or the bus would have been faster, but Frankie didn't like the idea of being crowded in with other people. She wanted to remain as she was, soaked, sopping—penance for her sins. The walk was long, arduous. Somewhere along the way she was reminded of that day in Venice, of the flood, when she had tried to reach the train station. For a moment she was transported back to that large chilly departures hall, so that she could see the ticket manager in front of her once again, all frowns and concern, warning her to get somewhere safe.

As if *she* had been the one in danger that day.

She laughed, a dark, sputtering noise that sounded halfway between a cough and a retch. A couple, several paces ahead, increased their gait and crossed the road. She must look mad, Frankie realized. And she was, wasn't she? Haunted by visions of Venice, of Gilly. The fragility of her mind fracturing once again. As she made her way back home, she wondered whether there was any way to mend it this time.

She stood, looking up at her house. The rain was falling swiftly now, with more force. She could feel it rappelling down her body, affecting her vision, so that the house seemed to be there one moment and gone the next. Suddenly she wanted nothing so much as to be inside. She thought of the large fireplace, of the warmth that it dutifully pulsed out, sending tendrils of heat to even the farthest corners.

She reached to turn the doorknob, but it resisted the motion. A laugh bubbled between her lips. She hadn't unlocked it yet. Rummaging around in her pocket, she withdrew her key. She slid it into the keyhole—only it wouldn't fit. It seemed like the key was too large, or was the lock too small? She struggled with it another minute or two, until her vision was drawn away, toward the window. To where the curtain was moving. She squinted—was there a figure standing just behind it, watching her? No, she was confused. That had been Venice, not here. And he was gone now. Maria's cousin. Back to the island where he had come from, safely tucked away at home once more.

"You blasted thing," she murmured now, doing her best to fit the key into the lock again.

No luck. She held the key in front of her. The wooden frame of the door tended to swell in the damp—was it possible for locks to do the same? Another few minutes of fumbling produced no further effects. By then, however, she was no longer alone. She had not heard them alight from the car behind her, but all of a sudden there they were—two looming shadows, two policemen, frowning at her as they approached.

"I was trying to get inside," she said, indicating the door. "My key won't work."

She saw a frown settle on one of the men's faces. "Name?" he asked.

"Frances Croy. But what does that matter?"

The man, the more sullen-looking of the two, ignored her question. The other one was now approaching the window, where Frankie had sworn she had seen something moving before. "Look at me, Mrs. Croy," the other officer intoned.

"Miss Croy," she snapped.

"Miss Croy," he amended, the frown settling in further. "What brings you here today?"

She started at the question. "I'm obviously trying to go home, but for some reason this bloody door refuses to work."

He tilted his head, as if considering her words, weighing up whether he believed them or not. "Is there someone we could call?" he asked.

"About the key?" she responded, not understanding. But then the man kept staring at her and she could feel herself shift under his gaze, as though she actually had done something wrong, and so she gave him Jack's name and telephone number, hoping that might put an end to the whole thing. And it seemed to, for a short time. The two men stood back, although they were obviously keeping an eye on her. Frankie, with nothing much else to do but wait and see what unfolded, sank down and sat on the brick path that led up to the door.

Minutes passed, half an hour likely, and then Jack was there, crouching beside her, a furrow between her brows. "Frankie, what's happening?"

Something was wrong, then. Frankie knew it, could taste it on her lips, acrid and burning. She stood, holding out her key. "It won't work," she offered, trying to ignore the glares from the policemen standing just behind her friend and the shadow standing just behind the window. She could feel them, the stares, the whispers. She gave a slight shudder, as if that would free her from their gaze, imagined taking a brush and running it along her back, her sides, wondered whether it would be enough to sweep them all away.

"Frankie, dear," her friend whispered, taking the key from her hand. "This isn't your home." Her friend pursed her lips. "Not anymore."

Frankie felt something wash over her—fear, she thought—felt it coat her completely, so that her skin burned and was chilled all in the same moment. It was as though she had just been awakened, as if her friend's words had dispelled whatever cloud had hovered over her before. She knew straightaway that her friend was right. That this wasn't her home. She stepped back, taking in the changes. The addition of fencing that marked the perimeter of the property, the change of the door, painted blue now, rather than red, and then perhaps the most noticeable of all: the absence of the garden that her mother had prided herself on. What was it that Jack had said? *Not anymore.*

"I don't know what I was thinking," she began, giving a shake of the head. She saw it then—the fear on the woman's face behind the window, the actual occupant of the house, the concerned look on the policemen, tinged with something else, annoyance, she thought, at having to deal with a dotty old woman. No, not old. But not young either, and not attractive enough for anyone to indulge her brand of lunacy. No one would care for Ophelia half so much had she been a woman in her forties, Frankie thought.

Jack was smiling and shaking her head, telling her friend *not to worry, that everything was fine, that these things happened.* But they didn't. Frankie knew that, just like she knew her friend was only trying to pacify her. The best she could do was nod her head in agreement, remain silent as Jack thanked the officers, as she promised to take care of her friend, that no more incidents like this would happen, and then head dutifully home at Jack's suggestion.

Home. She felt the word brush up against her, felt its comfort, its promise, before it vanished, leaving Frankie to wonder what it was and whether she had felt it, truly, in a long, long time.

At home, Jack paced. "You're soaking wet," she had exclaimed after ushering Frankie inside. The next few minutes were spent in a burst of anxious fussing, hanging up coats, shaking off the rain, making sure that Frankie's hands and feet weren't turned completely blue with cold.

"I got caught in the rain," Frankie explained.

"The rain stopped hours ago, Frankie." Jack's face folded into a frown. "I'll put the kettle on."

Frankie nodded, collapsing onto the sofa. Jack returned a few minutes later, handing her a cup of steaming tea and covering her lap with a blanket.

"Any warmer now?" Jack asked, watching her carefully.

"Yes, that's much better."

"Do you want me to start the fire?"

"Yes," Frankie responded, but she stood again, setting the tea aside, the blanket falling to her feet. She moved toward the window, peering out, her eyes sweeping up one side of the street and then the other, searching. Frankie could feel her friend's gaze burning into the nape of her neck.

"What's happening, Frankie?" she asked, her voice firm but gentle. "What were you doing before, at your old place?"

Frankie searched for an answer. "I wanted to see the stars." It was something her mother always said when they found her, late at night, standing in the garden. It rarely happened once the war had started. It was one of the things her mother had missed most, she knew, the ability to step out into her garden and look upward at the sky. She hadn't lived to do that again.

Jack whispered, "You're exhausted, Frankie."

Yes, she thought, as she allowed Jack to lead her up the narrow staircase, toward her bedroom. Perhaps that was all this was. Exhaustion. She would crawl into bed and get a good night's sleep and in the morning—what? In the morning Gilly's book, instead of her own, would still be headed to press. That would not change, and until it did, there was nothing that would make her feel better, not even Jack.

Her dreams were muddled, distorted.

One minute she was at home, at her flat in Crouch End, and the next she was back at the palazzo, in Venice, the water surging up to meet her. She stood, panicked, the stench of the lagoon rising as the water crept first to her ankles, then her calves. She looked down and saw pages in her hands—torn and shredded, falling to the ground like the maple seeds she threw in the air as a child. And just like then, she was unable to catch them, despite her outstretched arms, so that they fell into the water, one by one, the ink turning the water beneath her black. She covered her mouth as the smell, *that* smell, flooded the air around her, and she feared she might be sick, might suffocate, might never escape—only, she realized with a start, she wasn't the heroine.

When at last she woke, gasping for air, trying to shrug off the shroud of her nightmares, which she could still feel, heavy against her skin, she heard nothing but the sound of rain against the windowpane, and for a long, thick moment, she feared that she was still back there.

She opened her eyes, blinked against the darkness.

No, she was no longer in the palazzo—but nor was she at home, in Crouch End.

Holding out her hand in front of her, she was met with something dark and cold. She recoiled. "Jack?" she whispered, searching through the darkness for her friend.

That was when she heard it. The droning of noise from above—loud, insistent—so that it rattled everything below. She could feel it, in her bones, in her teeth. The first time it had happened, she was convinced that she could still feel the vibrations hours later, after the planes had disappeared. It was half the reason that she had become an air-raid warden, so that she did not have to sit in the fallout shelter in the dark, in the damp, groping her way blindly around. She would rather see the end coming than have it take her by surprise.

She could smell it now—the damp mustiness of the basement. The smell of the war and so similar to what had come off the lagoon in Venice. She wondered that she had never noticed it before.

There was a noise to her left. A shuffling, like the tiny sharp claws of rats. Frankie closed her eyes, exchanging one darkness for another. When she opened them again, the girl was there. A few feet away, huddled in the corner, knees tucked up underneath her as if she were still relaxing in a palazzo instead of hiding in a basement.

"What are you doing here?"

Gilly tilted her head.

She opened her mouth to further accuse the girl but was stopped as a piece of wall crumbled just above her. The shaking had begun again, alongside the screaming wails of the sirens. She had never known which one she hated more. Frankie looked back at the girl, who still sat silent, stony-faced, despite the onslaught of noise and movement.

"Why won't you let me go," Frankie whispered, desperate, her voice breaking.

Gilly stared back at her. "Why won't you *let* me, Frances?"

Frankie started at the girl's words—her own words too, for weren't they one and the same? She placed her head onto her arms, curling into a ball, just as they had been taught. Perhaps, she thought, that was at the root of it all, the reason that she could never forget, could never manage to leave the past behind. They were too entwined, too entangled, in life, in death, in the secrets they held, even in the novel that they had created. Gilly would always be with her because she *was* her, a part of her, and there was nothing that would tear them asunder.

She closed her eyes then, ready, willing the darkness to hurry up and claim her.

CHAPTER 28

Frankie inhaled, the dryness of her throat causing her to descend into a coughing fit.

"Relax, Frankie." The voice was familiar, but she couldn't place it. She shifted uncomfortably. Her mouth felt dry and gummy. "Drink this. Easy now."

The coolness of the water seemed to burn at Frankie's throat. She choked, coughed again, the liquid running down her neck, onto her chest. When at last she managed to open her eyes, they were flooded with light, although somehow she could tell that the curtains were drawn shut, the room shrouded more or less in darkness. Still, there was a pain behind her eyelids.

"Leonard?" she whispered, peering at the form in front of her.

"Yes," he said, leaning in closer. "Though I daresay you were speaking to someone else just now."

Gilly, she remembered. But had that been now or hours ago? "What did I say?" she asked, fearful.

"I haven't the slightest, my dear. There was a lot of mumbling, a lot of nonsense."

Frankie let out a laugh, her throat protesting against the action. "I've been told I talk in my sleep."

"Yes, she's a regular chatterbox," came another voice.

Frankie turned her head and saw Jack, leaning against the door-frame.

"Hello there," Jack said, coming into the room to stand next to Leonard. "You gave us a fright, you know."

"I'm sorry."

"The doctor gave you a little something to calm you down. Exhaustion was his official diagnosis, which seemed too terribly close to hysteria for my liking, so I sent him away."

"Thank you." She saw something flicker across her friend's face. "What is it?"

Jack hesitated. "I was so worried, Frankie. I thought maybe—" She stopped. "I rang Harold. I know you two haven't been getting on, but he was so concerned, it took all my powers of persuasion to convince him not to rush right over."

"It's fine, Jack," Frankie assured her friend. "I'm not cross."

Jack looked relieved. "He told me I should pass on some good news, when you were ready for it."

"Oh?"

"Yes, they made a decision about the title. They went with your suggestion. He said you would be pleased."

Frankie managed a smile, her lips cracking in protest.

"So what was it, then?" Leonard asked, leaning in.

"What?"

"The title you suggested."

Unable to meet either of their gazes, Frankie turned toward the window. "*The Impostor.*" As the words slipped from her mouth, she could feel her mind drifting, sleep pulling on her. She surrendered easily.

"I hear you've been unwell."

Frankie disliked the way the reporter was eyeing her—as if ready to jot down the first sign of illness, physical or otherwise, wondering how it would benefit his article, his career, if he was the first to report her decline. She cursed Harold for talking her into this, and then herself for relenting. Frankie sat straighter. "I'm fine now," she replied, working to push the chill out of her tone.

He paused, as if waiting for more. When she did not provide any further details, he only nodded. "Well, then I suppose we should get on."

"Yes, let's." Frankie did not smile.

He nodded again, looking down at the notebook in front of him, and when he did so she caught a glimpse of a receding hairline. It made him, she thought, appear somehow more desperate. As did the suit, which was too much in the watery sunlight of the chill spring day, the tweed too heavy, coupled with the bright-red waistcoat underneath, so that a line of perspiration had appeared on his forehead, causing her to blink and glance away. "Well." He cleared his throat louder than what she suspected was necessary. "I suppose I should begin by saying it must be such a relief." He looked up at her and grinned, expectant.

"Sorry, what is?"

His grin stayed in place, although there was something false about it, she thought, something mechanical. Practiced, she realized. He had practiced this before, no doubt in front of a mirror, or even on the train here. He had been waiting for this moment, and now that it was here, he had pulled out all of his performative tricks. "The reviews."

"What about them?"

"Well." Here he seemed to hesitate—the hesitation of an actor who had studied his cue. "They're decidedly favorable this time. Unlike—"

"Yes," Frankie cut in. "I understand what you mean."

A moment of silence passed.

"And so, are you—"

"Am I what, Mr. Burke?"

"Relieved. Are you relieved?"

She smiled but did not respond.

"I mean, surely it must have been a bit of a surprise," he said, thrusting his hand out, pen clutched between his fingers. "After the reception of your previous novel."

"I'm not hearing a question."

"I just thought, given the reviews for this one—"

"I won't answer any questions about anything other than the new novel, Mr. Burke. And I won't answer questions for longer than a half hour, which I'm sure you've already been told." Her eyes glanced to the mantel. "Which means you now have less than fifteen minutes left."

Frankie was glad then that she had insisted on using Harold's office for the interview. Initially, he had been rather insistent that it take place at her own flat, something that she had never done. "Think of it as a rebirth," Harold said, "as beginning again in a way, with something just as new and exciting as the first time." Her flat, he had reasoned, would be the perfect spot. A way to begin her career anew. Still, she knew what he was after. Making herself more accessible after years of doing the opposite, taking advantage of what had happened at the inquest and the public sentiment following her testimony. Apparently, the press had lapped up what she had said regarding the pressures of writing, about what the girl might have experienced in her final days. Public opinion had turned swiftly in favor and support of the young girl—and of Frankie herself, it seemed, for the stress and strain that both of them had recently endured, leading to one breakdown and one death. The review—that damn review that had set this whole thing in motion—was mentioned, as was the anonymous author, although this time it was to vilify, calling out their words, their right to judge what another person had toiled to create. A year ago, Frankie would have laughed with relief, with anger and hurt and the need for revenge. Now she felt nothing at all. Not even when Harold relayed the whole thing to her with something close to glee. The most she could manage was a brief nod, which he had quietly accepted, along with her refusal to hold any interviews in her own home. Something was broken between them, the friendly sparring from days past gone—the crack deep enough that she did not know whether it could ever be mended.

"Good for you," Jack had said, when Frankie told her of refusing Harold's plans. "You're the one who's been ill recently, Frankie, remember that."

Jack had been staying with her nearly every night since she had woken up, almost a fortnight now, nursing her back to health. And although she was still gathering her strength, Harold had insisted that they not waste any more time. "The book is set to be published soon, and there hasn't been a single interview."

She did not contradict him, although from what she could tell, it did not seem that anyone was likely to forget, at least anytime soon. The early reviews, based on the galley proofs, had been good, according to Harold, glowing even, and the bookshops had put in orders far exceeding those for her other books, so that her editor was already talking about going back to the printers. She had put off talk of interviews for as long as possible, Jack standing guard, ready to pounce whenever Harold became too insistent. Eventually, however, she began to concede that she could not avoid it forever. She told Harold to choose *one* and they would go from there. He had practically jumped from his chair, unable to conceal his excitement.

And so now his reporter of choice, from some important magazine that Frankie herself could never be bothered to read, sat across from her, eyes narrowed, lips pursed, looking slightly irritated at the whole event. Frankie wondered whether it was because she was a woman or because the interviewer himself happened to be a novelist, whose first book had gone largely unnoticed. She liked to think it was a bit of both.

"Well, could you at least tell our audience what inspired you to

try your hand at such a different style of novel? Was it perhaps because of what happened—I mean, what was it that influenced this
new avenue of writing for you?"

She rewarded him with a small smile. "I suppose I wanted to try
my hand at something new."

"So this wasn't in reaction or response—"

"No, absolutely not. I wouldn't give anyone the satisfaction of
changing just because they thought I should."

"Did the events of last year influence your decision?"

"I just said, the critics had nothing to do—"

"Not the critics."

"I don't understand, then."

"Well, you had a difficult time last year. In particular, there was
the incident where you attacked a woman at the—"

"I did not," Frankie interrupted.

"—which was followed by a stay at a country *retreat*."

Frankie was silent. She had not missed his emphasis on the last
word. How the man in front of her had managed to dig up that bit
of information, she had no idea, but her thoughts flickered briefly
toward Harold. "I don't see what this has to do with the reason
we're here today, Mr. Burke," she responded, doing her best to work
some of the coldness back into her exterior. The reporter grinned—
big and easy—and she knew immediately that she should have
shrugged, should have dismissed his comment. Instead, she had
looked alarmed and he had clamped on to it, like a terrier. In her
reaction, she had given him just what he wanted. Frankie rose from
her chair. "I think we're finished now."

He did not rise. "I think you'll find that I have another five
minutes, Miss Croy."

She gave a curt nod. "And you are more than welcome to spend
them here, alone."

As she reached the door, he called out to her. "You don't remember me, do you?"

She stilled at his words, wondering for only a moment if they were a bluff. "Should I?"

"I would say yes, but given the state you were in that night . . ."

Frankie peered at him more closely now, saw what it was that she had initially missed. She cursed herself. The waiter. The one from that night at the Savoy. The one who had turned out to be a reporter, who had printed everything she had said, everything she had done. Her mind raced at the realization—and whether Harold had known. Surely not. Even his penchant for press wouldn't extend this far. Besides, this reporter worked at a different publication from the one that had run that story. A promotion, she surmised. The thought made her ill.

"Do you know, I had the most interesting visit, shortly after we met." He paused, as if waiting for Frankie to guess. When she did not respond, he pushed on. "It was from the author of the review. The one that you were so rattled by. It turns out they were offended by my piece in the paper, thought I was making more out of it than I should have. I assured them that my facts were accurate, as I had witnessed it all firsthand. Still, they were upset."

"Why are you telling me this?"

"I thought you would be interested to know."

"Know what?" she asked through gritted teeth, wanting nothing more than to leave the room, to put as much distance between herself and this man as possible.

"Who wrote the review." He paused, a smile creeping over his features. "Isn't that what you were after the last time we spoke?"

Frankie almost laughed. The last time they spoke. As if they had exchanged greetings and witty banter over canapés, rather than her blabbering almost incoherently to a stranger, never assuming that he was transcribing each and every word she had uttered. It was true that the review had brought her to the precipice, but it had been his words, his so-called reporting, that had sent her over the edge, that had nearly destroyed the life that she had worked so hard to retain. She wondered now if he knew just what he had done to her, knew how much his words had almost wrecked everything. "Why would I believe a word that came out of your mouth?" she demanded.

"Have I ever lied?"

Her eyes shot to his face. No, his report had contained nothing of exaggeration, nothing of hyperbole. She saw the determination in his eyes now and knew that he was being honest—he knew who had written the review.

Frankie paused a moment, then shook her head. "I already know," she said, ignoring the expression on the reporter's face, which plainly asserted that he thought she was lying.

She was not.

Frankie held his gaze—and then she tossed her final words to him over her shoulder, not bothering to look back before she closed the door behind her.

"Gilly Larson wrote the review."

CHAPTER 29

The girl had confessed that day. Standing outside in the rain, water falling from above, water rising from below, she had pulled Frankie close and whispered into her ear. At first Frankie had struggled to understand them, the girl's words nearly lost in the rush of water and wind and the growing frenzy that surrounded them. But then a moment passed and then another and all at once she had understood—the answer to the question, to her question, the one she had put to the girl, in one form or another, ever since that first day they had met: *What are you doing here?* As soon as the words left Gilly's mouth, *I wrote the review,* Frankie knew it was the truth, because there was nothing else that made sense. It was as simple as that. Before she had been able to think further, before she had been able to respond, the girl had slipped away from her and into the waters of Venice, into the storm of the century, buried by the rush of water.

In the weeks and months that followed, the words had left Frankie with more questions than answers. If Gilly had written the review, had she come to Venice in order to watch the havoc her words had wreaked upon Frankie's life—or to apologize for them? Neither explanation satisfied Frankie. Whatever Gilly was, or had been, it was not cruel, it was not malicious—but nor was she particularly apologetic.

Sometimes Frankie wondered whether it had been simple curiosity that had led her to the city of bridges. If she had learned of Frankie's own presence there from the chatter of her father, of friends, and had decided to go and see, in light of everything that had happened. If it had been anyone else, Frankie would have scoffed at the idea. But the absurdity of it—no, the *oddity*—was what made her think it was closer to the truth than anything. There had always been something strange about the girl. She was something like a sprite, a changeling, even—something that appeared in place of what should be. That Frankie would never know exactly where she had come from or why was somehow fitting. She had been there, in Venice, with her, and that, she told herself, was enough.

It would have to be.

When she returned home, Jack had gone.

Frankie marked the emptiness, grateful to have a moment to collect herself. She leaned against the doorframe and inhaled slowly, counting her breaths as she released them. The scene with the reporter still reverberated within her, so that as she withdrew the gloves from her hands, she found they were still shaking.

Her eyes flickered to the clock. She was startled to find it was already half past seven.

Time had become a difficult thing for her over the last few weeks, ever since her episode. There were times when it seemed to drag on, so that a minute lasted an entire lifetime, and then there were the other times, when she found that minutes, sometimes hours, were lost to her. Now was such an example. She was almost certain that it had still been light out when she returned, the watery sun filtering into her flat as she made her way from sitting room to kitchen. But now a quick glance out the window confirmed that the clock was indeed correct and that evening was already well under way.

She had lost several hours.

She went to the kitchen, filling the kettle, reaching for her cup, the one with the chip at the edge that she couldn't bring herself to toss out. Halfway through pouring, she paused, the flow of water stopping between kettle and cup. There was something just there, she realized, in the pit of her stomach.

It took her a moment to recognize it as the growing feeling of dread.

Frankie did her best to push it out of her mind as she moved into the sitting room, taking a seat on the sofa, tea in hand. She looked toward the empty fire but could not convince herself to begin work on it. It seemed somehow too much effort, in the absence of her friend. Instead, she pulled a blanket over her lap and told herself that would be sufficient until Jack's return.

At some point, as she sat and waited, Frankie must have fallen asleep, for the next thing she knew her tea was cold and the room around her had fallen into darkness. She moved slowly, feeling the stiffness in her neck, in her joints, as she reached for the lamp. The light that sprang from the antique, a leftover from her very first bedsit, startled her and she blinked, unable at first to take in the shapes around her. She grew troubled when she realized the late hour, coupled with the fact that Jack had not returned. Frankie remembered her friend mentioning that she planned to go home for some clean clothes—and even though Jack didn't say so, Frankie knew she was also anxious to see Leonard again, having spent so much time away from him recently. Still, Frankie was surprised by the length of her absence.

It was just as she had finished lighting a fire that she heard her soft rap against the wooden frame.

She knew then what had happened.

For a moment Frankie remained still, watching the shadows cast by the glow of the lamp, made grotesque and macabre, allowing herself to believe she had got away with it. She let her mind drift, ignoring the knock on the door, which had grown more insistent, letting herself imagine what the future might hold with the new success of this most recent book, with her mended relationship with Jack and Leonard—instead of the fate she knew she deserved. Making her way toward the door, hand outstretched to the latch, she did her best to keep her head high, as though she were walking to stand before a firing squad.

She opened the door.

Jack's face was miserable, ashen. In her hand was a manila envelope. "This came in the post today," she began without preamble. "Maria sent it, thinking you had left it behind."

Frankie knew, without asking, what it contained. The pages that Gilly had brought over that night for her to read. She had wondered, every so often, what happened to them, had convinced herself, in lieu of an actual answer, that they too were lost to the flood. She realized now how careless she had been.

Jack withdrew a stack of bound pages. "You told me you wrote this here, in London. So how did these end up in Venice, where *your* manuscript was lost?"

Frankie paused, willed her hands to stop trembling, willed her heart to stop beating so madly. "Come inside, Jack. It's freezing out there."

Jack's face was pained as she stepped through the doorway. "Tell me the truth, Frankie." She turned to face her. "Did you write this book?"

Frankie folded her arms across her chest. "What a thing to ask."

Jack moved closer. "The thing is, Frankie, I've read everything you've ever written. Every draft, every sentence, before and after editing. I know your words just as well as I know you. And this"—she held the manuscript up between them—"this has never sounded like you."

Frankie paused, her smile frozen. And then, despite knowing that it was futile, that she would only make things worse, that Jack would never believe her, she said, "Well, that's the point, isn't it? Harold wanted something new, something unexpected."

Jack was already shaking her head.

"Oh, Jack. Don't be so dour," Frankie said, laughing, the shrillness of it echoing throughout the flat.

But Jack was only watching her with something like sadness, tears crowding her eyes. She held out a single piece of paper—the first of the manuscript. The one, Frankie recalled, that held a short, handwritten note:

> *To Frances.*
> *Hope you enjoy.*
> *XXX. Gilly.*

"What were you thinking, Frankie? What if she had come forward to claim it as her own? Or had you offered her something to stay quiet?"

Frankie felt her smile still, and then fall. And then, because she couldn't stand it any longer, lying to everyone about so many different things and to Jack, most of all, she said miserably, "I wasn't worried about her claiming it."

Jack laughed. "God, how cavalier you are, Frankie."

Frankie walked toward the fire, upending the pages that Jack had thrust in her hands into the flames. Her voice was quiet when she spoke again. "I didn't mean to. It just happened."

"How does something like this just happen?"

"It was Harold. You know how he is. He kept pushing and pushing. And I tried, Jack, to fix it. I went to the library and I wrote. I wrote every day and I poured myself into it, poured every ounce of myself and more. But it wasn't enough. They wanted something else. *Someone* else." She paused, gave a short laugh. "What was it you said in Venice? The reason you liked the girl? She was *young.* That's what they wanted as well."

Jack was silent, a look of horror creeping onto her face.

"Don't look at me like that. Please, I can't bear it." Frankie turned to the fire. "The funny thing is, I hate it. The book, I mean. I told her so too, that I didn't think anyone would ever want to publish it. Lacking narrative," Frankie said with a shake of her head. "That was what I told her. That's what an absolute fool I was. But she pushed me, Jack, just like Harold pushed me. I didn't even want to read it, but there wasn't any way that I could say no. We were stuck inside during that awful flood and there was nowhere to go. I kept trying, don't you see? I kept trying to get out of it all, but no one would let me. I was trapped." Frankie stopped, realized that Jack was staring at her, eyes widened, mouth slightly agape. "What?" she demanded. "What is it?"

Jack was shaking her head. "You said you didn't see her after Leonard and I left. You said she never came back to the palazzo. You said, you swore, that the last time you saw her was the morning after that night we all went out together."

Frankie rubbed her temples. "Did I?"

"Yes, yes, you did," Jack said. "In fact, you were adamant about it." Jack stumbled back. "Oh, God, Frankie, what—"

Frankie let her hands drop. "*What*, Jack?" She said it with more conviction than she felt, telling herself that Jack couldn't know, that it was impossible for her to think Frankie capable of such monstrosity, no matter what had happened with the book.

When Jack spoke again, her voice was little more than a whisper. "Why did you go to Rome, Frankie? Was it because—did something happen in Venice?"

"Happen?"

"With Gilly. Was her death—was it an accident?"

Frankie debated lying, knowing that it made the most sense. As strong as Jack was, the truth would devastate her, would devastate both of them. And as for Frankie, if her part in Gilly's death was ever known, if her culpability in the girl's death was ever known, another inquest would be held and she would be prosecuted. She was aware of these facts, every last horrible one. Despite this, she took a deep breath and told the truth. "I don't know."

All the air seemed to escape from the room at once.

Jack collapsed onto the sofa, a strangled sort of cry escaping from her. The noise was guttural, hideous. Frankie wanted nothing more than to run to her, to gather her into her arms and apologize for every last wretched and pitiful thing she had ever done. To beg Jack to forgive her, to ask her what she could do to put things right, to make her forget. But she didn't. Instead, Frankie remained standing by the fire, breathing slowly but quietly, waiting until Jack's racking sobs subsided into something quieter, something more manageable. She stood and watched as Jack wiped her face, as she pulled her coat tighter to her body, as if this would shield her from the cold that had settled throughout the room.

And then she was gone.

Frankie remained still. Jack had not said anything as she left, had not paused on the threshold of her flat. Frankie knew, instinctively, that she would never see her again.

CHAPTER 30

She went to the water, because that was the only thing she could
think to do.

Frankie boarded an early train, the first that left out of Victoria,
nodding and handing over the money at the ticket office, anxious
to be gone from the city. She did not let herself think of where she
was headed. Instead, she sat, content, the feeling of being on a train,
of being pointed in one direction, quieting her mind.

It took her several days.

On the last leg of the trip, just a few hours outside Venice, the
attendant appeared, holding out his hand in expectation. Frankie
riffled in her handbag for her ticket. "It means *come back again,* did
you know that?" she asked, glancing up, but he did not react, so that
she was unsure whether he understood. "Venice, I mean."

He still stared at her with that same blank expression.

At the train station, the damp sulfuric smell of the city rose
to greet her, making her stomach turn in anticipation. She took a
water bus over to the San Zaccaria station, the porters looking bewildered when she alighted without so much as a single bag. They
turned away in disappointment.

Frankie began to walk, unsure exactly where she was going but
knowing that there was somewhere she was headed. She walked

from the water's edge by the Danieli, up through the narrow cor-
ridors, the twisting streets, over bridges, alongside canals, her feet
echoing on paths that she remembered, surprised by her own rec-
ollection. She passed the Campo Santa Maria Formosa, watching
the children as they kicked around a football in the dying light,
watching an old man pause at the *fontanella* to take a drink of water.
It was all so familiar and yet none of it seemed like a place that she
had been, a life that she had once led. It was all so foreign and far-
away, as everything had been since the day of the flood.

She continued on, into the outer reaches of the Castello, into
the area that none of the tourists ever went, where green spaces
could be found, where one could, for a brief moment, forget where
they were, the hallmarks of Venice falling away around them. It
was the place that Frankie had taken Jack to, months ago now, in
another lifetime.

It was colder than she had anticipated and Frankie shivered,
pulling her scarf closer to her face. There were few people out, the
hour or the chill keeping them inside. She had left her watch at
home and she didn't know the time. It was impossible to tell. Venice was mischievous that way, making the world feel encased in a
darkness that was difficult to see through. No matter. Frankie had
little use for the light now.

Increasing her pace, hands jammed into her coat pockets, she
pushed against the cold, against the wind, moving closer to her
intended destination. The water's edge. The point where there was
no land to be seen, no palazzos, no bridges, only the lagoon stretching out into a vast, unending nothingness, so that it was possible to
believe one was standing on the shore of a vast sea. In the distance,
she could just make out the Isle of the Dead, as it was known to the
locals, a foggy haze wrapping itself around the tiny island.

Eventually, she stopped walking.

This was the place that she had remembered, that she had held
in her mind. She wasn't certain why, there was nothing remarkable

about it. Just a mooring, steps from the park, no evidence of either gondola or clients now. She had first noticed it that day she came with Jack, sipping on wine from the *sfuso*.

Today, she was the only one there. Venice was already fast asleep, Frankie knew.

She descended onto the first step.

And then the second.

The water was up to her ankles now and it burned, the chill painful against the hot flush of her skin. She took yet another step down, the water lapping against her knees and then her thighs. Everything around her was quiet, still, in that way that only Venice ever was. It was as if she was holding her breath—waiting.

In that moment, Frankie thought she might be the last woman on earth. There was no evidence to prove otherwise. Although perhaps that was not entirely true, she thought, feeling Gilly's hand as it slipped into her own. Frankie turned and looked at her, at the girl, who was smiling now, her red hair cascading down her shoulders, just as it had that first day they met. Frankie smiled back. And then together, hand in hand, they walked farther into the lagoon, until the sound of the waves, until the gentle lapping of the sea-green water below, reached up and obscured them altogether—until there was nothing left at all.

ACKNOWLEDGMENTS

First and foremost, thank you to Elisabeth Weed for reading each and every single draft I send her way—and for understanding when I decide to abandon one nearly completed manuscript in order to start on something new. Thank you to Zachary Wagman for his exceptionally keen eye, which helped shape *Palace of the Drowned* into this final version, and for bringing me along to his new home at Flatiron. To Richard Beswick and Zoe Gullen, thank you for all the advice and for helping my British characters be as British as possible. And to everyone that I hadn't yet met when I wrote the acknowledgments for my first novel (Meghan Deans, Miriam Parker, Sonya Cheuse, and Hayley Camis), and to everyone that I have yet to meet this time around at Flatiron: thank you all very much.

Thank you to all my brilliant friends and family who supported me throughout this process. To RK for listening to every idea, for reading every draft and always offering up advice and encouragement. To S and J for acting as my own personal travel guide to Venice—your insights into the city were invaluable. And S, for your help with the title, I am in your debt. To all my friends scattered across the globe for in turn reaching out to their friends scattered across the globe on matters of translation, thank you very much, indeed.

Last, a massive thank-you to all the librarians and booksellers and readers who supported my first novel. I am forever grateful.